Magic Flutes

Eva Ibbotson was born in Vienna, but when the Nazis came to power her family fled to England and she was sent to boarding school. She planned to become a physiologist, but hated doing experiments on animals, and was rescued from some fierce rabbits by her husband-to-be. She became a writer while bringing up her four children, and her bestselling novels for both adults and children have been published around the world. Her books have also won and been shortlisted for many prizes. *Journey to the River Sea* won the Nestlé Gold Award and was runner-up for the Whitbread Children's Book of the Year and the Guardian Fiction Award. *The Star of Kazan* won the Nestlé Silver Award and was shortlisted for the Carnegie Medal. Eva lives in Newcastle.

Also by Eva Ibbotson

A Company of Swans
A Song for Summer
The Morning Gift
The Secret Countess

For younger readers

Journey to the River Sea
The Star of Kazan
The Dragonfly Pool

The Beasts of Clawstone Castle
The Great Ghost Rescue
Which Witch?
The Haunting of Hiram
Not Just a Witch
The Secret of Platform 13
Dial a Ghost
Monster Mission

Magic Flutes

EVA IBBOTSON

YOUNG PICADOR

First published in Great Britain 1982 by Century Publishing Co. Ltd

This edition published 2009 by Young Picador
an imprint of Pan Macmillan Limited
20 New Wharf Road, London N1 9RR
Basingstoke and Oxford
Associated companies throughout the world
www.panmacmillan.com

ISBN 978-0-330-46263-1

3 5 7 9 8 6 4 2

A CIP catalogue record for this book is available from
the British Library.

Typeset by Intype Libra Limited
Printed and bound in the UK by CPI Mackays, Chatham ME5 8TD

To Aaron and Johanna

'*What do they celebrate, the magic flutes of love? Why,
tears and laughter*'

After Praxilla (fourth century BC)

Prologue

(Birth of a Hero)

They were both born under the sign of Gemini, and for those who believe in the stars as arbiters of fate this must have seemed the link that bound them. She herself was to invoke the heavens when at last they met. '*Could I be your Star Sister?*' she was to ask him, '*Could I at least be that?*'

Certainly it would seem to need the magic of star lore to link the life of the tiny, dark-eyed Austrian princess – born in a famous castle and burdened, in the presence of the Emperor Franz Joseph, with a dozen sonorous Christian names – with that of the abandoned, grey-blanketed bundle found on the quayside of a grim, industrial English town: a bundle opened to reveal a day-old, naked, furiously screaming baby boy.

Her birth thus was chronicled, documented and celebrated with fanfares (though she should have been a boy). But his . . .

It was the merest chance that he was found at all, for

the bundle was half concealed by sacking and the Tyne docks that mid-morning in 1891 were high-piled with packing cases waiting to be loaded on the boats for Scandinavia, with rusty barrels, coils of rope and coal from the barges. But among the shawled and clogged women on their way to work on the Fish Quay there was one who had sharp ears and detected above the screeching of the gulls another, more frantic and urgent cry.

An hour later, in the Central Police Station in New-castle upon Tyne, the contents of the bundle had been recorded in the register, found to be the fourteenth foundling abandoned in the city that month and noted to be male.

By the evening, the baby was in the arms of the matron of the Byker orphanage where, duly fed, bathed and clothed in the calico nightdress stitched by the ladies of the Christian Gentlefolk Association, it caused that excellent woman a certain puzzlement.

Bald, shading from puce to apricot and back again under the impact of his rage, the baby, squinting at her with the lascivious eyes of a Tunisian belly dancer, seemed to be made of a different, a denser, substance than any she had known. She was sure she had never seen a baby that sucked at its own wrist with such ferocity or screwed up its legs with such violence, and as she lowered it into the twelfth cot from the left she was already aware that the question she so often asked about abandoned babies, namely 'Will it survive?' was inappropriate. If there was a question to be posed about this latest addition to her orphanage, it was rather, would they survive him?

Matron followed her instincts about the occupant of cot number twelve when naming the baby, and rejected the list put out for her guidance by the Board of Governors. The compressed and explosive individual whose irate face appeared so incongruously above the scalloped edges of his nightgown was clearly no Albert or Edward and certainly no Algernon, and 'Attila the Hun', though suitable, was unlikely to be acceptable to the gentlemen on whom her livelihood depended. She called the baby 'Guy', and for his surname used that of a group of islands off the Northumbrian coast which she had visited as a child with her fisherman father: the Farnes.

A relative lull followed while Guy Farne primed his muscles, coordinated his limbs and secured a few basic necessities in the way of teeth and hair. Then, some three months earlier than expected, he began to crawl and subsequently to walk. Life had now begun in earnest.

Speculation about the ancestry of their babies was something that Matron and her hard-working assistants seldom permitted themselves. Not one of their foundlings had ever been traced or claimed, and in turning them out to be clean, God-fearing and suitable for work as domestic servants or labourers, the staff of the orphanage was doing all it could. With Guy Farne, however, it was different. As he progressed from child-battering to arson, including a little grievous bodily harm and possession of unlawful weapons on the way, there was an attempt to prove that this particular baby could not possibly have been English.

'Well, he doesn't look English, does he?' argued Matron's assistant. 'And him being found in the docks like that. I mean, there's boats from all over come in there.'

'Aye. He could be anything with those cheekbones and his eyes set like that.'

'There's all sorts you find where there are ships,' agreed cook. 'Even Lithuanians,' she added darkly.

A tendency to blame Lithuania increased amongst the staff of the Byker orphanage as Guy Farne reached the age of three, four, five . . .

'Though you can't really say there's any actual malice in him,' said Matron, bandaging the leg of a fat girl he had bitten in the calf. 'I mean, Maisie was bullying little Dora.'

This was true, but the staff found it cold comfort. It was also true that when Billy was carried in with concussion because Guy had knocked him against a brick wall, he had been tying a tin can to the tail of a puppy that belonged to Matron's sister. And that Guy had stolen a gold watch from a corpulent governor's back pocket only to present it immediately to the aged boiler-man who had a birthday. True, all true – but when Guy reached his sixth year Matron decided that enough was enough and looked about for a suitable victim.

Her choice fell, as in the manner of fairy stories, on a poor widow named Martha Hodge.

Mrs Hodge had lost her husband when very young in an accident in one of the shipyards; since then she had fostered, very successfully, one little girl with partial hearing for whom she had found a job with a kind lady as a housemaid and another girl who was now working happily in the country. Matron accordingly wrote a letter in her neat copperplate to Mrs Hodge, suggesting that she might like to foster another child and reminding her that the three and six paid weekly by the parish had now risen to a munificent five shillings, enabling those who took up fostering to make a reasonable profit.

Mrs Hodge had not found this to be so, but she nevertheless put on her hat and coat and on arrival at the orphanage told Matron respectfully that she was willing but it had to be a little girl.

'For without a man to help me, Ma'm, I divn't think I can deal with a wee lad.'

Matron repressed a sigh and said she saw her point. 'However, if you'll just look at the boy now you're here?'

Guy was led in, glowering, and stood before her. At the time of this encounter he was six and a half years old. Entirely without hope or expectation, he looked at Mrs Hodge. Small for his age, with the extraordinary air of compactness that characterized him, his chin lifted to receive the information that he was not acceptable, he waited. His knees, scrubbed to a godly cleanliness, shone scarred and raw; his naturally springy hair had been slicked down with several applications of vaseline and water and stuck relentlessly to his scalp.

Mrs Hodge looked at him and felt frail and tired and more mortal than usual. Force emanated from this strange-looking boy as visibly as beams from a lighthouse. It was impossible; she would never be able to cope with him.

The boy waited. His eyes, strangely and slantingly set above high cheekbones, were a curious deep green which sent Mrs Hodge in search of images that were beyond her: of malachite, of the opaque and clouded waters of the Nile.

Silence fell. Only the sudden descent of his left sock as the garter snapped revealed the tension that the child was concealing.

It was entirely without volition that the words Mrs Hodge now uttered issued from her mouth.

'All right,' she said, 'I'll have 'im. I'll give it a try.'

She had turned to the Matron as she spoke, and it was a few moments before she turned back to look at the boy. When she did so, she had to catch her breath. The child had not moved from where he stood, nor did he smile, yet he was utterly transformed. The mouth, sullen no longer, curved upward; the clenched fists had unfurled, and everything about him, every line of his body, seemed to express joy and a wholly unexpected grace. Most movingly of all, there had appeared in the strange green eyes a glimmer of the purest, the most celestial, blue.

It was then she suspected that she did not stand a chance.

The first month that Guy spent in Martha's 'back-to-back' in the narrow, cobbled road beside the shipyard passed in unnatural quiet. Every child knew that fostering or adoption was on a month's trial. Memories of cowed and defeated children returning with their bundles to the orphanage had been burned into Guy's mind when he was scarcely four years old. On the last day of February he packed his belongings, crept downstairs and said, 'I'm ready.' It was always thus with him – to anticipate the worst, to be prepared.

'Ready for what?'

'To go back,' said the little boy.

'Go *back*?' said Martha. 'Whatever for, you daft boy? Don't you want to stay?'

Guy did want to stay. By the time he had made this clear, his eyes undergoing that characteristic change from green to blue, Martha found herself knocked backwards on to the horsehair sofa, with broom sent flying and hairpins clattering on to the floor.

His violence and aggression now took a different direction. In the orphanage he had fought against the world, now he fought for Martha Hodge. When she explained that kicking, biting and twisting the limbs of children who had fallen foul of her in some way just would not do, he taught himself to box. While applying first aid to the bloodied noses of his victims, Martha wished she had held her tongue. Whether or not

Martha, long widowed and still comely, would have wished the fishmonger to kiss her when he came up the cobbled lane with fresh herrings was never put to the test, for no sooner had the tradesman's arms encircled her waist than Guy shot out from the coal bunker and – forming himself into a human battering ram – sent the unfortunate man sprawling.

School, for which Martha had thirsted like a spent hart for the thicket, provided scant relief, for despite returning with his behind in weals from the cane, Guy still seemed to have enough energy left for hours of mayhem before she got him into bed. Nevertheless, it was from this small, red-brick building between the slaughterhouse and the glue factory that deliverance came. Two years after Guy had come to her, Martha was sent for by the headmaster.

'He is a devil, Mrs Hodge,' said Mr Forster. 'A thoroughgoing, copper-bottomed fiend in hell.' He embarked upon a recital of the damage that Guy Farne had inflicted in his short time at Titley Street Board School. 'However . . .'

Martha, lifting her head at the 'however', was then informed that her foster-child had a remarkable capacity for learning: had, in short, more brains than any child that had passed through Mr Forster's hands in twenty years and could, in his opinion, win a scholarship to grammar school.

She came home, burst into tears and was discovered thus by Guy. Though disappointed that what she wanted of him was something as humdrum as a scholarship, when he was prepared to raise an army or build a fleet, Guy applied himself. Going out with her rolling pin one day to rescue a neighbour's little boy who was pinned against the sooty brick wall of the shipyard, Martha discovered that the child was warding off not Guy's threatened blows but his determination to explain the Second Law of Thermodynamics; then she knew that the battle was won.

When he got his scholarship, there was a street party and Guy, now sporting a black blazer with a tower on the pocket, went to the Royal Grammar School. Soon he became, as such children do, bilingual in English and Geordie. His passion was for science, but he had an ear for languages and the kind of maths-and-music brain that gives tensile strength to this type of high intelligence. He still fought at the slightest provocation, but now there were sports to channel his energy and though he was too wary to make friends, friends – cautiously – began to make him.

The scholarship to Cambridge was a surprise to no one except Guy himself. He went to Trinity for natural sciences, and Martha, just as she had braced herself through the years of his childhood for the reappearance of his lost parents, now prepared herself to let him go, without complaint, out of her life.

These preparations were unnecessary. No one was ever to come forward and claim kinship with Guy, nor did Guy himself now show the slightest signs of turning his back on his past. Though he spent the long vacation getting such work as he could to help pay for his clothes and extra expenses, he returned every Christmas and Easter, changing as the train steamed over the Tyne Bridge into his old ways and old dialect as easily as one changes coats. At nineteen, Guy Farne was still on the short side, still trailing his extraordinary strength and compactness as though his muscles were of a different clay. The springy dark hair, the pointed ears which Martha had bandaged to his skull in vain, combined with his high cheekbones to give him that puckish, foreign look that in the orphanage had been laid at the door of the Lithuanians, but his wide mouth and strong chin recalled a simpler, more pastoral heritage. Guy's eyes, during those years at Cambridge, were seldom without the glint of blue which signalled the well-being of his soul as he came into his own in scholarship, in sport and friendship. Only women he left alone, knowing – as men whose sexual power has never been in doubt do know – how to wait.

He got a First and went to the University of Vienna which, in the year 1911, was unrivalled for its work on the conduction of metallic ions through water. Martha Hodge never knew what happened during that year for which he left bursting with confidence and from which he returned, green-eyed and taciturn, with the information that he was no longer interested in academic life and had thrown up his studies. That he had been deeply hurt was obvious; that it was by a woman she did not find it difficult to guess. Wisely, she held her tongue and received, with her usual quiet attention, the information that nothing mattered except to be extremely rich.

The first million, they say, is the hardest. Guy made his by selling to the house of Rothschild (one of whose youthful members he had known in Vienna) a detailed and audacious scheme for the forward purchase of options on cargo shipping rights. Based on the prediction of a war which, owing to the almost equal balance of power in Europe, would be long, and presented to the amazed old banker in a red student's exercise book which was to become a family heirloom, it provided at minimum risk – for the down payments to the shipping companies were to be regarded as interest-free and recallable loans – an opportunity to corner the charter market within five years.

Extorting his reward, under the threat of publishing the details of his scheme, Guy left for South America where he spent three months exploring the backward and mineral-rich Minas Cerais. Within a year he had extracted from the Brazilian government an option on the mining rights of the Ouro Preto range, offering in exchange foreign investment and the building of roads and schools for the Indians. It was not the gold and emeralds which were his chief concern, but the cobalt, for he foresaw the western world's insatiable demand for high-grade steel.

Thus, in those first years, he established a pattern which was to make his success a legend: the use of his scientific training to predict events, the nerve to back his hunches and the direct and practical entrepreneurism of the man on the spot; for he was always to return to the products of the earth's crust and the adventure of their extraction.

By the time war came, he had a facienda on the Amazon and a diversity of interests from oil to real estate, but he chose to honour his commitment to the Indians and it was 1916 before he returned to England. Resisting the efforts of the War Office to recruit him on the staff, he joined the Northumberland Yeomanry, fighting with a detached ferocity directed not at the enemy but at the blundering fools who had made the war. A year later he was invalided out with a shattered leg and a Distinguished Service Order and set about forming his own investment company. By now he had a retinue, an international reputation and offices in a dozen capitals, but Martha Hodge – as he returned at intervals to install into the house she resolutely refused to leave, first running water, then electricity, then a bathroom – continued to be troubled by the colour of his eyes.

Then, in the spring of 1922, he returned to Vienna.

1

Guy returned to the capital of a dismembered empire: a city impoverished by defeat, in the grip of inflation but still beautiful. The theatres were open, the concert halls were packed. The Viennese still danced, still sang. Sometimes, as the new republic struggled with the shortages and disruptions left by the war, they even ate.

Guy took a suite at Sachers, saw that his stenographer and chauffeur were suitably housed nearby and allowed himself a week of the swashbuckling entrepreneurism that was his hallmark, wresting the copper concessions in the Eisen Gebirge from an Armenian syndicate after a spectacular battle, and gleefully beating a South African tycoon to the lignite deposits near Graz. After which, considerably refreshed, he presented himself at the Treasury and plunged into the work which had brought him to Vienna.

It was work shrouded in secrecy, as vital and exacting as it was outwardly unspectacular. For Austria was seeking a huge loan from the League of Nations, seeing in this her only chance to stabilize her currency and set off along the road to recovery. It was to assist the new republic in presenting her case to the League that Guy had been sent out by the British government, who feared that a permanently weakened Austria would seek union with Germany. No one seeing him, day after day, courteous and patient, would have imagined how irksome he found the ponderous bureaucracy and time-wasting social functions in the stuffy, grandiose rooms of the Hofburg.

Then, on a fine Saturday at the end of March, Guy, obeying a summons from his young secretary David Tremayne, left the city, dismissed his chauffeur and turned his car southward towards the fortress known as Pfaffenstein. This is the most famous castle in Burgenland, an emblem for the whole of Austria – the embodiment for close on a thousand years of defensive power, aggression, grandeur and pride.

The position alone is breathtaking. At the head of a dark green lake whose glacial waters chill the blood even in midsummer, is a great pinnacle of rock rising skyward from the pines which cling to its base. To the east the crag, split from top to bottom by a fault in the rock, drops sheer to the Hungarian plain. To the north are the wooded slopes and jagged peaks of the Pfaffenstein mountains whose passes it dominates; to the west, sloping more gently, are the vineyards and orchards which merge in the far distance with the snow crown of the Alps.

On the summit of this gigantic eyrie, the last outcrop

of the Pfaffenburg spur, the Franks built a fort at the time of Charlemagne, but even they were not the first. Two hundred years later, the Crusaders added a square of turreted towers, threw a drawbridge over the dizzying ravine to the east of the castle and rode out full panoplied against the infidel, bearing aloft the banner of the Pfaffensteins with its impaled griffin and crimson glove.

By the time Richard Coeur de Lion was brought there, pending his imprisonment at Durenstein, Burg Pfaffenstein was a thriving Romanesque citadel with a council chamber, a chapel and a village clinging humbly to the base of its crag. In subsequent centuries, as the Tartars invaded Hungary, the Hungarians invaded Austria and the Turks invaded both, its fame and importance increased as steadily as the power of its owners who became, by conquest and marriage, first counts, then margravines, then princes.

The rout of Sultan Mahomet's troops after the second siege of Vienna, which banished the Turks for ever from Christendom, set in train a riot of new building as cannon bastions and barrier walls were blown up and the years of imperial splendour under the ever mightier Habsburgs were reflected in Pfaffenstein's steadily increasing grandeur, opulence and pomp. Ignoring, but never quite managing to erase, the dungeons built deep into the rock, the torture chambers and oubliettes of the earlier fortress, the princes of Pfaffenstein built a palace along the southern front, the windows of its great state rooms sheer with the crag as it rose above the lake; blasted terraces out of the rock and threw pepper-pot turrets on to the flanking towers. A musical Pfaffenstein built a theatre, an Italianate one arcaded the courtyards, a prince of the Church enlarged the Romanesque chapel to form a soaring, gilded paean to the glory of God.

Larger than Hochosterwitz, more heavily fortified than the Esterhazy palace at Eisenstadt and far, far older than the castles that the poor mad Swan King Ludwig had built to the north in Bavaria, Burg Pfaffenstein, by the end of the nineteenth century, had become the subject of innumerable paintings and the inspiration of countless minor poets. The redoubtable Baedecker, when he arrived, gave it three stars.

To this castle, driving himself in his custom-built, tulip-wood Hispano-Suiza, came Guy Farne on a spring afternoon in 1922, with a view to purchase.

He came, as all who come from Vienna must, by the road which skirted the western side of the lake and as the fantastic, towering pile reared up before him, his wide mouth curved into an appreciative smile.

'Yes,' he said to the young man sitting beside him, 'it will do. Definitely, it will do. You've done well, David.'

His secretary, David Tremayne, whose fair good looks and puppyish desire to please concealed a tireless efficiency, turned a relieved face to his employer. 'I thought you'd like it, sir. I saw a few others but I don't know . . . This one put them all in the shade.'

'It certainly makes its own quiet statement,' said Guy sardonically.

16

But as he switched off the engine and got out of the car, he momentarily caught his breath. Burg Pfaffenstein's role as fortress, as refuge and as palace was evident in every stone. Now, in the still, green lake which mirrored with exquisite accuracy each tower and pinnacle and glistening spire, Guy saw it in another guise: as Valhalla or Venusberg – the castle as dream.

'You're certain the owners want to sell?'

'Absolutely, sir. There are only the two old ladies left now and a great-niece in Vienna.' And David fell silent, thinking with compassion of the proud, impoverished families he had visited in his search, all desperate to offer him their ducal Schloss or moated Wasserburg or hunting lodge.

Guy nodded, measuring the road which passed under the crag at the head of the lake and then vanished into the ravine.

'Let's see if we can make it without oxygen, then,' he said and climbed back into the car.

But as Guy drove skilfully round the hair-raising bends that led up to the Burg, David was frowning. His instructions had been simple: to find an impressive and imposing castle ('toffee-nosed' was the word his employer had used, reverting to his origins) which the owners were willing to rent or preferably to sell.

Only why? This was something Guy Farne had not chosen to reveal to his otherwise trusted secretary, and the whole enterprise seemed totally out of keeping with what David knew of his employer's tastes and inclinations. A millionaire he might be, and several times over, but his personal habits were spartan to a degree which caused deep pain to Morgan his chauffeur, to Miss Thisbe Purse, his stenographer, and at times to David himself. Farne's indifference to comfort, his ability to go without food or sleep, his detestation of pomp were a byword, nor had he troubled to conceal his contempt for those post-war profiteers who conned the newly-poor out of their houses and possessions. True, his sojourn in Austria was likely to be of some duration and he needed a base – but why this gigantic castle? In Brazil, where other men of his wealth had bought palaces, he had lived in a simple if lovely facienda by the river, his only extravagance a steam yacht with which he explored the mazed waterways of the Amazon. In London he lived in an apartment in the Albany, in Paris in a roof-top flat in the Ile St Louis which but for the glory of its plumbing might have belonged to any Left Bank painter or poet. Only on movement – elegant boats, fleet cars and (his latest acquisition) a small bi-plane – did Farne habitually spend the awe-inspiring sums which betrayed his stupendous wealth.

They had negotiated that last hairpin bend, crossed the drawbridge, been sneered at by the griffins on the gatehouse arch and now drew up in a vast and silent courtyard.

Ten minutes later, having followed an ancient retainer in the Pfaffenstein livery of crimson and bottle-green along an immense groin-vaulted corridor and through a series of shrouded and magnificent rooms, they found themselves in the presence of the two old ladies who were now the castle's sole occupants.

Augustine-Maria, Duchess of Breganzer, was in her eighties, her eagle's beak of a nose and fierce grey eyes dominating the wrinkled, parchment face. The Duchess wore a black lace dress to the hem of which there adhered a number of cobwebs and what appeared to be a piece of cheese. A cap of priceless and yellowing lace was set on her sparse hair and her rather dirty, arthritic hands rested on a magnificent ivory cane which had belonged to Marie Antoinette.

Her sister-in-law Mathilde, Margravine of Attendorf and Untersweg, was a little younger and in spite of recent shortages, resolutely round-faced and plump. Unlike the Duchess who had received them standing, the Margravine remained seated in order to embrace more efficiently the quivering, shivering form of a goggle-eyed and slightly malodorous pug whose lower extremities were wrapped in a gold-embroidered Medici cope.

Driven back room by room by their poverty, the demands of the war (which had turned Pfaffenstein into a military hospital) and their own increasing age and infirmity, the ladies had taken refuge in the West Tower, in what had been an ante-room connecting the great enfilade of state rooms on the southern facade with the kitchens.

Its round walls were hung with tapestries which Guy suspected had been chosen more for their capacity to exclude draughts than for their artistic content, for they mainly depicted people holding heads: Judith that of Holofernes, Salome of John the Baptist and St Jerome of a dismembered stag. The Meissen-tiled stove was unlit; dust lay on the carved arms of the vast chairs fashioned, it seemed, for the behinds of mountain ogres – but the condescension and graciousness of the ladies was absolute.

'Welcome to Pfaffenstein, Herr Farne. We trust you found your journey enjoyable.'

Guy, kissing the extended hand and replying suitably, noticed with pleasure that the Duchess spoke what was called 'Schönbrunner Deutsch', a dialect which the high nobility shared with the cab drivers of Vienna. And indeed both ladies had been attendant on the Emperor Franz Joseph's family in the palace of Schönbrunn outside Vienna where the gruelling Spanish ceremonial, the staggering absence of lavatories and the indifferent food had proved an excellent preparation for their present way of life.

Refreshment was offered and refused, the necessary courtesies were exchanged. Then Guy, whose German was fast and fluent, came to the point.

'You will know already that I would like to buy Burg Pfaffenstein. My solicitors have mentioned the terms?'

The Duchess inclined her head. 'They are fair,' she conceded, 'and we are willing. But as I have already informed your secretary, for a final decision we are awaiting a reply from Putzerl.'

Hearing the name, the pug shot like a squeezed pip from his golden cope and began to run round the room yapping excitedly, causing Guy to exchange an apprehensive glance with his secretary. If Putzerl was the name of the little dog they were in trouble.

The danger passed. For Putzerl, as the ladies now explained, was the great-niece in Vienna, more precisely the Princess of Pfaffenstein and (her mother having been an archduchess) of quite a few other places, and now the sole and legal owner of the castle with its dairies, sawmills, brewery, villages, salt-mine (now defunct) and 56,627 hectares of land.

'Because, you see, when her father went off to fight he managed to break the entail on the male heir and a great fuss it was. He had to go and see poor cousin Pippi in the end,' said the Margravine.

'But we're certain she'll agree. She's been urging us to sell. Putzerl is extremely modern,' said the Duchess. 'And of course the money will be invaluable for her dowry because poor Maxi really doesn't have a kreutzer to bless himself with.'

The dizzying capacity of the Austrians to refer to absolutely everybody by some appalling diminutive or nickname, which Guy had forgotten, now returned to his mind. Having gathered that cousin Pippi was Pope Pius XV, he was now informed, though he had been careful not to ask, that Maxi (alias Maximilian Ferdinand, Prince of Spittau and Neusiedel) was the young man they had picked for Putzerl to marry, there being – owing to the cruel war and the sordid revolutions in various places which had followed it – quite simply no one else.

'The Gastini-Bernardi boy would have done quite well, actually,' said the Duchess, on whom the thought of Maxi seemed to be working adversely. 'But he's dead. And I must say there always seems to be cholera in Trieste.'

'Or Schweini,' said the Margravine, her voice soft. 'Such a sweet-looking boy.'

'Don't be silly, Tilda. The Trautenstaufers only have twelve quarterings.'

'Still, they're in the *Almanach* . . .'

The argument that followed seemed a little pointless since Schweini, though destined for the Uhlans, had apparently been speared to death by one of his own boars before he could cover himself with glory. Guy, while not wishing to appear indifferent to Putzerl's matrimonial prospects, now felt free to indicate that he would like to look round the castle.

If he had hoped that he and David would be allowed to roam at will, his hopes were dashed. The retainer was rung for, the pug lowered on to the ground again; shawls, walking sticks and bunches of keys were fetched and the expedition set off.

Within ten minutes Guy realized that Pffaffenstein, inside and out, was exactly what he had been looking for. Its neglect, though spectacular, was recent. In the three months he had set aside for the task he could easily restore it to its former splendour. The huge, baroque state rooms with their breathtaking views over the lake were ideal for his purpose; the guest rooms in the loggia were sound and the outer courtyards with their stables, coachhouses and servants' quarters would house his workmen without inconveniencing the villagers. Above all, the private theatre with its aquamarine curtains, gilded boxes and ceiling frescoes by Tiepolo was a jewel which would be the perfect setting for the entertainment that was to set the seal on his plans.

But if he had seen enough to satisfy himself almost at once, there was no way of hurrying the ladies.

'This,' announced the Duchess unnecessarily as they entered a low building piled from floor to ceiling with skulls, 'is the charnel house.'

'Those skulls on the right are from the Black Death,' said the Margravine helpfully.

'And the ones on the left are Protestants,' said the Duchess, murmuring, as she recalled the probable Anglicanism of Guy and his secretary, that there had been a 'little bit of trouble' during the Thirty Years War.

But it was before a lone skull displayed on a plinth in a kind of bird-cage and still boasting fragments of a mummified ear, that both ladies stopped with an especial pride.

'Putzerl found this one when she climbed out through the dungeons on to the south face, the naughty girl.'

'She believes it's a Turk and we never had the heart to contradict her, though it is most unlikely. The Turks were all impaled on the eastern wall.'

'We think it was probably a commercial traveller who came to see her great-grandfather.'

'About saddle soap,' put in the Margravine.

'He came by the front entrance, you see. And poor Rudi was always so impulsive.'

They inspected the chapel with its Eichendorfer altar piece, climbed up yet another massive flight of stairs to the weapons room bristling with flintlock pistols and percussion guns; the museum packed with the heads of wolves, boars and the last auroch in the Forest of Pfaffenstein which Kaiser Wilhelm II had shot, only to be bitten in the leg by the three-year-old Putzerl for his pains . . . And down again, passing the well into which a seventeenth-century princess of Pfaffenstein, who had not cared for the matrimonial arrangements made on her behalf, had thrown herself on her wedding day.

'Which was extremely silly of her,' added the Duchess, 'because he would have had Modena and Parma had he lived.'

'Oh, Augustina, but he had no nose,' expostulated the gentler Margravine. 'It was all eaten away, you know,' she explained to Guy, blushing, 'by a . . . certain disease.'

'Putzerl used to sit here on the rim of the well for hours when she was little,' said the Duchess, 'waiting for a frog to come.'

'She wanted to throw it against the wall, like in the fairy tale, and turn it into a prince.'

'And then one day a frog really did come and she cried and cried and cried.'

'The frog was so much prettier than a prince, you see – even than Schweini, and *he* had the most lovely curls!'

'So she kept it in the oubliette as a pet. Now here,' continued the Duchess, opening a studded door from which a flight of slime-green steps led down into the darkness, 'we must be a little careful. But you'll be interested in the third Count's collection of torture instruments. It is arranged exactly as the Inquisition left it!'

But at last they were back in the tower room, solicitors' names exchanged, contracts mentioned and a bottle of Margaux '83 brought up from the cellar.

'And how soon would you wish us to leave?' asked the Duchess, her voice carefully expressionless.

Guy leaned back in his carved chair and, the ladies having given him permission to smoke, selected a Monte Cristo, rolled it between his long fingers and began the careful husbandry that precedes the lighting of a great cigar.

'There is no need for you to leave at present unless you wish to,' he said. 'On the contrary. In fact, you could say that in proposing to purchase Pfaffenstein I am endeavouring to secure your services.'

The ladies, whose small breath of relief had not escaped him, looked at him in puzzlement. 'What had you in mind, Herr Farne? Not tourists? Because I'm afraid we couldn't countenance that.'

'No, no,' said Guy soothingly. 'Nothing like that. I propose to give a house party here at Pfaffenstein. It will last for a week and include a ball, a banquet, possibly a regatta on the lake – and finish with an entertainment here in the theatre. And I want you to select the guests.'

'Us?' faltered the Duchess.

Guy inclined his head. 'I only ask that they should belong to your social circle.'

'You wish to entertain our friends to a banquet and a ball?' said the stunned Margravine.

'And a house party to follow,' repeated Guy. 'I myself shall bring only one guest: a lady.'

Guy's voice had been carefully expressionless but David leaned forward, aware that he had touched the heart of the mystery. At the same time he felt an inexplicable sense of unease.

'A lady to whom I hope to be married,' Guy continued. And answering David's look of bewilderment, the slight hurt in the boy's face, he added, 'She is the widow of an officer wounded in the war and her period of mourning will only end in June, so no formal engagement exists as yet.' He paused, and David saw the extraordinary change in the colour of his eyes as he remembered happiness. 'I knew her years ago in Vienna.'

'She is Austrian?' enquired the Duchess.

'No, English, but she loves your country. I should add perhaps that I am myself a foundling and was discovered in circumstances so disreputable that they must entirely preclude my seeking an entrée into the nobility. Indeed, my ambitions in that direction are non-existent. It is otherwise, however, with Mrs Hurlingham. Her aunt,' said Guy, who had been made well aware of the fact, 'was an Honourable.'

The ladies exchanged glances. 'That is not a very high rank, Herr Farne,' said the Duchess reprovingly.

'Nevertheless she wishes, most understandably, to take her place in society. And I,' he went on, his voice suddenly harsh, 'do not wish her to suffer from being married to a man who is not even low-born but not "born" at all.'

'It will be difficult,' stated the Duchess.

'She is not perhaps a Howard? Or a Percy – the aunt?' enquired the Margravine hopefully.

'I don't think so.'

'Oh, dear.' The Duchess was perplexed. Well versed in the ways of the world, she was aware that the attractive Herr Farne with his wealth and obvious indifference to what anybody thought of him would be accepted far more easily than a fiancée with aspirations. 'You see, our friends are rather particular. Prince Monteforelli, for example . . .'

Though highly entertained by the deep and ingrained snobbery of these old women, whose country on the map now looked like a severed and diminutive pancreas, whose court and emperor were totally defunct, Guy felt it was time he made his position clear. So leaning back, gently lowering a wedge of fragrant ash into the Louis Quatorze spittoon with which he had been provided, he said placidly that if they felt unable to introduce Mrs Hurlingham to European high society he regretted that the sale would be cancelled.

The ladies now retired behind a screen to confer. Though they spoke in whispers, they were sufficiently deaf for their deliberations to be perfectly clear to Guy, who gathered that their desire not to deprive Putzerl of her dowry, along with the lure of the word 'banquet' was fast overcoming their reluctance to offend their friends by introducing them to a lady whose aunt, though an Honourable, was unrelated to the great ducal families of Britain.

'Very well, Herr Farne,' said the Duchess with a sigh. 'We will present your friend.'

'Good,' said Guy. 'You should hear from my lawyers in a few days, by which time I trust your great-niece will have been in touch, and then I will send in the workmen. Mr Tremayne here,' he continued, grinning at David, 'will see to everything. There is one other condition. I want complete secrecy. My name is not to appear in the transaction; the deeds will be made out in the name of one of my companies. I would prefer that even the local people do not know that I am the new owner until everything is completed. I suggest June the eighteenth for the reception and the opening ball?'

'Very well, Herr Farne.'

'Oh, and I want to hire an opera company. Is there one that you can recommend?'

Even the ladies of Burg Pfaffenstein were impressed by the high-handedness of this.

'The International Opera Company in the Klostern Theatre is said to be very good. Putzerl often speaks of it.'

28

'And she's extremely musical. In fact she's studying music.'

Guy thanked them, removed a spider which had fallen into his wineglass and took his leave.

It was not until they were halfway back to Vienna, eating supper in the candle-lit dining room of the White Horse Inn, that Guy, crumbling a roll in his long fingers, chose to give his secretary some kind of explanation.

'You've been very patient, David. You must think I've gone quite mad. All that for a woman . . . Only, you see, she's had a rotten life – forced into an unhappy marriage, then watching the poor devil take four years to die.' He was silent for a moment, his eyes on the candle flame, the customary mocking look momentarily absent from his face. He looked years younger and to David, who worshipped him, suddenly and frighteningly vulnerable.

'I want her to have everything she wanted at seventeen, however absurd,' he went on. '*Everything*. She doesn't even realize I'm rich – we only met a fortnight before I came away and I didn't tell her. When I knew her before, I was twenty years old and penniless. I want her to come upon Pfaffenstein lit up for a ball and peopled with princes. I want her to walk into a fairy tale – and know that all of it is hers.'

'She must be very beautiful,' said David quietly.

'The most beautiful woman I've ever seen. She's lovely now but at seventeen – oh, God!'

And for the first time in his life, Guy began to speak of his love for the girl who had been Nerine Croft.

2

Whether it was the sheer beauty of the city, then at the
height of its imperial splendour: a city from whose
every window came music, a lazily grey and gold-
domed city framed in the cherished hills and vineyards
of the Wienerwald . . . whether it was Vienna itself or
the cosmopolitan society Guy experienced there, or the
fizz of new thought as Schönberg revolutionized music,
Klimt's golden, exotic ladies scandalized the world of
art and Sigmund Freud produced the outrageous theo-
ries which were to change men's views of themselves for
ever . . . or whether it was simply that he was young and
at the height of his powers, Guy now paused in the conquest of knowledge, the world, himself – and began
simply to enjoy life.

What happened next was of course inevitable, but to
Guy it was the miracle that a first love, truly and violently experienced, is to every man who is worthy of the
name.

Vienna, in those halcyon years, was not only a gay

and fashionable capital but also the centre of a thriving international industry: Europe's most popular marriage mart. To the finishing schools of Vienna came the daughters of American millionaires, British industrialists and the French nouveau riche, nominally to learn German, study music and appreciate art – actually to take the preliminary steps which would secure, in due course, a husband both nobly born and rich.

Housed generally in some magnificent Schloss whose owners had fallen on hard times, protected by high walls and splendid iron gates, these girls, who often could scarcely add two numbers together, nevertheless understood precisely the subtle arithmetic by which a German ritter with land might equal a Hungarian count without . . . how a French vicomte with a pedigree could nevertheless be set aside for an Italian marchese with factories discreetly out of sight somewhere which made him a millionaire. As for a prince, he needed nothing else. To be addressed as 'princess' these girls, well-trained by their mothers, would have embraced a man of fifty with dentures and the pox.

Meanwhile, enchantingly dressed in their muslins, frantically chaperoned by hatchet-faced and underpaid 'companions', the girls trooped through museums, attended concerts and military manoeuvres and took excursions into the surrounding countryside.

This beguiling, hot-house world was one to which normally Guy would never have had access. But coming into the university lobby in his first month in Vienna, he found a pale, frightened, long-haired young man pinned to the wall by two cropped louts from the Jew-baiting Burschenschaft who were questioning him about his ancestry.

Guy had been leading a life of exceptional docility but a look of pleasure now spread over his face. Taking one of the louts by the shoulder, he said he would be obliged if they would leave his friend alone.

The lout, swinging round to meet a pair of malachite eyes, asked what business it was of his? Guy, mustering his German, said that bullying did not amuse him, adding that if there was no objection to duelling with someone who had been found under a piece of sacking on the Fish Quay in Newcastle upon Tyne and was most unlikely to have been born in wedlock, then he would be delighted to meet him. Otherwise, if he did not go away, Guy would pulverize him into insensibility and knock his idiotic duelling scar into his earhole. The second lout, coming to trip him up, found himself rolling down the steps towards the Ringstrasse.

Nonplussed, the louts departed. The victim, who in spite of his tragic and semitic appearance was the scion of a noble Hungarian house, now became Guy's devoted slave and invited him to his family's box at the Opera. In the neighbouring box, displayed like the choicest flowers from Olympus for the gaze of the populace, was a group of girls from Frau von Edelnau's Academy. Pretty girls, striking girls – and one, in the seat nearest to Guy, who possessed that unique quality: an unequivocal and breathtaking beauty.

The English are a plain race but just occasionally,

borrowing usually from some Celtic ancestor, they achieve a breathtaking perfection. Nerine Croft's dusky, abundant ringlets were tied high with a golden thong to dance on her bare shoulders: the forget-me-nots embroidered on her white muslin dress mirrored the heavenly blue of her wide-set eyes and her small nose, as though to ward off the accusation of a cold perfection, was slightly, tantalizingly retroussée.

If it hadn't been *The Magic Flute* . . . if she had not, as the curtain rose, given the smallest of anticipatory sighs . . . if she had not, at the end of Pamino's miraculous aria of exalted love, turned in the soft dusk of the lôge and smiled at him.

But it was Mozart's masterpiece, and she did so turn. The parents of Guy's friend were acquainted with Frau Edelnau, and in the interval he was introduced. Nerine, delighted to find that he was English, said, yes, the singing had been wonderful and, yes, he could procure for her an ice.

So it began. It was spring: violets in the Prater; Strauss in the Stadtpark; the café tables with their bright, checked cloths spilling out on to the pavements once again. Bells rang in this enchanted city, the Kaiser drove out in a carriage with golden wheels . . . It was Frau Edelnau's policy to invite suitably vetted young men to private dances and outings with her girls. To this select band of officers and students Guy, who at twenty was a strangely compelling creature with his wolf's eyes and air of compressed energy, was now admitted. And Nerine, trained almost from birth to beguile and flirt and please, was enchanting to her young compatriot whose physical courage and intellectual brilliance were becoming something of a legend in the University.

And so, in a city which God might have designed for the purpose, Guy experienced the miracle, the transforming alchemy of total love. Every plumed spray of lilac in the Volksgarten, every caryatid supporting Vienna's innumerable pillars, every street-seller with her brazier of chestnuts seemed to him limned in light. He wrote songs to Nerine and sent them floating as paper boats down the River Wien; he kept vigil outside her window at night. Friends clustered round him like puppies, bemused by his happiness. He discovered the Secessionists, climbed the dizzying verdigris dome of the University, and hardly ever went to bed. That spring and summer of his twenty-first year, Guy was invincible.

Later, he was to ask himself how much Nerine had been affected. She was always enchanting, looking up at him with those artless, deep-blue eyes, and he was accepted by the other girls as 'hers'. But Frau von Edelnau and her minions had brought chaperonage to a fine art. Guy was allowed to waltz with her at private dances but never more than twice, to walk beside her carriage in the Prater, to procure lemonade at the manoeuvres and military parades so beloved of the Viennese, but it was impossible to be with her alone.

Until the picnic in the Vienna Woods . . .

The word 'picnic', which to the British suggests a casual and relaxed approach to eating, suggested to

34

Frau Edelnau something quite different. Rugs and hampers of food were piled into carriages; the ropy arms of the chaperones emerged from hastily donned dirndls, and the expedition set off for the ruined monastery on the Kahlenberg now suitably provided with wooden tables, carefully sited vantage points and hygienic toilets.

They arrived . . . picnicked . . . the chaperones dozed, overcome by salami and pumpernickl. The girls picked cornflowers and marguerites to twine into their hair.

'There can't be anything better than this,' said a freckle-faced, sunny American girl, looking at the tapestry of the green and gold-domed city below them.

'Yes, there can,' said Nerine.

'What, then?'

'Oh, being rich . . . having marvellous clothes . . . Dancing the night through with princes at a glittering ball. Living in a castle.'

Guy, as always, was beside her.

'I'll buy you a castle,' he said.

Nerine turned and stared at him, caught not by the words but by the tone in which they were spoken. It was almost as though this impecunious boy really had the power to grant wishes. She became dreamy, pensive . . . Guy had found a glade of wild orchids in which there danced a myriad golden butterflies. Now he offered to show it to the girls and a party set off. The others fell behind and in a sudden shaft of sunlight Nerine, dazzled, stumbled on a root.

35

Guy caught her and quite beside himself by now, kissed her with all the passion of his nature.

And Nerine kissed him back.

To Guy, adrift in a foreign city, reared by Martha Hodge, that kiss meant one thing and one thing only. When Nerine returned to England, he followed her and in a daze of happiness, presented himself at the Crofts' ornate and over-furnished villa in Twickenham to ask for her hand.

It is hard to see why they were not kind. So simple, surely, to have spoken of her youth, his need to complete his studies, their conviction that at seventeen their daughter could hardly know her own mind. Instead, the Crofts exhibited a cruelty and arrogance that he had not known existed.

'Insolent puppy!' snorted the empurpled Mr Croft, just returned from his city bank. 'How dare you! I ought to have you horse-whipped.'

'No birth, no family and no prospects,' sneered Nerine's brother, a pallid young man of Guy's own age. 'I must say you've got a nerve!'

'And penniless!' roared Mr Croft, to whom poverty was the ultimate crime.

'Are you aware that Nerine's aunt is an Honourable?' enquired Mrs Croft, a small, tight-lipped woman with calculating eyes.

Unable to lift a finger against the relatives of his beloved, Guy stood stock-still in the centre of the drawing-room with its draped piano legs and over-stuffed cushions. But the footman, coming forward in response to Mr Croft's instructions to 'Throw him out, James', found himself reeling against the wall, nursing his arm.

Nerine was not present at the interview. His subsequent letters were returned.

That had been ten years ago. To say that the wound had never healed might seem absurd. If Guy was deflected, now, from the path of scholarship and determined to become rich enough to be revenged on the Crofts of this world, it was a decision he never regretted. Three years later he was in the Amazon, entertaining a string of lovely women on his yacht, and in the years that followed he had innumerable affairs. But he never again fell in love – and he never forgot.

Then, just two weeks before he left for Vienna, he had come out of the new, seven-storey office block in the Strand which housed his Associated Investment Company when he heard a soft voice say, 'Guy!' – and there she was.

Nerine was in half-mourning, her raven hair piled high under a plumed velvet hat. She had filled out, there were now a few lines round her lovely eyes, but Guy, as he gazed at her, was gazing at his youth.

She was pleased to see him, pleased and surprised, she made that clear, having no idea what had become of him. Her own story was sad: marriage to the son of a baronet who should have inherited a title and a comfortable life as a landowner – and had instead died by slow degrees of a wound received in Flanders.

'So I'm back home,' said Nerine, lifting a face full of

courage and resignation to his. 'And you, Guy? How are you?'

'I'm just off to Vienna, as a matter of fact,' said Guy, when he could trust his voice again.

'Ah, Vienna! I was so happy there! Do you remember . . . ?' Guy remembered.

Nerine's father was dead. Her brother had speculated unwisely. In the villa at Twickenham, Guy, though he kept his wealth a secret, was now a welcome guest. When he left for Austria, it was with Nerine's promise to join him, with her brother, as soon as she was out of mourning. Though nothing could be settled until then, he had returned to Vienna as a man who, against all expectations, was to achieve his heart's desire.

3

Though she was both emancipated and in a hurry, Tessa began the day by brushing, with three hundred regular strokes, her almost knee-length, toffee-coloured hair. Her country upbringing had been strict and even though her glorious new life in Vienna was now devoted to the service of art in general and opera in particular, she found it hard to break the habits of her childhood. Moreover, it was true that lacking the height, the Rubenesque and potentially heaving bosom and the Roman nose she so desperately craved, she could find a certain consolation in the rich, fawn tresses which she could most comfortably have sat on had her employer, Jacob Witzler, ever given her the time.

Whether Tessa would have appeared on the payroll of the International Opera Company as under wardrobe mistress, assistant lighting engineer, deputy wigmaker, A.S.M., prompter or errand girl, remained a theoretical question since she did not, in fact, get any pay. That it was an inestimable privilege to be allowed to work in the opera house and learn her craft, Tessa, her auburn eyes burning with artistic fervour, had assured Herr Witzler – a view which he entirely shared and had in fact suggested to her in the first place. And though she did not actually have any money to speak of, it had all worked out marvellously because Frau Witzler, a former Rhinemaiden and spear-carrying soprano of distinction, had found a family in the Wipplingerstrasse who, in exchange for a little help with their three young children, had offered Tessa one of the old servants' attics. A beautiful room, she thought it, with its views over the roofs of the Inner City and the soaring spire of the Stefansdom.

Now she quickly braided and pinned her hair, washed her hands and face, dressed in her working smock of unbleached linen, and ran downstairs to where the three infant Kugelheimers in their cots greeted her with cries of satisfaction.

During the next half-hour she changed the baby, lugged the three-year-old Klara on to the gigantic, rose-adorned chamber-pot, ran into the kitchen to heat some milk, dressed the four-year-old Franzerl, made coffee for Frau Kugelheimer – and, finally, grabbing a letter from the postman which she thrust unread into her pocket, was safely out into the street.

It was just growing light, the city lifting itself out of sleep. A row of tiny choristers walked across the cobbles to sing Mass in the Peterskirche; the pigeons on the Plague Memorial, safe again after years of being potted at by hungry citizens, began to preen themselves for the day. A baker, pulling up his shutters, called 'Grüss Gott!' and Tessa gave him a smile of such radiance that he stood watching her like a man warming himself in a sudden shaft of sun until she turned into the Kärntner-strasse. It never failed her, this sense of awe and wonder at belonging . . . at working here in this city which had been Schubert's and Mozart's, and now was hers.

The Klostern Theatre, which now housed the International Opera Company, had once been the private theatre of a nobleman whose adjoining palace had been pulled down at the time the old ramparts were destroyed and the Ringstrasse built. The auditorium with its enchanted painted ceiling of obese and ecstatic nymphs, its red velvet boxes and gold proscenium arch, invariably wrung a sigh of pleasure from connoisseurs of Austrian high baroque. Backstage, the theatre resembled a cross between the Black Hole of Calcutta and the public lavatory of an abandoned railway terminus. The pit was too small for the orchestra, the manager's office was a windowless kennel, merely to approach the dimmer board was to take one's life in one's hands. Everyone who worked there cursed the place from morning to night and resisted with vituperative ferocity all suggestions of a move to more salubrious quarters.

Tessa let herself in by the stage door, sighing happily at the familiar smell of glue and size and paint and dust. As always she was the first to arrive and the sense of the sleeping theatre, dark and cold, waiting to be brought to life – and by her – was an ever-recurring delight. Today was a particularly exciting day: the last day of

41

Lucia di Lammermoor in which Raisa Romola, losing her reason as only a two-hundred-kilo, red-haired Rumanian soprano knew how, had scored a triumph; then the announcement by Herr Witzler, after curtain down, of the new opera they would begin to rehearse next week.

Quickly she sorted the mail into the appropriate pigeonholes, took the director's letters upstairs to his office, emptied the mousetraps under his desk, riddled and filled the ancient, rusty stove. Then downstairs again to the front of the house to turn on the light, admit the cleaning ladies and ring the police to inform them that a handbag containing three thousand kroner and a ticket to Karlsbad had been left in row D of the stalls.

Then she hurried back through the orchestra pit, pausing to tidy up the poker school which the trombonists had set up under the stage . . . up two flights again, round a curving iron staircase to the star soprano's dressing-room, to change the water for Raisa Romola's roses, scrub out her dachshund's feeding bowl and collect for repair the bloodstained Act Three nightdress through which an idiot stage hand had put his foot as the heaving diva waited in the wings to take her curtain call.

And downstairs again to find that the wigmaker, Boris Slatarski, had arrived and was staring gloomily at 'The Mother'.

Boris was a Bulgarian and thus committed to longevity and yoghurt. The latter he made from a culture of great ethnicity and ripeness which originated in some shepherd-infested village in the Mirrovaroan Hills. Known as 'The Mother', it lived in a jamjar on the draining-board of the laundry room, smelling vilely, flocculating, turning blue and generally showing all the signs of the artistic temperament.

'I don't like the look of her this morning, Tessa,' he said now, unwinding his long, yellow face and bald skull from the folds of a gigantic muffler. 'She's precipitating much too fast.' He rummaged in a hamper, ripped the muslin sleeve out of a peasant blouse from *The Bartered Bride* and began to filter The Mother through it. 'Have you got the milk yet?'

'I'm just going,' said Tessa. She fetched the can, ran to the dairy three streets away, and back, hiding the egg she had managed to wheedle out of the dairyman in a box labelled 'Spats'.

The theatre was fully awake now. Hammering resounded from the scene dock, pieces of scenery suddenly flew upward. Cries of 'Where's Tessa?' came with increasing frequency – from Frau Pollack, the wardrobe mistress, who wanted to know why Tessa had not brought down the costumes for *Tosca*, had not sorted out the buckle box, had not made the coffee . . . from the lighting assistant who wanted her to hold a spot, from the carpenter who had a splinter in his eye.

At eleven the Herr Direktor, Jacob Witzler, arrived and began to go through the pile of bills, of notices threatening to cut off the water, the telephone and the electricity, which constituted his morning mail.

This frog-eyed Moravian Jew, with his ulcer and his despair, quite simply *was* the International Opera Company. Jacob's dedication, his sacrifices, his chicanery, cajoling and bullying had steered this unsubsidized company for over twenty years through crisis after financial crisis, through war and inflation and the machinations of his rivals.

In a way the whole thing had been bad luck. Jacob came of a wealthy and not particularly musical family of leather merchants in the Moravian town of Sprotz. His life was marked out almost from birth – a serene progress from bar mitzvah to entry into the family firm, marriage to a nice Jewish girl already selected by his mother, a partnership . . .

Jacob was deprived of this comfortable future in a single afternoon when at the age of eleven he was taken, scrubbed to the eyeballs and in his sailor suit, to a touring company's performance of *Carmen*.

All around him, dragged in by their culture-hungry parents, sat other little boys and girls, Christian and Jewish, Moravian and Czech, wriggling and fidgeting, longing for the interval, thirsting for lemonade, bursting for the lavatory.

Not so Jacob. The Hippopotamus-sized mezzo dropped her castanets, Escamillo fell over his dagger, the orchestra was short of two trumpets, three violins and the timpani. No matter. Alone of all the infants of Moravia Jacob Witzler was struck down, and fatally, by the disease known as Opera.

Now, some thirty years later, his fortune gone, his

health ruined, his faith abandoned, he reached for a dyspepsia pill and settled down to work. The claque was clamouring to be paid but that was absurd of course. Raisa would get enough applause tonight; the mad scene always got them and next week they were alternating *Tosca* with *Fledermaus*, old war horses both. Frau Kievenholler had put in a perfectly ludicrous claim for cab fares for her harp . . .

The phone rang: a tenor wanting to audition for the chorus. And rang again: someone was coming round to inspect the fire precautions! And rang again . . .

At noon Jacob put down his pen and sent for Tessa.

'Good morning, Herr Witzler.'

The under wardrobe mistress stood respectfully before him. There was a smut on her small and surprisingly serious nose, her hair was coming down and her smock was liberally spattered with paint, but as he looked at the little figure emitting as always an almost epic willingness to be of use, Jacob at once felt better. His blood pressure descended; his ulcer composed itself for sleep.

Allowing Tessa to come and work for him was one of the best things he had done and if the police did come for her one day he, Jacob, was going to fight for her tooth and nail. True, she had obviously lied to him about her age – he doubted if she was twenty, let alone the twenty-three she had laid claim to. Nor had she remembered to respond, within half an hour of her interview, to the surname she had offered him. She

45

appeared to have no relatives to vouch for her, no documents, certainly no references of any sort; that she had run away from some institution in the country seemed clear enough. He had told himself that he was mad to take her on, but he knew this was not true.

Since then his hunch had paid off a thousand times. It was not simply that this fragile looking waif with her earth-brown eyes worked a fifteen-hour day, trotting indefatigably through the labyrinthine corridors with loads which would have tired a mountain pony. Nor, even, that she herself had no personal ambition to sing or act or dance but only and always to help and to learn. It was, perhaps, that her patent ecstasy at being allowed to serve art somehow vindicated his own absurd and obsessive life. He and this foundling were fellow sufferers from the same disease.

'Have you seen to Miss Romola's bouquet for tonight?' he began.

'Yes, Herr Witzler. It's ordered and I'm going to fetch it after lunch.'

'You don't think we could make it a bit smaller?'

Raisa's bouquets had been steadily shrinking on the principle of the horse from whose feed one removes each day a single oat. It was Tessa's opinion, now delicately voiced, that they were down to the stage where the horse was in danger of dropping dead.

'But I could get Herr Klasky's buttonhole out of it, I think,' she said, referring to the conductor, 'which would save a little?'

'Good, do that. What about the wine for the party tonight?'

'It's just arrived and I've put it in the wig oven, very low, to make it chambré.'

'And you've remembered my wife's reservations at Baden-Baden?'

'Yes, Herr Witzler. A room for one week from June the eighteenth at the Hotel Park, with a cot for your son.'

Jacob nodded gloomily. He had married Leopoldine Goertl-Eisen after that lady, suspended aloft (and in the act of singing 'Weie, Wiege, Wage die Welle') had been horribly precipitated by the snapping of her steel cable on to the stage of the Klostern Theatre during a matinee of *Rheingold*. If he had espoused the massive, bruised Silesian soprano mainly to stop her from suing the International Opera Company, there was no doubt that the marriage was a success. Understandably, however, his Rhinemaiden's nerves had been affected. When they gave *Rheingold* anywhere in Vienna, Jacob was compelled to send her to Baden-Baden and the expense was appalling.

'Then there's a tenor auditioning at three,' he went on. 'Respini can't come, so you'll have to accompany him.'

'Ah, but I don't play well enough.'

'For a tenor you play well enough,' said Jacob firmly. He sighed. 'I was wondering about a ballet for *Tosca*?'

Tessa screwed up her waif-like countenance, pondering. Sylphides in the torture scene? Swans in the prison yard?

Jacob's efforts to insert a ballet into almost everything were herculean and disinterested since he himself was indifferent to 'the Dance'. He employed, however, three delectably pretty and available ballet girls known collectively as The Heidis (since two of them were christened thus) in the hope that their presence would lure in the rich patron he so desperately craved.

'If the Heidis were in the stage box dressed in their tutus with rosebud wreaths and some gauze on their shoulders, you know?' suggested Tessa. 'We could keep the lôge light on low above them. Then the gentlemen could see them and if they wished to . . . afterwards . . . they could . . .'

Jacob beamed. 'Yes! That's what we'll do. Now that leaves the new *Fledermaus* programmes to be fetched from the printers, and I want you to go round and tell Grabenheimer that if I don't get those poster designs by Friday I'm not interested and if he's in the Turkish bath, get him *out!*'

At six the conductor arrived and demanded his button-hole. Zoltan Klasky was a Hungarian with tormented eyes, a shock of long, dark hair and the kind of divine and profound discontent which has sent Magyars through countless centuries galloping westwards and giving everybody hell. He was a brilliant musician who loathed sopranos, tenors and everything that both moved and sang except the occasional nasal and impoverished Gypsy.

Though he conducted even the lightest operettas with maniacal expertise and care, Klasky's own being

48

was dedicated to the composition of an expressionist opera, now in its seventh year of labour. The libretto of this work, authentically based on a newspaper clipping, concerned the wife of a village policeman who is seduced by a millowner, bears him a son and hangs herself, after which the policeman goes mad and tries to murder the baby and serve it to the millowner in a fricassée.

While Tessa had doubts about the operatic qualities of the fricassée, like the rest of the company she was a staunch believer in Klasky's opera which was scored for strings, mandolins and thirty percussion instruments and would herald a new era in atonal music drama, when it was at last performed.

Now, however, there was a peremptory screech from the star dressing-room, announcing Raisa Romola's arrival. Within five minutes, Raisa's dachshund (who inexplicably had remained uneaten during the hardest years of the war) had made a puddle, the state of her head notes made it impossible for her to go on and the tenor, Pino Mastrini, had accused her of stealing his egg.

Tessa dealt with the dachshund, rushed down to the spats box to fetch the egg so vital to the tenor's larynx, ran up to the chorus dressing-room to help Lucia's clansmen with their tartan plaids . . .

And the curtain went up.

Three hours later Tessa, leaning humbly against an upstage tombstone holding her glass of wine, heard Jacob Witzler announce that their new production would be Debussy's lyrical masterpiece, *Pelleas and Melisande*.

The clock was striking two when she let herself back into the house in the Wipplingerstrasse. It was not until she was standing at her attic window, once again brushing her hair, that she remembered the letter which had come that morning and was still unread in the pocket of her smock.

She opened it, noting with approval that her aunt had learned to address her in the way that Tessa had instructed, read it through once, then read it through again.

The news was wholly and absolutely good. It was necessary for Tessa to repeat this to herself with resolution because there was no denying that she did feel . . . well, a *pang*, and that her stomach seemed to be plunging about in a rather uncomfortable way. It was rather as though the whole of her childhood had suddenly dropped into a void. But that was absurd, of course; just sentiment and a failure of courage – and anyway she had no choice. The thing to hold on to was that she was free now . . . free for work, for art, for life!

And opening the window, allowing her long hair to ripple over the sill, the Princess Theresa-Maria of Pfaffenstein leaned her head on her arms, blinked away the foolish tears that threatened her and smiled at the moon.

4

In the breakfast room of Schloss Spittau, watched from the banks of the moat by a pair of moulting swans, Dorothea, Princess of Spittau, was reading a letter.

From the turreted windows of the room, as from all the windows of the castle, one looked out on water. Spittau's long, low, yellow-stuccoed main front, with its flanking pepper-pot towers, was lapped by the waters of the Neusiedler See, a large, reedy and melancholy lake stretching away to the Hungarian border. The north, west and south sides of the ancient Wasserburg were surrounded by a wide and scummy moat. Only a single causeway connected the castle with the swampy, pool-infested marsh, which in that desolate, aqueous region had to pass for land.

'Pfaffenstein is sold!' said the princess now, looking across the table at her son. 'And well sold. To a foreigner. A millionaire!'

Prince Maximilian of Spittau, thus addressed,

momentarily stopped chewing and said, 'Putzerl will be pleased.'

'Not only pleased,' said his mother, 'but rich. There is no longer anything to wait for. You must act, Maxi. *Act*!'

Maxi's blue, poached eyes bulged with a certain apprehension; his vestigial forehead creased into furrows. He was in fact a man of action, having shot a large number of people during the war, and, with the cessation of hostilities, an infinitely larger number of snipe, mallard, teal, godwall, pochard and geese which he pursued virtually from dawn to dusk in punts, rowing boats and waders. Even now his feet, under the table, rested on a huddle of soaking wet pointers, retrievers and setters who had been out with him since sunrise.

But action as understood by his mother was a different thing.

That the prince had been dropped on his head as a baby was unlikely. Kaiser Wilhelm II had attended his christening; a series of starched and iron-willed nurses had handed him from room to room in the gargantuan palace in Schleswig-Holstein, now confiscated by the Allies, in which he had been born. His lack of cerebral matter seemed rather to be inborn, the price he had paid for being related to both Joan the Mad who brought Castile and Aragon to the House of Austria, and to the Emperor Charles II whose Habsburg chin and Bourbon nose had locked in a manner that made the ingestion of food almost impossible. But though his intellectual activity was limited to weekly visits to the village hall in Neusiedl where they showed the latest films from Hollywood, there was nothing unattractive about Maxi. True, his duelling scar had gone awry a little, but enough of it was visible above his left eye to give him a slightly rakish look; his blond moustache waved pleasantly and except when he was dealing with his mother, his expression was amiable and relaxed.

'I have been very patient with you, Maxi,' continued his mother, whose nickname 'The Swan Princess' referred rather to her beady eye and savage beak than to any grace or beauty, 'and so have Putzerl's aunts. But enough is enough. There is going to be a house party at Pfaffenstein in June. Putzerl is sure to be there for that, so you must propose to her formally then and announce your engagement on the spot.'

'But, Mother, I have proposed to Putzerl three times. When you told me to, on her eighteenth birthday, and then again that spring. And only three months ago, when I was in Vienna, I invited her out for lunch and proposed again. Without you telling me! She doesn't,' said Maxi, a trace of pardonable puzzlement in his voice, 'love me.'

'Don't talk like a waiter,' snapped the princess. 'Putzerl knows perfectly well that she must marry you. I must say she isn't quite what I had hoped for from the point of view of character, but her lineage is impeccable, and with the money she brings in from Pfaffenstein we will be able to shore up the east wing and mend the roof. Anyway, no one not bred to the life would fit in at Spittau.'

This was certainly true. Schloss Spittau, almost afloat on water, was not for the faint-hearted. In winter, mist enshrouded it; frozen birds honked drearily on the ice. The coughing of retainers bent double with rheumatism mingled, as spring advanced, with the plopping of evil-eyed pike in the moat. Pieces of stucco fell suddenly into the lake, and in the summer enormous, muscular mosquitoes moved in like the Grande Armée.

Maxi continued to look depressed. He was perfectly aware of the advantages of marrying Putzerl. He liked her. When you took Putzerl out on to the lake there was no need to take a call duck. She could imitate, like no one he had ever met, the cry of a mallard ready to mate. There was no girl who was a better sport than the Princess of Pfaffenstein. But all this proposing got at a man's pride . . .

Then suddenly he brightened and pulled at the soft ears of the dog nearest to him, a German pointer with beseeching amber eyes. 'If I could take the dogs to Pfaffenstein?' he suggested. 'To the house party? Don't you think Putzerl might agree to marry me then? You know how she is about the dogs.'

The princess looked at the five dogs now thumping their wet tails on the floor and trembling with anticipation. She opened her mouth to tell Maxi not to be silly – and closed it again.

For it seemed to her that, for once, Maxi had a point. Whatever her feelings about her intended bridegroom, the Princess of Pfaffenstein really did love the dogs.

'I cannot zink in French!' declared Raisa Romola the morning after Jacob's announcement.

'There are no tunes in Debussy,' declared Pino. 'It is not what my public expects.'

'I shall go to Schalk!' stated Raisa – and Jacob blenched. Schalk was the director of Vienna's most prestigious institution, the heavily subsidized State Opera. Saying 'Schalk' to Jacob was like saying 'Boots' to a struggling British retail chemist.

Rallying, he launched into an impassioned speech in praise of Debussy's subtle, impressionistic score, its contrapuntal texture, its throbbing beauty . . .

The idea of throbbing beautifully had a slightly calming effect on Raisa, who narrowed her greedy almond eyes and said that if Jacob was prepared to consider a bonus, 'zinking' in French might just be possible.

To all this Tessa, busy repainting a flat for *Tosca* in the wings, listened with eager interest. True, there were strange things in *Pelleas and Melisande*. One never knew, for example, who exactly Melisande was. Was she a mortal or a being from another world? Had she in fact deceived her husband, Gollaud, with his handsome younger brother Pelleas? And why did she keep losing quite so many things down wells – her crown, her golden ball, her wedding ring? But the whole opera, played largely behind a gauze and subtly and romantically lit, was the very stuff of poetry – and modern too.

She was therefore a little disappointed when Boris, spooning yoghurt on to his plate at lunchtime, said gloomily, 'You know what *Pelleas* means, don't you? It means hair. And hair, right now, spells trouble.'

Boris was right. For the outstanding feature of Melisande which makes her mysterious, haunting beauty unforgettable, is her knee-length shimmering, streaming, golden hair. With this hair, as she lets it fall from her window, the lovesick Pelleas besottedly toys; with this hair Gollaud, her jealous husband, humiliates her, pulling her by it back and forth across the stage. The same hair surrounds her, an incandescent aureole, as she lies dying.

Hair for wigs comes traditionally from nuns. Italian nuns, mostly, since the Italians are noted for being both hirsute and religious, and postulants by the hundred are shorn to become brides of Christ. But her Italian possessions had been wrested from Austria, as had Moravia, Czechoslovakia, Hungary, Yugoslavia and all the other countries which had once humbly supplied the capital with everything from paprika to the tresses of their young girls. Of late, Boris had been driven to do business with the local convents, which had been anything but easy – with the fall of the monarchy and the urgings of the new republic, the religious vocation of Vienna's jeunes filles had declined disastrously.

Any hope that they would get away with horsehair dipped in peroxide, or an old wig from *Meistersinger*, was dispelled at the first rehearsal. Max Regensburg, the young director called in for the production, was a realist through and through. 'This Melisande must be flesh and blood,' he declared, and the company, envisaging Raisa's bulk, felt he had a point.

On a cold morning during the second week of rehearsals, Tessa accordingly set off on the long tram ride which took her to the lower slopes of the Leopoldsberg and trudged up a steep, tree-lined avenue to the Convent of the Sacred Heart – only to be met at the gate by a distraught Mother Superior.

'My dear, I'm so sorry but I'm afraid the girl I spoke of has turned out to be quite unfit to take her final vows!' She lowered her voice. 'We found her with the carpenter who came to fix one of the prie-dieux. Such a scandal! We had to send her straight home!'

Two days later Tessa arrived at the Convent of the Annunciation in the working-class district of Ottakring, only to find that she had been beaten by a Swiss merchant who had appeared the day before and bought up the entire crop of hair.

'He paid in Swiss currency, you see,' the Mistress of Postulants apologized, 'and our Order is very poor.'

The Convent of the Blessed Virgin was in quarantine for typhus. The Convent of the Resurrection yielded a single, meagre hank of hair at which Boris looked in disgust.

'I can fudge the colour, but I've got to have the length,' he said gloomily.

With a week to go to the dress rehearsal, Boris grew

frantic. The making of a wig is a most delicate business, for some four thousand strands of hair have to be knotted painstakingly into the lace.

'What am I going to do?' he enquired. 'Jesus Maria, what am I going to do?'

Tessa, who was sewing silver stars on to Melisande's cloak, lifted her head and rather sadly told him.

At Pfaffenstein, everything was going ahead as Guy had planned. The absent Putzerl had given her consent to the sale; the workmen, much impressed by the dollars with which they were paid, had promised to carry out the necessary repairs in the minimum of time and David, left in charge at the Pfaffenstein Arms, was following his employer's orders to spare no expense in preparing for the house party in June.

Guy meanwhile had returned to Vienna and immersed himself once more in the gruelling work connected with the loan, and it was not until he had finished his report on the first stage of the negotiations that he felt free to turn his attention to the matter of the opera.

That music was to play a main part in the entertainment of his guests went without saying: there would be an orchestra to play for the ball and to accompany the fireworks; there would be chamber music at night for those who cared for it. But for the climax of his house party, Guy intended to do no less than stage, in the theatre at Pfaffenstein, the opera at which he had first seen Nerine.

At the beginning of every love affair there is a moment when the timeless essence of the beloved is somehow encapsulated, crystallized and fixed in the mind for ever. It may be no more than the way she bends to a flower or touches the head of a passing child, yet in that instant the lover will perceive the uniqueness and wonder of her whole life. For Guy, this moment had come when Nerine gave that first, small, anticipatory sigh as the curtain rose on the dream landscape of Mozart's *Magic Flute*. To share with her once more the music of a composer he worshipped above all others, to meet her eyes again over Pamino's avowal of undying love – that would be to set the seal, like nothing else he could imagine, on the joy and miracle of their reunion.

Now, in his suite at Sachers, he rang for Thisbe Purse.

The woman who arrived in response to his summons was a grim-faced spinster with a greying bun of hair and steel-rimmed spectacles. The prize pupil in her year at Mr Pitman's Academy for typing and shorthand, she travelled everywhere with Guy – forming with Morgan, his chauffeur-valet, and David Tremayne, the trio of indispensables who enjoyed Guy's confidence and trust.

'I want tickets for the opera, Thisbe, please. For tonight.'

'Yes, Mr Farne,' said Thisbe, who lived in constant hope of an earthquake, flood or fire from which – with her teeth if necessary – she could rescue her employer. 'For the State Opera or the Volksoper?'

'Neither. There's a company called the International Opera Company, I believe?'

'Yes, sir. They're in the Klostern Theatre, in the Braungasse.' Her employer's passion for music was such that she made it her habit to investigate all musical events in any city in which they arrived. 'I'll go and look in the paper.'

'It's *Pellas and Melisande*,' she said, returning with the *Wiener Presse*. 'By Debussy. A première.'

Guy's eyebrows rose in surprise. From a small and unsubsidized company he had expected rather another *Waltz Dream* or *Merry Widow*.

'All right. That will do. Get me a ticket, please.'

'Not a box, sir?'

'No, I'm going alone. One ticket. Centre stalls.'

'Yes, sir,' said Thisbe Purse. That there might not be a ticket for a première occurred to her but she did not mention it. If Mr Farne wanted a ticket, he got it. No one who worked for him was left in doubt of that.

The theatre, with its baroque insouciance, pleased Guy. Still in his opera cloak, for public buildings were still very poorly heated, he skimmed the programme and joined in the applause for the conductor whose tormented eyes, as he acknowledged it, seemed to imply a dreadful martyrdom ahead.

The introduction began and Guy relaxed. The orchestra was good; the interpretation sensitive and precise. The curtain rose . . .

Melisande crouched, lost and frightened, by the

moonlit well. 'Ne me touchez pas, ne me touchez pas,' cried Raisa, managing after all to 'zink' in French. But Gollaud did touch her, married her, took her back to his gloomy castle to be loved and destroyed by Pelleas. Of the tenor, Pino Mastrini, even the producer had not demanded that he *act*, only that he should sing the actual notes which had been written. The glorious voice that God had seen fit to place in the throat of this Milanese bullock did the rest.

The production interested Guy. The scene where Melisande lowered her hair from the window and Pelleas toyed with it came over remarkably well. Lovely hair, it was, but real – not the excessive, overdone Rapunzel stuff he had seen in some productions. With its soft, blown look it made the love scene very moving, and even Pino Mastrini knew how to *toy*. Long before the curtain came down on Melisande's death bed, Guy knew that the International Opera Company would do.

At the stage door he parted the waiting crowd of students and admirers, presented his card and asked to see the director. But once inside the theatre he did not hurry to follow the directions that the doorman (rendered obsequious by Guy's air of authority) had given him, but wandered along enjoying the notices on the call board and the rueful graffiti pencilled on the bleak, tiled walls. Some of Guy's happiest moments had been spent in freezing theatre corridors like this: waiting for the delectable Claudine from the Paris Opera Ballet when he was on leave in France, for a Spanish chanteuse from the Teatra Amazonas in Manaus, for a Russian girl from the Ballets Russes who had been his mistress for a year in London.

Avoiding the babble from Raisa Romola's dressing-room, he turned left, then right and down a flight of curving, rickety stairs.

And stopped suddenly.

The sound he had heard, though soft, was unmistakable and in these dungeon-like depths below the level of the street, curiously unnerving. Someone, behind the peeling, dark green door he had just passed, was crying.

He turned, threw open the door and went in.

The room, lit by a single, naked bulb, was entirely crammed with wigs on stands, trays of moustaches, switches of hair, hat boxes piled on shelves. There was an ironing-board, a sink, a table littered with scissors, glue, rolls of ribbon . . . On the draining-board stood a jar of sour milk and a battered samovar and everywhere on the floor were wicker baskets overflowing with clothes.

However, it was only gradually that Guy took in this clutter, for his eyes were immediately drawn to the only occupant of the room: a girl who could scarcely have been out of her teens. A girl in a rumpled, paint-stained smock, crouched on the lid of an enormous hamper, who, as he entered, put down the mirror she had been holding and looked up to reveal a small, startled face somewhat dramatically streaked with dust and tears. A face with huge eyes the colour of a Stradivarius, eyes which might have been put in by the thumb of Titian himself when he grew too old for detail and was concerned only with the extreme condition of the human soul.

'Oh! I'm sorry!' She started up, trying to rub away the tears with fingers so dusty that they merely accentuated the anguished mottling of her cheeks. 'I'm afraid you've come to the wrong place. Miss Romola's dressing-room is upstairs. Or did you want one of The Heidis?'

Guy, standing debonair and faultlessly attired in the doorway, continued to stare in a most uncharacteristic way. Not at the girl's great smudged eyes, not at her hands – the hands of an Altendorfer Madonna on a painting spree – nor at her ragamuffin clothes. No, what held him riveted was her hair – or rather, the place where normally one would have expected hair to be. For this miniature Countess of Monte Cristo, immured in the depths of one of Vienna's most ancient edifices, seemed to have no hair. Above her anguished, lemur eyes and high forehead were only tufts such as certain capuchin monkeys achieve in their maturity, and her ears, which had the pricked look one finds in ferns and cyclamen, rested on an area of ravaged stubble. A stubble whose colouring – a warm beige shading to bronze – nevertheless seemed curiously familiar to Guy. And suddenly understanding, he said, 'My God! That was *your* hair that Melisande was wearing. But why?'

Quickly, stammeringly, Tessa explained. 'I was glad to do it, honestly. After all, Cosima cut off all her hair when Wagner died and put it in his grave so it was the least I could do. Only . . . just now I looked in the mirror – I didn't really have time before, you know how it is before a première – and I suddenly realized . . . I mean, it isn't as though I have anything else.'

She sketched with small and extraordinarily expressive hands the longed-for curves, the Amazonian bosom which her maker had so relentlessly withheld.

Guy studied her. In a sense she spoke the truth, but only in a sense. The dirty ragamuffin with her butchered hair did in fact have something, but it was not something to which at this late hour he could easily put a name. Style? No, it was something more intimate that Guy now chased through the painters he most loved. An image of innocence with the sad eyes of experience; of someone very young acquiescing in their fate. And moving from the tiny, rigid Infantas of Velasquez enduring their silken bandages of pomp to the grave, coiffed girls of Holbein, he came to rest on a Murillo urchin: the one who stands always in the shadows watching the others eat the cherries, the slice of water melon, the hunk of bread.

'Where do you live?' he asked abruptly, for the child looked utterly exhausted.

'In the Wipplingerstrasse.'

'And who is taking you home?'

'Taking me? Goodness, no one takes me! It's only half an hour's walk. I've just got to sweep up and take Miss Romola's dachshund out and set the mousetraps and then I'm going.'

'My car is outside,' said Guy. 'I'll give you twenty minutes while I talk to your director. Then I'll take you back.'

'Oh no, I really couldn't!' Tessa was aghast at the idea of depriving this stylish and powerful-looking foreigner, with his winged eyebrows and inky, velvet-collared cloak, of his scheduled night of pleasure.

Guy smiled at her. 'Don't worry; I haven't any designs on you, I promise.'

What she said next moved him absurdly.

'As though you could have,' she said, brushing her fingers over her butchered hair. '*Now*.'

Guy's interview with the director left Jacob in a state of jubilation bordering on delirium. It had happened! At last, at last, materializing out of the night as mysteriously as the stranger who had commissioned Mozart's *Requiem*, the rich patron had come. Parodying Jacob's wildest dreams he had offered to engage the company for a week in summer, to house and feed them and to finance the new production of an opera! And what an opera! Not some schmaltzy operetta or fashionable salon piece but *The Magic Flute*! Surprised in his bed by the Angel of Death and told he could bring one work with him to Paradise, Jacob in his nightshirt might have hovered between *Figaro*, *Don Giovanni* or *The Flute*, but it would have been with a score by Mozart in his palsied hand that he would have sought to meet his maker.

Great things would come of this commission, Jacob was sure of it. What the Esterhazys had been to Haydn, the mysterious Madam von Meck to Tchaikovsky, Herr Farne would be to the International Opera Company.

So the man was English and had probably bayoneted babies . . . so he wished the company's destination and his own part in the transaction to remain a secret which would make everything devilishly complicated . . . *So!* For the money Herr Farne was offering, Jacob would have secreted the Golden Horde.

The theatre at Pfaffenstein, said to be the loveliest in Austria with acoustics which were a legend! And in June, when attendances always fell off disastrously and just the week he would have had to send the Rhinemaiden to Baden-Baden! Was it Raisa who had wrought this miracle? He had been worried about her determination to play Melisande barefoot, but clearly the diva's bunions had not cooled the ardour of the Englishman. Or was it to a Heidi's tip-tilted profile that they owed this munificence?

Joyfully squeezing himself into his galoshes, Jacob prepared to go home and tell his Rhinemaiden that it would not be necessary, now, for her to pawn her pearls.

Returning to the wig room Guy found her waiting, her face scrubbed to a shining cleanliness – and seeing her attire, his sardonic eyebrows lifted appreciatively.

'*La Bohème?*' he enquired.

She nodded and pulled the blue velvet cloak with its gathered hood more closely round her. 'From Act Three, you know, where she waits for Rudolfo in the snow and coughs.' She gazed wistfully out at him like a dormouse in a yurt. 'It's a little big, perhaps?'

'Well, a little,' said Guy, as she attempted to pull still tighter the voluminous folds of the cloak designed for Raisa's ample Rumanian form. 'But not noticeably so. The muff is from *Bohème* too?'

'Yes. But the gloves are from *Traviata*. Where she is back to being a courtesan and enormously elegant.' She stretched out a small hand, quite drowned in a sea of stylishly wrinkled kid. 'No one can see my hair now – no one can see anything – so perhaps I won't disgrace you?'

'There is no possible way that you could disgrace me,' said Guy gently. 'But I should like to know your name.'

'Tessa,' she said.

'Just Tessa?'

She nodded and let him lead her in silence from the theatre. But at the car, parked under a lamp-post across the street, she gasped with admiration. 'Oh!' she said. 'How beautiful! Are you perhaps extremely rich?'

'Well, fairly extremely. I'm glad you like it. Get in.'

Morgan, Guy's chauffeur, was holding open the door. Impeccable and correct, he would never at any time have allowed himself to betray so extreme an emotion as surprise. But though it had been his habit to conduct females of all kinds from stage doors to whatever abode his master considered suitable – a chambre séparée at Maxims, a suite at the Ritz – he had never seen anything like this strange, dusty and submerged little creature.

But as she climbed into the car and he tucked the rug

round her knees, she smiled and said with unexpected dignity, 'Thank you, you are very kind.'

Guy spun round, for she had spoken in English. And if there are two words in the English language that test the pronunciation of the foreigner, they are 'Thank you'. Words which this minion from the nether regions of a minor opera house had spoken in an English both unaccented and educated.

He changed also to his native tongue. 'How is it that you speak English?'

'I had an English grandmother and I spent a lot of time with her when I was small. She was a marvellous woman. I loved her most dearly.'

Guy had given Morgan his instructions and the car set off. 'Tell me about her.'

'She came from the very north of England where there are lots of sheep. More sheep, she said, than people, and moors with purple heather. She lived in Carinthia with my grandfather but she was always homesick, I think.'

Only a very slight increase in care, an almost imperceptible stress on certain words, betrayed the fact that she no longer spoke her native tongue.

'And she's dead now?'

'Yes. At the end of the war. She had lived in the same village all her married life and done so much good. But the peasants – of course it's no good blaming them, but they started saying that the English . . . that they boiled corpses to make oil and . . . well, you know.'

'Yes, indeed I do know,' said Guy bitterly. 'Our side produced exactly the same kind of pernicious rubbish.'

'They say people can't really die of a broken heart,' she continued, 'and of course that's true. But they can just wait for an excuse. And with her it was the flu epidemic three years ago. It killed my mother too.'

'And your father?'

She shrugged. 'He was killed in 1914 at Tannenberg.' Then, conscious of her duty to this distinguished-looking foreigner, 'Have you been in Vienna before?'

'Yes.'

She glanced up quickly, caught by something in his voice, but when she spoke it was to say, 'In that case, you know that we are just passing the house where Mozart's sister-in-law first saw the score of *Don Giovanni*.'

Guy, aware that he was about to get a view of Vienna hitherto denied him, said he had not known that and Tessa obligingly pointed out in the lamplit streets the place where Anton Bruckner bought his manuscript paper, the café where Schönberg got his idea for 'Verklarte Nacht' and – as they turned into the Kärntnerstrasse – the shop where the prima donna of the State Opera got her underwear.

'Oh, it's good to see the lamplight again. Everything is beginning, don't you feel it?' Her voice had changed, she had forgotten her hair. This was the Murillo urchin who *got* the cherries, who *played* the mandolin. 'There will be no more wars and art will make everybody equal and free,' said the wardrobe mistress, her eyes shining.

'And to be allowed to work! I cannot tell you how marvellous that is.'

Wondering what sort of childhood made it a privilege to work as a drudge to the International Opera Company, Guy listened to her prattle and was suddenly astonished when she said quietly, 'Were you very happy, then, the last time you were in Vienna?'

There was a pause. Then, 'Yes,' said Guy. 'Happier than I've ever been in my life.'

She nodded, well pleased with this tribute to her city, and was off again.

'People always tell you that this is where they keep the hearts of the Habsburgs, the ones that are buried in the Kapuziner crypt,' she said, waving a hand drowned in its wrinkled kid at the moonlit spire of the Augustinerkirche, 'but what is really interesting, I think, is that Brahms's housekeeper used to come here every day to light a candle when Brahms had a liver complaint. Every single day she came!'

They drove on through small squares, as quiet and enclosed as rooms, down narrow cobbled streets, taking in apparently the place where William Gluck's little dog had almost been run over by a hansom cab and the house of the hairdresser whose father had dyed Johann Strauss's moustache.

But the biggest treat was still to come.

'Do you think we could stop for just a moment?' she said as they drove across the Michaelerplatz. 'In that little street on the left, about half-way down?'

Guy gave instructions and the car drew to a halt.

70

They were opposite a small and fusty-looking café from which a dim, pink light shone out on to the pavement. Beside him, Guy felt Tessa tense in a momentary anxiety; then she relaxed and said, 'Yes, there she is. Look, in that corner by the aspidistra. Can you see her?'

Sitting alone, an ancient lady dressed in black was consuming with apparent dedication a large slab of yellow cake.

'She comes here every night and has a cup of coffee and a piece of gugelhupf. Even in the war when food was so difficult, the proprietor always kept one for her.'

'Who is she?'

Tessa sighed with fulfilment and with awe. 'Schubert's great-niece,' she said rapturously. '*In the flesh.*'

To his surprise, Guy was sorry when the car drew up in front of the house where she lived. As she got out and turned to thank him, her hood fell back and instinctively she reached up to pull it back over her savaged hair.

'No!' Guy's hand came down over hers, pulling it away. He turned her head so as to catch the lamplight and stood for a moment, studying the narrow, fine-boned little face. Then he nodded. 'You've nothing to worry about. It will be a triumph when it's cut, you'll see.'

'Cut! But surely I must grow it again?'

'On no account,' said Guy. He opened the door for her – and was gone.

Left alone in the lobby, Tessa stood for a moment, frowning and bewildered. She knew about phantom limbs: that the place where they had been went on aching even after they had been cut off. Her cheek, where the Englishman's fingers had been, did not exactly ache . . . but very strangely, most curiously . . . it *felt*.

5

Guy was mistaken in thinking that Nerine was unaware of his wealth. Ever since her brother Arthur, an avid reader of the *Financial Times*, had suggested that the Farne who appeared so frequently and impressively in its columns might be the young man who had had the effrontery to propose to her all those years ago, Nerine had never rested. Arthur was despatched to make enquiries in the City and returned with the information that in addition to the enterprises which bore his name, Guy Farne was chairman of Ouro Preto Inc., had a controlling interest in nine other companies, and was regarded as one of the richest as well as the most brilliant men in Europe.

'He's in for a knighthood too, they say,' he added, 'despite the fact that he's so young.'

'A knighthood!' Nerine was shaken. It looked as though her family had been hopelessly wrong in their assessment of her youthful suitor.

Her meeting with Guy outside the Associated

Investment building was thus most carefully contrived, for Nerine's first attempt at a brilliant marriage had been a disastrous failure. That her parents had forced her to marry Charles Hurlingham was not strictly true. Mrs Croft in particular, whose snobbery was so intense as to amount almost to a religious vocation, had been resolute in advising Nerine to wait for bigger prey. But it so happened that in the space of three weeks, the French girl who had been Nerine's friend in Vienna wrote that she was marrying a marquis and the freckle-faced American sent ten pages of rapture about her engagement to a young industrialist. To be beaten to the altar by two girls who were, in every possible way, grossly her inferiors was not to Nerine's taste. Charles was heir to a baronetcy and a famous estate in Wilt-shire; she accepted him and had to endure the four years' martyrdom that followed his injury in Flanders. Unspeakable years, walled up in the country with Charles who seemed to expect her to stay with him con-stantly though he had excellent nurses, and who followed her with his devoted, doggy eyes whenever she left the room. Oh, God, the waste of those years, the boredom, the frustration!

Well, that was over. Charles was dead and Guy – she had seen this within minutes of meeting him again – was hers for the asking.

'I suppose you know what you're doing,' said Mrs Croft plaintively, 'but I cannot approve. Not only found under a piece of sacking, but a piece of sacking in Newcastle upon Tyne! I'm sure you would do better to accept Lord Frith.'

The drawing-room of the villa in Twickenham had scarcely altered since Guy had all but broken the arm of the footman instructed to eject him. The same draped piano legs, the same over-stuffed cushions and looped, mauve curtains; the same brown portraits of dead and portly Crofts . . .

'Compared with Guy, Frith is a pauper,' said Nerine, who was making a list of the clothes she would need for Austria. But she had not finally refused the young Scottish nobleman pining for her so flatteringly in his crenellated tower in the Grampians, for this journey to Vienna was only a way of testing the ground. If Guy, in spite of his wealth, proved to be tight-fisted or attempted to make her mix with the company of her inferiors, there was still time to change her mind. Her period of mourning, about which she had purposefully been a little vague, had come in very useful there.

'And that dreadful foster-mother,' continued Mrs Croft. 'You don't mean to visit her, surely?'

'No, of course not. Guy only hinted at it. I shall send her a nice note when the engagement is announced. *If* it is announced.' Nerine's exquisitely arched eyebrows drew together, but briefly, for never frowning had helped her to keep her marvellously youthful skin. Guy's fondness for Mrs Hodge, who seemed to be some kind of washerwoman, was certainly a drawback but she did not believe that he would foist the company of such a person on his future wife.

'I only hope that Farne knows what he's doing,' said Arthur. 'They say he lived like a labourer in Brazil. I shall take some Keatings powder. And some Andrews Liver Salts. One cannot be too careful.'

Guy had written to say that he had engaged a suite for them at the Grand Hotel, making it clear that he himself would remain at Sachers. So far, so good – but after that they were to go into the country to join some kind of house party and it was this part of the programme that Arthur regarded with particular apprehension.

Nerine's brother was the kind of young man intended from birth to be middle-aged. Though only two years older than his sister, he was already going bald; his fleshy cheeks, pendulous stomach and the flat feet that had kept him out of the army, represented a complete rout of those genes which had given substance to the glorious being which was his sister.

'You must not expect to meet distinguished people while you are there,' pursued Mrs Croft, for it was her brother who, by marrying the daughter of a baron, had acquired the aunt who was an Honourable. 'No one well-connected is likely to receive a man with Farne's origins and European high society is very exclusive. But once they know who *you* are . . .'

'Don't worry, Mother. Just leave it to me.'

'I can't say that I'm looking forward to this adventure,' said Arthur. 'I'm not at all sure that I shall be able to get the *Financial Times* abroad.'

'There's no need for you to come, Arthur, I've told you. I'm taking my maid – I shall be perfectly all right.'

But in the abacus that served Arthur for a brain there was room for a correct and protective attitude towards his sister. That he should let her travel without escort to a country full of people who were not only foreigners but practically Huns, and join an adventurer who was most unlikely to know how to behave was out of the question.

Nerine had put down her pencil and was looking into the shell-encrusted mirror opposite, her gaze settling on her own reflection with the sense of homecoming experienced by a great pianist as he lowers his hands on to the keyboard of a perfectly tuned Steinway. She was seldom out of sight of a looking-glass, for she knew that her beauty was a gift bestowed by the gods, a kind of divine trust, and that to grudge any time of expense in caring for it would be selfishness indeed.

But all was well. The three dusky curls that she had trained to tumble from her high-piled hair on to her forehead still held their spring; her upper lashes – each one a burnished, raven scimitar – still soared away from her sapphire eyes. Her nose was matt, her mouth crimsoned and glossy, even without the bite on each lip which she now bestowed with her pearly teeth.

How she would reward Guy if he proved generous! Nothing would be too much trouble, nothing! Even now, uncomplainingly, she was preparing to spend every farthing she had wrested from the awful, stingy Hurlinghams on clothes for the journey, and then . . . !

In Paris, in Vienna and all the capitals of Europe she would endure, patient and uncomplaining, the endless fittings at couture houses, the painstaking selection of suitable jewels and accessories which would make Guy, in possessing her, the envy of the fashionable world.

'I think I'll take some Jeyes Fluid too,' said Arthur, who had been pursuing his own reflections. 'You can never trust foreigners when it comes to drains.'

Two weeks after the première of *Pelleas*, Miss Thisbe Purse appeared in Jacob's office and was greeted by him with sighs of relief. Guy Farne, materializing out of the night like the Prince of Darkness, might have been a dream conjured out of Jacob's own need, but no one could have dreamed up Miss Thisbe Purse.

At the hands of this gaunt and comically English spinster, Jacob now received the contract between the International Opera Company and a syndicate entitled 'Associated Investments Ltd'. He received also the measurements of the theatre in which they were to per-form, a preliminary cheque which brought tears of emotion to his eyes – and an envelope containing a single sheet of paper which informed him that an appointment had been made for one of his employees, by name Tessa, at Anita's in the Kärntnerstrasse at 3 p.m. that afternoon to have her hair styled. The fee had been taken care of. Mr Farne's name was not to appear in the matter.

Jacob was left staring in puzzlement at these some-what autocratically worded instructions when Miss

Purse had gone. Tessa? How had Herr Farne even seen Tessa? Could she be the explanation of the Englishman's interest in the company? Impossible, surely? But if so . . . if she had that kind of potential, something must be done. Could he, perhaps, put her in a ballet?

Tessa, when he finally found her in the workshop, was painting the ballcock and chain of a derelict lavatory cistern with silver paint and as he gazed at her, Jacob's bewilderment increased. Since the première of *Pelleas* she had taken to wearing a blue beret and now resembled both Jackie Coogan in *The Kid* and the smaller kind of French railway porter. Surely it was not conceivable that this foreign multi-millionaire with his power and sexuality intended to make her the object of his attentions?

'Anita!' shrieked Tessa when she heard what was to befall her. 'I can't afford Anita! And anyway, I have to finish this ball and chain for Cavaradossi and then I must go and get some manuscript paper for Herr Klasky and fetch the velvet samples from the warehouse because Frau Pollack has a migraine.'

Jacob frowned. The senior wardrobe mistress had been in a state of almost constant prostration since she had eaten – or very nearly eaten – the ashes of her great-uncle Sandor which had arrived from Budapest for burial and been supposed by her to be an ersatz meat powder of the kind much used in the last years of the war. 'It's an order,' he said to Tessa. 'The company is paying. Three o'clock.'

Three o'clock accordingly saw Tessa, dressed in a

blue skirt and embroidered blouse from *Pagliacci* and carrying, for some reason, a large biscuit tin, enter the sacred portals of what was arguably the most expensive hairdresser in Europe.

'Impossible!' declared Anita, a platinum-blonde Berliner with a contempt for the easy-going Viennese. 'It is out of the question that I can do anything with you. The hair has not been cut; it has been butchered. I am not a magician. It is too short.'

'I know, I'm sorry,' said Tessa. 'They made me come, but I'll go.' She tried to get out of the chair. 'I'll grow it again.'

'Grow it!' sneered Anita, pushing her down. 'Are you mad? Do you want to look like an Austrian strudel girl with earphones?' She gestured to an assistant. 'A fringe I must have to emphasize the eyes but my God, the back . . . And of course a Nestlé's out of the question with that face.'

She began savagely to comb, to slash, to complain . . .

An hour later Tessa crept out of the shop. The biscuit tin was still clutched under her arm but there was a bewildered look in her eyes. 'The simplicity which costs no less than everything' is a phrase much beloved of saints and mystics who use it to describe the pursuit of a spiritual life. This simplicity Anita had brought to Tessa's hair. The minutely calculated sweep of the silken fringe above the eyes, the curving fronds lapping the pointed ears, the soft strands nestling into the hollow at the back of the neck suggested now a very different kind of urchin: a winged messenger, the young Mercury perhaps, or Ariel.

'You look charming.'

It had not been Guy's intention to pursue his acquaintance with Witzler's under wardrobe mistress. But leaving the Treasury on a personal errand he had recalled his instructions to Thisbe and, on an impulse, crossed the road to Anita's. Now he too was startled. Tessa had been not so much transformed as revealed. The vulnerable little face, the delicate bones, the strange air of puzzlement as she tried to comprehend what the mirror had shown her moved Guy strangely. He had the absurd feeling that as one can see in young babies the throbbing of their pulse beneath the fontanelle, so he could put his hand on the bronze and shining head and feel the beating of her soul.

'She is not ready,' thought Guy. 'Poor child, what have I done?' And lightly he said, 'May I relieve you of your burden?' For the tin she was carrying, adorned with a painting of the former Empress Elizabeth in a tiara, was large.

'Oh no, thank you. I'm just going to the Stadtpark to release the mice.'

'The mice?' said Guy, nevertheless taking the tin.

Tessa nodded. 'You see, when I first came to work in the theatre they had those traps that break their backs, only sometimes . . . they . . . didn't. So I borrowed some of those where the mice go in through those bristle tunnels that point backwards, you know, and then they can't get out. Only then, of course, you have the mice.'

Guy, steering her across the road with a light hand under her elbow, said he saw this.

'So I let them out in the Stadtpark,' she said, 'when I can get away. But please . . . I'm sure I'm delaying you?'

'Not at all. I was only going to buy a birthday present for my foster-mother in England.'

They had entered the park where lilacs mingled their heavy, fragrant clusters with the golden tresses of the laburnums, little girls bowled their hoops and a troop of firemen in Ruritanian uniforms were marching towards the bandstand.

'Are they musical mice?' Guy enquired. 'I mean, are we making for the Johann Strauss statue? Or the Schubert Memorial?'

Tessa smiled and shook her head. 'I usually try to get down to the banks of the river – it's steep there, a sort of cutting and not many people go. It's the river Wien, did you know? Mostly it flows underground but here it comes to the surface for a little.'

'Yes.' Guy did know. He had come here with his poems to Nerine and floated them down the sluggish, sleepy little river which was nevertheless more truly Vienna's own than the Danube, for the city had been named for it.

'Here?' he asked.

Tessa nodded and Guy opened the box.

'I don't want you to think I'm sentimental,' she said as six damp and not noticeably grateful mice lurched away over the gravel. 'If it were possible to eat them, I wouldn't mind killing them. But I don't think it is?'

'No,' said Guy gravely, as the last of the thumb-sized rodents vanished behind the stones. 'I don't see them as a really useful source of meat.' But he wondered, suddenly, if the girl was ever actually hungry. Well, at least for a week at Pfaffenstein he would see that she was decently housed and fed.

As they scrambled up the bank, the band began to play. A waltz, of course . . . And drawn by the music, smiling at the firemen perspiring in their uniforms, they came to a halt before the bandstand at which Strauss himself had played.

'I know the words in English,' said Tessa proudly. And in a small, true voice she sang the self-congratulatory, foolish refrain.

'Oh, what a *piece* of *Heaven* is this!
Vienna is *bliss*, Vienna is *bliss*!'

She smiled up at him. 'Not very poetical, is it?'

'No . . . all the same.' He looked down at the small, sleek head striking fire from the sun. 'Is it like that for you? A piece of heaven, this city?'

'Yes,' she said. 'Sometimes it is like that for me. Heaven in springtime. Heaven in C major. Yes, sometimes it is like that for me.'

The next moment her dreamy pensive look had gone. An ex-serviceman on crutches had come up to beg and as he saw the note Guy put in his hand he exploded into fulsome gratitude.

'Thank you, Herr Baron. God bless the Herr Baron. May the Herr Baron know nothing but happiness.'

'Oh!' said Tessa, her eyes kindling, when the man had hobbled away. 'You shouldn't let him do that!'

'Do what?'

'Grovel like that! Call you Herr Baron. This is a republic. Titles were abolished officially two years ago.'

'I don't think you will change human nature with political decrees,' said Guy, who had always been rather amused by the Viennese habit of conferring titles on anyone they wished to flatter. 'People will always be snobs.'

'No, they won't! They can be educated. When I am the first woman director of the Burg Theatre I'm going to put on plays which—' she broke off. 'I'm sorry, that was rude. Only, I am a very deep republican. You were on your way to buy a present?'

Guy accepted the change of topic. He nodded and they began to stroll towards the gate. 'For my foster-mother. The woman who brought me up.' He frowned. Guy had sent sables and mink and diamonds in a spate to the little house in Byker to which Martha stuck with quiet obstinacy. She received these with every protestation of delight, but he knew full well that they went into a cupboard in the back room until some friend or neighbour needed them for a wedding or a funeral. 'I've sent her all the usual things: fur coats, jewels, but she just puts everything away.'

'What is she like?'

Guy hesitated. 'Sandy hair. Grey eyes. Plump. Talks broad Tyneside, smells of green soap . . .' His voice grew warmer as he began to describe the woman who was Martha Hodge.

Tessa was silent when he had finished. 'And she brought you up?' she said at last. 'You were really and truly an orphan?'

Guy laughed at the palpable longing in her voice.

'Really and truly.' He described his origins. 'And I feel bound to tell you that it is most unlikely that I shall turn out to be a nobleman in disguise. Lost princes are extremely thin on the ground in Tyneside.'

But Tessa's sense of humour had temporarily deserted her. 'You're so fortunate! To make your own life . . . always to have been free.' Her dark eyes were shadowed with longing. 'As for your Mrs Hodge, I know exactly what she would like. But you must think only about pleasing her.'

'What?'

Tessa told him.

'Good God,' said Guy, outraged. 'I couldn't do that.'

Tessa shrugged. 'Very well. Get her another mink.'

The little packet arrived at 12 Front Street, Byker, a fortnight later. 'I am advised,' said the covering note in Guy's looped hand, 'that you would like this, so have endeavoured to overcome my scruples.'

Martha, removing the layers of tissue, found a

85

delicate filigree locket containing what she had begged for vainly every time he came: his photograph.

'I am advised.' Only a girl could thus have advised him. He had found her, then: the girl in Vienna who had sent him off to South America looking the way he had looked when she first saw him in the orphanage – closed and defensive and hurt beyond belief. Guy had never spoken of her, but Martha had guessed and been wicked enough to hate her for what she had done to him.

Well, she had been wrong. Guy had gone back and found her and she was the right one; she understood.

With hands that trembled a little, she fastened the locket around her neck. She was to wear it until the day she died.

At Burg Pfaffenstein, David Tremayne was achieving the miracles that Guy expected and for which he paid him. The rooms in the arcaded Fountain Courtyard were refurbished, the stonework cleaned, new lighting and new stoves were installed. Girls with their dirndl aprons hitched over their knees scrubbed and chattered their way through the great rooms. The one hundred and thirty-seven clocks were wound, the three hundred and eighteen mirrors polished. The leaking boats which belonged to the castle were repaired and repainted for the pleasure of the expected guests. Chefs were summoned, horses hired.

The Duchess and the Margravine viewed these preparations with benevolence. Though minutely concerned with the seating precedence of the hundred or so expected visitors, they would appear suddenly on an upturned crate sharing a sandwich with one of the stonemasons or be found bandaging a labourer's cut hand. As for David, he was soon a favourite with them and bidden to call them Tante Augustine and Tante Tilda.

Since Guy, determined to completely surprise Nerine, still kept his identity a secret, it was inevitable that quite a mythology sprang up round Pfaffenstein's new owner, glimpsed only as a Mephistophelean figure in a chariot of tulip wood. That he was foreign was regrettable but the villagers, seeing the castle brought back to its former glory, were very willing to don their green and crimson liveries and show him how things should be done.

'Though they're all very sad that it will mean saying goodbye to the Princess,' said David, reporting to his employer as he did once a week at Sachers.

Guy leaned back on the red plush sofa, his fingers laced behind his head.

'Ah, yes, the ubiquitous Putzerl. Is she to honour us with her presence then?'

The Princess of Pfaffenstein had promptly signed the documents she had been sent but had shown no further sign of life.

'I don't know. I imagine so, surely? Her aunts certainly hope that she will come. It's her birthday on the eighteenth – the day of the ball.'

Guy's eyebrows rose in faint surprise. Martha

celebrated the nineteenth as his birthday, but that was the day he had been found.

David sighed. He was a susceptible and romantic young man who had been much moved by the way the people of Pfaffenstein spoke of the princess. 'She sounds a most taking little thing. It isn't just her aunts – everyone seems to tell me of some good thing she has done. Not taking soup to the poor and all that stuff, but real things.'

He broke off, recalling the vignettes that the villagers had conjured up for him in the dialect he was just beginning to understand. The tiny, six-year-old princess, in a white frilled nightdress, eluding her nurse to walk barefoot at night down the crazy, tortuous footpath which wound round the crag on the far side of the drawbridge, in order to bring the innkeeper's daughter – ill with scarlet fever – one of her own dolls. The suddenly halted carriage, containing a screeching archduchess and a prostrate governess, from which the child had leapt in order to wade into the lake and rescue a kitten some boys were trying to drown. And a later, graver image: the princess at thirteen, walking through the great hall of the castle where the wounded officers lay, cared for by coiffed and nobly born nurses, ceaselessly asking, 'But where are the men? Who's nursing the *men*?'

'She sounds as though there's not an ounce of snootiness in her. And full of pluck!'

'Come, David. You're not trying to cut out the vacuous prince, surely?'

David flushed. 'No. Though that's one of the things they most regret, that they won't see her wedding.'

With five weeks to go, the invitations to the house party began to home like gold-limned doves into the homes of Austria's high nobility and were everywhere received with pleasure and excitement. If Pfaffenstein could be sold to a millionaire reputed, varyingly, to be an American shipping magnate, an Armenian oil tycoon and a banker from Basle, why not Schloss Landsberg whose marble hall of mirrors was fast sinking on to the terrace below, or Malk, along whose famous topiary allée an ever-diminishing posse of gardeners clipped their way from dawn to dusk. The Countess of Witten-furt, known as the meanest woman in Europe, bought a new dress; the ninety-two-year-old Prince Monteforelli had himself injected with fresh monkey gland. Even the appalling Archduchess Frederica, tottering through her ruined palace on Spanish heels and demanding that the bailiffs leave her presence backwards, pronounced herself willing to attend – and the Archduke Sava, exiled to Graz, asked if he could bring his bear.

'Putzerl will be pleased.' The comment first uttered by her intended husband, Maxi, was repeated continually as octogenarians examined their emblazoned carriages, landgravines looked out their lace and the nobility everywhere prepared to converge on Pfaffen-stein for a week of good living at someone else's expense.

It says much for the esprit de corps which made up the old Empire's crème de la crème that not one of them grudged the young Princess of Pfaffenstein her good fortune; nor did even one of the mothers of marginally eligible sons so much as consider trying to secure the newly rich princess for their own offspring. For the fact that Putzerl was destined – and soon now – for Maxi and his moated Wasserburg had been known to every one of them since the day she had been carried, screaming and empurpled, to the christening font in Schönbrunn Palace and the Emperor had smiled and said he hoped she would not grow too hot to handle.

'You must simply assume that Putzerl is going to marry you,' said the Princess of Spittau, on the day the invitation reached her. 'It mustn't be a question of whether but simply of when.'

'Yes, Mother,' said Prince Maximilian.

Late spring was always a trying time at the Wasserburg. The ice cracked and more people than usual fell into the water. Frost-damaged tiles slid off the roof. The longer days gave strength to the germs which had been frozen during the winter months: people who had mere colds developed influenza; those who had been suffering from influenza got bronchitis or pneumonia. The Prince's housemaids became pregnant, also his bitches. Frogspawn covered the moat.

The old princess looked at her son. How to make him take a more manly role, that was the question. Because he *had* to marry Putzerl. With the money she brought from Pfaffenstein they could keep going for a while. There would be children, too, the line would be preserved, thought the Swan Princess, making a note

that something would have to be done about the nursery block, a kind of fortress in an inner courtyard in
which the Spittau babies were immured till old enough
to swim.

'Which uniforms are you going to take to Pfaffenstein?' she asked her son.

Maxi brightened. 'I thought the Tyrolean Rifles for
the banquet and the Hussars for the opera. And for the
reception and the opening ball, the Artillery. That's
Putzerl's favourite.'

'An infantry regiment for the banquet?' said his
mother, shocked. 'Still, that's not until the last day. If
you haven't got hold of Putzerl by then, God help us all.
Let's go and have a look.'

But when the arthritic old princess, leaning heavily
on her son, reached the huge, painted cupboard in
which Maxi's uniforms were kept, disaster awaited
them. Mildew had mottled the splendid silver green of
the Tyrolean Rifles; some biologically interesting but
unsavoury fungi had colonized the pink breeches of the
Hussars . . .

Furiously, the princess tugged at the bell-rope and
the prince's valet appeared.

'The prince's uniforms must be taken to the drying
room at once,' she ordered. 'How dare you let them get
into such a state!'

The valet pointed to the walls, running with moisture,
and shrugged. 'What can you do, Highness?' he said, and
gathered up the offending garments, forebearing to point
out that the drying room was now unheated.

'The Artillery's all right,' said Maxi, relieved, fingering the sumptuous, braided uniform with its beguiling slender lines in the style of the Crown Prince Rudolf, which had won first prize at the Paris World Fair as the most beautiful uniform on earth. Yes, he would propose to Putzerl in that. It was not as though she was the sort of girl who would expect him to go down on his knees, something which the tightness of the trousers rendered quite impossible.

Or would it after all be better done in mufti? In some private spot in the forest? With, of course, the dogs . . . ?

'As for me,' declared the princess, 'it doesn't matter what I wear, because I still have my pearls.'

But almost immediately she frowned. For if Maxi did not get hold of Putzerl, the pearls would have to go.

'I always stab the air with my left hand,' said Pino Mastrini, greatly offended at being asked to extend his acting range. 'Always. I stab – so – and then I drop down on my left knee, so. Always.'

'That's exactly what I'm complaining about,' said Jacob, wiping the perspiration from his forehead.

'In zis bodice I cannot zink! I cannot zink even 'igh C, and 'igh F you can forget absolutely it,' complained Raisa, erupting from the wings, followed by an infuriated Frau Pollack with her mouth full of pins.

'The starcloth will have to be cut down, Herr Witzler. It's half a metre too long.'

The International Opera Company was preparing for its mysterious assignment in June. Jacob had kept

Farne's secret, and no one knew who their patron was or whither they were bound. But underlying the speculation and the rumours was a growing sense of excitement, as though this was the chance that they had all been waiting for.

And so they worked. *The Magic Flute* had been in the repertory for years, but now they prepared to study Mozart's immortal singspiel as though it had at that moment just been composed.

Jacob himself was in a white heat of expectation. He had seen pictures of Pfaffenstein rearing romantically on its crag above the lake, heard descriptions of the enchanting theatre. Now he dreamed of the Perfect Performance in the Perfect Setting in the presence of the Perfect Patron who would lead the company from financial darkness into light. In the cafés, among his acquaintances, Jacob showed off and swaggered; he ran up new bills and defaulted on his creditors, but over his opera he dreamed true. And because of this, though they might complain and argue, nobody failed him.

'Where's Bubi?' cried the Rhinemaiden, who had come along to help.

'I have him, Frau Witzler.'

Tessa appeared briefly in the pit carrying the Witzler's three-year-old son on one arm and a plate piled high with sandwiches in the other. She emerged in the rehearsal room where Klasky – cursing the violins in Hungarian, the cellos in Czech and the woodwind in Serbo-Croat – appeared to be preparing Mozart's score for an audience of ranking cherubim.

'Thank you. Put them over there,' said Klasky, glaring at the orchestra who, having rehearsed for five hours without a break, now foolishly assumed that they could eat. He passed a moist hand absently over Bubi's blond curls and smiled at Tessa. She was a nice little thing, always willing to help. Perfect pitch, too . . . Pity there was never any time. Still, perhaps it was just as well. Like Chopin, who believed that to approach George Sands in love was to deprive the world of an étude, Klasky was convinced that women drained away a man's creativity and it would never do to dissipate his energy. For in spite of the recent spate of rehearsals, Klasky had made a real breakthrough with his own opera. By changing the wronged husband from a policeman to a railway porter, he had unblocked his imagination in a most amazing way. A chorus for plate-layers and signalmen had come to him in a single flash of inspiration; a soliloquy for an engine-greaser, a kind of Holy Fool who would speak for the oppressed proletariat, virtually wrote itself.

And sighing, for the girl was charming, he picked up his baton once again. 'From the letter D, gentlemen. And remember that sostenuto means *sostenuto*. Even for Herr Katzenbirger it means sostenuto.'

As the time drew nearer for their departure, the company's preparations grew more frantic.

'I am not a canary,' announced Raisa, arriving for a morning rehearsal. 'I cannot zink at ten o'clock,' but she sang. The coloratura Jacob had filched from Dresden to play the Queen of the Night fell off her

94

stepladder, twisted an ankle, and climbed up again to sing 'O Zittere Nicht' in a way that had the orchestra banging on their music stands. Boris stayed up until 3 a.m. creating exotic head-dresses for Sarastro's priest. Even Frau Pollack, presented with new fabrics after years of making do, forgot her almost-eaten great-uncle and trod the treadle of her sewing-machine like a Valkyrie.

As for Tessa, she was everywhere: prompting, copying, sewing, ironing and only once, very quietly and unnoticed, fainting in the laundry room when she had missed a little more food, a little more sleep than her small frame could endure.

On a Saturday evening, just five days before they were due to leave, Jacob received a phone call in his office which sent him hurrying in search of his under wardrobe mistress.

'I've just had a call from Herr Klasky, Tessa. He's conducting at the Musikverein at eight-thirty and he's forgotten The Button!'

'Oh no!' Tessa's eyes were wide with concern. 'Is it a première?'

Jacob nodded. 'Berg's Concerto. We must get it to him. It would be a disaster if he got upset now, so soon before the tour.'

All performing artists are superstitious and Klasky, though technically sane, could only conduct a première while in possession of a small, mottled object suggesting, with its faint air of decay and transparency, the shed milk tooth of an undernourished child, but authenticated without a doubt as the waistcoat button of Ludwig van Beethoven himself.

'He's rung his housekeeper,' Jacob continued. 'He wants you to run round quickly and fetch it and leave it at Sachers at the reception desk. He's dining there now on his way to the hall. Can you manage that?'

A faint shadow had crossed Tessa's face at the mention of Austria's most famous hotel, once the favourite haunt of the aristocracy, which the terrifying Frau Sacher still ran with a complete disregard for recent changes. But she only said, 'Yes, Herr Witzler,' and was presently found by the Littlest Heidi, rummaging hastily in a wicker skip for something to replace her paint-encrusted smock.

Heidi Schlumberger was not only the smallest but the prettiest and sweetest of the Three Heidis, her blue eyes permanently widened in admiration of the world.

'I've got a *Sylphides* dress that's spotless,' she said now, taking Tessa by the hand. 'Come along, I'll show you.'

'Is it suitable, do you think?' said Tessa, when she had slipped it on and stood looking at herself, white, gauzy and rose-embroidered in the mirror of the chorus dressing-room.

But what was suitable for the delivery of Beethoven's waistcoat button to Sachers? – and anyway, there was no more time. Thanking Heidi profusely, Tessa ran out into the street.

Guy had spent the day before Nerine's arrival in a kind of Odyssey, revisiting the places where he had been with her. The old hunting pavilion in the Prater where he had picked her a bunch of early scillas like little sapphire stars . . . the chesnut tree by the gates of the Academy where he had watched for her light at dawn . . . the room in the Kunsthistorisches Museum with its famed and fabulous Breughels in which Nerine – hiding from the other girls – had stood beside him to gaze enraptured at the master's complete and all-embracing world.

Now, strolling back through the Inner City past scalloped fountains, equestrian statues and the quiet facades of palaces warm in the golden light of evening, he could almost believe that the city, like himself, was waiting for his love.

He crossed the Albertina Platz, exchanged bows with the Minister of Trade who was assisting his portly wife into a fiacre, turned down the Philharmonikerstrasse and entered his hotel.

The foyer was almost deserted, for they had begun to serve the evening meal. But at the far side, between two Venetian mirrors, he glimpsed a small figure in white backed against the red-damask covered wall. A figure imprisoned by the fat, spread-eagled arms of a bald gentleman in evening clothes, his back to Guy, who was bending over her.

Guy approached and as he did so, the anguished face of Witzler's under wardrobe mistress appeared briefly from behind the bulk of her captor, lit up in recognition of Guy and vanished once again.

A certain melancholy settled on Guy. The man endeavouring to pin her to the wall was old, unsteady

97

on his feet and probably quite genuinely under a misapprehension for the glimpse of Tessa, her throat and bare shoulders rising from a cloud of white, hardly suggested a respectable Viennese hausfrau waiting for her spouse. Which was a pity – for Guy, penned for weeks in the Treasury, was in the mood to do justice to a prolonged, well-matched and bloody fight.

Now he merely seized the man by the shoulder, spun him round and in tones as polite as they were menacing, said, 'This lady is with me.'

Rubbing his shoulder and muttering angrily, the old gentleman tottered away. Guy, left looking down at Tessa's fragile, serious little face, transcending the absurd romanticism of the costume, was more than ever inclined to exonerate her tormentor.

'How old are you?' he asked abruptly.

'Twenty. Well, almost.'

Guy, who had been toying with the 'I am old enough to be your father' approach, abandoned it. At eleven he had not really been prepared for parenthood.

'You shouldn't be here alone,' he said, his voice still harsh. 'It's most unsuitable, you must know that.'

'Yes . . . I'm sorry.' Only the ghost of a sniff, a finger pressed against the corner of one eye as if to hold back an impending tear, betrayed her recent strain. 'I had to deliver something for Herr Witzler.'

Guy's thick brows drew together in a frown. What did Witzler mean by exposing her to this? Was the child never supposed to eat or sleep?

'You had better stay and have some supper. My secretary's probably waiting in the dining-room. She's a formidable lady, but she's got a heart of gold. Come and join us.'

Tessa shook her head. 'No, really, I couldn't.'

But at that moment a service door opened somewhere at the back and lifting her head, her nostrils flaring in the manner of Baudelaire when he smelled the fleurs du mal, she said raptly, 'Rindfleisch suppe!'

It was too much, and abandoning further protest she let herself be led to the double doors of the dining-room.

Inside, however, a reverse awaited them. The terrifying Frau Sacher, black-clad and omnipresent, came towards them, stared at Tessa and hissed angrily to Guy, 'You cannot bring *her* into the public dining room!'

Fury gripped Guy. Surely the woman could see that Tessa, though dressed like a dancing-girl, was not of their kind? But anxious above all not to subject the child to a scene, he allowed himself to be led upstairs and within moments the door was opened on an image from one of Tessa's most fervent dreams.

'Oh!' she breathed. 'All my life I have wanted to dine in a chambre séparée.'

Entranced, she looked at the red plush walls, the snowy damask, the alcove with its discreetly looped curtains of gold-tasselled brocade. This was life as she had conceived it: Sarah Bernhardt, the Duse, were now sisters under the skin.

But when she had sat for a while in a chair that Guy

had pulled out for her, she fell silent. A cloud passed over her face.

'Is anything the matter?'

'No . . . Only . . . would you mind very much if we changed places?' Guy, following her gaze, found that Tessa was confronting the portrait of an obese and haughty lady whose plump bosom was bisected by the Order of St Boniface. Narrowing his eyes to read the title, he learned that he was in the presence of Her Imperial Highness, the Archduchess Frederica.

'Certainly.' Guy rose and the change was effected. 'Your republicanism again?' he enquired politely.

Tessa nodded. She was now staring with every appearance of pleasure at a painting of Leda welcoming with unmistakable concupiscence the attentions of the swan.

'Yes, but this lady at least is enjoying herself,' she said, answering Guy's grin.

It was an agreeable meal. Someone, somewhere, had taught this waif the art of conversation. Tessa touched him with her ardent belief in art as the passport to man's freedom and happiness, but she could be very funny about the International Opera Company's preparations for their exciting and mysterious assignment. And she could listen. Guy, telling her about his travels in Brazil, saw her almost visibly drinking in his descriptions of that fabled, exotic land.

But as the meal drew towards its close, he noticed her small face slewing round more and more to the object only partially concealed by the half-drawn curtains in the alcove: an object which, without blazoning it to the world, was not really a couch or a sofa – was, by its width, the humped softness of its pillows . . . was, in short . . . a bed.

The waiter brought coffee and a liqueur for Guy, and closed the door with finality. Requesting permission to smoke, Guy watched, concealing his amusement, as the highly expressive face of the little wardrobe mistress registered in rapid succession a series of emotions: apprehension, followed by resolution, followed again by a flicker of despair.

'Do people often bother you like that?' he said, deciding to force the issue. 'Like that old man just now?'

'Well, a bit. It's worse since Anita cut my hair.' Her eyes slid back to the bed. It was awful not knowing how to behave, what was correct. That so handsome and wealthy a man – a man who clearly could have any woman he wished – should have any real interest in her seemed most unlikely. On the other hand, that so handsome a man – any man – should buy her a dinner, a three-course dinner with rindfleisch suppe and kalbsbraten which nowadays cost a week's wages, and want nothing in return, seemed equally unlikely. Caught thus between Scylla and Charybdis, Tessa reached for her wineglass, gulped and plunged.

'It is very difficult. You see, I believe that one must be completely generous. One must be like Sonia in *Crime and Punishment* when she went to Siberia with Raskalnikov, and like Isadora Duncan. I mean, not

101

dancing in bare feet but giving. And like Madame Walewska with Napoleon. Everything must be given freely – money, property . . . oneself. But though I believe this absolutely when anyone . . . the second double-bass player or the electrician . . . or anyone wishes to,' she went on, looking suddenly extremely miserable and somewhat wringing Guy's withers, 'I can't, I absolutely *can't*.'

Overcome by failure, she bent her head. Silky lashes curtained downcast eyes, and in the whispered murmur which now escaped her Guy, hair-raisingly, caught the name of Professor Freud.

With some regret, for it was burning beautifully, Guy now extinguished his cigar. Then he leaned over and laid his strong, chiselled fingers briefly on Tessa's clenched knuckles, whitened by confession and strain.

'Tessa, I promise you that one day it will not be like that. One day somebody will come – not the second double-bass player or the electrician, but somebody. And you won't have to think about being like Isadora Duncan or going to Siberia and you certainly won't have to trouble poor Professor Freud. When that person comes, whoever he is, all the fear and doubt will go and you'll know.'

'Will I?' Her face, wistful yet trusting, was turned to his. 'Are you sure?' Yet even as she spoke she felt, with a strange kind of puzzlement, that the question already belonged to the past.

'I'm sure,' said Guy. And meaning only to reassure her, he added, 'as for me, my dear, I promise I mean you no harm. In fact, I am waiting for someone to join me here in Vienna – someone I love and hope soon to marry.' He paused and Tessa drew in her breath, seeing what Martha had first seen in the child of six: the lightening of his eyes to a lyrical and tender blue. Then he rose and pulled the red curtains firmly across the alcove. 'So you see, you are perfectly safe!'

Tessa smiled. 'I'm glad,' she said, and took one of the crystallized plums from the box he held out to her.

She was glad. She was very glad. She was *happy*. Nothing was going to happen, not ever. He loved someone else.

Odd, though, that happiness should feel so much like a weight pressing against her chest; odd that the room looked suddenly a little misty.

Odd, too, that when she so much liked Karlsbad plums, the one she was eating should taste as if it had been dug out of an Egyptian tomb.

6

Nerine and her brother arrived in Vienna with fourteen pieces of luggage and a cowed maid called Pooley. Nerine was pleased with the suite Guy had engaged for them at the Grand Hotel, rather less pleased when only three days later he informed them that they were leaving for the country.

The country – even the dazzlingly beautiful landscape of Lower Austria – did not figure high on Nerine's list of priorities. Though Vienna was sadly changed from the Imperial capital she had known as a girl, there were always amusements of some sort to be found in the city.

Nevertheless, she made no attempt to delay their departure. Guy had been a courteous host in Vienna but he had not, so to speak, shown his hand. True, there were flowers in her hotel room but no gift of jewels, no offer to take her shopping, no hint of the fabled wealth with which he had been credited. If, as seemed likely, he now expected her to join some drunken businessmen in

104

a damp hunting lodge somewhere in a forest, or don a dirndl and act the village maiden, he would find himself disappointed. Marie Antoinette playing at being a milk-maid was not to Nerine's taste. And if things went wrong there was always Lord Frith, languishing for love of her in Scotland.

Now she sat beside Guy who was driving the Hispano-Suiza himself, with Arthur dozing in the back. A second car, driven by Morgan and carrying the rest of the luggage, followed behind. It was the seventeenth of June and the countryside through which they drove was straight out of one of Schubert's more ecstatic songs. Mill-wheels raced in emerald rivers; larks ascended, linden trees spread their murmuring crowns over ancient wells – and in the distance, glimpsed for an instant and then lost again, was the snow-glitter of the Alps.

She threw a glance at Guy, who was unusually silent, and sighed. He really was amazingly attractive with that caged-wild-beast look, those strong hands lying so easily on the steering wheel. No one, looking at him, would ever guess that he had been found in the gutter. That was one thing she would have to cure him of, telling everyone about his birth. It did no good, that kind of thing, it only embarrassed people.

They lunched in the courtyard of an inn from whose every window there tumbled petunias, geraniums and tousled orange marigolds, and then continued their journey.

The golden morning was turning into a wild grey

afternoon, the peaks shrouded in cloud, and now with the suddenness of mountain weather, the sky opened to release a torrent of rain.

Guy, driving carefully through the downpour, listening to the windscreen-wiper's slow adagio, had to fight down a sudden sense of desolation. He had hazarded so much on Nerine's first glimpse.

Then, as dramatically as it had begun, the rain stopped, the clouds parted and in the new-washed, azure sky there appeared a perfect rainbow.

It was thus that Nerine, stepping out of the car where Guy had halted it beside the lake, first saw the castle: its towering, fairy-tale pinnacles spanned by a radiant, multi-coloured arc.

'Good heavens, Guy, that's Pfaffenstein, isn't it?' Her lovely head was tilted upward, her voice reverent. 'Frau von Edelnau had a picture of it in her dining-room.'

'Yes, that's Pfaffenstein,' said Guy, making obeisance to the gods, for the skyscape framing the fortress was breathtaking.

Arthur climbed out ponderously and joined them. His finger in his Baedecker, he was able to inform them that parts of the castle dated back to the year 909, that it had been in the possession of the Pfaffenstein family since 1353, that it comprised the demesnes of Hohenstein, Untersweg, Breganzer and Pilgarten, and that the original ramparts measured two kilometres in circumference.

'It's staggering,' said Nerine. 'There's nothing

106

remotely like it in England, is there?' Forgetting for once her determination never to screw up her eyes for fear of wrinkles, she peered at the gatehouse tower looking for the family flag. 'Do they still own it, the Pfaffensteins?'

'No,' said Guy.

It was coming, the moment to which his whole will, his whole being had been directed . . . the moment which had had its birth in the Vienna Woods so many years ago.

'Who does, then?' And as Guy was silent, she persisted, 'Whose is it, then?'

He turned his back to the castle, wanting to see nothing but her face.

'Mine.'

She did not understand him at first; it was too incredible. 'What do you mean, Guy?'

'I mean that I have bought Burg Pfaffenstein,' he said carefully. 'It is mine and – if you wish it – yours.'

If ever a man had his reward, Guy had it then. Nerine's eyes widened, she drew in her breath; her face became transfigured and in the first spontaneous gesture of love that she had shown him, she let her head fall against his shoulder.

'Oh, Guy,' she breathed. 'Oh, darling!' All doubts left her, the spectre of Frith vanished into the mists of his native air. 'I can't believe it.'

Arthur, stunned into tact, retreated. Guy, closing his arms around her, feeling her hair against his cheek, hearing her whispers of gratitude, had that sense of complete 'arrival', of 'being there', which human beings continually crave and hardly ever actually experience.

He belonged to the old tradition of knight errant: the chevaliers sans peur et sans reproche who ask of their lady only that she is beautiful and willing to be served in order to ride to the ends of the earth at her bidding. Valiant, selfless – and generally slain – the Lochinvars and Lancelots of this world, however, were not granted the benison that was now to be bestowed on Guy: a prolonged, close and domestic sojourn with the beloved.

'Come!' said Guy now, holding open the door of the car. 'I want to show you everything.'

She smiled up at him, lovely as daybreak. 'Yes,' she said. 'Oh yes, my darling. Yes.'

But in the room in the West Tower where the Duchess and the Margravine were waiting with David Tremayne to greet them, anticipation and excitement had suddenly drained from the day.

'She can't come at all?' said the Margravine, her plump face puckered. 'Not even for the reception and the ball? Not for her birthday?'

'I've read you what she says,' said the Duchess, holding out the letter which had just been delivered. She was regally dressed for the occasion in a grey silk dress entirely devoid of cobwebs or even the smallest piece of clinging cheese, but the hooded old grey eyes were suddenly bleak and lifeless. 'She has asked her professor for leave, but she is needed in Vienna; she cannot be spared.'

The Margravine groped for her handkerchief and surreptitiously wiped her cheeks. 'It won't be the same without Putzerl,' she said, and the pug – hearing the name which meant walks, games and being scratched in exactly the right place on the stomach – shot out of his cope and (as was his wont) began to slither, yapping, round the floor.

David was silent, but he too had to fight down a sudden sense of desolation. He had worked unstintingly over the past three months, turning Pfaffenstein into a place in which Le Roi Soleil himself would have been pleased to dally during a summer progress through the countryside. But though he had worked for Guy and thus for the woman at whose feet Guy wished to lay the castle, it was the image of the small princess of whom everyone spoke with such warmth that he had held in his mind. It was the thought of pleasing her, of showing her that her home was in good hands, which had given a special zest to his labours. Now, suddenly, everything seemed pointless and flat.

'She will come later,' said the Duchess, laying down the letter. 'She promises that.'

But she was eighty-one, her sister-in-law only two years younger. The word 'later' was entirely without significance for them. They wanted their great-niece, with her loving heart, her power to make them laugh, in the only time that they still counted on; the present – now.

'Oh, be quiet, Quin-Quin!' snapped the Margravine as the agitated dog continued to yap and ricochet off the furniture.

But as they recaptured the pug the eyes of the old ladies met, anticipating another and even more formidable disappointment. All the guests due to arrive on the following day would miss Putzerl badly, but for Maxi and his mother her absence would be a disaster. Maxi was definitely going to settle things with Putzerl, the Swan Princess had made this clear. Maxi was serious. He was bringing the dogs.

'They are here,' said David. His sharp ears had heard a car drive into the main courtyard. The servants would already be mustering in welcome. Time, then, to go forward and greet Pfaffenstein's new master and his chosen bride.

Nerine had been assigned the state bedroom in the main facade with three long windows overlooking the lake. An incredible room with its vast bed carved with cupids and peacocks and canopied in yellow, hand-painted Lyons silk. The jewelled Sèvres toilet set of sixty pieces which Marie Antoinette had sent to an earlier Princess of Pfaffenstein lay on the rosewood and ivory dressing-table. Drifts of sandalwood rose from a pair of agate perfume burners and curled languorously between the glittering drops of the chandeliers.

'It used to be Putzerl's room – our great-niece's room,' explained the Duchess. 'She inherited it when her father died.'

'But we used to find her sleeping on the floor,' put in the Margravine.

'So she moved to a room in the West Tower,' said the Duchess.

'Thank you, the room is quite delightful,' said Nerine in the careful German that no one could fail to learn under the strict tutelage of Frau von Edelnau.

'The Archduchess Frederica usually has it when she comes but—' the Duchess broke off for the 'but'. Though unpleasant to contemplate, this was no longer her affair. Pfaffenstein now belonged to Herr Farne and the task of explaining to this most disagreeable of relations that she had been ousted by the Englishwoman would fall to him or his nice young secretary.

The ladies departed and Nerine, despatching her maid to unpack in the dressing-room, was left alone.

It was unbelievable . . . staggering! Pfaffenstein was hers! *Pfaffenstein!* If only her mother could see her, and those girls at Frau von Edelnau's who made such a fuss every time they danced with a count! Well, they would see her! Everyone would see her. She would be married here, of course. To think she had almost accepted poor Frith with his draughty tower and gloomy moors.

But she must not be idle. She must be generous. She must give. In twenty-four hours she would stand beside Guy at the reception, welcoming in ownership a veritable *Almanach de Gotha* of guests.

Like a general checking the supplies before a battle, Nerine surveyed the room. Yes, there were plenty of mirrors. The oval one, framed in porcelain flowers, on the dressing-table; three hand mirrors in the Sèvres toilet set; a large Venetian one set between the silk panels on the wall and a free-standing cheval glass on clawed legs which could be turned to the light. With the small magnifying mirror that travelled with her everywhere and the built-in double mirrors of the painted wardrobe in the dressing-room, she ought to be secure.

She glanced at her watch. There was no time to lose: in an hour Guy was coming to give her 'The Ring': 'I want everyone to know that you're mine,' he had said as they drove up to the castle. 'Everyone. And *now*.'

The ring, he had explained, was part of a parure. He was going to give her the necklace before some opera or other which he was staging in the theatre and the earrings on their wedding morning. How she loved such gestures! The romance of it all . . .

She seated herself at the dressing-table and began to smooth her eyebrows. 'Quick, Pooley,' she called. 'I want the yellow peignoir – it will take up the colour of the bed hangings. And I want my hair dressed very high.'

'Yes, ma'am. Would you want the yellow mules as well, or the gold sandals?'

'The mules. I want everything very informal, flowery . . . no jewels. Hurry, girl, for heaven's sake!'

Pooley loosened her mistress's hair, and the knee-length, unbelievably luxuriant blue-black tresses mantled the snowy shoulders and flowed down her back. The Bible was right, Nerine thought, there was power in hair like that. She would never follow the fashion for short hair, *never*! Staring eagle-eyed into the mirror, she watched as Pooley braided her hair and dressed it in shining coils. Then, as the last pin was in place, she changed her mind.

'Undo it again. Brush it out.' She had not yet meant to let Guy see the full glory of her unbound hair. But Pfaffenstein . . . In procession she saw in her mind the incredible rooms through which they had come. The great hall with its domed ceiling . . . the blue salon . . . the vast marble staircase – what an entrance she would make down those stairs! Yes, her impulse was right. She would be wholly giving: he should see even her hair.

'I will sit in that gilt chair by the window. Put it so that the light falls on my left side. Good heavens, girl, how many times do I have to tell you, the *left* side!' There was a small beauty-spot on Nerine's left cheek, God's last blessing on his handiwork. 'Yes, that's good,' she said, pulling the pleated silk robe closer. 'I might have known about the furnishings when I bought it. Give me the mirror and the comb.' Guy would think he had come too early, she would start a little, turn . . . There should be flowers near: that bowl of roses and lilies. Could she hold a rose in her hand? No, not if she was combing her hair. Or wear one behind her ear? No, because she wanted the dishabille look: 'Beauty Surprised'. But suppose she had been overcome by the loveliness of the rose as she combed her hair?

'Quickly, one of those roses in the bowl. No, you idiot, a pale one. Yes, that's right. Now you can go.'

Thus Guy, entering the room a few minutes later,

saw the woman who held his heart. She sat, fresh as the morning, by the open window with the light shining on the heart-rending perfection of her curved cheek. Her incredible hair streamed over her shoulders; her face was pensive, serene, and she was looking down at a flower cupped in her hands – on a rose whose fragrance had made her forget her toilette. She was like the lady in the unicorn tapestry at Cluny, caught in her enclosed garden, dreaming, forgetful of her beauty.

'I'm sorry – am I early?'

'Oh Guy, you startled me!' She smiled up at him. 'How could you be early, my dearest? I'm always happy when you come.'

Joy welled up in Guy. She was worthy of every guerdon; nothing he had done had been excessive. A thousand castles, a million banquets would not be too many to lay at her feet.

But Nerine had put down her rose and was looking at the small box he carried – a box which he now opened and placed wordlessly in her hand.

'*Oh!*' For a moment she was speechless. She could not remember when she had been so moved. This surely must be the largest, the most valuable diamond in the world. 'Guy,' she said. 'Oh, Guy, darling!'

Gravely, Guy bent and slipped the jewel on her finger. Then, in a gesture as old as love itself, he knelt at her feet and put his head, almost as dark as hers, into her silken lap.

And in the mirror, Nerine smiled.

*

114

'Where is The Mother?' cried Boris for the seventh time that morning.

'She's inside the wig basket,' soothed Tessa. 'Screwed down very tight and wrapped in Pamino's petticoat with lots of padding.'

'Mind your backs, please! Mind your backs . . .'

The International Opera Company was loading to go on its mystery assignment and in the narrow lane behind the theatre the confusion was incredible. A huge covered lorry, advertising itself as the first motorized pantechnicon in Europe and looking as though it would soon be the last, was parked half on the pavement. An old army truck and something resembling a gigantic hearse were parked close behind. Jacob was rushing about with a list, so was the stage manager: everyone, in fact, had lists.

Though the chorus, orchestra and principals were to follow by train, several of the artistes had come to see the fun and were busy getting in the way of the men carrying the scenery and props out of the theatre.

'Herr Klasky has just phoned,' screamed the Rhine-maiden from the stage door. 'He wants to know if Tessa has his towelling robe.'

'Yes, I have it, Frau Witzler,' called Tessa. 'He left it in the Green Room.' She snatched the tottering Bubi from the path of an oncoming trolley, ran back to fasten the windows of the dressing-rooms and administered aspirin to Frau Pollack who was getting ready for her travelling migraine.

'The cyclorama!' yelled Witzler. 'My God, the cyclo-rama!'

Gradually the chaos subsided. Tessa, Boris and the stage manager climbed into the pantechnicon. Jacob shut the door and seated himself in the cab beside the driver and – to the screams of Bubi who wanted to go in the lorry with Tessa – the company took to the road.

They crossed the Ringstrasse and headed south, Jacob frowning in a rare moment of contrition as he recalled his last glimpse of the under wardrobe mistress curled up between a pile of flats, her shorn head jammed against the pillars of Sarastro's temple. Perhaps he should have let her have the twenty-four-hours' leave she had requested: she had looked very troubled when he had refused. But the truth was, he simply could not face the get-in without her. Klasky had Beethoven's waistcoat button but he, as he was beginning to realize, had Tessa. There was also the matter of his little son. The Rhinemaiden could lift a piano but her nerves were delicate and Bubi adored Tessa. In fact, he had thought of suggesting that Tessa might like to have Bubi's cot in her room at Pfaffenstein.

Well, it was done now. He forgot it, thoroughly pleased with the way he had kept Farne's secret. No one but himself and the driver knew their destination. Even the principals would only receive their instructions when they got to the station. Not many people could do that but *he* had done it. And now for a week of glory!

Tessa, in the back, rested her head more comfortably on the rolled-up starcloth. She had been very miserable

116

when Jacob had refused her leave, knowing how disappointed the aunts would be. But if it was not to be, it was not to be and there was something very *real* about spending one's birthday like this. Jacob had said she could have leave later and she would go home then – except that it was no longer 'home'. Being unpaid, she could take leave whenever she wished, but that had not for a moment occurred either to her or to her employer.

In the darkness of the windowless van she could just make out Boris leaning against a cut-out tree. He had unpacked The Mother and was speaking to her softly in Bulgarian, promising her milk.

There was nothing to do, thought Tessa dreamily . . . not for hours. She could think, or rest or *sleep* . . .

Tessa's sleep debt was boundless. In her attic in the Wipplingerstrasse, to which often she did not return until the small hours, she was at the beck and call of the little Kugelheimers who regarded her bed as a perfect refuge from the tigers and spooks that inhabited their nursery. She was the first to reach the theatre and the last to leave at night . . . sleep for Tessa was what salvation is to the sinner, enlightenment to the mystic: mostly unattainable and infinitely desired.

Her eyes closed, her small hands uncurled. She was in a red plush-lined room and Mozart was looking down at her. She knew it was Mozart because of the radiance that shone from him. 'I wrote it for you,' he said, and handed her the score of *Figaro* but when she opened it, it was a box of Karlsbad plums.

Thus Tessa slept and smiled and slept . . . slept as

they drove through Neustadt and Feldberg . . . slept as they paused for Frau Pollack to be sick beside a railway siding in Oberwent . . . slept as Boris covered her carefully with his own overcoat. She was still deeply and utterly asleep when the lorry stopped and Witzler climbed down, opened the double doors and said, 'We're there.'

'Good God!' Boris had climbed out and was looking at the vast courtyard, the soaring towers, the lowered flag with its gold griffin and scarlet glove. 'It's Pfaffenstein, isn't it? I came here once on an excursion.'

A chorus of 'Pfaffenstein! We're at Pfaffenstein!' echoed round the castle walls as the stage-hands and carpenters climbed out of the other covered lorries and examined their surroundings.

'Yes,' said Jacob proudly. 'It's Burg Pfaffenstein.' He peered into the pantechnicon and saw Tessa, pale as a snowdrop, still curled in sleep. 'We'll leave her for a bit,' he said, feeling contrition touch him once again, and turned to find David Tremayne coming towards them, followed by a posse of retainers: tall craggy men with war ribbons pinned to their liveries of crimson and green.

'Mr Farne thought you might like to see your rooms first,' said David when he had introduced himself. 'We have managed to get the whole company into the Fountain Courtyard – that's through the archway. The theatre's over there.' He pointed to the huge double doors at the end of the great south facade. 'We're rather keen to get the lorries away by six because the reception begins then, so I've brought along some men to help your people unload and show them where things are. They're old castle servants and absolutely trustworthy.'

Jacob thanked him and with Boris and the still ailing Frau Pollack, followed the young Englishman into the arcaded courtyard with its creeper-covered colonnades. The company, he saw at once, had been royally treated. The rooms were light and most comfortably furnished; a double bed for himself and his Rhinemaiden had been specially brought in and the room assigned to Raisa was, tactfully, the largest and filled with flowers.

Well pleased, conveying his thanks to Herr Farne, Jacob returned to supervise the unloading. And saw at once that something was wrong. The men were not working; they were standing round the pantechnicon, scowling and furious, and when they saw Witzler they swarmed round him, their mood so ugly that some absurd idea of a strike or revolution crossed Jacob's mind.

'They've taken Tessa!'

'Kidnapped her!'

'Frog-marched her away. Those louts in green and red uniforms.'

'She didn't stand a chance. They just climbed into the back to unpack and then grabbed her.'

'We tried to stop them and they went for us. One of them had a sort of staff and he clouted Stefan.'

'They took her through that iron door there.'

Witzler turned pale. It had happened then. He had been half-expecting it, but why *here* for heaven's sake?

Guilt stabbed him. If only he had let her have the leave she had asked for . . .

'I'll see what I can do,' he said heavily. Only what could he do if she had run away and was in trouble with the police?

On the gatehouse the griffin flag climbed slowly up the mast and fluttered gaily in the breeze. It was a sight the staff of the International Opera Company perceived without the slightest sign of pleasure.

'Nothing will go right now,' said the junior carpenter gloomily. 'Not without Tessa. You'll see.'

7

The great hall at Pfaffenstein, two storeys high, with its columns of agate-coloured marble, its statue-packed niches and ceiling frescoes by Tiepolo, was reached from the main courtyard by a set of massive double doors. Opposite this another set of doors, emblazoned with the Pfaffenstein arms in hammered gold, led to the ballroom which looked over the lake. At the far end, however, to the right as one entered, the hall ended in that apogee of baroque ceremonial: the grand staircase. It was at the foot of this staircase with its wide balustrade, its stone griffins, its famous jewelled corona lit by a hundred and twenty lamps, that Guy now stood with Nerine beside him to receive his guests.

The aunts had advised on the maximum of formality for the reception preceding the opening ball. Even relations they had dandled on their knees were to approach in order of rank, to be announced, and introduced by them to Pfaffenstein's new owner. Later, they had suggested, Guy could follow his own inclinations but if a foundling, however gifted, intelligent and rich wished to establish his lady with the nobility, he would do well to call on all the protocol that was available. Guy himself, always and only concerned for Nerine, had concurred in their arrangements and had further heightened the theatricality of the occasion by remaining out of sight until this moment, instructing David and Thisbe to see to the welfare of his guests.

Now, standing on one side of the dais made by the wide sweep of the lowest step, he looked down at the assembled throng, concealing his amusement.

If the most potent scent in the room was not of the ladies' perfume or the men's pomade, but of moth-balls, the massed effect was nevertheless most spectacular. The men in crimson and light blue and felden green with their gold epaulettes, their braid and rows of medals, were the most impressive, but the ladies in their brocade and lace, wearing those of their jewels that still remained unpawned, were no mean sight either. Only a professional grouser would have pointed out the piece of astrakhan apparently chewed out of the aged Prince Monteforelli's frogged tunic, or the streaks of oil on the satin train of the Countess Waaltraut as she pushed her gout-ridden mother's decrepit bath chair closer for a look at Farne.

For the new owner of Pfaffenstein was undoubtedly a surprise. The munificence of the entertainments laid on for them, coupled with the tasteful arrangements made for their comfort, had already deprived his guests of the hope that the Englishman would provide good sport by being vulgar and uncouth. A man whose secretary could provide accommodation for the Archduke Sava's bear and persuade the Archduchess Frederica, who was outranked only by the Princess of Pfaffenstein, that a move from the State Bedroom would benefit her health, was clearly a man to be reckoned with, and the rumours at first discredited that he was engaged in some kind of cloak-and-dagger business with the Chancellor on Austria's behalf were fast gaining ground. Not that he was handsome – but in the dark evening clothes which contrasted so strongly with the glittering uniforms of the men, he had an air of undoubted distinction, and the slight look of arrogance on his sombre face did him no harm in the eyes of his audience. As for the fiancée, men and women alike saw no mystery there. Here was beauty, unquestionable and absolute – the reward since time began for power, achievement and wealth.

Guy turned to smile at Nerine, wanting to share a moment of intimacy before the ceremony began. But Nerine, dazzling in gold brocade with slashed sapphire-velvet sleeves, was absorbed in her moment of triumph, her lips moving rapidly in a litany of rank. It was unbelievable, all of it! She and Arthur had watched from his window most of the day as princes and dukes and cardinals rumbled into the courtyard in their carriages and cars. Only when the theatre company had arrived, in their shabby lorries, had she been able to tear herself away and had gone to dress. Now, down among the guests, Arthur was blissfully counting . . . Five princes in his part of the hall alone . . . twenty-three flunkeys . . . two hundred bottles of champagne . . .

Guy glanced at his watch and raised enquiring eyebrows at the Duchess and the Margravine. If they were to get through the hundred or so people assembled there before supper and the ball, it was surely time to begin?

'Yes . . . yes.' The eyes of the ladies were bright and eager. They were looking at him with tremendous expectancy and he had the absurd feeling that they had some special surprise in store for him, a kind of rabbit they were going to pull out of their hat. Earlier this had not been so. They had seemed depressed; the arrogance and aplomb he admired in them had been dimmed, and David too, though nothing could impair his efficiency, had seemed downcast. But then, just after Witzler's troupe had arrived, everything had taken off and the kind of happy expectancy which precedes a party was everywhere.

The master of ceremonies, sumptuously braided, stepped forward. But before he could announce the first of the guests, something happened.

A ripple spread through the hall, an excited murmur – and then, in a single motion like a wave, every woman sank into a curtsy and every gentleman bowed his head.

Mystified, Guy turned in the sudden hush and, tilting his head upward, saw that the oak-studded door which led from the first-floor vestibule into the mediaeval West Tower had opened to reveal a small figure in white who stood for a moment, perfectly still, in the frame of the dark stone arch. His first image – that of a banished child disturbed in sleep coming for solace – was dismissed as she moved forward across the landing, turned to gather the train of her dress with practised ease, and began her slow descent.

Down below, the master of ceremonies tapped his staff and cleared his throat, but was stilled by a single shake of the head from the slim figure on the stairs. But if, by thus silencing her former steward, Her Highness the Princess Theresa-Maria of Pfaffenstein, Princess of Breganzer, Duchess of Unterthur, Countess of Malk, of Zeeberg and of Freischule, hoped to enter unobtrusively, her hope was to be unfulfilled. The eye of every curtsying woman was upon her; every man, his head respectfully bowed, awaited her.

'Mein Gott, her hair!' hissed the Archduchess Frederica above the hush of absorbed expectancy.

Still moving very slowly, one hand guiding her skirt into a perfect fall, she continued her descent. The blue sash of the order of St Hubert, awarded only to descendants of ruling houses, bisected her small breasts; the jewelled wheel of light above her head struck fire from the tiara set on the shorn, sleek head.

Guy alone of all the men had failed to bow his head. The first shock, which sent the blood from his face, had not for an instant broken his scrutiny. He felt, as if in his own bones, every movement she made; saw, as she came closer, her gravity, the degree of her concentration. How small she was against the vastness of the staircase, how slight – yet never dwarfed. She held it all in the hollow of her hand: this place, these people – and for a moment his throat tightened in pity and an exalted awe.

She had reached the bottom. A smile broke like a grace-note across the serious little face and as she raised her hand, in its white satin glove, every woman present rose from her curtsy, every man straightened his head.

It was that imperious gesture in the smooth white glove, so different from the wrinkled kid from *Traviata* she had worn on the first night he saw her, that changed Guy's mood to sudden fury. How could he have been so blind, so idiotic as to miss the clues that had been left for him everywhere? Her perfect English, her exquisite courtesy to Morgan . . . Frau Sacher's admonition – for of course, that staunch royalist must have recognized her. This was the girl he had wanted to protect and succour: this girl at whose finger-flick the nobility rose and fell like ninepins! How dared she trick him like that – how *dared* she?

And Nerine, whose moment of triumph this should have been – dear God, he had actually forgotten Nerine!

Tessa had turned and was coming towards her aunts whose unguarded faces as they watched her betrayed, for a moment, the full extent of their love. But as she reached them, they composed themselves and the Duchess said, 'Theresa, we would like to present to you the new owner of Pfaffenstein, Herr Farne.'

It was only now that she saw him and joy, overwhelming and unbidden, blazed in her face. Guy, the owner of Pfaffenstein! Guy, the man who had so miraculously restored her home, who would make, she knew already, the best possible master for the castle.

Radiantly she smiled up at him and extended her hand for his kiss.

'I am honoured, Your Highness.' The words were cold, the eyes as he straightened again as glacial and green as the waters of the Pfaffenstein See.

The happiness drained from her face. She looked at him, puzzled.

But Tante Augustine was now presenting the woman who stood beside Guy and who, as she sketched a curtsy, still kept her left hand, bearing its gigantic diamond, with firm ownership on Guy's arm.

Tessa scarcely heard the name because the woman, in her magnificent gold dress, was the most beautiful she had ever seen. Tall as Tessa herself was not, full-breasted as Tessa yearned uselessly to be, with an enchanting, heart-shaped face, long-lashed gentian eyes and jet-black hair. Thick, high-piled hair which caught the highlights from the chandeliers and would, when unloosed, reach to her knees in a ravishing cascade, thought Tessa as one of her own white-gloved hands stole for an instant to her own bare nape.

How stupid not to have remembered earlier Guy's words at Sachers: 'As for me, Tessa, I am waiting for someone I love and hope soon to marry.'

It was for this woman who was everything that Tessa herself could never be, that Guy had bought her home. This was the new mistress of Pfaffenstein.

And of course it had to be so. A man like Guy would love only a woman as beautiful as this, would want, when he had her by his side, to have nothing to do with someone like herself.

Fighting down the desolation which threatened her, she spoke a few friendly words to Nerine and then the reception began.

Ponderously announced, the guests came forward to be introduced to Guy and welcomed by him to Pfaffenstein. The obese Archduchess Frederica . . . the red-bearded Archduke Sava, smelling of bear . . . the aged, cadaverous Prince Monteforelli, squinting down the lovely widow's décolletage . . .

Tessa faultlessly played her part, for she was in familiar country. How often in her short life had she stood thus, clamping down personal misery, to pursue a tedious and interminable duty.

'His Highness, Prince Maximilian of Spittau,' announced the master of ceremonies, and Maxi advanced.

All had gone well with Maxi. Only one of the dogs had been sick on the train, his uniforms had been redeemed from the ravages of mildew, his mother was incapacitated with a migraine. Of course there had been that panic when they thought Putzerl was not coming, but here she was and looking very fetching too. His mother had been shocked by her hair, but Maxi liked it.

Always correct, he kissed first of all the small hand of his intended (for Putzerl outranked her aunts), then those of the aunts themselves, and was introduced to

Herr Farne and the luscious fiancée. The Englishman surprised him; he spoke excellent German and if one had not known better one would have taken him for a gentleman.

But it was Putzerl's welcome that warmed Maxi's manly and bemedalled chest. She really seemed pleased to see him.

And indeed she was. Too much had happened to Tessa that day, more overwhelmed than she realized by the sight of the home she would soon leave for ever. The shock of suddenly finding herself at Pfaffenstein, of being forced by her aunts' eager entreaties into her old role, and the hurt of Guy's rejection had left her, beneath the inbred poise, defenceless and forlorn.

So Maxi, coming towards her in the absurd Artillery uniform he loved so much, was safety and familiarity, was the whole landscape of childhood with its escapades and jokes. All the others were dead, the boys she had played with, but here now was Maxi.

The young Princess of Pfaffenstein, trained from the age of three in etiquette and protocol, gave no outward distinguishing sign of pleasure but her eyes were warm, the smile she gave him came from her heart, and as Maxi prepared to cede his place to the Duke of Oberkirchen, she leaned forward and whispered very softly, 'Have you brought the dogs?'

8

In the arcaded Fountain Courtyard, the members of the International Opera Company were preparing for bed.

Their spirits were low. They had eaten excellently, for Guy had ordered that the same food should be served to the company as to the guests who were dining in the banqueting hall. But as they sat at the trestle tables put out in the courtyard, washing down the roast veal, the raspberries and cream, the luscious cheeses still unobtainable in Vienna, with unlimited supplies of Pfaffenstein's wild, white wine, conversation was desultory and the nightingales who presently trilled from the darkening woods trilled in vain. For there was no news of Tessa and in her absence this first night, which should have been a triumph, had turned to ashes.

Witzler had spent the afternoon rushing through the castle, questioning every servant he could find, making a nuisance of himself to the steward and to Farne's own staff. But no one had seen a vanished wardrobe mistress or seemed unduly interested in her fate. Boris had run down to the village to question the local policeman; Jacob had rung the mayor in Oberwent. No one had seen anything suspicious or found anything to report and the men who had marched her away had gone off duty and were nowhere to be found.

'Herr Tremayne will find her in the morning,' soothed the Rhinemaiden now, lowering her vast bulk, encased in a nightdress of shirred mattress ticking, on to the bed and allowing her flaxen hair to ripple over the pillows in a way that her husband frequently found soothing.

But nothing at that moment could soothe Jacob, who blamed himself ceaselessly for Tessa's fate.

There was a knock on the door and Klasky's dark and tortured face appeared.

'Any news?'

Jacob shook his head.

'Capitalist swine,' said the conductor, a dedicated Marxist. 'She's probably in a dungeon somewhere.' Entering gloomily, ignoring the Rhinemaiden in bed, he proved – despite his political principles – to be wearing jet-black silk pyjamas monogrammed in gold, and to be carrying a briefcase containing his opera. He flinched as the sound of 'Wiener Blut', played by the local hired band, wafted over the battlements and closed the Witzlers' window without asking permission. Tomorrow he was taking over the music. His orchestra would play during the firework display; he himself had agreed to accompany Raisa in a recital of lieder – but without Tessa, now, to turn the music. Only Tessa turned the pages at the right time. Only Tessa did not have to be grimaced at for being too late or too soon.

'There has been heard nothing?' enquired Pino, arriving in a resplendent Paisley dressing-gown lightly streaked with egg.

The stage-hands, in their dormitory under the rafters, were still muttering mutinously.

'If they've done anything to her I'll murder them. I'll murder the whole lot of them,' said Stefan.

'Do you remember that night we took her to the jazz club and she danced till four in the morning and then we found her asleep in the cloakroom curled up on her coat?' said Georg.

But at last sleep overtook the company which had, after all, laboured since dawn. In his room Jacob slumbered, one hirsute arm buried in the tresses of his Rhinemaiden. Boris slept, The Mother flocculating quietly on his bedside table. Frau Pollack slept, whimpering and wracked by her dreams. Klasky, his ears stuffed with cotton-wool against the noise of the yokel band, finally put down the pencil-stabbed score of his opera before he, too, closed his eyes.

But in his cot in the small room assigned to Witzler's under wardrobe mistress, Bubi, the Witzlers' infant son, now woke.

The nightlight, glowing on soul-filled, coal-black eyes and an ear strangulated by the blond curl he was winding desperately round it, illuminated a scene of despair. Bubi was wearing new, utterly masculine pyjamas that replaced his infantile nightdress and had been

132

bought in the flush of affluence that Guy's commission had brought to his papa. Bubi had cleaned his teeth; he had prayed; everything that could be done had been done and where was she? They had said that if he went to sleep like a good boy she would be there when he woke – and he had, and she was not there. The unfairness of it was beyond belief. He had been promised Tessa. She was going to tell him about the giant whose stomach rumbles caused the thunderstorms; she was going to play the game where he crawled under the bedclothes and she had to guess what animal he was being. She was going to be there all night!

And where was she? Nowhere. Her bed was flat and empty: there were no clothes on it, nothing.

Pondering on the wickedness of mankind and on promises betrayed, Bubi, biting his lip, now heard the soft but unmistakable sound of music. Unwinding a fat finger from the coil of his hair, he listened. Hope dawned. Music meant people, and rows of chairs to crawl between. It meant men with hammers who let him bang things – and it meant Tessa.

Carefully he climbed out of his cot, padded along the landing and emerged in the courtyard. There were lanterns in brackets lighting the fountain, and flares in the archway from which the sound of music came. Hitching up his striped pyjamas, which had been bought to last, he set off resolutely across the cobbles. Bubi's first word after 'Mama', 'Papa' and 'No' had been 'Bailiffs' and men in bowler hats still made him cry, but the shadows behind the flaring lamps held no terrors for him.

Passing through an arch he found himself in an even larger courtyard; at the sight of the vast, dark expanse which faced him, and the looming statue of someone on a horse, he did for a moment hesitate. But it was from the long building opposite, with the light streaming from the windows, that music came, and with a last resolute hitch of his pyjama trousers Bubi set off staunchly in the direction of the open double doors.

'Oh, Guy, isn't it wonderful!' breathed Nerine, circling the brilliantly lit ballroom in Guy's arms.

'You're happy, then?' he asked, looking down at her tenderly.

'Happy! My dearest, you can't imagine . . .' she gazed reverently at the vast, brocaded backside of the Archduchess Frederica undulating two feet away in the heroic clasp of the Prince of Spittau. 'All these people here – and as your guests!'

'Our guests, Nerine. All this is for you.'

She looked up at him under her lashes, smiling – that long, slow, curving smile which had entranced him all those years ago. 'You spoil me, darling.'

It was all worthwhile, he told himself again. He would have endured for eternity the company of these relics of the *Almanach de Gotha* (now proposing to eat him out of house and home) to see her look like that.

The Pfaffenstein Serenaders, engaged for the first night so as not to offend the susceptibilities of the locals, paused for an instant to wipe their perspiring faces before thundering into the 'Gold and Silver Waltz'. Guy, steering Nerine between the couples, resolutely ignoring the spectacle of the Princess of Pfaffenstein supporting, without seeming to, the creaking form of the aged Prince Monteforelli while that disgusting old creature whispered his gallantries into her small, pricked ear, pulled his fiancée closer and said:

'Do you remember, darling? This is the first waltz we ever danced to? At the Academy . . .'

The high, bare room, the young girls in their pale dresses, the Hungarian killed on the Eastern Front who had been his friend and loved the freckle-faced American . . . that incredible moment when the music allowed him to do what would otherwise have been unthinkable: to take Nerine into his arms . . .

'Do you remember?' he asked again.

Panic flickered for a moment in Nerine's eyes. Guy had been asking her if she remembered things ever since they had come to Vienna, and the long and the short of it was that she did not.

'What was I wearing?' she prompted.

Guy frowned in concentration. 'Something pink . . . soft . . . floating.'

Relief spread across Nerine's face. Of course: the rose georgette, high-waisted, with puffed sleeves. The maid at the Academy had made an appalling mess of ironing the flounces and she had had to be very sharp with her.

'Yes, yes, my dear,' she said happily. 'I do indeed remember.'

The Unconscious, lately discovered by Professor Freud and used by others to store their joys, fears and frustrations, was for Nerine a gigantic subterranean wardrobe.

Nerine's brother was hardly less ecstatic than his sister. True, the oil-stained lady with whom he was dancing resembled nothing so much as a stranded sea cow patiently awaiting a gift of fish; true, her moist round eyes seemed unable to tear themselves from Farne – but what did it matter? She was the Countess Waaltraut von Waneck and could trace her descent back to Bohemian kings. Of course, to dance with the Princess of Pfaffenstein would really be something, but there was not much hope there. They were queueing up for her in order of rank, as was proper. Incredible, the catch Farne had turned out to be! What must all this be costing him, thought Arthur, and began happily to calculate again.

'Jolly good show, this,' said a captain of the Uhlans who was stranded, on account of a wooden leg, beside the Bath chair of Waaltraut's mother. 'Everything being done just as it should be. And the fellow seems to know how to behave too.'

The gouty old countess nodded. 'If he hadn't been engaged,' she said, 'I might almost have let Waaltraut demean herself.'

'Oh, I say, no!' said the Uhlan, shocked.

David Tremayne, standing unobtrusively by the

136

great double doors, keeping an eye on everything, was satisfied. There had been numerous problems, and even this afternoon the director of the opera company had pursued him with some complaint about a missing wardrobe mistress – a complaint which David found hard to take seriously. Surely massive Viennese sewing ladies did not vanish into thin air? But now everything felt right. Farne's guests were clearly having the time of their lives and Farne himself, waltzing with the lovely widow, must surely tonight be the happiest of men? How beautiful she was – staggeringly so, thought David – and turned to look yet again at the Princess of Pfaffenstein.

Already it seemed incredible to him that when she had first appeared in the aunts' Tower Room just before the reception, sleepy and bewildered, he had been disappointed. From the talk which had preceded her, he had imagined someone sweetly pretty with curls and dimples, and the grave, narrow little face and shorn head had come as a shock. Then she had hugged the aunts and smiled at them and it was as though a flame had been lit inside her. Long before her old nurse had come and led her away, protesting, to dress, he had not imagined how she could look otherwise.

Since then he had admired, increasingly, her determination to stay out of the limelight. She had refused to let the band serenade her for her birthday, and had left the ballroom on some pretext before the first dance so that Mrs Hurlingham and Guy could open the ball alone. Not that it helped, thought David. Those dotty aristocrats, one and all, seemed to adore her.

Now he watched as she deposited her ancient, creaking kinsman in a gold-backed chair beside her aunts – and was immediately claimed by the man everyone said she was going to marry, the Prince of Spittau.

'Nice tune, isn't it?' said Maxi happily, as the band broke into yet another waltz.

'Yes,' said Tessa. 'Though I must say, Maxi, I would simply love to Charleston.'

'To Charleston! Can you?' Maxi was shocked. No wonder his mother worried about Putzerl!

'A bit. Some friends took me to a jazz club and they taught me.'

But Maxi was bent on business. The music was heady and he would have been foolish not to know that in his sky-blue tunic and white trousers piped in red, he was looking his best. If he could propose and be accepted now, even without the dogs, he could really settle down and enjoy the house party.

'They should make a very suitable couple, shouldn't they?' said Nerine as Maxi and Tessa drew level. Her rage at Tessa's entry had been soothed by Arthur, who had informed her that the Princess was soon to be removed, and permanently, to the Prince of Spittau's Wasserburg. 'The prince so handsome and she – thanks to you – so rich.'

'She won't have all that much,' said Guy. 'Her father left a pile of debts.' Though not naturally an ostentatious dancer, he now performed a chain of double reverse-turns which took them rapidly to the other end of the ballroom.

'Putzerl, you know how fond I've always been of you,' Maxi began.

'And I of you, Maxi.'

Oh, please, not tonight, thought Tessa. My head aches so much and I just can't face hurting him again. It seemed to her that the ball had been going on for ever and Guy had not spoken a single word to her all evening, had not once glanced her way.

But it looked as though there was no way of avoiding it. Maxi had tightened his arm and his duelling scar was pulsating, always a sign of deep emotion. There was no doubt about it, he was going to propose.

'Putzerl, don't you think you could—'

The prince was halted by a scuffle and the sound of laughter. Then, eluding two flunkeys in crimson and green, a tiny boy in awesomely striped pyjamas tottered barefoot into the ballroom and stopped, blinking in the light of the chandeliers.

Bubi, having gained his objective, now took stock. The people were there, and the music, but where were the men with the hammers, where the rows of seats? And where was *she*?

A lady in a red dress tried to seize him but Bubi, used to nipping between scene-shifters, easily wriggled free. The laughter was growing now; more and more dancers had stopped and now the music, too, came to an end.

Had he made a mistake? Bubi's lower lip jutted out, began to tremble . . .

'Bubi!'

In an instant the little boy's face was transformed. Joy and relief shone in the coal-black eyes. It was her voice. She was here! And then she was bending over him and as she picked him up and he put his arms round her, he heard the words he longed above all others to hear.

'You've got *pyjamas*, Bubi,' said Tessa, her voice full of awe. 'Real, proper, grown-up, striped pyjamas!'

Thus the Rhinemaiden, alerted by some sixth sense to her son's disappearance and making a Wagnerian entrance, a shawl over her nightdress, put aside the images of Bubi impaled on iron spikes or drowned in a dark well, and saw him safe in the arms of a slim girl in white satin, light dancing from the tiara on her lovingly bent head . . .

And saw, too, that the search for their under wardrobe mistress had ended.

Tessa slept badly the night after the ball and not because Bubi, refusing to be parted from her, shared her bed in the turret in the West Tower.

Shortly before daybreak she rose, carried the still-sleeping child to her nurse next door and extracted the working smock which the old woman, clucking with disapproval, had washed, dried and ironed the previous day. Then slipping it on, she crept downstairs.

In the castle no one was stirring yet, but carrying up from the village she heard the familiar sounds of a country dawn: a cockerel crowing, the clank of a bucket, the creak of bolts pulled back on a stable door.

She passed the chapel, hesitated and went on. God, she felt, would not be very pleased with her this morning, and crossing the main courtyard she passed through the gatehouse arch, crossed the drawbridge and climbed the worn, stone steps which led to the eastern ramparts. The sunrise place, she had always called it, as she now stood looking out to where, from the rim of the plain whose inhabitants had once brought devastation and sorrow to her house, a silver disc of brightness had begun to lift itself above the haze.

It was not sensible, after all, thought Tessa, feeling the first rays of warmth touch her face, to feel so hurt, so *finished*, because a man had been rude to her. It was natural, after all, that he did not want to dance with her, that he had no use for her in the presence of a woman so beautiful that he could only resent anyone who seemed to intrude.

Only, I didn't want to intrude, thought Tessa bleakly; I just wanted to be friends. Surely he could have spared me a few words when he has everything: Pfaffenstein, the woman he loves, untold wealth and this power that makes everyone, even poor silly Waaltraut in a single evening, want to be where he is? Could he not be generous, having so much?

She leaned her cheek against the cool stone. This was the oldest part of the castle, the part she loved as she could not love the baroque grandeur of the south facade. Yes, after all, it would be hard to leave: harder than she had dreamed it could be.

She was turning to go when she heard footsteps and saw a solitary man seeking the eastern ramparts as she had done, for the glory of the sunrise.

'Good morning, Your Highness.' The Lithuanian look, much commented on in Byker, was greatly in evidence, the voice still cold.

'Why do you call me that?' she said wretchedly. 'When you know . . .'

'Know what? That you are a staunch republican?' Tessa, he noted, was looking pinched and plain, a fact that gave him an obscure satisfaction.

She caught her breath. 'I don't understand why you are like this. In Vienna you were so kind.'

'I don't mean to be unkind. But you must see that this masquerade of yours is apt to annoy people when it's discovered. Dear God,' he said, rage overtaking him again when he remembered her entry on the previous night, her upstaging of Nerine, 'the way you came down that staircase!'

Tessa had turned her face to the horizon but as she spoke one small hand traced, with unconscious familiarity, the pattern of a lily carved deep into the stone. 'Yes,' she said tonelessly, 'I know how to come down a staircase. They began to teach me when I was five. I had a book on my head – Plotinus, usually, bound in Spanish leather – and my skirt was too long on purpose. If I dropped the book, or stumbled, I was sent to bed without supper. There's a marble staircase they use at

Schönbrunn; it's kept specially polished so as to be slippery. I used to think that if you looked at the little red flecks in the marble you'd find they were bits of dried blood shed by the children who have come down that staircase.' She finished tracing a lily stem, laid her hand flat on the wall. 'So you see, I know how to come down a staircase. This useful accomplishment I have.'

The bitterness in her voice held Guy silent for a while. 'Were you often at Schönbrunn?'

She nodded. 'My father was in the Emperor's suite. Pfaffenstein was all right, one could always escape into the woods, but Schönbrunn . . . it was so lonely, like being in a prison. The long corridors and the *rules*. If your curtsy wasn't quite deep enough, if you didn't put your fork down the second the Emperor had finished, it was a scandal. My parents wanted a boy, of course. They went on hoping, but there weren't any more children so I was always a disappointment. I used to go and talk to a little girl in a picture. She was pretty, not like me, but I knew she felt the same. The Infanta Margarita, she was called, by Velasquez – do you know her?'

The sun was fully up now, turning the pigeons wheeling below them into triangles of light. Guy nodded, calling to mind the little Infanta kept captive in the Escorial outside Madrid until she was ready to ship as a bride to the boring, pompous Leopold of Austria.

'Sometimes my mother used to take me driving, sitting very stiff, you know, with footmen everywhere, and I'd see all those ordinary children belonging to each

143

other . . . and to the world. Really *belonging*. Playing in the park or eating ices in a café . . . I remember, once, there was a pair of twins with bright red curls sitting on the rim of a fountain in the Volksgarten with their mother. She had an arm round each of them and they were splashing in the water and laughing. I started to beat on the window . . . I wanted the coach to stop and to get out and ask them to let me just be there . . . just to be there and belong.'

'Go on.'

'Then my parents died and Pfaffenstein belonged to me. But the money had gone too and I was always failing everyone. I'd ride round to visit my parishioners and I'd see an old lady with a hole in her roof and I'd send for the steward and say, why haven't you mended Frau Keller's roof? And he'd say I have only ten men, Highness, to do the work that two hundred did before, and he'd show me their time-sheets. We'd begun already on that hopeless business: selling off pictures, selling off forests . . . So then I knew that the only thing I could do för Pfaffenstein was to leave it, and I told my aunts to sell.'

'Yes,' said Guy, 'I see.' His anger had evaporated and he regretted its passing. It had been an effective armour against the troubles of this child. 'And music? Has it always meant so much to you?'

She nodded. 'Ever since I can remember. Once when I was at Schönbrunn – I was about six, I suppose – the Vienna Choir came to give a concert. I was standing by the window in my room when these voices came from the chapel. It was only a little Schubert song, 'Auf dem Wasser zu Singen', but it just stabbed me. It was an absolute coup de foudre. You know what music is like when you aren't expecting it . . . when you *overhear* it? And I thought then that if I could just serve music . . . sort of help it to happen . . . I could bear it.'

'Bear what?' Guy wanted to say, but refrained, for after all he did know. Once, in London, he had spoken to one of Diaghilev's ballerinas about her fabled grace and lightness, wondering to what extent these qualities were 'natural'. He could remember her huge, Byzantine eyes turned on him, the slightly pitying shrug as she said, 'Dancing hurts, my friend. It hurts all the time.' Now, looking at Tessa's fawn head turning to copper in the risen sun, he realized that she could say the same about being a princess.

Suddenly impatient, irked by the understanding she had forced on him, he began to make his way down the steps, impelling her to follow him. As they crossed the drawbridge he noticed another lily, spare and formalized, carved into the gatehouse arch. A strange emblem for the bloodthirsty Pfaffensteins, he thought, for he had noticed this flower also worked into the gaudy standard with its impaled golden griffin and scarlet glove.

'What will you do with the money from Pfaffenstein?' he asked abruptly.

'Well, half will go to the aunts, of course.'

'I doubt if they will countenance that. They intend it for your dowry.'

'My dowry?'

'For your marriage to Prince Maximilian of Spittau. The only man, they informed me, with enough quarterings to aspire to your hand.'

The harshness was back in his voice and hearing it Tessa closed her eyes in sudden weariness.

'It's no use being angry with them; they're old, they cling to the old ways. But there's no question—'

She broke off and Guy watched her face suddenly light up with a pure and shining joy. The next second Prince Maximilian, in lederhosen, a woodcock feather in his loden hat, came round the corner.

'Oh, goodness, how lovely! Rinty, how you've grown! Down, Hector, *down* . . . Yes, yes, Samson, I know how you feel; you *are* the oldest.' Talking tenderly in her own language, laughing, Tessa let herself be submerged in a sea of wagging, thumping, blissfully slobbering dogs. She stroked the black muzzle of the wise old labrador, fondled the ears of the pointer with her velvet mouth and loving eyes, fielded the quicksilver ecstacy of Maxi's new, half-grown red setter – and was felled by the wolfhound bred for the prince's rare hunting excursions on to dry land. 'I've missed you all so much,' she said. 'It's really awful not being able to have dogs in Vienna.' Freeing an arm, she pulled in the Irish water spaniel, whose liver-coloured clown's face had begun to quiver with impending rejection, and swivelled round to smile at Guy, wanting to share with him the happy innocent world of these working dogs.

But Lithuania had reclaimed the new owner of Pfaffenstein. He scowled, answered the prince's, 'Good morning' curtly, and strode away across the courtyard.

'What's the matter with him?' said the prince, some-what offended, for he had been well-disposed towards the Englishman.

Tessa shrugged. 'He's like that,' she said. But it wasn't true; to everyone else he was polite and friendly. It's only me he doesn't like, she thought, and buried her face in the labrador's sturdy neck.

'I wondered if you would like to come for a walk,' said Maxi. There was going to be a pigeon shoot, fol-lowed by an English breakfast: kidneys were rumoured, and scrambled eggs and kedgeree. The English were swine of course, everyone knew that, but they did understand breakfast. But he was willing to forego all this in order to get things settled with Putzerl. His mother, recovered from her migraine, had already man-aged to make herself unpleasant about Maxi's failure on the previous night. And now, in the freshness of the morning, with the dogs looking really very well indeed, it seemed to him he had an excellent chance.

'Maxi, I can't,' said Tessa. 'I have to work.'

'Work?' said Maxi, his long Bourbon jaw hanging open. 'What do you mean?'

It occurred to him that Putzerl was oddly dressed. Was she perhaps going to milk a cow? He looked anx-iously behind him but the great courtyard was reassuringly devoid of cattle.

'I work for the International Opera Company,' said Tessa, rubbing the wolfhound's stomach while returning the caresses of the setter caught in a frenzy of adolescent adoration. 'We're going to perform *The Magic Flute* in the theatre and there's a terrible lot to do.'

'You mean you're directing this opera?' said Maxi, puzzled. There had been artistic Pfaffensteins, he knew, and queer blood like that did sometimes turn up again.

Tessa laughed. 'No, Maxi. I work backstage.' Turning her attention to the water spaniel, she explained her duties.

'You're joking?' said Maxi nervously. 'You don't really let them order you about? Ordinary carpenters and people like that?'

'Maxi, I've told you—'

'Yes, yes.' Hastily he averted the expected information that all men were created equal and that the Princess of Pfaffenstein herself was a devout republican. But really it was all a bit much. No wonder his mother worried about Putzerl and thought her fast. 'Couldn't you come out just for an hour?'

Tessa shook her head. 'I'm sorry, Maxi. There's so much to do, and I promised to have coffee with the aunts.'

Maxi's face fell. He had spent five minutes arranging the feather in his hat at an angle which would give pleasure to his intended and though he tried not to be vain about his legs he would have been foolish not to know that few men could carry off lederhosen the way he could. But if Putzerl absolutely wouldn't, he might as well go and fetch his gun – and try the English breakfast.

'I shall never forget it, never in my life!' said the Rhine-maiden, sitting astride an Act One rock and throwing out a spear-carrying arm at her audience. 'There she was, in white satin and a tiara, with princes and cardinals absolutely grovelling to her. And then, when she picked up Bubi and the flunkeys ran forward to take him from her, she just shook her head once like this,' continued Frau Witzler, moving her massive Silesian head from right to left and back again, 'and they fell back and escorted her upstairs. Six of them in uniform, clearing a way for her!'

The International Opera Company were assembled in the theatre at an unaccustomed early hour. Orchestral players who were rumoured not to have seen daylight in ten years were wandering round the pit, stage-hands stood about in clusters in the wings; on stage, Witzler and his principals sat about holding coffee-cups. The first rehearsal had been called for ten-thirty but no one was even pretending to begin. There were the usual difficulties in a new theatre: lost keys, dried-out dimmers . . . but that was not what was delaying them. It was the news conveyed by the Rhinemaiden at breakfast and repeated again and again as new members of the company turned up who had not yet heard it. Had anyone else informed them that their under wardrobe mistress was the Princess of Pfaffenstein, they might have been sceptical, but the Rhinemaiden's Nordic truthfulness was notorious.

'Well, that's that,' thought Boris. No more laughs in the wig room, no more milk for The Mother. Only Tessa had been able to wheedle a regular supply of milk out of the dairyman. I shall die young without yoghurt, thought the wig-master, giving in to trans-Danubian despair, and what does it matter?

'I must have a replacement,' said Frau Pollack. 'It is quite impossible for me to do all that work alone.' Boris shot her a look of loathing – who on earth could replace Tessa? He could see her now, sitting on an upturned crate, that pretty fawn hair of hers rippling to the ground, saying resolutely, 'Cut, Boris. Go on, just do it. *Cut.*'

Klasky, pencilling Hungarian insults into the wood-wind scores, was scowling. When the revolution came Tessa would be rounded up with the rest of the aristo-crats who had ground the faces of the poor and would be almost certainly imprisoned, but he found that the thought gave him amazingly little satisfaction.

'I lent her a dress,' thought the Littlest Heidi deliri-ously, leaning in the fourth position against a pillar. 'She was my *friend*.' Heidi's grandmother had gone into black on the day that the Crown Prince Rudolf shot himself and had remained thus ever since, and Heidi was a passionate royalist.

'Who will bring my footstool now?' thought Pino morosely. The little tenor was a head shorter than Raisa and Tessa's tactful way of inserting a footstool behind the tombstone, rock or sofa on which he found himself had earned his deepest gratitude.

But it was Jacob who was most badly hit. Of course he could turn the whole thing to the company's advantage. If he talked to the press, told them who Tessa was and released some poignant photographs of her performing some menial task, it would undoubtedly be excellent publicity and for a while improve their bookings. But only for a while. Against that, he had lost Tessa. No more glimpses of the small figure in her paint-stained smock grinning up at him as she trotted through the corridors; no one to catch his thoughts almost before he had thought them.

'All right, everybody, that's enough,' he shouted now. 'We'll do a straight run-through of Act One. The Three Ladies on stage, please, and you, Pino – everyone else off and remember—'

He broke off, aware that nobody was listening. A hush had fallen and all eyes were on the auditorium.

Coming up the centre aisle, dressed exactly as usual and carrying in one hand a can of milk, in the other a straw-lined basket filled with brown eggs, came their under wardrobe mistress.

'Good morning, Herr Witzler.' Tessa's eyes were anxious, for she was late. It had taken far longer than she had expected to explain her work in Vienna to the aunts. Not that she had lied to them exactly . . . not *exactly*.

'Good morning, Your Highness.'

Tessa reached the pit, vanished beneath the footlights

and reappeared beside the Herr Direktor on the stage. Raisa had lowered her vast bulk into a curtsy, the Littlest Heidi had sunk completely to the ground.

Tessa looked critically round the set. 'The cleat for that batten is above the dimmer-board. Shall I fix it? And then shall I unpack the Papageno costumes, because the feathers will need curling again and—'

Jacob had cleared his throat. 'Your Highness, it is absolutely out of the question that you continue to work for us. Absolutely out of the question – you must see that.'

Tessa had turned very pale. 'No,' she said quietly, 'I don't see it.'

'Please.' Jacob passed a plump hand over what had once been his hair. 'The embarrassment . . . Your father was equerry to the Emperor.' Only a man who had begged his way systematically through the ranks of the nobility, year after year, as Witzler had done, could gauge the extent of the lese majesty. 'It would be impossible for the men to continue to give you orders.'

'Not to mention the bad language,' put in the Rhinemaiden.

Tessa looked round at the stage-hands, old friends now looking at her with the cowed respect she had so often encountered in the past. Not seeing her, seeing some shape, some label to be revered or hated according to their creed.

Swallowing down the lump in her throat, she said, 'Herr Witzler, I have lost my home. I have nothing left except my work. Must I lose that also?'

Jacob shrugged wearily and flinched as his ulcer expressed its views on what was going on.

'It is impossible, Your Highness. There are three hundred years of privilege which cannot be wiped out. The position of your family . . . your rank. I'm sorry, your work is excellent,' said Jacob, 'but you cannot remain with us.'

'I see.'

Tessa put down her can of milk, her basket of eggs. Instinctively she had moved upstage and now, turning, commanded them all. When she spoke it was quietly, but the children of Schönbrunn had been taught not only to walk down a staircase, but also to be heard at whatever distance and in whatever place they chose.

'You make me ashamed,' she said, and the quiet voice cut like a whip. 'Deeply and bitterly ashamed. All of you.'

They stared at her. Klasky put down his score. A stage-hand stepped backwards as though to escape the anger in her face. Was this the little waif, the ever-willing girl who would do anything for anyone?

They were not to blame for their amazement. No one here had seen the Emperor of Germany hopping round the courtyard, nursing his bitten leg after he had shot the last auroch left in the forests of Pfaffenstein. No one had watched the procession of stretchers carried up from the straw barns of the outlying farms, bringing the wounded men to be nursed inside the castle, at the command of the thirteen-year-old princess.

'I believed what you said,' Tessa's low implacable

voice went on. 'I believed what Herr Witzler said about music making everybody equal. I believed Herr Klasky when he rehearsed the prisoners' chorus in *Fidelio* . . . when he made them sing that chorus for four hours because what Beethoven said in it about freedom and brotherhood was sacred. I actually believed him. And now . . . in this production. In *The Magic Flute*.' She looked at Witzler, then at the old bass who sang the High Priest, Sarastro, who was staring at her with an open mouth. 'Only two days ago, when Herr Berger gave up his lunch and his tea to make that recitative perfect; that part where he says that Tamino is more than a prince because he is a *man* . . . Dear God, when you said that that was the keynote of the opera, I *believed* you.'

No one spoke. A door opened at the back of the hall as Farne slipped in to greet the company. No one heard him, no head turned. There was nobody in the theatre except that slight, pale, implacable figure accusing them.

'I believed it. I believed it all,' said Tessa. 'That you served music, all of you, because it was above pettiness and rank. Because it makes everybody one: rich and poor, sick and well. Because it comes to us from God. *I* believed it – but not you. Not one of you.'

She paused and momentarily passed a hand across her eyes.

'The Princess Lichnovsky knelt to Beethoven; she knelt to beg him to give back the score of *Fidelio* which the Viennese had sneered at. She knelt, and she was right to kneel. Well, I won't kneel for my right to work. I won't kneel because I don't kneel to hypocrites and time-servers and *snobs*!'

Silence. Total, unbroken silence as Tessa bent to pick up her basket, her can of milk. Then, suddenly, it began. The stage-hands started it, clapping first; then stamping and shouting as if the theatre was packed to the roof, and the orchestra banging on their music stands and Boris, dabbing his eyes with the end of his muffler and leading the yells of 'Bravo!' and 'Bis!'

It was left to Raisa to bring some sense into the proceedings. Ovations were all very well but they belonged, in general, to her.

''er 'ighness is being perfectly correct,' she stated. 'In art all is being of equalness.' She pushed aside the people now crowding round Tessa and said firmly, 'In zis bodice 'ighness, I cannot zink. I cannot zink even an 'igh C, and an 'igh F you can forget absolutely it.'

Tessa finished blowing her nose on Jacob's handkerchief and turned a radiant countenance on the soprano. 'Yes, Frau Romola. I quite understand, Frau Romola. If you will give me the bodice now, I can have it ready for this evening. It only needs a gusset . . .'

9

The forest that stretched away on the spur behind the castle might have been invented by the Brothers Grimm. Pines and ferns, larches, moss, little rills of crystal water, shafts of sunlight on silvered cones, the tang of resin . . .

And in a clearing the feathers of pigeons drifting to the ground and the scent of gunpowder, as Guy provided for his guests such limited sport as the month of June offered. In felden green with silver buttons, in lederhosen or field uniforms, all those of his guests who could walk and had not preferred fishing or billiards were in the forest cheerfully pursuing birds whose lowly status did not prevent them from being amazingly difficult to hit.

Guy, sharing a hide with Prince Maximilian and despatching with accuracy but relatively little enthusiasm such pigeons as fell to his lot, found himself an unwilling recipient for Maxi's low-voiced confidences.

'Jolly good party, this,' said Maxi. 'Everyone says

what a good party this is. Everything laid on as it should be.'

Temporarily exhausted by so much conversation, he aimed and brought down his bird. That he should have left the dogs behind merely because they were unnecessary for this type of sport was not to be expected. Now he sent off the pointer, directed the labrador to a runner in the bushes, whistled the water spaniel out of the stream and spoke a manly word of sympathy to the wolfhound rendered gloomy by the lack of serious booty.

'I'm glad you're enjoying it.'

In the distance the Countess Waaltraut, who had been steering her mother's Bath chair between the larches in relentless pursuit of Guy, was brought to a halt by the silver ribbon of a stream and stood, melancholy and baulked, staring at the trees which hid him from her sight.

'Pity Putzerl couldn't come. Tessa, I mean.'

'Does she care for shooting?'

'No, she doesn't,' said Maxi, frowning down at his half-grown setter bitch. 'She's a jolly good shot, though. Her father taught her. I taught her too, at Spittau. Had her out in a punt when she was six. You wouldn't believe it,' said Maxi earnestly, 'but she can imitate a mallard like no one I've ever met. Got a perfect ear. You don't need a call duck in the boat if you've got Putzerl. It's uncanny. It's all that music she goes in for, I suppose.'

He sighed. His mother would not be at all pleased

about this business with the opera company. 'And the dogs,' he continued, taking the bird out of the pointer's mouth and looking with surprise at the dead squirrel brought in by the labrador. 'You wouldn't think it, because she's so little and quiet, but they'd do anything for her.'

'Really?'

Guy's cool and slightly contemptuous tone was lost on Maxi who patted the pointer, commended the labrador, told the spaniel to stay . . . and aimed once more and hit once more, sending the whole cavalcade in motion once again. 'They're trained for the water, of course,' he commented. Then continued, 'It's all this art and music I worry about. She'll grow out of it, I suppose?'

'Do you want her to?'

'Well . . . when we're married . . . Spittau isn't . . . Of course, she could play the piano. It's a bit warped but I expect it could be put right. Spittau,' he explained, 'is very low-lying.'

Guy did not answer. 'When we are married', the prince had said. Everyone was right, then, to take the engagement for granted. Well, it was none of his business. He too aimed; he, too, fired and hit – and in the lull that followed, turned to attend to the sprightly, skeletal Prince Monteforelli, fresh from his morning's injection of monkey gland, and to parry with courtesy and skill the old courtier's questions about Guy's business with the Chancellery.

By the time Guy's guests met at luncheon, a meal

served informally at small tables in the yellow salon, there was no doubt that the house party was a resounding success. The buzz of talk, the laughter, the popping of champagne corks bespoke a total satisfaction with the hospitality of the Englishman. The members of the shooting party did not find themselves impeded, by the consumption of their English breakfast, from partaking of the staggering quantities of food fetched for them from the sideboard. The guests who had been fishing commented on the excellence of the catch, those who had played billiards on the beautifully renovated tables.

The presence of an entire opera company was also noted with approval. This was a return to the great days of patronage to which they themselves had once been accustomed. A glimpse from his bedroom window of the Middle Heidi doing her pliés had affected the Uhlan captain with the wooden leg so powerfully that he had choked on his Odol mouthwash, and the Archduke Sava, sitting beside Monteforelli, was in a state of glazed fulfilment. On the way to visiting his bear in the stables, he had crossed the Fountain Courtyard and found Raisa Romola splayed on a rush mat, sunbathing. A music lover and a bosom man, finding his two passions thus united in a single body had proved almost too much for the Archduke who, with gestures, was trying to convey to the old prince just what the sight had meant to him.

Only on the table containing the aunts, the Swan Princess and the Archduchess Frederica, was there a slightly less abandoned and roistering air. Not that the

Archduchess was off her food: on the contrary, she was systematically concealing in a bag specially brought down for the purpose, all the more durable delicacies which the servants piled on her plate. But the revelation of Putzerl's activities in Vienna had naturally come as something of a shock, and Tante Augustine and Tante Tilda could not help feeling that their niece, dearly as they loved her, had been a little bit inaccurate in her description of her work, for 'studying music' did not seem adequately to describe the moving of furniture, combing of wigs and stitching of hems.

'If only we could see her settled,' said the Duchess. 'Of course she will always have a home with us but . . .'

'Don't worry,' said the Swan Princess grimly, beckoning the flunkey to demand another slice of ham. 'Maxi knows his duty. We shall have an announcement any minute now.'

Nerine, sitting between Guy and her brother Arthur, looked round with utter satisfaction. Twenty-four hours had completely changed her view of Guy. For Mama had been mistaken about him: low-born or not, he seemed to have an extraordinary power of attracting people – and not only young Tremayne and the rest of his staff who obviously worshipped him. One could say that Guy had simply bought the company of these aristocrats, but she could see in none of his guests the slightest sign of contempt despite the fact that he made no secret of his origins. In fact, some of the women were already being extremely silly: that oil-stained dowd and the fat Italian marchesa who had fluttered her eyelashes at him at the ball. As for the young Princess of Pfaffenstein, Nerine intended to make sure that she never set foot in the castle after the house party was over, which meant that her aunts, too, would have to go. True, Guy in explaining their past encounter had spoken of her with obvious dislike, but Nerine had seen Tessa's face when she had first caught sight of him – and there was going to be no more of *that*!

Yes, Guy must marry her here and marry her soon, thought Nerine. Later, of course, they would return to England: 'abroad' was never quite the same, but as a setting for a wedding, Pfaffenstein was unbeatable. She would need a few months to get an adequate trousseau together, but then . . . And turning to her brother Arthur, she found that he was able to inform her of the exact cost of the fireworks purchased for the night's display.

The aunts had offered to accompany Guy on a tour of the picture gallery, suggesting that he and his fiancée might care to know a little of the history and background of the family. After luncheon, therefore, they set off – together with David Tremayne who was now almost as familiar with the castle as the ladies themselves – for the long, panelled room which adjoined the great hall and connected it, on the eastern side, with the ante-room to the theatre.

'We're sorry our great-niece has so little time,' said the Duchess as the sound of violins, followed by Hungarian expletives, floated towards them.

'We would have liked her to show you everything, but she is so occupied with her work,' said the Margravine who was carrying the pug, informally wrapped for daytime in a quatrocento dressing-gown.

Nerine, who was delighted that the princess intended to spend her days out of sight grubbing about in a dirty theatre, replied suitably and they entered the gallery.

Row upon row of Pfaffensteins confronted them. Men in every possible uniform stretching back through time: men in the sombre black of the House of Spain with their lace ruffs and intricate daggers, men in the service of the Austrian court sporting their medals and sashes . . . There were Pfaffensteins astride rearing horses, Pfaffensteins with their wives or more often, with their dogs . . . Pfaffensteins in the scarlet of cardinals, in armour, in opera cloaks, in tails . . .

A supercilious lot of devils, thought Guy, noting again and again among the men in slashed hose and doublet, the women in hooped skirts or riding habits, the fawn, almost amber hair of Witzler's under wardrobe mistress, her auburn eyes.

Nerine, never bored when there were clothes to be studied, was walking gravely along the rows. There were one or two useful ideas here. That muslin cape over the brocaded sleeve was very effective: gossamer lightness against the firmness. She liked the way that chain of gold beads was looped over the low bodice . . . and that coif-like head-dress – if she had that copied and sewn with sequins for evening it would suggest a very special sort of innocence. And at every third or

162

fourth picture she paused, carefully studying her own reflection in the glass. Yes, she had been right to wear only a cool, white blouse open at the throat, a simple navy pleated skirt, so that the eye sated by the splendour of the pictures would return to her own fresh simplicity.

'We could never get her to sit still,' said the Duchess to David Tremayne, who had paused at a simple pencil sketch of a child with tumbled hair. Her voice, as always when she spoke of her great-niece, had softened and grown warm. 'But there's a painting of her by Scharnach in my bedroom if you'd care to see it.'

'In her confirmation dress,' put in the Margravine.

Guy, who had passed the drawing of the young princess with studied indifference, was examining something which interested him more than the actual portraits. The same motif in many of the carved and gilded picture frames, on the shields and flags held aloft by the sitters, and again worked into the mosaic of the gallery's lovely birchwood and maple floor: a lily, stylized and graceful, a surprisingly peaceful emblem for these warlike princes.

'I was wondering about this flower,' he said, tracing the pattern on the floor with the tip of his shoe. 'It seems to turn up everywhere. Even on the battlements of the Old Fort over the drawbridge.'

The aunts exchanged glances.

'There is a legend . . .' began the Margravine, and looked at her august sister-in-law for permission to continue. 'From the time of the Third Crusade. Count

Johannes was ruler here then and he had a wife, the Lady Isabella, who was very, very beautiful. He loved her very much and she loved him. They loved each other greatly.' She looked a little anxiously at her audience, wondering if she had gone too far, for they were English and known to be cold.

'Then in the year 1311 the call came from the true Church to go on a crusade against the Infidel,' said the Margravine, 'and Count Johannes rode away to war.'

'The Lady Isabella was quite distraught, but he promised to return and bring her all the spoils of battle. "It is in your name that I go to recapture Jerusalem," he said to her.' The Margravine had unwrapped the pug and lowered him to the ground in order to do justice, with fervent gestures, to the story.

'He fought very bravely,' the Margravine continued. 'Heroically. But at the Siege of Acre he was hit by an arrow and mortally wounded.'

'And as he lay there with the blood draining from his body he saw, growing quite close to him, a single flower. A lily. The Lily of Paradise.'

'Lilium auriculum,' put in the Duchess, always happy when returning to fact. 'White, very fragrant, on a leafless stem.'

'Count Johannes managed to drag himself towards it and pick it, then he turned to his squire and said, "Take this flower to my lady and tell her that I died with her name on my lips." The Margravine paused, quite overcome with the drama of it all. 'So the squire took the flower and spurred his horse and galloped to Smyrna.

164

For days and days he rode in the hot sun but the flower didn't droop or wither. *Not at all*. And in Smyrna he took a galley to Venice and the journey lasted for weeks and all the time – *all that long time* – the lily stayed as fresh as when it had been picked.'

'That is the legend,' put in the Duchess.

The Margravine's soft blue eyes rested reproachfully on her sister-in-law. 'Even when he took horse from Venice to Vienna,' she continued, 'even then the flower stayed fresh and fragrant. And then at last he reached the castle. He expected a welcome and food and warmth but the castle was silent and shrouded. Everyone inside it was grieving. The Lady Isabella had fallen ill, you see – gravely ill – on exactly the same day as her husband was wounded, though she knew nothing about it, of course.'

'They were *sternengeschwister*, you see,' explained the Duchess.

The ladies' German had been getting too rapid for David and Nerine.

'Star siblings?' David translated, puzzled.

The Duchess nodded. 'Don't you have that in English? People who are born under the same sign. He was her Star Brother, she was his Star Sister. They were heavenly twins. Gemini. Even in England you must have that?'

'Yes,' said David as Guy turned away, frowning, 'we do.'

'Anyway, the squire ran to the Lady Isabella's bedchamber where she was lying, just holding on to life.

Waiting . . . waiting . . . for what she did not know. And he knelt down and handed her the flower and said, "Your husband sends you this and asked me to tell you that he died speaking your name." And she took it and smiled because she understood what she had been waiting for, and then she died.'

'And it was only then—'

'Only after she died—'

'That the lily wilted.'

They waited for the effect of the story, nodding in a satisfied way at each other, and were rewarded by smiles from David and Nerine.

'Since then the husband and wife at Pfaffenstein have often been astrological twins. The first Prince, who married a cousin of Louis the Fourteenth and was faithful to her for fifty years, and the fifth Prince who—'

'No, Tilda, that's rubbish. Tessa is a Gemini and Maxi is a Pisces and they are excellently suited in every way.'

'Yes, yes, of course. I didn't mean—'

'Goodness, how romantic!' The story had appealed greatly to Nerine. 'I'm an Aquarian. What about you, Guy?' She looked at him, smiling, a delicious dimple in her cheek.

But Guy had turned away. 'Why ask me?' he said gruffly. 'You know I don't know when I was born. Or where.'

'Well, but roughly.'

'Nerine, please don't bother me with that kind of

rubbish. If there's one thing I hold in utter contempt, it's astrology.'

She drew in her breath. Guy had never spoken to her like that, never! 'Well, really,' she began.

But the pug had begun to bark and wag his tail and Guy, who happened to be looking at David, saw the young man's face light up in a way which gave him considerable disquiet.

'Putzerl!' The Margravine's face was illumined. 'We were just telling Herr Farne and Frau Hurlingham the story of the Pfaffenstein Lily.'

Tessa, still in her working smock, had taken a short cut to the kitchens and was carrying a pile of velvet cloaks for steaming. How can she go round looking like that, thought Nerine. How *can* she?

'Yes, it's a nice story,' said Tessa. 'They're both in the crypt of the church here in effigy. Very formal, you know, and kneeling in prayer, but so close their noses are practically touching. Although . . .'

Her voice died away.

'Although?' prompted David.

Tessa shrugged. 'It's just that he rode away, you know, with her favour on his saddle and her name on his lips. "In your name I will conquer Jerusalem," he said. But did he ask her if she wanted Jerusalem, or the heads of the infidels or the spoils of war? I imagine her always leaning out of the window with her long plaits hanging against the stone and wanting none of the things he was getting for her. Fame, glory, the jewels of

Saladin. Wanting only that he should stay and be with her. How could she want anything but that?'

'But surely men have always got things for women. I mean, it's chivalry, isn't it?' said Nerine.

'Yes.' Tessa shook herself free of her thoughts. 'It's chivalry, certainly.' She smiled at Nerine over her pile of velvets. 'I will see that you have it. That you get it on your wedding day.'

'Have what?'

'The Lily. The Lily of Pfaffenstein.' She appealed to the aunts. 'Didn't you tell her?'

'We were just going to. You see, after the Lady Isabella died they made a copy of the Lily of Paradise in silver. And the tradition is that it is handed to every bride who comes to Pfaffenstein on the morning of her wedding.'

'Oh!' Nerine's eyes widened with pleasure. 'Where is it, then?'

'It's in the bank in Vienna,' said Tessa. 'I took it when I left. It's the only thing I took from Pfaffenstein.'

'But how will you get it here?' said Nerine. 'You obviously won't,' she added firmly, 'want to come yourself.'

David looked sharply at his employer. Surely he intended to ask the princess, and the aunts who had been so helpful, to his wedding? But Farne was silent and forbidding, in his most 'Mr Rochester' mood.

'I'll see that you get it,' said Tessa quietly. 'I'll find someone to bring it to you. Someone suitable.' She looked up suddenly, her face glowing with an idea which pleased her, and addressed Guy for the first time. 'Your foster-mother!' she said. 'Martha Hodge! She'll be coming for the wedding, won't she? And travelling through Vienna? I'll give it to her! She sounds exactly right as a bearer of lilies.' She moved to the door and as David hurried to open it for her, she turned and said, 'We are making a lovely opera for you. A truly *lovely* opera!' And thanking David, was gone.

'What is all this about an opera, dearest?' enquired Nerine an hour later as she walked beside Guy along the path that climbed upward from the postern gate, through flower-studded meadows towards the woods. 'What did she mean? What exactly is happening in the theatre?' She had delayed Guy only long enough to place a navy tam o'shanter aslant on her curls and was in a most relaxed and gracious mood.

Guy turned to her eagerly, his eyes at their bluest. 'I wanted it to be a surprise but that's absurd, needless to say. You'll have heard them rehearsing already. It's *The Magic Flute*, of course – what else could it be?'

She waited, holding her smile as she had learned to do before the mirror. It was important to get this right.

'I couldn't resist hearing it once again with you. Only having you really beside me, not separated by a wretched wall.'

Of course. They had met at the opera, she had remembered that. So it must have been *The Magic Flute*. But the whole scene was not quite clear to her yet and since it obviously meant so much to Guy she prompted gently:

'What was I—'

But Guy, fortunately, was already telling her. Describing his first sight of her with her dark ringlets dancing on her shoulders, the white dress with little blue flowers, the way she had smiled at him over her fan – and now she could remember it all. The box at the Imperial Opera, the French girl who had bet her that she couldn't get the Hungarian count in the next box to come over in the interval . . . So she had smiled and he had come, but with Guy, and the relief of finding that Guy spoke English . . . And really, how well it had all worked out!

'. . . and the way Selma Kurz made her voice sound so totally disembodied – I've never heard such unselfish singing!'

Nerine, nodding absently, was suddenly filled with excitement. She had had a most wonderful idea! This opera was obviously meant as a climax to the house party. Arthur had worked out the sums involved in hiring a whole opera company and they were quite simply staggering. So she would reward Guy by reproducing, exactly, the effect she had made on that first night! There was no problem with her hair – she could still carry off ringlets in the Greek style – and she happened to have a dress with tiny blue flowers; that kind of fashion never dated. Not forget-me-nots, it was true, but fleurs de lys – still, that would do. The gold ribbons were no problem, nor the sandals, and she could manage the tiny posy of blue and white fresh flowers she had tucked behind her ear. But the fan . . . was there time to send to Vienna for a white, pearl-encrusted fan? And what about jewellery? She had worn none then owing to the stuffiness of Frau von Edelnau, but would the effect be too understated without any? After all, every eye would be upon her.

But Guy had stopped talking about music and it was necessary once more to listen.

'How much time shall you want to spend here, do you suppose?' They had entered the forest and he was looking round critically, aware of how much essential work was concealed beneath the romantically lichen-silvered trees. 'I'm tied to Austria for a while on this business for the League, but after that we could travel.'

'Travel? Where?'

'Oh, anywhere! The Amazon. The Gobi desert. Peru. The world is yours, my love.'

She laughed, aware that Guy was joking. 'I'd like to go to Paris in the spring, of course, for the collections. And be in London for the Season. But I think we could do much of our entertaining here and of course it's the perfect place to be married. I thought the end of October for the wedding – would that do?'

'Perfectly.'

'I shall write to my relations tomorrow.' She paused. 'What about your old nurse, Mrs Hodge? She won't really want to travel abroad, will she?'

'She's not my nurse, Nerine. She's my foster-mother, she brought me up. I shall certainly ask her to come. I think perhaps she will, even though she's never been abroad before. She always swore she'd see me married.'

Nerine repressed a sigh. It was going to be awkward, but no doubt she would find a way round it.

They had reached a small, still pool beneath the larches and Nerine paused, now, to study her reflection in the still water. A wave of her scent, cool and fresh, a movement of her head, sent Guy back in memory to that day in the Vienna Woods and suddenly, more than anything, he wanted to kiss her. He put his hands on her shoulders and turned her towards him, only to be halted by an anguished and piteous cry.

'Oh, no, *no*! Oh, Guy, look!'

He stared at her desperate face. Tears had actually sprung into those enchanting eyes, and her lips trembled.

'What is it? For heaven's sake, Nerine, what's happened?'

'There! Look! Can't you see?' She was staring, horrified, at something inside the lapel of her blouse.

Guy looked. Low down on Nerine's throat, just where the swell of her breasts began, the white skin was disfigured by a pink and rapidly swelling blob.

Relief making his voice light, almost teasing, Guy said, 'It's only a mosquito bite, my dear, and nothing at all to worry about in this climate. In the tropics it would be different, but there's been no malaria round here for ages.'

'*Nothing to worry about!*' Nerine was watching with utter hopelessness the mottled disfiguration still spreading in hideously irregular patches across her skin. Did no one understand the cost of beauty? The yellow satin she had planned to wear that evening was extremely décolletée. And her surprise – her lovely surprise for the opera would be completely ruined! It would be days before the bite was invisible: days and days and days . . .

Piteously, she laid a hand on his arm and in a voice she just managed to keep from breaking, said, 'Take me back, Guy. Just take me back.'

'Well?' said the Swan Princess. 'Have you spoken? Have you settled it between you? Or do you mean to let her spend the rest of her life grubbing about backstage like a kitchenmaid?'

Maxi looked in a hurt manner at his mother. Assembled in the round room of the West Tower with the Duchess and the Margravine, an hour before dinner, she seemed to be part of a phalanx of 'Older Womanhood' and the kind of thing he found most difficult to bear.

'I tried to get her to come for a walk this morning but she said she had to work,' said Maxi, on whom the memory of this statement still had its effect. 'And she's been cooped up in the theatre ever since.'

He frowned and his frown was repeated on the faces of the ladies.

'We would be so happy to feel that everything was understood between you,' said the Duchess. 'As you know, it was her parents' dearest wish.'

She sighed. Herr Farne had reiterated his invitation to them to stay in the West Tower, making it clear that once the house party was over there would hardly be a shortage of space. But Mrs Hurlingham, though politeness itself, had not seconded her fiancée's words. The eyes of the beautiful widow had been cool and appraising as they rested on Tilda and herself and it seemed likely that their days at Pfaffenstein were numbered. Somehow they would always contrive to make a home for Putzerl, but to see her married and suitably established before they died was the one desire now left to them.

'I hope you are not going to be feeble, Maxi,' said the Swan Princess. 'If there is one thing a high-spirited girl cannot stand, it is feebleness.'

'No, Mother. I mean, yes, Mother. I won't be feeble,' said Maxi. 'I thought I'd ask her tonight during the firework display. Of course, I won't have the dogs . . .' He paused, pondering his strategy.

'Ah, yes, that will be so romantic!' said the Margravine approvingly. 'By the lake . . . with the orchestra playing.'

'You'd better see if you can get her away from the theatre now, dear,' said the Duchess. 'It's time she came in and changed for dinner.'

'And for heaven's sake, Maxi, go and comb your hair. And your moustache. You look like a spaniel,' said the Swan Princess.

'Yes, Mother. I mean, no, Mother,' said Maxi, and went.

But when he entered the theatre there was no sign of Tessa. There seemed, rather, to be pandemonium everywhere. On stage, a bald little man was rushing about shouting at people; coloured lights flashed on and off and the sound of oaths came from above.

Deeply shocked by the environment in which his beloved spent her days, the prince asked for Her Highness and was directed down some iron stairs by the laconic thumb of a carpenter. Tessa, when he ran her to ground, was in a kind of cubby-hole, kneeling with her mouth full of pins, while on a low table stood a figure in a pleated, golden dress.

Jacob had not dared to put a ballet in *The Magic Flute*. What was fair game for Puccini and Donizetti was out of the question for a man who ranked only a millimetre below God himself. This did not mean, however, that he had left behind the Heidis. They were to appear in beguiling animal skins as the wild beasts who cavorted to the sound of Tamino's magic flute. But Jacob, studying the libretto, had also been reminded that the temple of the high priest, Sarastro, was dedicated to Wisdom, Industry and Art. It was therefore as statues representing these three virtues that the Heidis were to appear in Act One.

Having had this brainwave Jacob, in pursuit of musical perfection, had largely forgotten it and it was left to Tessa, at the eleventh hour, to complete their costumes. Fitting the two elder Heidis had been no trouble but Heidi Schlumberger was proving difficult. The discovery of Tessa's identity had thrown the Littlest Heidi into a stupor of servility. She could not bear Tessa to do anything for her and now, supposedly standing still to be

pinned, was wringing her hands in an excess of outraged serfdom.

'But Your Highness shouldn't be doing this. Your
Highness should let me—'

'Heidi, please will you shut up and stand still!' said
Tessa. 'How can I get the hem straight if you keep bob-
bing about?' She turned, feeling the draught of the open
door. 'Good heavens, Maxi, what on earth are you
doing here?'

'I came to fetch you. The aunts say it's time to
change for dinner.'

He surveyed his beloved, who looked as though a
good deal of changing would be necessary before she
could take her place between Monteforelli and the
Archduke Sava in the state dining-room.

'I can't come until I've finished this, Maxi. I'm not
even sure that we're stopping for dinner at all.' She had
lost the morning's pallor, for the excitement of work as
they prepared for this most crucial of performances was
like ambrosia. 'Oh, I'm sorry, how rude! Maxi, this is
Heidi Schlumberger, one of our dancers. Heidi, this is
my friend, Prince Maximilian of Spittau.'

Maxi, taking his eyes off Tessa for the first time,
looked up. Looked, stared . . . and flushed a dusky red
as emotion took him by the throat.

The girl he was looking at, standing with bare arms
in a gold bodice and sculptured, golden skirt, was not
merely pretty; she was enchantment itself. Blonde curls,
as fat and shiny as butter, tumbled on to her shoulders;
her eyes were huge and blue and long-lashed; her cheeks

were dimpled, her mouth a rosebud. Not only that but her look, demure yet coy, the slight parting of the lips, called to his mind the woman who embodied for him everything that was most desirable in the female sex: Mary Pickford stood before him, in the flesh.

'Enchanted, Fräulein,' he said, and bowed.

The Littlest Heidi, equally rapt, returned his regard. That long and handsome face, the duelling scar, the luxuriant moustache! So manly, and a prince!

'I am honoured, Your Highness,' she said. And gracefully, delightfully, still on her pedestal, sank into a curtsy.

10

The firework display was going splendidly. A dozen barrels of wine sent down by Guy at the beginning of the evening had secured the enthusiastic cooperation of the villagers, now assembled on a strip of beach below the road. From the three islands in the middle of the lake, there erupted a succession of rockets, Roman candles and exotic set-pieces which trailed a blazing path across the sky, dimming the stars themselves. Chinese lanterns were strung between the trees, braziers with roasting chestnuts glowed on the shingle, and on a platform constructed near the bathing huts the orchestra played Handel.

'My dear, you must have spent a fortune,' said Nerine, standing with Guy and a group of guests, still in their evening clothes, beside the water's edge. Like most of the younger members of the house party, she had come down to the lakeside after dinner, leaving the older people to watch from the comfort of the terrace.

Guy shrugged. 'It is no good being stingy with

fireworks,' he said, watching with approval the coordi-nation between David, Morgan and the head forester, who were each in charge on a different island.

Tessa, standing at the other end of the beach close to the wooden jetty which ran out across the darkness of the water, was watching with parted lips, her republican principles not noticeably outraged by this wanton dis-play of extravagance. That she was looking extremely pretty was not her fault, for it had been her intention to miss dinner and slip down later, still in her working clothes. In this she had been foiled by her old nurse, who had never been interested in the question of whether Tessa was or was not grown-up, and had dragged her upstairs, immersed her in a bath, and released her in a long, full-skirted dress of cream taffeta, with satin pumps on her feet and a rose on a velvet ribbon around her throat.

'Putzerl,' said Maxi, who had been glued to her side all evening. 'Tessa . . .' The orchestra had come to the end of its piece and there was a lull in the pyrotechnics. Now was the moment. He took her arm. 'I've been absolutely longing to talk to you alone—'

'Hush! Listen, Maxi!' Tessa had turned away from him, her gaze on the row of trees fringing the shore. 'Don't you hear it?'

Maxi did. A strange, coughing noise, then a low growl . . . And then a dark shape shambling out of the trees . . . pausing . . . the great head swaying in confu-sion and fright.

'Oh, Lord, it's Mishka!' Tessa's voice was breathless

with concern. 'He must have broken down the door. And Uncle Sava's not here, he's taken Frau Romola for a drive! They were going to watch the fireworks from High Pfaffenstein.'

'The devil!' Maxi was well aware of the danger. The Archduke's bear had been found as a cub in a fair in Novgorod with a firecracker tied to his tail. Normally he was docile enough, but now . . .

A piece of frayed rope dangling from his collar, the bear slithered down on to the shingle and a group of children ran screaming in the direction of the bathing huts. For a moment he paused uncertainly, his eyes glowing red in the light of the braziers. But ahead of him was darkness and quiet, and now he lumbered on to the jetty and moved down to the end, sniffing the water.

Only the dark and the quietness were deceptive. The fireworks were starting up again and as a burst of rockets went up from the nearest island, he turned with a roar of terror and stood, growling and swaying, facing the shore.

'Oh, poor thing, he's so frightened!'

'There's nothing you can do, Tessa. Look, those men have gone for—'

But Tessa was no longer by his side. She had picked up her skirts, was running towards the jetty, had reached it and now slowed down, moving quietly along the planking, holding out her hand. 'It's all right, Mishka: don't be frightened. It's all right—'

The next moment her arms were seized from behind,

she was viciously jerked backwards and a furious voice said, 'Are you mad? Come back at once!'

Guy. Only it couldn't be Guy. She had just seen him standing on the far side of the beach. No one could have run as fast as that.

'Let me go!' Desperately she tried to wriggle free, bracing herself against him, kicking out with her satin slippers.

The attempt of this freshly bathed and bird-boned infant to get the better of him might have amused Guy at some other time, but it did not amuse him now. His hold tightened. 'You will move slowly round behind me and get back to the shore.' Keeping his eye steadily on the bear, taking care to make no further sudden movements, the anger that possessed him was concentrated wholly in his voice.

'No, I will *not*.' A strand of her hair had caught in the stud of his dress shirt. Savagely, she wrenched it free. 'He knows me, he won't hurt me! It's you he'll go for – you're a stranger.'

'A terrified animal knows no one.'

As if in echo to his words, there came a fresh shower of rockets from the lake and the bear, roaring in renewed terror, reared up on his hind legs.

For a moment, confronted by the animal's appalling height and his vicious canines, hearing the screams from the shore, Tessa went limp and Guy appeared to loosen his hold. At once she rallied and seeing her chance, began to move forward again.

This was a mistake. Guy had merely been adjusting

his grasp. Now he gripped her elbows as if in a vice, lifted her up into the air and threw her, without the slightest sign of effort, far out into the lake.

The shock of the icy water, the struggle to surface in her voluminous dress, gave Tessa a few moments of immunity. Then she kicked off her shoes, trod water and opened her eyes to see . . . Maxi wading with idiotic chivalry into the lake towards her . . . some men approaching with a muzzle and chains . . . and then – because in the end she *had* to look – the bear on all fours and Guy, holding the rope, leading it quietly back towards the shore.

At which point, the Princess of Pfaffenstein drew breath, gave vent to a volley of Serbo-Croatian oaths learned from her father's groom, swallowed a large quantity of water – and sank.

As might be expected, the incident was wholly to the liking of the villagers, few of whom went sober to their beds. In throwing their beloved princess fully clothed into the waters of the lake and calming (in English) a savage bear, Herr Farne had shown himself a fitting successor to the seventh prince who had decapitated a card-sharp in the Turkish bath at Vilna, and the fifth prince who had been inseparable from his camel.

That the Swan Princess, the following morning, should view the matter in the same light was not to be expected.

'You realize that there are only four days left?' she said, whacking at the wolfhound who was dribbling on her shoe. Though seated most pleasantly between a fig tree and a statue of Aphrodite and facing, from the terrace, one of the loveliest views in Austria, her expression as always was grim. 'It really is quite amazing, Maxi, how inept and ineffectual you can be.'

She was growing desperate. It was not just the money or Putzerl's lineage, it was the succession. She had been old when she had Maxi, and Maxi was the only son. There had to be babies, there *had* to be! It was unthinkable that the seed of Barbarossa should run into the ground. At the thought of the nursery block full of tumbling babies, the beady eye of the Swan Princess softened for a moment. Whether Maxi's mother did or did not have a single redeeming feature was a point which had been much argued among the nobility of the Holy Roman Empire. If she did, it was probably her genuine and deep-seated love of babies. Even those who looked like uncooked buns or emerged from lace shawls like hirsute marmosets peering through balls of oakum, could bring a smile to that testy and cantankerous old face.

'I went over this morning,' said Maxi, conscious of deep injustice, for Casanova himself could not have proposed to Putzerl as she emerged shivering and spitting like a kitten from the lake. 'As soon as I'd let out the dogs, but the theatre was shut with notices all over it saying 'Silence' and 'Keep Out' and what-have-you. Anyway, it wouldn't have been any good digging her out; she's absolutely besotted about this opera.'

The Swan Princess scowled. 'I don't know what

Tilda and Augustine are doing, letting her carry on like that. Associating with those people! Running errands.'

Maxi shrugged. 'I don't suppose they could stop her. You know what Putzerl's like. Say a sharp word to her or show her a bird that's fallen out of a nest and she just shrivels. But when she's decided to do something she thinks is right . . .'

'All the Pfaffensteins are pig-headed,' said the Swan Princess gloomily. 'It's the blood of Charlemagne.'

'I'll try again tonight,' promised Maxi. 'There's a lieder recital after dinner,' he added, a look of misery passing over his kind, long face. 'I'll go to that.' It was the ultimate sacrifice, but he would make it.

'Well, make sure you do, Maximilian. Just make sure you do,' said the Swan Princess, and she stabbed her cane at the fig tree, which unaccountably continued to be covered in fruit.

'Ah, the nature, how she is beautiful!' cried Raisa, crashing barefoot across a flower-studded alm behind the castle. Attired in a Central European sack massively embroidered in cross-stitch, her piggy eyes glowed with well-being and her vast, freckled arms, thrown out in Rumanian ecstacy, narrowly missed Pino Mastrini's butterfly-net as the little tenor, his thighs bulging like delicious Parma hams beneath his linen shorts, pursued a Camberwell Beauty.

Never had Witzler's troupe been so happy, so cared-for and so well-fed, as in these last few days at Pfaffenstein. The beauty of the castle, the sunshine, the endless supply of delicious food brought forth a steady chorus of praise. Some of the lower-paid members of the company still experienced, in Vienna, real poverty and hardship. Now there was a surfeit and release. With The Mother growing sleek and fat on a window-sill in the dairy, Boris, his longevity assured, was taking yodelling lessons from one of the grooms. Bubi, who now slept in the room next to Tessa with her old nurse, paid monseigneurial visits to his parents and could be seen, his blond curls just clearing the feathered grass-heads, being taught the names of the flowers by the country-bred Rhinemaiden. And on the battlements, lean-ing against the railings on which thirty of his country-men had been impaled, Klasky composed his opera.

It was as well that the company was in such a state of contentment because Jacob, in rehearsals, was really going a little mad. The discovery that Tessa was safe, her dramatic return, had seemed to Witzler yet another sign from heaven. There was nothing now to prevent this from being the performance of a lifetime. Again and again he hounded the principals back into the theatre to go over parts they believed note perfect; again and again he repeated scene changes, altered little bits of business; again and again he demanded another ounce, another effort.

'You want to eat?' he could be heard yelling at the unfortunate coloratura, the sheep-like hausfrau he had kidnapped from Dresden. 'Sleep? What do you want to *sleep* for?' he demanded, at two in the morning, of the venerable bass who sang Sarastro. And in a voice of outrage to a member of the chorus, 'The lavatory! In the middle of Isis and Osiris you want to go to the lavatory!'

But they were nearly there. All of them were artists to their finger-tips – the money-grubbing Raisa, ridiculous Pino with his eggs – and they knew it. That indefinable something was in the air, like electricity, like the beating of wings. Barring an unexpected disaster, it would come.

'I thought you would like to know, Your Highness,' said Maxi's valet, easing the skin-tight trousers of the Hussar uniform over his master's calves. 'Eight-thirty in the village hall.'

Maxi, standing passive in his corset, turned mournful eyes on his servant. 'Yes, you did quite right to tell me, Franz. All the same, it's a devilish business. I have to go to this concert.'

Melancholy gripped him by the throat. If there was one thing that really got him down it was a lieder recital. Those awful, pigeon-chested women in purple satin or green silk with trailing scarves and an idiotic, wispy handkerchief dribbling from their clasped hands. The way they closed their eyes and *felt* the music . . . the arch way they translated the stuff if it was in a foreign language. And then, just when one thought it was over, the torture of those interminable encores.

Well, he would endure it for Putzerl's sake. He would sit beside her until she was softened up and then they would slip away and let the dogs out for their evening

186

run and he would propose. But did God really have to arrange things so that on the very same evening, down in the village, they were showing *Broken Blossoms* with Lilian Gish?

He stretched out his arm for the frogged tunic whose buttons had kept Franz busy for the best part of the afternoon. 'You're going, I suppose?' he enquired of his valet. 'Yes, Your Highness.'

Maxi's brows drew together, indicating thought. There was a quotation that fitted here. Something Latin and classy which the gladiators had said when they were about to go in among the lions and wished to salute those who were going to have a nice time and stay alive. But he could not quite remember how it went, and anyway it was way above Franz's head. Arranging a strand of his perfectly pomaded hair to frame his duelling scar, Maxi went down to dinner.

Two hours later he sat in the picture gallery, keeping a vacant place beside him for Putzerl. Though the room was crowded, no one attempted to commandeer the chair, for the romance between the Prince of Spittau and the Princess of Pfaffenstein was most dear to everybody's heart.

'Ah, keeping a chair for Putzerl, are you?' said Monteforelli approvingly, hobbling past, and even the Archduchess Frederica deigned to smile at him.

But a hush had fallen and the concert was about to begin. Where on earth was Tessa? The Rumanian diva came in – dressed in purple satin as Maxi had foreseen – and behind her the Magyar, reasonably shaved for once. And then . . . good God, it was unbelievable! Tessa, carrying a pile of music and seating herself beside the Magyar at the piano. She was going to turn over for him! She was going to be there all evening, miles away, out of reach!

It was too much. There were sacrifices that one made and sacrifices that were just plain silly. The first notes of Strauss's 'Morgen' were just floating over the audience when Maxi reached the door and fled.

Fifteen minutes later, having run down the Narrenweg – which, with its thirteen wayside shrines, wound round the pinnacle of rock on the far side of the drawbridge – and hurried along the road which skirted the lake, Maxi entered the Pfaffenstein village hall.

The place was packed but the white screen at the far end was still mercifully blank. Old women he had known since childhood called greetings, the men saluted – but without servility, for this was a meeting of acolytes in which rank, for a while, was set aside.

Maxi walked down the aisle looking for an empty seat. Near the middle of the hall, he stopped. Could it be? It was! In a rose-pink dirndl with a snowy apron and blouse, sat Heidi Schlumberger.

'Will you permit me to sit with you, Fräulein?'

Heidi lifted a rapt countenance. The Prince was in his Hussar uniform, the whole image overwhelming.

'Oh, yes, Your Highness. Please.'

Maxi slipped into his seat.

'Have you seen it before?' she enquired shyly. 'Broken Blossoms, I mean?'

'Five times,' said Maxi, waving a careless hand.

Heidi nodded. It was right that a man of such magnificence should have beaten her. 'I've only seen it four times,' she said meekly. 'I've brought an extra handkerchief. That part where she looks up and sees the Angel of Death . . .'

'And where she puts her hand on her heart like this,' said the Prince, suiting the action to the words.

'Yes.' They fell silent, in tribute to the miracle that was Lilian Gish. Then, 'What about *Intolerance*, have you seen that, too?' asked Heidi.

'Seven times,' said Maxi proudly. 'At Spittau I made them show it every night.'

'Oh! You can do that?'

Maxi nodded. 'We had *Less Than The Dust* for two whole weeks,' he boasted.

'Ah, Mary Pickford!' The Littlest Heidi sighed. 'I've seen *Pollyanna* eight times. I went every afternoon in Vienna, sometimes twice.'

Should he tell her how much she resembled the famous heroine? No, not yet. 'And *The Little Princess*?' Maxi enquired.

'I like that even better, I think.'

'Yes, that's the very best of all.'

Maxi cleared his throat. 'You don't . . . by any chance . . . like cowboy films?'

'But I do! I absolutely adore Tom Mix. When he rises in his stirrups like this,' said the Littlest Heidi, lifting her entrancing bottom marginally from the seat, 'and then shades his eyes with his hand – so . . . And in *Child of the Prairie*, where that Indian crawls out from behind the rock and he doesn't even *look* but just whips out his gun!'

Maxi stared at her. A twin soul! It was incredible. But now the lights were going out. The lady at the piano began a stirring march. Not only *Broken Blossoms* but a Chaplin two-reeler first! He glanced down at Heidi's hand nestling like a plump, delicious fledgling in the folds of her apron. Could he? Dared he?

Diffidently, flutteringly, in the dusk of the hall, the small hand crept closer. With the questing tentative grace that distinguishes the born cocotte, it raised itself a soupçon. Maxi grasped it. Then the screen flashed to life. The little man in the baggy trousers came marching down the street – and in the village hall of Pfaffenstein they were no longer prince and ballet girl and peasant but only a rapt and adoring audience, welded by laughter into one whole.

Tessa rose very early on the following day. There was a visit she wished to pay before she left, and while the rest of the company still slept she was approaching a small wooden house in a clearing in the forest, a mile or so behind the castle.

She knocked and entered. The room was small but spotless: a stove with a bench round it, a limewood table, a spinning wheel – and in the carved bed in the corner an old lady, as old as time itself. Her filmed eyes seemed almost sightless but she knew her visitor at once.

'Your Highness!' The smile transformed the wrinkled face. 'You're back, then. It's true what they said.'

'Yes.' Tessa sat down on the bed, took the brown, transparent hand into her own. 'Yes, I'm back, Grossmutterle, and I've brought you some nice things to eat so don't turn into a wolf and eat me up.'

The toothless smile came first, then the whole body shook with laughter. Laughter which turned suddenly into a grimace of grief.

'You're going then, Your Highness? The castle is really sold?'

'Yes, but it is sold to such a nice man, Grossmutterle. You'll like him very much.'

'Foreign, they say?'

'Yes, but he speaks German like a native. He'll be a good master, you'll see.'

The bent shoulders rose in a faint shrug. 'Maybe. But without you . . . without Your Highness . . .' She was crying now, the easy, utterly justified tears of old age. 'Well, I'm glad to have seen you once again. Let me kiss your hand.'

But the old lady did not get a hand to kiss. Tessa's arm came round her, she was hugging her. 'Don't cry, Grossmutterle! Ah, please don't cry!' begged Tessa.

When she came out, her own eyes too were wet and she did not for a moment recognize the figure on horseback coming along the bridle path. When she did, she drew back, but it was too late. Guy had seen her and turned his horse aside.

'Good morning.'

She looked up at him, sitting easily but entirely without the sartorial trappings of horsemanship, astride the tall, black mare. It was the first time she had seen him since the incident of the bear and at the memory of the things she had called him – albeit in Serbo-Croat – a blush came to her cheek. Trying to conceal it, she said quickly, 'I didn't know you rode.'

The wrong remark again. His brows rose. 'Oh yes, even bastards ride sometimes. I found it a useful way of getting about when I was abroad. And you? Have you been paying visits?'

'Yes, I've been to see my father's old nurse.'

'To say goodbye?' He was close enough now to see the tear stains on her face and, dismounting, he began to walk beside her.

She nodded. 'There are a lot of people like that, Guy . . . people who've lived here all their lives.'

He looked up quickly. He had used her Christian name from the start, but this was the first time she had called him Guy.

Now she had begun to talk about Nerine, saying how glad she was that Nerine would be there to take over the visiting. 'It's the people who live in the isolated places: there's an old woodcutter in the next valley who is completely paralyzed – a most marvellous man, so *wise*. The factor knows them all, of course; she has only to ask him.' And as Guy was silent she flushed and said, 'I'm sorry, I don't mean to interfere.'

'You're not interfering.' They walked on for a

192

moment along the cone-strewn path. 'Will you come back?' he asked after a while.

'No.'

She left the word bleak and unadorned and Guy was silent, accepting her decision. If Nerine was to take her rightful place as mistress of Pfaffenstein, Tessa had to stay away. Guy had not failed to notice that wherever Tessa appeared, engaged in however menial a task for Witzler, she was greeted not only by the salutes and curtsies due to her rank, but by smiles which lingered long after she had gone. It was not only the inmates of the castle, it was the whole village, all her people, that the Princess of Pfaffenstein held in the hollow of her hand.

'Perhaps it's as well,' he said now. 'Because I mean to make considerable changes.'

She turned her head enquiringly. 'What sort of changes?'

'I can't stand toys,' said Guy. His face had the taut, absorbed look that David and Thisbe Purse knew all too well. 'This place must pay if we're to live here even for part of the year; it must *work*.'

'Yes,' she said eagerly. 'But how, the forests are not very productive and—'

He shook his head impatiently. 'No, no! Forestry and agriculture will help, of course, but that's not enough. But there's tungsten in the rock, did you know? In the Stielbach valley. I had the geological report yesterday and I've just been over to look. I intend to mine for it.' He waited for her protest, but apart from a quick intake of breath Tessa was silent. 'The main deposits are on the far side of the spur so you won't see it from the castle. But, yes, though I shall make tree-breaks and site the workings carefully, there will be a gash in the hill. Yes, I shall spoil the beauty of the countryside. I happen to think that it would be better for your people to have independent jobs instead of bowing and scraping to the owners of the castle, but I'd do it anyway because I can make it pay. So you see, it's a good job you won't be here.'

'Yes,' she said quietly. 'It's a good job I'll be out of the way. But not because of that. I think you're right: jobs must be made that are not to do with feudalism or the land. My father would never see it, but if I had known how to set about it, I would have done it too.'

They had reached a fork in the path. The wider track led back to the castle; the narrower, mossy and overgrown, plunged back into the woods. Tessa paused, hesitating, seeming to make up her mind.

'Have you got a few moments more?' she said shyly. 'There's a place I'd like to show you.'

Guy smiled. 'Yes, indeed. Nerine gets up late and frankly I can wait to be reunited with some of my guests.'

'We'll leave her here, then,' said Tessa, patting the mare, and they hitched the bridle to a tree and took the narrow path back into the heart of the woods. The forest was denser here; boulders covered with moss like green velvet seemed to swim in the darkness; sudden

194

shafts of light turned the bright toadstools into exotic jewels and from a great, jagged pine, a cuckoo called.

'You know what the Jesuits say,' said Tessa, 'that if you give them a child for the first seven years of its life, you can have it for the rest of the time because it will already be theirs?' And as Guy nodded, 'Well, I think it's like that with landscape. What you know and love when you're a small child is always the way a landscape should be. For me, it will be the woods if I live to be ninety. But my grandmother was always homesick for the sea. The proper sea, with tides and wind and rain. She didn't count the Mediterranean or the Baltic – no tides, no waves.'

'Who was she?'

'Her father was the Duke of Bewick. She lived near the Scottish border on the coast.'

'Yes, I know it.' A great, gaunt, wind-lashed pile, Bewick Castle, the lair of king-makers and Mercian rogues. He had visited it from school once, as a child. 'It's the same with me. My first outings with Martha were all to the Northumbrian coast and you can keep the mimosa and the lemon trees.'

'It's where one would go back to die, I suppose,' said Tessa.

The path had been growing ever narrower and more overgrown. Now they pushed through the last of the encroaching trees and with a sigh of satisfaction, Tessa stopped.

They had come out in a clearing of unsurpassed and Arcadian loveliness. The golden light of morning

195

streamed over the emerald grass and lit the clusters of gentians and starry white anemones. Dragonflies skimmed over a stream that danced over iridescent stones and paused to make a still, deep pool on which the leaves of water-lilies quietly swung. A single, ancient crab-apple trailed a golden tangle of honeysuckle through the candelabra of its branches.

But Tessa was looking for something, searching the ground. Kneeling, now, to part a clump of tiny trifoliate leaves, so exquisitely wrought that the peers of England have taken them for their coronets.

'Yes,' she said happily. 'It's a bit early but some are ripe.' And carefully, absorbed like a child, she picked the small, flecked barely scarlet berries and held them out to him. Wild strawberries – the most prized, most fragrant and heart-stirring fruit in the world.

'In Sweden,' she said, rising to stand beside him and speaking very seriously, 'they have a word for a place like this. It's called a "smultronställe". A "wild straw-berry place." A place like that is special, it's the most special place there is.'

Guy looked down at the berries she had tipped into his hand. Their scent, subtle yet piercing, seemed to overwhelm him with its sweetness.

'Only it isn't just literally a wild strawberry place,' Tessa went on. 'A *smultronställe* is any place that's absolutely private and special and your own. A place where life is . . . an epiphany. Like that very quiet room in the Kunsthistorisches Museum where the Vermeers are. Or that marvellous bit where the flute plays that golden music at the beginning of *L'Après-midi d'un faune.*'

'The nave of King's College chapel at Evensong,' said Guy.

'The place in the Prater behind the hunting lodge where the first scillas come in spring.'

'The garden act of *Figaro.*'

'The Lippizzaners doing a capriole, in the winter, when there's no one there.'

It was very quiet in the clearing, the murmuring of the stream the only sound.

'You must bring your children here,' said Tessa. 'But never, never anyone you don't love.' Unaware of the implications of her words, she bent her head and touched one of the berries he still held cupped in his hand. 'Eat!' she admonished him.

But Guy, suddenly, was in another smultronställe. Martha Hodge's small, dark kitchen in Newcastle – the smell of gingerbread in the oven, the kettle on the hob. A place where the obstinate, confused boy he had been had tasted his first wisdom and goodness and certainty.

'Oh, God!' thought Guy, overcome by longing for that uncomplicated world – and ate.

11

Guy spent the morning, on the fifth day of his house party, performing a task he had meant to attend to days earlier: writing to tell Martha Hodge about his engagement and his great happiness.

'. . . The wedding,' wrote Guy in his large, looped hand, 'will be here at Pfaffenstein at the end of October. I know how you feel about "abroad", Martha dear, and about travel. However, I wish to make it absolutely clear that there is no question whatsoever of my getting married without you. I shall send Morgan or David to bring you here, or I shall come myself if I can get that wretched business with the Treasury wound up by then – but come you must . . .'

Nerine, too, was attending to her correspondence. She had written exultantly to Mama, to Uncle Edgar, to her father's cousin Clarence Dimcaster, and most importantly, to the aunt who was an Honourable, Aunt Dorothy. But she had not yet written to Lord Frith.

Nerine's anguish after her walk in the forest had

been misplaced. Both her yellow satin and the dress she meant to wear for the opera comfortably cleared the mosquito bite, and Guy's lovely surprise was safe and sound. Now, lifting her head momentarily to observe that the bow on her polka-dotted muslin blouse was still uncrumpled, she pondered. She ought, of course, to tell Frith about her coming marriage. It was not as though she still had the slightest doubts about Guy. On the other hand, poor Frith, sitting alone in his northern fortress while his pipers marched round his solitary table, was a sad case. Frith really adored her. Perhaps it would be rather unkind to say anything until the knot was tied between her and Guy. Fate could be so unexpectedly cruel. If anything should happen to Guy, with his habit of flying about in dangerous aeroplanes or driving very fast in high-powered cars, well, she could still possibly make poor Frith the happiest of men. Yes, a friendly note simply saying that she was extending her visit to Austria would be best. There was never any point in inflicting unnecessary pain.

Meanwhile, behind the locked doors of the theatre, the dress rehearsal of *The Magic Flute* was going as Witzler intended: badly!

Herr Berger, the bass who sang Sarastro, missed his entrance; the stage lift stuck half-way, leaving the Queen of the Night with her head and shoulders sticking out of the trap-door. Pino stumbled over his footstool and began his duet with Pamina flat on his back. Klasky halted the 'March of the Priests' three times to hurl insults at his orchestra, and Raisa's dachshund entered stage left and tried to lift his leg against a tree.

At five in the afternoon, Raisa said, 'I go to Schalk,' and flounced off, to be brought back by Jacob who said that when he had told her she had sung like a piglet with the croup, he merely meant that she had not given absolutely of her best. At six, a portly gentleman in the chorus fainted. At nine, the A.S.M. gave notice and the coloratura from Dresden was apprehended on her way across the drawbridge in an attempt to return to her native town. At ten, Frau Kievenholler's cousin broke a harpsichord string and had hysterics . . .

At two in the morning Jacob brought down the curtain, informed them that they had one and all brought ruin and disgrace to the art of opera, and said he would dismiss any performer who appeared before six p.m. the following day.

'Not too bad, eh?' he said to Klasky, rubbing his hands, as they walked back across the Fountain Courtyard. And having left everyone nicely keyed up, the wily old fox put on his pyjamas, pillowed his bald perspiring head on the bosom of his Rhinemaiden, and fell asleep.

Though she had been to bed late, Tessa woke early on the day of the performance. Woke and stretched in the wooden bed in her room high in the West Tower, and walked over to the window to look at the much-loved view of shimmering water and soft blue hills which, in two days' time, she would leave for ever.

200

'Oh, let it work, tonight,' she prayed. 'Let it go as we hope!'

For Nerine, receiving her breakfast tray in the canopied four-poster, the day ahead was one of unremitting labour. Not only that, but her preparations would have to be made in secrecy. Now, sipping her coffee, she considered her strategy. A long rest, then a massage, followed by a face-pack and scented pads behind the elbows and knees. Her hair would have to remain in curlers until the last minute: ringlets à la Grecque demanded a very tight curl. Probably it would be best if she had a light supper sent up and just appeared to Guy in the lôge itself. Yes, that was the thing to do. She would part the curtains and just stand there. He would turn, unable to believe his eyes!

She put down her cup and reached for the mirror, ready to begin.

'Oh, God, *no*!' Her heart began to pound and droplets of perspiration broke out on her forehead. It couldn't be – no, it couldn't be! Not now, at the eleventh hour, a spot on her chin!

She leaned forward, peered, passed a hand over the glass – and fell back on the pillows, sighing with relief. It was just a speck of dust on the mirror – those dratted castle maids not dusting properly. What a fright she had had! But it would be all right now, it would be a triumph!

Thus Nerine prepared to recreate for this all-important night, with selfless dedication, her seventeen-year-old self.

By midday, the castle courtyard was a-bustle with carriages and cars as more visitors arrived from Vienna or Neustadt for the performance. Men staggered across the courtyard with tubs of oleanders to decorate the foyer, an awning was erected to the theatre door. Baskets of nectarines and peaches were carried up from the village to augment the cold collation and champagne set out for the party after the show. Bouquets were carried to the dressing-rooms . . .

At six-thirty there was a knock on Nerine's door.

'No!' she cried. 'I absolutely cannot be disturbed!'

But when Pooley returned, it was with a dark blue box and a note scrawled in Guy's hand: 'This is for tonight which is, after all, our anniversary. I shall be waiting impatiently. Guy.'

She opened it, and gasped. A diamond necklace – but a necklace out of a fairy tale, a dream! He had said her engagement ring was part of a parure . . .

Happiness overwhelmed her. That was the one thing which had worried her a little: that, dressed as she had been at seventeen, she would be a little too simple, too understated. Now the necklace would add the last, entrancing touch. Young, yes; girlish and unaffected, yes; but also cherished, valued, adored.

Oh, fortunate, fortunate Guy to see what he would see tonight!

'I cannot go on!' announced Raisa, squirting throat spray across the dressing-room. 'My uvula it is septicked with pimpules and my head she explodes!'

'I've forgotten every single line,' declared Herr Berger, emerging yet again from the lavatory. 'I can't remember a single word. After "In diesen heil'gen Hallen", I can remember nothing.'

'Yes, you can, Herr Berger,' said Tessa soothingly to the shivering bass. 'After "In diesen heil'gen Hallen" comes "kennt man die Rache nicht", and anyway Herr Witzler himself will be in the wings.'

'I am schweatink like a porker; I am ill . . .'

'Where's Papageno's bird-cage, Tessa – for Christ's sake, where has it gone?'

'That blasted flautist's drunk again. Can you rustle up some black coffee, 'ighness – and quick!'

'The Button!' screamed Klasky. 'Where's Beethoven's button?'

'I have it here, Herr Klasky.' Tessa, as always, was everywhere; comforting, contriving, finding what was lost.

'First call for beginners, ladies and gentlemen. First call for beginners.'

Jacob wiped his brow. 'Stay with me, Mozart,' he begged.

'He will, Herr Witzler, I know he will,' said Tessa fervently. 'I can feel him sort of floating over the theatre, wishing us well.'

Jacob smiled at his under wardrobe mistress and, in a rare gesture of affection, laid his hand briefly on the silken head. 'You must go out front now or your aunts will be worried.'

'No. Let me stay, please. I belong here now.'

But Jacob was adamant. 'No. We shall need you in the interval, but now get into your box, my little princess, and we will play to you.'

The third prince had built his theatre after a visit to Versailles. Dazzled by the blue-green marble, the aquamarine silk curtains, the Corinthian columns with which the Sun King had adorned his opera house, the prince had copied the sumptuous colour scheme of blue and gold, hung a hundred Bohemian chandeliers across the auditorium and ordered his griffin, his lily and his glove to be emblazoned on the front of every box.

It was in this exquisite theatre that Guy's guests now waited to hear an opera that was the quintessence of Austrian life. For the composer, whom the ancestors of this very audience had spurned, insulted and underpaid, was now more uniquely 'theirs' than any other. Prince Monteforelli could remember his grandfather telling of the time he had been taken, as a little boy, to the Theater an der Wieden on the night when Mozart himself went backstage to play Papageno's glockenspiel. Now, deaf or not, he intended to hear his thirty-second *Magic Flute*, if need be through his very bones.

How distinguished he looks, thought Waaltraut, down in the stalls, craning her head yet again at the main box, canopied in gold, in which Farne sat. So dark, so brooding. But why is he alone?

The same question was on the lips of most of the audience as they gazed at the solitary figure of the Englishman who, even in repose, seemed to have a knack of commanding attention in every gathering in which he found himself. Where was the widow?

'Ah, Putzerl,' said Maxi as Tessa, who had been way-laid by her old nurse wielding a hairbrush, slipped into the box which Maxi was sharing with the aunts. She was in dark green velvet with a big lace collar, her auburn eyes shining with excitement, and even Maxi, unmusical as he was, suddenly found himself looking forward to what lay ahead.

It was time, now. The audience was falling silent. And then a rustle as heads tilted to look up at Farne, whispers of 'There she is!'

And in the box set aside for Pfaffenstein's princes Guy turned, rose and caught his breath.

Nerine continued to stand quite still, one hand holding back the blue silk of the curtain. Her eyes were on his – wide, questing, the mouth a little tremulous.

It was she, now, who said softly, 'Do you remember?'

Guy could not speak at first, only reach for her hand and carry it to his cheek. She was dressed exactly as she had been then: the same dusky ringlets danced on her bare throat; the dress with its tiny, starry flowers was the same; she held, as she had held then, the smallest, most delicate of fans. Standing there, seeking his approval, his delight, she was seventeen again; the world had just begun – all life, all hope was before them.

'I remember,' said Guy – and she had never heard in any man's voice what was now in his.

205

The orchestra entered, followed by Herr Klasky. Guy pulled out a chair and, smiling her thanks, she seated herself. The conductor raised his baton.

And in that moment, deeply, utterly and most enchantingly, Nerine sighed.

What makes a truly great performance? What blend of grinding work, talent and sheer luck? Is there a conjunction of planets that needs to be evoked? Does the audience send back, across the footlights, some mysterious wave of empathy which the players absorb into themselves?

What alchemy, on this night of nights, turned the fat little Italian, Mastrini, into a prince able to express a love so pure, so ardent that it transcended passion itself? What made the hausfrau from Dresden give to the Queen of the Night's aria, with its cruel F in alt, an icy, brilliant glitter that brought a shiver to her listeners? And Papageno, the birdcatcher, whose simple ditties have become folk-song all over Europe . . . Papageno can be a clown, a simpleton, the Common Man. This Papageno, an unknown baritone whom Witzler had promoted from the chorus, was all of these and much, much more. As he finished 'Ein Vogelfanger bin Ich, ja' – the song that Mozart himself hummed through cracked lips as he lay dying – the audience stirred like the sea, and Monteforelli dabbed his eyes.

The Queen of the Night vanished into the split rock, the stage lift worked, the prince and the birdcatcher set out on their adventures. The scene changed and in a room in Sarastro's palace lay Pamina, abandoned and afraid. And here was alchemy again as the quarrelsome, rapacious Raisa became a young girl whose simplicity and seriousness was affirmed in every limpid note.

Felicity followed felicity. The duet between Pamina and the birdcatcher as they preached a tender sermon on conjugal love ended in a torrent of clapping which Klasky dissolved as he took his players forward into the solemnity and seriousness of the High Priest's temple. Darkened by trombones, by muted trumpets and muffled drums, the music spoke now of the poetry of man's existence, of the necessity of suffering and endurance in the creation of a perfect love.

'I will be nicer to Mother,' thought the Countess Waaltraut, and the acid-penned critic Mendelov, who had come from Vienna, closed his notebook and shook a wondering head.

Guy was beyond thought. He had forgotten even Nerine, held as if in a vice by the miracle that was this music.

Solemnity dissolved once more in laughter as Papageno played his magic bells and the delectable animals that were the Heidis danced to Tamino's flute. And then Sarastro himself, for whom Mozart wrote the most profound and fiendishly difficult arias in all music, singing of ordeals to be overcome and trials to be met before the lovers could be united . . . the great C major chorus extolling courage and virtue . . . and the curtain fell on Act One of Jacob Witzler's *Magic Flute*.

It came down to a thunderclap of applause, to the

stamping of ancient, rheumatic feet, to a chorus of 'Bravo!' and 'Bis!' Guy caught a glimpse of the small shape that was Tessa slipping out of the neighbouring box before he turned to Nerine.

'I won't ask you how you enjoyed it,' he said when he could trust himself to speak again. 'I can see it all in your eyes.'

'Yes,' she breathed. 'Oh yes.' A hand was pressed against the diamonds at her throat as though to hold back the emotion which otherwise might have choked her.

'I think we should go backstage now and congratulate them. It's quite a long interval and you haven't met Witzler yet, have you? We won't stay long, but I'd like to say a few words.'

Nerine smiled. 'You go, my dear. They will want to see you. But I need a few moments . . . quite alone.'

'Are you sure?' Guy looked at her tenderly. 'I can easily wait.'

'I'm sure.'

She waited until Guy had left the box before gathering up her skirts and running to the powder room. It had been an anxious moment. The theatre was warm and she was almost certain that a drop of perspiration had run down her throat. She had felt her hair go limp, too, just at that part where all those priests were marching about. And if the neck of her dress had moved even a fraction, it would have revealed the remnants of the mosquito bite. She had instructed Pooley to wait for her and, yes, there she was.

'Hurry, girl!' ordered Nerine. 'That ringlet's not right. And I'll want fresh powder on my shoulders . . . and lots here on that wretched bite . . .'

'Wait!' The peremptory voice halted Tessa, already through the baize-lined door and into the corridor which led backstage.

She turned, saw Guy, and without thought or volition ran like a child into his arms.

'Oh, wasn't it marvellous? Wasn't it beyond belief! You must be so *proud*,' she said, her head against his chest.

'Proud? *I*? It's you who have to be proud. I've never heard anything like it, Tessa. Never in my life.'

'I know.' She lifted her face to his, rubbed her eyes with a small fist. 'Isn't it stupid to want to cry because one is so glad and glad and *glad* to be alive!'

If Guy had let her go then, while they were just two people united in homage to something that was greater than them both, all would have been well. But Guy did her an injury. He went on holding her, made no movement to loosen his arm or draw away – did not appear, in fact, to have understood that she was a being separate from himself.

His foolishness lasted only a few moments before he did, after all, collect himself and let her go. But those few moments were to cost Tessa dear.

Witzler, when Guy reached him, tried desperately to maintain the pessimism and gloom his race demanded.

'This act wasn't too bad,' he admitted, 'but who knows what may happen in the last one? There is Sarastro's larghetto and the cyclorama for the fire and water scene . . . Oh, many things can go wrong still – many, many things!'

But his eyes, as he shook hands with Guy, shone with an unquenchable happiness. One perfect act, at least, thought Witzler. They cannot take that away from me. One act behind which I can stand when I get up there and meet him.' And 'him' – it is often so with those who practise music – was Wolfgang Amadeus, not God.

But nothing was taken from Witzler that night. Guy returned to find Nerine already seated, her profile tilted attentively to the stage. Klasky entered, the curtain rose, and the enchantment of this performance – which was to become an operatic legend – held. The slow march for the priests unfolded with an awe-inspiring majesty; Herr Springer, sober for the first time in months, played his flute solo like an archangel. Sarastro's sublime 'In diesen heil'gen Hallen' had the Uhlan captain vowing to foreswear roulette and the Archduchess Frederica wishing she had not bullied the pearls out of her late husband's niece. Raisa sang her G minor lament, 'Ach Ich füls! with a despairingly, unearthly grief and the orchestra consoled her in a postlude of heavenly tenderness.

The thunder thundered, the lightning flashed, the 'star-flaming Queen' re-entered, and traditional disaster after disaster was avoided as trap-doors opened as

smoothly as silk and costume changes lasting two minutes were effortlessly accomplished. The dreadful old
crone who had appeared to Papageno was transformed
into an adorable young girl and then – the very heart of
the opera now – the lovers, united again, faced and
overcame their ordeals. And with a last, exultant chorus
– Mozart standing up to be counted in E-flat major –
the opera ended.

It was now that the audience paid their greatest tribute. For the curtain did not fall on a burst of applause.
As Klasky dropped his head in weariness over the score,
there fell over the entire theatre a total stillness. In that
solemn and magical hush, the spectators took hold of
their departed souls and admitted them once more into
their bodies.

It was in that moment of utter silence before the
applause which would presently raise the roof, that Guy
turned to the woman for whom this miracle had been
wrought.

She sat with her dark head leaning against the blue
silk draperies of the lôge. One lovely arm lay relaxed
and still on the arm of the gilt chair, the hand with the
great diamond hanging free. The marvellous eyes were
sealed by luxuriant, dusky lashes; her bosom rose and
fell, softly, rhythmically. Her breathing was steady, but
every now and then a small, incongruous and not
entirely pleasant snuffling noise came from between her
parted lips.

Guy leaned forward, suddenly anxious. Had she
been overcome? Had she fainted?

But, no. There was no cause for alarm and certainly none for the black despair which now overwhelmed him. Naturally and – but for the small snores she emitted – gracefully, Nerine Hurlingham lay deep in sleep.

12

Refreshments and champagne had been laid out in the great hall for the cast and those who cared to join them. However when they had eaten and – more particularly – drunk, they were inclined to wander back to the theatre where they felt at home and, carrying bottles and glasses, to come to rest amongst the scenery – lolling contentedly against pieces of temple, sprawling across pillars.

Everyone was exhausted, tipsy and for these few hours completely happy. For their triumph was as tangible, as unmistakable, as a seam of gold in a rock face, or as the discovery of a new planet, or the act of love. Tomorrow there would be tensions and rivalries again – and hard work as they struck the set and prepared for the journey back to Vienna. But tonight belonged to the gods and even Jacob who never paused, paused now. Even Jacob who never praised, now praised.

'No, no, Savachka!' said Raisa firmly. She removed the Archduke's glass and handed him her large, scuffed and overflowing shoe. 'It is from *zis* zat you must drink champagne!'

'Ah, if only Mama could have been here tonight,' sighed Pino, his arm around the Middle Heidi. 'How that woman loved me!'

'It came quite suddenly you see, this terrible *twang* – and then I fell and all I remember is my silver tail rolling, rolling away over the footlights before everything went black!' declared the Rhinemaiden, recounting her historic mishap to the sympathetic David Tremayne.

But again and again they returned to the performance, recalling its felicities like people telling their beads so that they would not forget this night.

To the happiness and contentment pervading the party there was a notable exception: Prince Maximilian of Spittau, scrambling frantically over pieces of scenery and looking for his love.

For Tessa, Maxi could not help feeling, had behaved most shabbily. Not only had she rushed backstage during the interval, but as soon as the applause started after curtain down she had shot off again, declaring that she had to help clear up. And since then he had seen no sign of her.

But he was going to find her. He was going to find her and bring this proposing business to a head if it took all night. Enough was enough. Now, his glass clutched in his hand, he stumbled over entwined couples, fell over Raisa's dachshund and enquired with increasing desperation for the Princess of Pfaffenstein.

No one could help him. Even Boris, who regarded Tessa as his special charge, had no idea where she was and Klasky, when questioned, opened an eye, said vaguely, 'Dear little thing . . . brought The Button to Sachers . . .' and passed out at the foot of a cut-out tree.

'Going to find her,' said Maxi, draining his glass. 'Going to *find* her . . . *going* to –' and lurched away in the direction of the dressing-rooms.

At first Tessa had been buoyed up and sustained by the general jubilation that followed the fall of the curtain. But slowly, inexorably, the pain that had been lying in wait for her crept closer, could not be ignored and soon took over her whole self in a way which seemed entirely physical.

As soon as she had tidied up backstage, she slipped away to the West Tower. But before she could be alone, she had to go and say good night to the aunts for she was aware how badly she had neglected them during the past week.

She found them preparing for bed, their grey plaits hanging down their backs and, as always, their faces lit up at the sight of her. But when she had left again to go up to her room they turned to each other, suddenly stricken and helpless.

'What is it?' enquired Tante Tilda piteously. 'What makes her look like that? Her eyes . . .'

Tante Augustine shook her head in bewilderment. 'Before,' she said gruffly, 'one could at least brush her hair for her. But now . . .'

'She'll be all right when she's married to Maxi?' said Tante Tilda beseechingly. 'She'll be all right then, won't she, Augustine?'

But the Duchess was silent. Tomorrow she would forget again, would continue to press for the marriage that was so suitable, so dynastically right. But tonight she was still caught by the music's truth and she did not speak.

Tessa had reached her room, but she did not prepare for bed – instead, she climbed the round, stone steps which led up to the tower roof. It was for this view, this freedom, that she had chosen the plain, round room out of all the others in the castle, and now, stepping out, she found herself under a brilliant canopy of stars.

She was alone now and there was no escape. No more than one can ignore what Van Gogh saw in an olive tree or Rembrandt in the lineaments of age, could she forget what had happened to her when Guy had held her in his arms.

Here it was, then. Love. Love as strong, as specific, as if it were some metallurgical process welding her thoughts, her desires, her soul to a man who scarcely knew she existed. All those celestial shriekings in *Tristan and Isolde*, all those swords plunged by heaving tenors into their own chests, had been nothing more than case histories, describing this thing which was as real, as hard as stone.

Oh, God, thought Tessa; *why?* The uselessness of it when he loved Nerine and would, in any case, never have stooped to her. To 'why?' there was no answer except in the whim of fate. *When*, then? This was easier to answer. Almost at once, had she known enough to read the signs. That first time when he had taken her home and placed his fingers against her cheek, measuring the line of her hair . . . And again in the Stadtpark when he spoke of his foster-mother and his voice had grown so warm and tender . . . And at Sachers. Yes, she had certainly known at Sachers.

And I wanted to consult Professor Freud, thought Tessa. Well, the joke's on me. With the appalling clarity of her condition, she saw Guy's hand as he pushed a lock of hair impatiently from his forehead, saw his mocking smile as he drew the curtains of the alcove at Sachers, the curve of his throat as he bent to take the strawberries from her in the woods.

Do I know everything about him already? she thought, bewildered. And back came the answer: everything. You are branded with this knowledge, you will have it for the rest of time.

But this was too much. She took a deep breath, inhaling the night air scented with hay, with honeysuckle and the rich waters of the lake, listened to the music and laughter coming from the theatre and tilted her head at the stars. She had never seen them so brilliant and clear. Cassiopeia, Orion, the great girdle of the Milky Way – and her own birth sign, Gemini. With such staggering beauty in the world, how could anyone not rejoice?

It seemed, however, that 'anyone' could. For at once came the age-old cry of lovers since time began. 'What are the stars if I am not gazing at them with him? What is beauty except something that we share?'

Alone and appalled, Tessa stared at the meaningless heavens. 'This,' said the Princess Theresa-Maria Rodolphe Caroline of Pfaffenstein, lifting her chin, 'this I will *fight*.'

'May I help Your Highness?' The Littlest Heidi stood before Maxi as he clambered over yet another pile of scenery in his relentless, and so far hopeless, search for his beloved.

'I'm looking for the Princess of Pfaffenstein. For Tessa,' he added, for he was endeavouring to embrace democracy.

But his eyes rested, with a pleasure he found it impossible to conceal, on the entrancement that was Heidi Schlumberger dressed as a rabbit. It was thus that she had danced to Tamino's flute. Now, though she had removed her mask, she was still encased in soft, beige fur with a white fluffy tail. The huge blue eyes, the golden curls tumbling over her pelt, were almost too much for Maxi. He had not sought her out since they met at the film show but the little dancer had seldom been absent from what passed, in Maxi's mind, for thoughts.

'I haven't seen her for quite a while,' said Heidi. 'Shall I help you look? She may still be doing something in one of the dressing-rooms. You can't imagine how hard she works.'

Maxi, who could imagine it all too well, wrinkled

the nose which came to him straight from Phillip II of Spain and said he would be grateful. It was necessary, he said, for him to speak to Tessa that very night.

So they searched the dressing-rooms, the wardrobe, the Green Room, but there was no sign of Tessa.

'Could I perhaps get Your Highness some more champagne?' suggested the Littlest Heidi when they returned, defeated, to the stage. 'There are still bottles and bottles in the great hall.'

Like everybody else, she knew that the prince was to marry Tessa and thoroughly approved the match. She was a modest girl and when she gazed as she gazed now – rapt and awed – into his face, it was not marriage that she had in mind.

Maxi indicated his approval. 'Only you will want some too. We'll go together.' Damn it, there were limits to what a fellow could do and there was still tomorrow. 'I know a short cut,' he said.

The 'short cut' – through the trophy room, the picture gallery and the library – was, perhaps, not a sensational time-saver but Heidi made no demur. For the library, when they reached it, was quite deserted and splendidly provided with statues, niches and literary nooks. At exactly the right moment, she stumbled over a fluffy Afghan rug and was prevented from falling by the heroic prince. With exactly the right, almost imperceptible wriggle she indicated that his hands, now resting on the indescribable delights of the softly rounded rabbit tail, were not giving offence. And because the prince's hands were now engaged, she felt

219

emboldened to enquire whether His Highness would not wish her to loosen his collar, knowing how much the military suffered in their uniforms.

'You can call me . . . Maximilian,' murmured the Prince, as her plump little hands fluttered up to his throat.

But this the Littlest Heidi, though otherwise so totally obliging, felt unable to do.

Nerine was feeling aggrieved. She had worked ceaselessly and unstintingly all that day on her surprise for Guy. After all, she was not seventeen any longer; it had been no easy task to produce the miracle that was her own appearance en grande tenue. Then, just because she had dozed off for a few minutes at the end of that absolutely interminable opera, Guy was in a mood. She could tell he was although he had said nothing, only escorted her up to the boudoir which adjoined the state bedroom. Naturally, she had not been able to face a party which consisted largely of drunken theatricals, but though Guy had accompanied her upstairs, accepting the excuse that she was tired, he showed no inclination to leave her alone and let her prepare for bed.

'Are you cross because I dropped off for a minute?' she asked. 'Because really I can't see why. I've never pretended to be brainy, you know.'

'No, I'm not cross. Only . . . Nerine, just how much does music mean to you?'

She shrugged and suppressed a yawn. If she did not

get a full eight hours' sleep she would have rings under her eyes tomorrow, and there was still the farewell banquet on the following night.

'Well, I like it very much. To dance to, I mean. And when Charles was so ill and I never got about, Mama took me to *Chu Chin Chow* and I enjoyed that very much. In fact, that was where I met Lord Frith,' said Nerine, but saw that this was not a point to pursue. 'Mama went to *Chu Chin Chow* four times, actually, so you can't say we're not a musical family. But after all, dear, I *am* English.'

'English?' echoed Guy.

'Yes, dear, English,' said Nerine with quiet pride. 'And the English have never been fond of opera, have they? It's foreigners, really, who go in for that. Germans and Italians like opera and Russians like ballet. But in England it's not like that. You don't have to go to the opera socially, like you do in Vienna, to be seen. You go to Ascot and Henley and Goodwood. Of course, I'll come with you while we're living here – to the Vienna Opera, I mean. I quite see that it's necessary here. But quite honestly, all those priests droning on and that rather ridiculous birdcatcher . . .'

'Yes.' Guy was perfectly aware, at one level, of the absurdity of the art he loved, and saw without rancour what Nerine meant. 'Idiotic of me not to have asked you. You see, when we met that first time at the opera . . .' He broke off and stood twisting a candlestick over and over in his hands. 'I always remembered how

221

you sighed when the curtain went up. Always, I remembered that.'

'Well, so would you sigh,' said Nerine, suddenly exasperated, 'if you faced nearly four hours of boredom. Good heavens, Guy, it never ended at that academy. Concerts where funny little men almost fell off their piano stools, all that interminable trudging through museums in the heat . . . I never pretended,' cried Nerine, 'to be intellectual and clever. I never *pretended* it!'

Guy bowed his head. The truth of what she said was absolute, she had not pretended. The foolishness, the idiocy, had all been his. He had fallen in love not just with her appearance but with a response – wholly imagined, he could see now – to beauty and art. Tessa's coup de foudre as she overheard the choirboys at Schönbrunn, Jacob's experience at *Carmen*, had had its counterpoint when Martha took him to the pantomime in Newcastle for the first time. Just seven years old, Guy had emerged from the dirty, Doric portico of the Theatre Royal in a state of trance and had not come down to earth for several days. But what did his own passion for music and the theatre have to do with Nerine? He had been blind and foolish, and worse than that, for to twist another person into one's own image is to do them an incalculable injury.

Well, she should not suffer. Never would he reveal his mistake nor tell her what hopes he had had of a future in which his wealth would serve the purposes of art. From now on he would take her as she was: a lovely woman who had promised him nothing and owed him nothing but her own existence.

He put down the candlestick and picked up one of her hands. 'No, you never pretended and you shall never need to,' he said, playing with her fingers. 'As for operas – we'll have no more of them!'

She smiled, relieved. 'Well, frankly, dear, I think Mama and Aunt Dorothy would be a bit horrified if they found they had to sit through an opera when they came to the wedding. And really, there's no harm done, is there? Your guests enjoyed tonight and the company have been well paid – too well paid, I shouldn't wonder. They will probably boast of their week at Pfaffenstein for the rest of their lives. But since we're talking about music, dearest,' said Nerine, pleased to show that she did after all know something about the subject, 'which would you prefer at our wedding? The Mendelssohn March? Or the one from *Lohengrin*?'

Guy smiled: a smile that did not quite manage to reach his eyes. 'I leave that to you, my dear. Either will do perfectly well for me.'

13

On the last day of Guy's house party, the green and glacial waters of Lake Pfaffenstein saw two momentous though disconnected events.

Not far from the southern shore of the lake lay a wooded island on which the fifth Prince of Pfaffenstein had built a classic temple, following his return from the Grand Tour. Boats to journey to this and other islands, and boatmen to row them, had been provided by Guy for his guests. At an hour when most of them still slept, Klasky, carrying a briefcase full of manuscript paper and wearing his habitual dark suit, silk socks which had belonged to Gustav Mahler and patent leather shoes, was rowed across to this peaceful spot.

Dismissing the boatman, instructing him to return at lunchtime, Klasky repaired to the bench in front of the temple. Nature, always abundant in the month of June, smiled at the Hungarian but she smiled in vain. Cuckoos called, dragonflies shimmered, marguerites, balsam and meadow-sweet scented the grass by the water's edge, but all to no avail. Klasky's impassioned eyes were turned on a wholly inward vision as his thin white fingers raced across the lined paper. Sometimes he hummed – a distracted sound as of a deprived and atonal bee – sometimes he whistled. Midges bit him, lavender beetles dashed across his shoe. Caught in a white heat of creative fervour, he saw nothing that did not come from within.

For it was coming! The breakthrough when he had changed the hero from a policeman to a railway porter had been followed by one even more fundamental, when he had discovered that by changing the B flat in his tone row to G the whole musical structure of the work fell into place. Since then, he had lacked only the vision for the chorus that would conclude his opera. The heroine, betrayed by the mill-owner, has hanged herself. Her husband, the railway porter, has gone mad. The mill-owner, wrongly believing that he has consumed his child in a fricassée, has jumped out of the window. The action then is over, but it is left to the plate-layers, engine-greasers and lavatory attendants who represent the simple, uncorrupted spirit of the people, devoid of capitalism and desire, to sum up the inner meaning of the tragedy.

The theme of this last chorus had continued to elude the composer. The lament of the captive Israelites in *Nabucco*, the paean of the prisoners in *Fidelio*, were to pale into insignificance beside the yea-saying life-enhancement of these signalmen and engine-greasers assembled on a railway platform somewhere between Vlodz and Kranislav.

Klasky had despaired of doing justice to this last, all-important vision. But as Witzler had hoped, the fresh air, the excellent food, above all the absence of Klasky's latest mistress – a voracious Burg Theatre actress – had done the trick. His élan vital undisturbed, Klasky, in spite of the previous night's excesses, had woken at dawn with the chorus in his mind. Now, discord followed meaningful discord as the voices of the oppressed came to him in an unbroken stream of sound.

The boatman returned and was waved away by the perspiring Hungarian. The shadows lengthened . . .

At five he stabbed a last cluster of quavers on to the paper, closed his brief-case and reeled sightlessly towards the landing stage. The opera was finished.

There was no boat, but that was of no importance. He turned to look at the little temple. Would they transport it as they had transported the summer-house where Mozart had written *The Magic Flute*? Would there be a Klaskeum like the Mozarteum at Salzburg, or would people merely come to Pfaffenstein in charabancs to see where he had worked? No, where he had *lived*. There could be no doubt but that Farne, after last night, would install them here.

His mind raced ahead to the production. He would need a much larger bass drum than any they possessed, thought the composer, wondering if even now, in some fertile alm above the castle, there grazed two outsize and expiring cows whose hides would give the neces-

226

sary sound. Or simply two cows, expiring or not, since it was after all perfectly possible to shoot them.

At this point he perceived, not far away, a rowing-boat containing Tessa, the Prince of Spittau and a quantity of dogs.

Should he hail them? But no. The dogs seemed to be wet and there were a great many of them. Extracting a leberwurst sandwich from his pocket, Klasky prepared to wait.

Whether it was the uplifting effect of Mozart's master-piece or just a flash of arbitrary inspiration from above, Maxi had woken on the last day of the house party knowing exactly where to propose to Tessa.

For just as Mexicans prefer to eat, sleep and make love in the place they have been accustomed to from birth, namely a hammock, so Prince Maximilian was happiest performing life's functions on the water. It was in a boat, therefore, that the prince decided to put his happiness to the test – and this time he would brook no opposition. Putzerl should, and would, hear him out.

But Tessa had in any case given up the fight. The opera was over and tomorrow she would leave Pfaffen-stein for good. She could not avoid a tête à tête with Maxi for ever.

Four o'clock, therefore, saw Maxi rowing strongly towards the centre of the lake, the Princess of Pfaffen-stein captive in the stern. Not only did he have Tessa, and in a most romantic setting – for the castle rearing up behind him looked, in the slanting, golden light, more like something out of a fairy tale than ever – but he had the dogs. To get five dogs into a small rowing-boat is not easy, but he had managed it and though the animals were a little bit on edge owing to the unfortunate proximity of a brace of mallard and a swan, they were behaving well. The red setter had her head in Tessa's lap and was dribbling affectionately on her dress, while the water spaniel lay across her feet. To emphasize even more that his business was love and not sport, Maxi had left behind not only his gun but also his rod, and this despite the fact that the lake, cruelly underfished since the decline of the Pfaffenstein fortunes, was teeming with trout.

If Maxi supposed, however, that by taking to the water he would be unobserved, he was mistaken. The news that the prince was about to put his fortunes to the test had spread like wildfire round the castle. In the West Tower his mother, the Swan Princess, was stationed behind the late Prince of Pfaffenstein's telescope, which she had securely trained on her son. Putzerl's aunts, though they would not have stooped to such tactics, stood on either side of her, more than ready to receive details at second hand. The Archduke Sava, aware of the importance of the occasion, had abandoned his watch on the sunbathing soprano and carried *his* telescope into Monteforelli's bedroom which faced the lake. Maxi's valet, exceptionally keen-sighted, had climbed on to the balustrade outside the servants' attics and was relaying information back to the castle maids.

And down on the terrace overhanging the lake,

Nerine picked up the field-glasses Guy had left when he went for his interview with Witzler. This was better than looking at some red-legged hawk as Guy had wanted her to do!

'He's doing it!' cried the Swan Princess. 'He's proposing, I'm sure! He's stopped rowing!'

And indeed the Prince of Spittau had, at that moment, shipped his oars.

'Putzerl,' he began. 'Tessa . . .'

The Princess of Pfaffenstein, who had been sitting quietly in the stern with her hands on the tiller lines, raised her head. Maxi's eyes were deeply poached, his duelling scar throbbed like a wound. It was coming, then. Steeling herself, feeling the familiar guilt creep over her, Tessa said, 'Yes, Maxi?'

'Putzerl, you know how fond of you I've always been,' said Maxi, and indeed he spoke the truth. No one had played 'Cowboys and Indians' as willingly and as often as she had done.

'I'm very fond of you, too,' said Tessa, repressing a sigh.

A trout, a five-pounder by the sound of it, rose very close to them. Maxi resolutely ignored it, as did the older dogs who were perfectly trained. Not so the young setter, who raised her head from Tessa's lap and moaned with agitation, setting off the swan who approached hissing in fury, causing the labrador who was of a heroic turn of mind to rush to the stern and emit a fusillade of barks. A period of considerable confusion followed as they beat off the swan, restrained the wolfhound who had scrambled over the oars to aid his friend, and shipped a considerable amount of water.

For a moment Maxi wondered whether, after all, it had been such a good idea to bring the dogs. Tessa now seemed more worried about the wolfhound, who had scratched his nose on a rowlock, than she was about him. She was also, as he was himself, extremely wet.

'So don't you think . . . Tessa . . . please? I know I've asked you before, but now Pfaffenstein's sold . . . I mean, you can't go on working for the opera company for ever, and—' He broke off. 'Sit!' he ordered furiously.

The pointer, who had leapt to her feet and was gazing with an air of quivering attention at the wooded island, turned a reproachful head. She had, she wished to make this clear, *heard* something.

'So Tessa, do please marry me. I would be so happy. Everyone would be so pleased. And we get on so well.'

Tessa had picked up the bailer and was trying to reduce the pool of water in which they sat and Maxi, determined to pursue his advantage – for she had not yet said 'No' – plunged into the delights of Spittau. 'We would have such great times together. You could breed water spaniels, you know how you love them. Of course, I know Mother's a bit difficult but . . . And I mean it isn't as though you're liable to rheumatism. You're healthy, Putzerl, although you're so little. That's one of the things I like about you.'

The mallards now returned and foolishly approached the boat, quacking and fussing, while the dogs turned with desperate appeal to their master. Was nothing going to happen? How long were they expected to endure it?

Not for ever, it seemed. A long, high-pitched whistle sounded from the wooded island and without a second's hesitation the pointer, the labrador and the spaniel leapt into the water.

'Idiot! Half-wit! Moron!' yelled Maxi, shaking his fist in the direction of the island, with its little temple, from which the sound had come.

Yet no one was to blame. That the noise, a piercing A flat, emitted by one of Klasky's characters (the engine-greaser who has a fit in the second act) was the same as the whistle to which Maxi had trained his dogs, was a coincidence no one could have foreseen.

'They're having a little bit of trouble,' reported the Swan Princess as the puzzled faces of the dogs, hauled back into the boat by an irate Maxi, swam into focus, followed by a dangerous rocking as the animals shook themselves. 'But it's all right now. Tessa's got hold of the dogs and Maxi's rowing again.'

And indeed Maxi was now in a state of desperation when nothing could stop him. Bracing his feet against the wolfhound and rowing strongly away from the island, he said, 'And after all, we're both descended from—' But here he veered off again, because it was no good talking to Putzerl about lineage and breeding and all that. The fact that he could trace his descent straight back to Barbarossa cut absolutely no ice with Tessa, who was apt to go off at half-cock when he mentioned anything like that. He returned to the subject of Spittau. 'Maybe we could put in some central heating . . .'

He flushed, on delicate ground, and Tessa, on whose lap the soaking and frustrated water spaniel had settled, felt the familiar guilt intensify.

Guy had paid generously for Pfaffenstein. The cheque she had been handed, signed by the Associated Investment Company, in these inflationary times ran into millions of kroner. Half of this would go in trust for the aunts, and there were debts to be paid, but even so it left her with enough money to shore up Maxi's imperilled Wasserburg and put heating into the mouldering rooms.

'Maxi, I haven't got quite as much money as your mother thinks, perhaps. My father left a lot of debts and they have to be paid. But I've enough all the same to—' She tried again. 'Would you let me help a little with Spittau? Do the roof at least, so that it can be preserved? I mean, we're almost relatives, aren't we?'

Maxi's eyes became vibrantly convex; his duelling scar turned livid. His manhood had been outraged, his honour impugned. 'How can you suggest such a thing, Putzerl?'

'I'm sorry, Maxi. I didn't mean any harm. Only, I don't know any other way to marry except for love. A particular kind of love. And that isn't . . . how I love you,' said Tessa, her voice very low.

'But Tessa, we aren't like that. Like ordinary people. I mean, being in love.'

'I'm an ordinary person.'

He sighed. Her republicanism again.

'I don't think I am going to marry at all, Maxi. I think I'm going to live for art and bring music and theatre into people's lives.'

A slight tightening of the jaw – the beginning of a yawn, which always attacked him at the mention of art – now troubled the prince. Bending to conceal it, he incited the wolfhound who caught Maxi rather painfully under the chin as he reared up in hope of land.

'Are you sure, Putzerl? Are you absolutely sure?' said Maxi when he had quietened the animal. 'Couldn't you please, *please* say yes?'

Tessa's heart smote her. She knew only too well what Maxi would have to endure if his suit did not prosper. 'I'm so sorry, Maxi.' She put down the tiller lines, pushed the spaniel gently from her lap and, over-whelmed by pity, leaned forward to kiss him on the forehead. She too could perform life's most varied actions in a boat.

The kiss was seen by Nerine on the terrace, by the Swan Princess and thus the aunts in the West Tower, by Monteforelli and Maxi's valet and many others in the castle – and misinterpreted by all of them.

Witzler sat in the small room in the East Tower, adjoining the theatre, which he had used as an office since he came to Pfaffenstein. Out in the courtyard the men were loading scenery. The stage crew would leave at dawn for Vienna, with the principals and orchestra following by train.

But only for a while, Jacob was sure of that. His eyes closed in a moment of blissful remembrance. If he lived to be a hundred, nothing could dim the triumph of the previous night: old Monteforelli, that reprobate who knew every Mozart score by heart, hobbling backstage to throw his arms round him . . . the Comte d'Antibes throwing his diamond tie-pin on to the stage . . . But it was not only that, or the half-hour of applause, or the quick emotional handshake of Mendelov before that acid-penned critic went back to Vienna. It was the justification of a life spent in pursuit of an ideal. The journey that had begun with the visit of that tatty touring company playing *Carmen* had been justified last night.

What a week it had been altogether! Bubi was sunburnt and well, the Rhinemaiden's nerves were such that she could probably sustain an entire performance of *The Ring*. And this morning Klasky had stolen off with his brief-case and a look in his eyes that Jacob, who had nursed many talents, had recognized with excitement. If this glorious week should also see the completion of Klasky's opera!

Should he suggest to Farne that he install the company permanently at Pfaffenstein, or would it be best to keep a base in Vienna? Suppose he bought a little house in the village? They could keep a cow; Bubi would go to bed in time and wear lederhosen, mused Jacob, as the sound of Boris practising his yodelling floated in at the window. Everyone was out there waiting for the result of his interview. He glanced at his watch, but punctual to the minute Farne knocked and entered.

Guy, too, was sunburnt and fit. Since the previous night's conversation with Nerine, he had taken a satisfactory amount of exercise: a pre-breakfast game of squash, tennis with one of his guests, then a ride in a neighbouring valley. Nevertheless, it was not the picture of a sporting gentleman relaxing on his estate that Guy suggested to Jacob, who felt rather that he was about to be interviewed by some beast of prey.

He rallied, however, and said, 'Well, Herr Farne, you are satisfied, I think, eh?'

'Yes. The performance was outstanding! I told you so last night. The interpretation was right, the balance, the detail too. I've never seen a better *Magic Flute* and I never will.'

He had got out his cheque book but even this object, so beautiful in Jacob's eyes, did not deflect the impresario into hasty or impatient greed.

'Of course, in this theatre, *Figaro* would be perfect. *The Marriage of Figaro* for your marriage.' He waxed eloquent on the scoring, the ensemble writing of this most human and moving of operas. 'Though of course it would be unwise to concentrate too much on Mozart because of competition with Salzburg. And in any case you may prefer something very light. Rossini, say . . . *The Barber* . . .

Once again he elaborated and only noticed after a while that Guy was silent. He had unscrewed his fountain-pen and was writing a cheque. 'This is the balance of what I owe you. Will you see that it is correct?'

'Yes,' said Jacob, looking down. 'It's perfectly correct. Thank you.'

But for once money, so deeply a part of Jacob's life, was not what he wanted to discuss. Indeed, Farne's pragmatic and almost mercenary attitude shocked him a little. Genuinely, vociferously, Jacob was gripped by the vision of the music he and the Englishman would make here at Pfaffenstein.

'Of course it would be possible, for the actual wedding, to stage a performance out of doors. On the lake, even, on a raft as in Boden. I don't usually care for this because of standards and it will be difficult to persuade Klasky: the acoustics . . . the mosquitos . . . and he cannot swim. But if you wished—'

Guy had screwed up his pen, returned it to his pocket and straightened up. His voice when it came was harsh, his appearance more Mephistophelean than ever.

'Let me make myself clear, Witzler. There will be no more opera staged here at Pfaffenstein . . . And no more music. Not for my wedding. Not ever.'

Jacob stared at him, sweat breaking out on his forehead. His ulcer, which he had hardly noticed during the last few days, bit agonizingly into his gut.

'There was something wrong?' he stammered. 'Was it because Sarastro did not sing the E below stave? You see, I think what Mozart wanted there was not a trick but—'

'I have told you,' interrupted Guy, 'the opera was

perfect. That has nothing to do with it. My contract with your company is now terminated and it will not be renewed.'

The round little Jew sat down. He seemed suddenly to have shrunk, and one pudgy hand rubbed at his forehead as though to erase a pain.

'Could one ask why?' he said after a while.

'That is my business, surely?'

Jacob nodded. 'Yes . . .' he said. 'I'm sorry . . . Yes . . .'

Guy had walked to the turret window. He had dismissed hundreds of people in his time, blasted them and forgotten them. But he knew what he had bought when he bought the International Opera Company: the dedication, the ceaseless, gruelling work, the hopes . . .

He turned. 'My fiancée doesn't care for music,' he said, his voice expressionless.

Jacob looked up in surprise. 'But I thought . . . I thought it was because . . .' He saw Guy's face and fell silent.

'Then you thought wrongly,' said Guy silkily.

It was then that, seeking escape from Jacob's archetypally tortured-looking face, Guy turned back to stare out of the turret window. More keen-sighted even than Maxi's valet, he saw the boat on the lake, saw the occupants surrounded by a gaggle of multi-coloured dogs . . . saw Tessa drop the tiller lines and lean over to kiss – with a tenderness undiminished by distance – the Prince of Spittau on the brow.

*

237

The news of Maxi's engagement spread, like the good news from Aix to Ghent, with amazing speed. In the West Tower the arthritic Swan Princess, abandoning her telescope, managed to caper round the room and to embrace the aunts whose faces shone with relief and joy. They were presently joined by Monteforelli, the Archduke Sava and the Archduchess Frederica, and since the prince happened to have a bottle of champagne with him, a happy party was soon assembled and to the agitated barks of the pug, dynasties were cemented and wedding plans laid.

The Countess Waaltraut, pushing her mother across the courtyard, heard of Maxi's successful courtship from the Uhlan captain with the wooden leg, who had heard it from Raisa Romola who had been sunbathing on the battlements and seen the kiss. The Comte d'Antibes heard it from his valet, who heard it from the gardener who had been clipping the yew hedge on the terrace overhanging the lake.

The Littlest Heidi heard the news as it spread through the opera company, and managed to be glad for she was a girl with a good heart; David Tremayne, who heard it from Thisbe Purse, who heard it from the Archduchess Frederica's maid, managed to be glad too for it appalled him to think that when she left here, Tessa would no longer have a home.

Guy Farne heard it from Nerine.

'They're engaged, Guy! Tessa and the Prince of Spittau! Isn't it splendid news!' And indeed, Nerine's lovely face glowed with happiness. Not only was the princess

leaving the castle for good but she was marrying someone else! No more dramatic entrances, no more of those
friendly, intimate looks at Guy, those boring conversations about music from which Nerine had felt herself
excluded.

'Yes,' said Guy. 'I'd heard. Or rather seen. I'm sure
they will suit each other excellently.'

He then excused himself to go to the gymnasium.
His morning's squash and tennis, the long ride, having
naturally left him short of exercise, Guy now indulged
in a ferocious bout of fencing with a young cavalry
officer who, having taken on the Englishman out of
politeness, found himself two hours later thoroughly
trounced. It was as Guy was returning to his room,
showered and sleek and unpleasantly vulpine looking,
that he found the double doors of the theatre open and
Witzler's under wardrobe mistress carrying a wicker
skip out to the waiting lorry.

The sight of her small figure in the same smock,
packing up as though nothing had happened, as though
she was still the unassuming child he had befriended in
Vienna, made him suddenly choke with an almost
blinding rage.

'I have to congratulate you, then,' he said, blocking
her path. 'And indeed you are most heartily to be con-
gratulated. You certainly took me in, in a most
impressive way. You know, I actually believed what you
said.'

'What I said?' repeated Tessa, completely bewildered. She put down the basket and stared at him.

'Your remarks about being a republican. About art making everybody equal. Doesn't your own hypocrisy ever sicken you? All that rubbish about Schönbrunn: how constrained you were, how unhappy.'

'I didn't . . .' But it seemed impossible to speak. The lump in her throat was too obtrusive – and anyway Guy was far too angry to hear a word she said.

'No doubt you will find it amusing, but I actually believed you for a while. I thought you truly wanted to escape from the limitations of your upbringing. I thought you wanted to be free – that all this clap-trap of rank and ceremony meant nothing to you.' He laughed, and it was an amazingly unattractive sound. 'Yes, I believed you. I was quite touched. I even believed what you told me at Sachers.'

She flushed, staggered at his bad manners in refer-ring to her confidence. 'What . . . have I done?' she managed to falter. 'Why are you like this?'

'Oh, you've done nothing. All is as it should be,' he jeered. 'Sixteen quarterings – or is it thirty-two? An impeccable lineage, rejoicing all round.'

'I cannot help . . . my lineage.'

'It doesn't happen to be your lineage that I am refer-ring to.'

But it was necessary now to curtail this interview before his mind registered what his eyes were already seeing: a weary child leaning her head against the side of the lorry as though the weight of it was suddenly too much for her to bear. Did it matter, after all, that she had succumbed to the pressure of her relatives? Maximilian was a fool but he was neither venal nor cruel.

He shrugged. 'Well, I hope you'll be happy,' he said.

Boris, coming out a few minutes later, found Tessa still leaning against the lorry. Not crying, just standing there with the wicker basket lying at her feet.

'Jesus!' said Boris, looking at her face, and led her away.

Installed in Boris's cubby-hole behind the stage, Tessa dutifully swallowed the scalding tea he brewed for her on his samovar, but when he handed her a saucer of yoghurt she managed a ghost of a smile and shook her head.

'Thank you, you are very kind,' she said carefully. 'But I don't think . . . I really want to live to be very old. You eat it, Boris.'

Boris, as he took the spoon from her, continued to stare at her in consternation. What was all this? Like everyone else he had heard about the events in the rowing-boat, but when she had come up from the lake Tessa had said nothing, just begun in her usual way to throw herself into her work, and no one in the company had ventured to congratulate her, waiting for the news to be official. Then Witzler had come with his bombshell: the news of Farne's rejection and instructions that they were to pack and leave at once. Even then, in the misery and disappointment that had followed, the tears of the Rhinemaiden, the hurt and shock on the artists' faces, Boris had held on to the idea that Tessa, at least, would be all right. But if being engaged to the Prince of Spittau was going to make her look like that . . .

'You don't have to do anything you don't want to,' he said now. 'No one can force you.'

But Tessa had not really heard him, caught as she was in the toils of her private nightmare. A nightmare out of which she now visibly tried to lift herself, putting a hand on his arm to say, 'It will be all right about the company, Boris, I'm sure. Herr Witzler's so clever. He'll work something out, you'll see.'

'Yes,' said Boris to reassure her. But he knew rather more about the company's finances than she did and his view of the future was bleak indeed. 'I'll never learn to yodel now,' thought Boris, and began to eat.

An hour later, the farewell banquet was in full swing. A mood of particular elation and jollity was evident among the guests. The news of Putzerl's engagement, along with the desire to eat and drink as much as possible before they had to depart and take up the burden of their lives again, kept them happily absorbed. Never had uniforms glittered so brightly, jokes been so deliciously risqué, flirtations so skilfully pursued.

Herr Farne, beside his lovely widow, seemed as everyone noted to be in particularly high spirits. Presently he rose to make a speech: witty, brilliant, of exactly the right length. He announced the date of his own wedding, at the end of October, thanked all those present for the pleasure of their company and with a gallant bow raised his glass to the health and happiness of 'Absent Friends'.

'Absent Friends!' cried the guests, following suit, raising their glasses with meaningful glances and nudges at the two empty places on the long centre table with its priceless epergne, fluted napery and bowls of roses. For both the Prince of Spittau and the Princess of Pfaffenstein were absent from their usual places, a circumstance which the guests found both delightful and amusing.

'Do you remember,' whispered the Count of Winterthur to his portly wife, 'how we crept away after we were engaged? Your Papa tried to find us but we were hiding away in the orangery?'

'They'll be in the woods somewhere, hand in hand,' cooed the Archduchess Frederica, in a good mood for once.

Here she was partly correct. Maxi *was* in the woods, but not with Tessa. It was the Littlest Heidi who was cradled in his arms, the Littlest Heidi who soothed his hurt and promised to keep secret the news of his rejection until the guests had left and everyone was home again.

'It's the fuss,' said the weary prince. 'I just can't face the fuss.'

'I understand, Your Highness,' said Heidi and did indeed keep her promise. And when she had comforted him in the only way she knew (and there is certainly no better) they spoke not of the future but of Tom Mix and Buck Jones and the incomparable Pearl White in *The*

Perils of Pauline and Maxi, stroking the golden curls, was comforted and soothed.

For Tessa the way was harder. She had waited until everybody was at dinner before slipping into the deserted chapel, and now knelt at the altar rail with her head in her hands. In the light of the candles, the church sang with gold: gold on the haloes of the saints, gold on the ceiling, on the chalices and goblets on the altar. Gold soaring and swirling on the pillars, on the family crests decorating the pew ends, on the Virgin's mantle, as though in the darkness someone was giving a great party for God.

'Help me to bear it,' prayed Tessa. With her shorn head, her smock, she might have been a lone shepherd boy come down from the hills. 'Help me not to make a fuss. Help me not to let anyone see how I feel. Help me just to work hard – to work and to work and not to ask anything else. And please, God, keep them safe here, all of them.'

She rose and fetched three votive candles from the box. Carefully, she lit them and placed them in their holders. One for the aunts she was leaving and whom she loved. One for the people she had cared for here. And one other, the tallest, which she did not offer up even in her mind, knowing that God would understand.

There was nothing left to do now except pack a small bag, leave a note in her room and make her way to the station. There was a last train which stopped at Pfaffenstein Halt before crawling on to Neustadt. She would catch that and wait there for the milk train to Vienna. Nothing mattered now except to get away.

Thus Guy, waking next morning with a heavy head, looked out of the window at the gatehouse tower and frowned. What was it that was different? Of course – the bright flag, with its griffin, its lily, its crimson glove, was gone.

14

Guy's guests departed with considerable reluctance. The Uhlan captain left his spare leg, in striped socks and regimental boots, leaning against the Bühl commode in his room until the last moment, as though in hope of a reprieve from banishment to his leaking hunting lodge in Styria. The Countess Waaltraut snuffled her way, with many a backwards glance, towards the embossed automobile into which her mother's Bath chair was being lifted. The Archduke Sava thanked Guy, with tears in his eyes, for saving his bear, and promised him the best wolf-hunting in Archangelskaya as soon as the Bolsheviks had been deposed.

But at last they left; the castle fell silent, for the opera company too had gone and the aunts kept to the West Tower.

To Guy, the departure of his guests was nothing but a relief and he made no secret of it to David as he thanked his young secretary for what he had done.

'You were a Trojan, David. Everything went off

splendidly. Even the Archduchess Frederica was kind enough to tell me that she had enjoyed herself.'

David smiled. 'Yes, it seems to have gone off all right. And —' he looked sideways at his employer, 'Mrs Hurlingham was happy? It all worked out, didn't it?'

'Yes. It worked out exactly as I had anticipated,' said Guy, looking with total absorption at a buzzard wheeling above the chapel roof. 'I'm off to Vienna on Monday; I've managed to persuade those lazy brutes from the Treasury to cut short their holiday and do some work, and I want to have the documents ready for the League by the end of September. I shall want you to come with me – there are enough people here to look after things and I'm not wasting you on any more of this domestic stuff. I've a few ideas about the Metallic Mining Consortium in Bayern, but we shall have to move fast if we're to get ahead of those Armenian twisters . . .'

He put his arm round the young man's shoulders and led him away, his voice carrying the familiar adventuring note as he anticipated the battles to come and David listened, immensely relieved. He had not relished the idea of staying behind to see to the wedding.

'It's good to be alone, isn't it?' said Guy to his fiancée that evening. 'I hardly had a chance to talk to you while all those people were around.'

'Yes. Yes, it's lovely. Only, Guy, if you're really off to Vienna next week, what am I going to do? I shall be awfully bored without you.'

She smiled caressingly at him, but Guy's face as he

looked at her expressed only amazement. That one could be bored in a three-hundred-room castle, surrounded by forests and mountains, beside a lake full of boats, with a stable full of horses and a vast library, had simply not occurred to him.

'I thought you might like to get to know the tenants and learn the ropes generally. Visit the local people, perhaps? There's a list in the factor's office. And I imagined you'd want to make some arrangements for the wedding.'

'Yes, I'll do that, certainly. But visiting . . . I don't know, Guy, I don't think they really expect it any more. And it would be a bit silly to go into one of those stuffy little houses and risk picking up an infection. No, what I thought was, why don't I come with you to Vienna? Mummy and Aunt Dorothy and the others won't be coming for a while. I could stay at the Grand again with Arthur, it would be perfectly correct.'

'Well, of course, I would be delighted. But what will you do while I'm working? I'm liable to put in a twelve-hour day.'

'Shop!' she said.

The following week, therefore, saw Nerine installed in the Grand Hotel and shopping for her trousseau. 'I won't waste your money, Guy,' she had assured him. 'You'll see. You'll be so proud of me!' And Guy had smiled and said he was proud of her already and, more importantly, had opened accounts for her in all the better shops.

To the pursuit of her favourite activity, Nerine

brought a dedication that was truly impressive. As Ithaca to the wandering Ulysses or Mecca to the Faithful, so were the fitting-rooms of couture houses – with their marvellously reliable supply of full-length mirrors – to Nerine. While shopping she was patient, dedicated, devout. Standing in lace cami-knickers did not chill her, nor did she become overheated when swathed in furs. The distractions that troubled lesser ladies as they stood captive in cubicles – the thought that outside the birds were singing, the glorious summer day passing unseen – never troubled Nerine nor forced her into a hasty choice.

Vienna had always been famous for its taste and though the war had changed many things, the city was still the centre for goods from all over the erstwhile Empire. Now, chauffeured by Morgan and accompanied by Thisbe Purse whom Guy had dragooned into the role of duenna, she bought an evening dress of panelled white satin; another, daringly bare-backed, in tiered blue chiffon, a third in pleated moonbeam taffeta. She bought a hand-painted theatre cape in silver gauze, a plaid suit with a hem a brave ten inches off the ground and (after only the briefest of hesitations) a pair of flame silk lounge pyjamas.

By now she had found women who could copy a Paris design in two days and tiny shops tucked away behind the Graben: a blouse shop which was an Aladdin's cave of handmade lace and delicate embroidery, a shoe shop where she bought pumps in pigskin and in kid, gold-thonged sandals, lizard court shoes with matching handbags . . .

Never had Nerine been so happy. Freed from the constraints of mourning and the stinginess of the Hurlinghams, she glowed with well-being and health. As she entered the restaurant of the Grand, where Guy came each night to dine with her, every eye in the room followed her to her place.

'You're so good to me, darling,' she would say to him. 'You spoil me so.'

But Nerine did not only gush. She also freely shared her problems with Guy. One evening, for example, though attacking her schnitzel with undiminished relish, she admitted to being perplexed. That afternoon he had, she told Guy, tried on a full-length chinchilla coat whose soft blue-grey lustre took up, really quite uncannily, the colour of her eyes. She had already made up her mind to buy it when the wretched furrier had produced another coat – a high-collared Russian sable – which had quite simply taken her breath away.

'What shall I do, Guy? Which one shall I buy? After all, I'm doing all this for you.'

Guy, detaching his mind from a complex calculation involving the land debt of Voralberg, gave the matter his consideration.

'Buy them both,' he said.

It was probably the most beautiful thing that anyone had ever said to Nerine, who went on to buy also a sauterne-dyed cape of Bukhara karakul and a jacket of Canadian lynx.

Arthur, meanwhile, had returned to England to escort Mama and Aunt Dorothy to Pfaffenstein for the wedding, but Nerine hardly noticed his departure for she had embarked on a new and profitable venture. Nowadays genteel ladies, mostly old and dressed in black, were often shown into her suite and after low, muffled conversations, departed without the sapphire heart pendant they had had on the day of their engagement, or the pearls their grandmothers had danced in at the Opera Ball. Sometimes she went further afield to visit shrouded villas in Hitzing or Heiligenstadt, returning with yards of priceless lace or small black boxes which she handed to the hotel manager to put in his safe.

After three weeks of chaperoning Nerine, Thisbe cracked.

'My work's piling up,' she said to Guy. 'I've got half a dozen reports to type. And I'm no good at this kind of thing, sir. Someone else who's interested in clothes ought to go along. She could take her maid. And I can't—'

But here the devoted Thisbe broke off, unable to criticize Nerine to the employer she adored. It was Morgan, threatening to resign if he was compelled to stand around outside any more fashion houses, who said bluntly, 'And to my mind it isn't right, sir, dunning those poor devils out of their possessions. A bargain's a bargain, but conning an old woman out of her pearls for the price of three hot dinners isn't right. No wonder they hate us for being British if we carry on like that.'

'Nerine, I must insist that you ask me for exactly what you need for your purchases,' said Guy that evening, as they drove in a fiacre down the Prater Hauptallee. 'We shouldn't take advantage of these people. Heaven knows, things are enough in our favour as it is. These old women don't know what things are worth.'

The satisfied languorous look that had been on Nerine's face ever since she came to shop, left her abruptly.

'Guy, if your servants intend to snoop and spy on me, I think you should dismiss them. I was only trying to save you money.'

'Well, don't, Nerine. I have enough money,' said Guy.

For a while they drove in silence between the magnificent chestnuts. Then, 'You mean you don't mind me actually buying the things?' said Nerine, peeping at him from under an enchanting cartwheel hat. 'That isn't what you mind?'

'No, why should I? But I'm here on behalf of the British government. We have to play fair and be seen to play fair. I'll open a personal account for you at my bank,' said Guy, almost absently.

Relief flooded Nerine. She could go on, spend more! Looking about her animatedly, she said, 'Look, Guy – I'm sure we've been here before, with Frau Edelnau. That old pavilion over there, don't you recognize it? It was some kind of feast day.'

'Yes, it was Easter Sunday and a most glorious day. I picked you a bunch of blue scillas and an old man came and shook his fist at me. Quite right, too. They weren't really wild, they were planted.'

Nerine was making a tremendous effort but the past did not quite yield itself, as yet, with the clarity she hoped for.

'What was I wearing?' she asked.

There was a moment of silence. Then, 'I don't remember,' said Guy.

'You mean Putzerl has refused you!' shrieked the Swan Princess. 'I don't believe it! I simply don't believe it! Why, I saw with my own eyes—'

But here the princess shut her beak with a snap, for much as she might despise her son she did not care to admit that she had watched his courtship through a telescope.

Aided by the discretion of the Littlest Heidi, and by Tessa's nocturnal departure from Pfaffenstein, Maxi had been able to postpone the announcement of his failure until his return to Spittau. Now, however, the day of reckoning had come. Standing on the causeway which alone connected Spittau to the land, the Swan Princess (though swathed almost from top to toe in mosquito netting) nevertheless managed to stare with an amazing amount of venom at her son. Around them the dogs frisked and splashed; frogs plopped incessantly in and out of the moat.

'I did my best, Mother. I said she could breed water spaniels,' said Maxi moodily, massaging the labrador's stomach with his foot.

'You know what this is,' said the Swan Princess. 'This is the end. Even if I sell my pearls it is the end.'

'She offered me some money. To repair the roof.'

'And?' enquired the Swan Princess sharply.

'I refused, of course,' said Maxi, flushing at the memory of this insult to his masculinity.

'Foolish, obstinate girl. I blame Tilda and Augustine. Letting her run wild in Vienna. All that rubbish about art and music.'

'I could marry someone else,' suggested Maxi, pulling a burr out of the wolfhound's ear.

Beneath the netting, his mother screwed up her ravaged countenance. 'Waaltraut might be acceptable as regards lineage, I suppose. But there's no money. And she is almost certainly too old to breed.'

'I thought maybe an American,' said Maxi, who had turned pale at the mention of the oil-stained countess. 'An heiress, of course.' he added hastily.

'Never!' declared the Swan Princess. 'Never a commoner. Never, never, *never*!' She stood looking out over the vast, grey, melancholy lake. 'We shall have to sell,' she pronounced in failing accents. 'After nine hundred years there will be no more Spittaus at Spittau.'

'If we were very careful, couldn't we manage . . .'

'Not without a roof,' snapped the princess. 'And I must say, Maxi, I think it was remiss of you not to accept Tessa's offer. With the roof mended we might have hung on, but as it is . . .'

Maxi looked bravely at the long, ochre, water-lapped pile: the last of the castles which his illustrious family still owned. So Spittau would go the same way as Hammerfelden with its four hundred rooms; the Pomeranian fortress on the River Oder; the palace in Vienna . . .

'Well, if I have the misfortune to have given birth to a milksop who cannot get a girl without beauty or distinction to marry him, I shall just have to suffer,' said the Swan Princess. 'Do it, then. Put Spittau up for sale.'

So Maxi wrote to the agents in Vienna, who sent down a man to take pictures, and Spittau was added to the many palaces and castles and pleasure domes whose fading photographs were displayed in the window of their office in the Schubertring. And that, for the time being, was that.

Witzler was back in his dog kennel at the Klostern Theatre, throwing into the waste-paper basket the usual pile of bills, threatening letters and abusive notices which constituted his morning mail.

He was, in fact, in rather more serious trouble than he cared to contemplate. On the strength of his commission from Guy, and certain hints he had put out as to the future of the company under the millionaire's protection, Witzler had borrowed extensively and the wolves were closing in on him. Not only that, but in October the lease of the theatre expired. The owners would undoubtedly increase the rent by a substantial amount and he had enemies who would be only too glad to deprive him of his theatre.

He crumpled up another bill and contemplated the

next three months. *Bohème, Traviata* and *Fledermaus*: one couldn't get more popular than that. He would have to try to keep open all through the summer, however poor the houses; he didn't dare risk a break now.

Sighing, he drew towards him for the fifth time that morning the score which Klasky had laid before him the day they had returned to Vienna. *Fricassée*, scored for fifteen mandolins, strings and thirty-seven percussion instruments was a modest work by contemporary standards. Klasky had not demanded typewriters in the orchestra, nor steam trains. Yet even so, this undoubted masterpiece would cost infinitely more to put on than Jacob could possibly raise.

He put his head in his hands, then reached for another dyspepsia pill. *Fricassée* was his responsibility, his dream-child. For seven long years, he had badgered Klasky to finish it and at Pfaffenstein, that Paradise for ever lost to them, the Hungarian had finally given birth. And what could he, Jacob, do? Nothing . . . *nothing*. He could not even afford the tubular steel scaffolding (expressing the rigidity of capitalist society) on which the action took place.

It was at this point that there was a shy and familiar knock on the door.

'Come in!' called Witzler, looking up eagerly.

Yes, it was Tessa! A feeling of relief flooded through him. There had been no sign of his under wardrobe mistress since their return to Vienna, and believing her to be preparing for her wedding Jacob had not been surprised, but her absence had added to the feeling of let-down and increased the apprehensions which had lately gnawed at him.

'May I speak to you?' said Tessa, entering the room. 'Have you got time?'

'Of course. Sit down.'

The Princess of Pfaffenstein, he noted, was dressed in an unaccustomed manner; in other words, conventionally and correctly in a brown skirt and crisp white blouse.

'It's about Herr Klasky's opera,' she said, pulling out a stool. 'Is it true . . . that there is not a great deal of money and that . . . Herr Farne is not going to engage the company again?'

'It is true,' said Witzler heavily.

'Well, I was wondering if you would let me help?' She parted her fringe, now badly in need of a trim, and looked out at him as though expecting a rebuff. 'To put on Herr Klasky's opera, I mean? I have some money now, you see. Not vast amounts because of my father's debts, but quite a bit. That's why I wasn't here last week; I was opening a bank account and sorting things out with my lawyers.'

'You wish to finance Klasky's opera?' repeated Jacob. The room reeled. Providence; an angel from heaven; the hand of God! Then his heart smote him. The child sat before him, defenceless, innocent and young. So had he once been – and prosperous into the bargain, able to walk past his bank manager with his head held high. The leather goods business had gone in the first three years – then the tannery he had inherited from his cousin – *that* went on a full cycle of Wagner's *Ring*. The life insurance had gone on a modern-dress *Turandot* – what a flop that had been! And when, for once, a production made some money, the profits were immediately swallowed up in the next one or the next.

'What does the prince feel about it?' he enquired. 'Would he be willing?'

'The prince?' said Tessa, bewildered.

'The Prince of Spittau. Your fiancé.'

'Good Lord, he's not my fiancé. I am not going to marry Maxi.'

'But everyone . . . it is generally assumed . . .' stammered Jacob.

He stared at Tessa. Her small hand was ringless, her expression, it had to be admitted, was not that of someone contemplating nuptial bliss.

Tessa sighed. 'Well, I'm not going to marry him. Or anyone else. I'm perfectly free to spend my money as I wish.'

Desperately, Jacob struggled for integrity – and lost.

He himself was ruined, yes; his wife slept on her pearls, one of his son's first words had been 'Bailiffs'. Yet he would do it all again, all of it. For *The Magic Flute* at Pfaffenstein, for the young Raisa's radiant, unearthly monologue in *Rosenkavalier* on the night that war was declared . . . So why deny Tessa the right to do as he had done?

'I am anxious,' Tessa now explained carefully, 'to involve myself. To be busy. I think people are best . . . when they don't have any free time at all.'

Jacob shot her a glance from under his bushy brows. But all he said was, 'I'm meeting Klasky tonight at the Griechenbeisl. You'd better come too and we'll talk things over.'

But the party that gathered on the pavement terrace of the famous restaurant needed four tables pushed together to accommodate it, for the news that Klasky's opera was to be financed by Witzler's under wardrobe mistress had spread like wildfire through the theatre and out into the musical circles of Vienna. Raisa was there with her new lover, a pallid young man with a brown coal mine in the Herzgebiet, as were Pino, the man who had produced *Pelleas* and the critic Mendelov. The Rhinemaiden was there and Bubi, enveloped in a gigantic table napkin and consuming a mound of kartoffel puffer, also a young journalist from the *Wiener Presse* who planned to write a piece on The Patroness Princess . . .

And Klasky, burning-eyed, palpitating with gratitude, and presently rising to make a speech. The Viennese, said Klasky, could forgive anything but greatness. 'Not three streets from here,' said the Hungarian, waving his arm, 'Mozart starved, Beethoven was humiliated and Hugo Wolf went mad. This, too, would have been my own fate as a genius,' he continued modestly, 'were it not for the heaven sent appearance of this young girl in whose slender body there burns the heart of a Razumovsky, an Esterhazy, a Frederick the Great.'

Much applause greeted him, including that from some of the passers-by who now decided to join the party. Tessa was unable to rise because Bubi, overcome by potato croquettes and the lateness of the hour, had climbed into her lap and fallen asleep, but she replied in kind, adding that she had seen herself more in the role of Madame von Meck, the lady who had supported Tchaikovsky for many years, but at a distance and without interfering in any way. At which the more musically informed people present exchanged glances of slight unease. Madame von Meck, Tchaikovsky's patroness, had been an ample, fierce-eyed, queenly widow, much sustained financially by a quantity of railway lines, paper mills and other business interests. Tessa, who had added a blue kerchief from *The Gypsy Baron* to her white blouse, did not really look like Madame von Meck.

But Tessa herself was delighted with the evening. This was *La Vie Bohème* as she had always dreamed of it. She had not thought of Guy for at least a quarter of an hour . . . well, ten minutes. And at the end of the evening she had the honour of signing, with a flourish, the bill for five kasenockerl mit sauerkraut, three plates of kartoffel puffer, four helpings of risibisi, six bottles of gumpoldskirchener, and a bottle of Vichy water which the waiter, appraised of her new status, placed before her.

It was an honour with which she was to become increasingly familiar.

Rehearsals for the new opera began immediately, despite the fact that they were playing their full repertory each night. Enthusiasm ran high for what was undoubtedly a work of genius but, as always, there were those who scoffed. Notably Frau Pollack, asking testily, 'What *is* a fricassée, anyway?'

'It's a sort of stew . . . meat chopped up very small in a white sauce,' said Tessa, cutting the legs off a boiler suit intended for the Littlest Heidi. Though promoted to the role of patroness, she continued to work exactly as before. 'It's sort of symbolic, too, because it's about the disintegration of capitalist society.'

'I don't fancy all this chopping up babies and eating them,' said Boris, shaking The Mother who had not cared for the return to Vienna and was going through a Blue Period.

'But the baby doesn't really get chopped up,' explained Tessa. 'The porter means to kill it but then the chief engine-greaser – that's the one who's a kind of Holy Fool – has this fit and one of the cleaning ladies saves it. The mill-owner thinks he's eaten it, which is why he jumps out of the window, but he hasn't.'

'Thinking's bad enough,' said Frau Pollack darkly, remembering the episode of her great-uncle Sandor's ashes, and continued to refer to the opera gloomily as 'Stew'.

Any doubts that Raisa might have had about tackling an atonal role were set aside by Jacob, who said that if she did not feel up to the part of the railway porter's wife, he was sure that the young soprano who had done so well as Papagena would be willing to try. As for Pino, nothing on earth would have induced him to relinquish a role in which he was on stage, alone, for

261

fifteen minutes, going mad to the sound of thirty-seven percussion instruments.

Nevertheless, there were difficulties. The Oldest Heidi fell off the tubular steel scaffolding, turning her ankle, and when her protector (an influential geheimrat) threatened to sue Jacob, the entire set was scrapped. Klasky proved extremely cooperative about the débâcle and said he was perfectly prepared to have a more realistic set, provided it was designed by Rayner-Meierhof and no one else. The famous constructivist was summoned from Düsseldorf and built a set on five different levels, using significant skeletal structures which could become railway platforms, signal boxes, decadent mill-owner's apartments or lunatic asylums, always supposing they did not jam the turntable or get stuck in the lifts.

Through the whole of July and August, while houses fell disasterously in the summer heat and there were ten empty rows even for *Fledermaus*, work on *Fricassée* continued at fever pitch. And the pivot, the centre of this turning world, was an object which took on an increasing and almost mystical significance to the members of Witzler's company: Tessa's cheque book.

It lived, tattered, paint-spattered and lightly smeared with chocolate (for Bubi regarded it as especially his own) in the pocket of her smock. Often mislaid, for she was liable to pencil measurements on its covers, it was rushed back to her, much as an unweaned baby kangaroo might be hurried back to the maternal pouch. And several times a week, Tessa would repair upstairs to be settled solemnly at a table in Jacob's office and sign cheques.

She signed a cheque for the steel scaffolding and for the wages of the men who subsequently took it away for scrap. She signed a cheque for nine hundred yards of denim, for twenty singers engaged to augment the plate-layers' chorus, for a gigantic kettle-drum (two outsize Tyrolean cows having given their lives for the cause). She signed a cheque for Rayner-Meierhof's awe-inspiring fee and for the bonus he had demanded for kindly casting his eye over the old sets for *Traviata* and pronouncing them disgusting. Sometimes, too, she was allowed to help a little with other productions, signing a cheque for Raisa's claque – who had reorganized along trade union lines – and for new costumes for the ball scene in *Fledermaus* in the hope (unrealized) that these would improve attendances.

And as each cheque book was reduced to a battered collection of stubs, Tessa, her head held high, went out to the bank to fetch another and another and another.

That something ailed their patroness and under wardrobe mistress was first put to the company by Boris and listened to with attention, for he was regarded as something of an expert on the Princess of Pfaffenstein.

'I tell you, there's something the matter with her,' he said. Tessa had gone out to negotiate for three dozen luggage trolleys from Austrian Railways and some of the company were in the fitting-rooms, kitting out the principals.

'Yes, I think you are right,' said Pino, pulling a pair

of dungarees over his portly stomach. 'During *Fricassée* rehearsals she is all right, but last night when she was in the wings waiting to blow out Mimi's candle she looked like my grandmother has looked when they have told her that my grandfather was buried in the earthquake.'

Raisa nodded. 'And in *Traviata*, in Act Two, when I am up-giffing Alfredo, and she waits to make *ze* noise for *ze* 'orses – she 'as been crying zen, I tink.'

'And in "Addio del passato",' put in the tenor, his head vanishing under a peaked porter's cap, 'where you are dying and think you will see me no more; I am waiting to go on then and though you are a quarter-tone flat, she has looked terrible.'

Witzler and Klasky, who had come to supervise the fittings, frowned.

'She's as thin as a cat, too,' said Boris. 'I tell you, she'll crack up if we aren't careful.'

'Is she ill, do you think?' Jacob demanded.

'No!' Raisa's eyes flashed. 'It is badder zan zat, my friends. She is in *lof*!'

There was a stunned silence. Then, as her listeners pieced together their own vignettes of Tessa since the company's return from Pfaffenstein, Klasky's black, dishevelled head, Jacob's bald one and Boris's yellow skull nodded agreement.

'Mein Gott!' Jacob was shaken. Having failed to marry the nice Jewish girl selected by his mother, Jacob, though riddled with guilt, had found plenty of rewards with his Rhinemaiden. But this was something else.

'We must protect her,' said Boris. Years and years

ago, when he was a small boy in Sofia, he had fallen over and grazed his knee. A small blonde girl in white knee socks had come up to him and said 'Does it hurt?' looking at him with wide, sad eyes. It had been a devastating experience, quite shattering, and in no way connected with the life he now shared with a typist in a flat in Ottakring.

Klasky's exopthalmic eyes bulged even more violently than usual. That his patroness should be taken in this way was deplorable. Screwing up his Magyar countenance, he remembered suddenly a girl with chestnut pigtails who had sat next to him at the Academy of Music in Budapest. Klasky had been precocious and attended the harmony class while still in shorts. The impact of the fronded end of Ildi's pigtail on his bare thigh had been quite terrible, and he had suffered agonies of love for a whole year. Nothing so painful had ever happened to him again.

'I vill make zo zat lazy porkling, Zia, bring to me my wrapping robe,' said Raisa, referring to her lethargic dresser. 'Zen Tessa must not 'ear me zink "Adio del passato" – in vich I am *never* flat!'

'I'll keep her down in the laundry room in Act One of *Bohème*,' said Frau Pollack. 'One of the stage-hands can blow out Mimi's candle.'

But even as they prepared to protect Tessa from the pangs of music, the question that Klasky now asked was in all their minds.

'But with *whom* is she in love? It can't be the Prince

of Spittau. Everyone knows he spent the whole time trying to propose to her.'

The deepest of gloom had spread over Jacob's face. He was remembering the matter of Anita's . . . his own idea of putting Tessa in a ballet.

'I think I know,' he said ponderously. 'But if I'm right, it's a bad business. A very bad business indeed.'

And he told them . . .

15

On a particularly hot and stuffy day towards the end of July, Guy, leaving the Treasury early for once and strolling down the Schubertring, was halted by the sight of a large photograph in a house agent's window.

He passed this way frequently and was familiar with the picture of Malk, towering dramatically over the Danube and bearing, underneath, a wholly imaginary account of its amenities prepared by Countess Waaltraut's mother. He had noticed the yellowing portrait of the Archduchess Frederica's leaning palace at Potzerhofen, and registered that no purchaser had yet been found for Schloss Landsberg, near Graz, which was as well since the Archduke Sava was holed up in its coach-house with his bear.

But the castle which now had pride of place in the agent's window was new to him: a long, low, stuccoed edifice, apparently afloat on a reedy lake, one of its towers obscured by a large and moulting swan.

he read, and cast his eyes down the notice informing him of the salubrious situation, historical associations and excellent facilities for water sports which awaited the fortunate purchaser.

Guy stared at the window, frowning. What the devil? Surely it was to save his decaying Wasserburg that the prince had become engaged to Tessa?

He had begun to turn away, still puzzling, when a figure shot out of the agent's door and bounced up to him.

'Thought it was you!' said the Prince of Spittau with satisfaction. 'Saw you from the inside.'

Nothing had been able to erase from Maxi's mind the conviction that Guy was deeply devoted to him. Beaming, pumping the Englishman's hand, he said, 'Have to come up to Vienna a lot these days on business. Pretty hopeless, though.' He turned to survey the portrait of his ancestral home. 'It's been up for sale for a fortnight and they haven't even had a nibble.'

Guy commiserated but said, 'Why on earth are you selling? I thought Tessa was bringing you enough to do it up. Doesn't she care for the place?'

'Oh, she cares for it all right. Tessa's very fond of Spittau, always was. Likes the frogs and all those things. Fond of the people, too. And the dogs, of course. She offered me some money to do the roof, but of course I couldn't take it. If she'd been going to marry

268

me it would have been different, but a man's got his pride.'

Guy stared at him. 'What on earth do you mean? Surely you and Tessa *are* engaged to be married?'

'No, we aren't.'

'But everybody—'

'Everybody,' said Maxi, with unaccustomed asperity, 'seems to have been watching out of some telescope or other and saw Tessa give me a kiss. But it was just her way of saying she was sorry. I'm absolutely sick of people coming up and congratulating me.'

'Yes, I can see that.' An image of Tessa leaning against the lorry, white and silent, while he upbraided her, rose up before him. He dismissed it and said, 'What's she doing, then?'

'Well, that's just it. She's financing that blasted Hungarian, and if I'd known—'

'You mean she's living with Klasky?' said Guy, and at his voice Maxi looked up, his forehead wrinkled. What was the matter with the chap? He was supposed to be so cool and clever.

The prince shook his head. 'She's back with Witzler's company and she's supporting this opera about . . .' But at the thought of what *Fricassée* was about, he gave up. 'You've never heard such stuff. Railway porters and engine-greasers with fits, and music like a lot of cats with a throat disease. Got poor Little Heidi in a boiler suit—' But here the prince broke off, for as a matter of fact Heidi in dungarees with a spanner had looked quite peculiarly ravishing. 'And Tessa's

269

paying for it all. Does nothing but sign cheques all day long and looks as peaked as a starved rat, and if you tell her she's a fool, she just bites off your head and says it's a privilege to serve art and people like us ought to do it.'

'Oh, my God!' said Guy.

'That's exactly it,' agreed Maxi. 'My uncle ruined himself with a ballet company, and opera's a damn sight worse. They say Witzler's in all sorts of trouble. Borrowed like mad because he thought you were going to set him up at Pfaffenstein and now they're closing in on him. Shouldn't be surprised if they don't all end up in jail, and Tessa along with them, and what Mother will say then . . .'

Guy was standing perfectly still, staring down at the contours of the paving stones.

'Fortunately, she's left half her money in trust for her aunts,' Maxi continued, 'so she'll get that when they die. But if I'd known what she was going to do, I'll be damned if I wouldn't have let her repair the roof. At least she would have had somewhere to come to if she was in trouble.'

Guy lifted his head. 'Would you still marry her, even now? Even if she loses all her share of the money?'

Maxi flushed. 'Certainly I would. I'd marry Putzerl any time. I'm dashed fond of her. If you've got Putzerl in a boat you don't need a—'

But Guy, unequal to hearing about Putzerl's ability to imitate a call duck, now interrupted him to say, 'You owned a number of other properties, didn't you?

270

Places that were confiscated by the Allies. Where were they?'

'Well, there was one at Hammerfelden, that's near Kiel; and there was Pstattin, on the Oder, in Pomerania. The palace here in the Himmelgasse was sold by my father before the war, unfortunately.'

Guy shook his head. 'We won't get any change out of Berlin. Wasn't there anything in the Affiliated Zones? Alsace-Lorraine? Trieste? Somewhere outside the direct military areas?'

'There was a chateau in Alsace,' Maxi admitted. The Chateau d'Arboras. Quite a small place – not more than eighty rooms, I'd say, but the land was good. About twenty thousand hectares, mostly vineyards. We used to make a very decent sort of wine.'

'And you've never claimed compensation from the Land Redistribution Trust in Strasbourg?'

Maxi shook his head. 'I asked our lawyers if anything could be done, but they said it was hopeless.'

'Who are they?'

'Schweinhofer and Brillerman, in the Kohlmarkt. They're a very old firm.'

'Old, idle and useless,' said Guy tersely. He had taken out his notebook and begun to write. 'You've got a chance, I'd say quite a good one. You'll have to plead loss of livelihood but the vineyards will come in handy there. Take this to Hermann Rattinger at Number 12, Borseplatz, and tell him to look particularly at paragraph 8 in section 15. Don't let anyone except Rattinger touch it.' He looked up and saw Maxi's face contorted by the effort of taking in so much information. 'I'll give him a ring myself, tomorrow. You won't get much, but if you can do the necessary repairs you ought to get by and when your mother dies I dare say you'll find something to do with the place – run it as a hotel or something. None of us can look too far ahead with the hens' breakfast they've made of the Peace Treaty.'

He tore the leaf out of his notebook, handed it to Maxi and ruthlessly cutting down the prince's fulsome expressions of gratitude, strode away down the Ring.

Maxi, left behind on the pavement, was a happy man. The possibility of a little bit of cash, coupled with Guy's casual assumption that the Swan Princess would not live for ever, produced a feeling of light-headedness in the prince. First thing tomorrow, he would present himself at the address that Guy had written down for him. Now, however, he strolled at a leisurely pace to a quiet street near the Danube canal, where presently he knocked at the door of a modest Biedemayer house and was taken through into a courtyard and up some wooden steps to a little apartment which, in the past few weeks, had become home to him.

And there, among the plump cushions and teddy-bears and ornamental feathers in shell-encrusted jars which Heidi Schlumberger had lovingly collected, lulled by the hooting of the tugboats which came to them through the closed green shutters, the prince and his

little dancer gave way to their unquenchable compati-
bility.

The heat of August defeated even Nerine's passion for
shopping. She returned to Pfaffenstein and Guy, though
he kept his suite at Sachers, came with her.

They found the West Tower empty except for Tessa's
old nurse, for the Duchess and the Margravine, leaving
a letter of gratitude for Guy, had moved to Vienna to
make a home for their niece. Nerine was delighted at
their departure and Guy, though he missed the old
ladies, shared her relief, for he wanted Tessa back at
Pfaffenstein no more than his fiancée did.

He was, in any case, still fiendishly busy. Though the
Austrian Parliament was in recess, officials continued to
come from the Treasury, some remaining as house
guests, and there were long sessions in the library
preparing the final drafts of the immensely complicated
documents they would present in Geneva. When Guy
did emerge from the interminable, stuffy meetings, he
took exercise, a point on which Morgan happened to
comment when he met David Tremayne returning from
the squash court before dinner.

'Been playin' 'im again, 'ave you?' Morgan enquired,
anointing the Hispano-Suiza with a polish he mixed to
a secret recipe of his own.

David nodded. 'Got thoroughly beaten, of course.
He's doing a work-out in the gym now.'

Morgan, still polishing, nodded. 'Taking a lot of

exercise, is Mr Farne. Yes, a lot of exercise. Mind you, he's a man who's always kept himself fit.'

'But not as fit as this?' prompted David. Morgan had been Guy's batman in the war and knew him as well as any man.

'Oh, I dunno. 'e 'as patches. I remember after Passchendaele . . . Young Whittaker got 'is chips then and Mr Farne thought 'e should 'ave got 'im out. Well, 'e did; 'e went over the line and brought 'im back but there wasn't much to *bring* back. We went on leave after that and Mr Farne took a lot of exercise then. Squash, tennis, work with the dumb-bells oh, yes, he was very fit that summer. And, of course, when we went up to Newcastle because Mrs Hodge was in 'ospital. Peritonitis, it was, and they got to 'er late because she was looking after a neighbour's little girl and didn't like to say she felt poorly. Touch and go it was, for a week, and Mr Farne got 'imself very fit then. Oh, yes. Five 'undred lengths in the swimming baths and beat 'is old fencing master with the sabres. And went up those bloomin' Cheviots like a bat in hell – covered in snow they were, too. It's nothing unusual for Mr Farne to take a lot of exercise.'

Silence fell.

'It will be this loan,' said David. 'It must be a great anxiety to him.'

'That's what it must be,' agreed Morgan. 'Though 'e didn't seem to notice much that time he took on the Argentinians over the Olinda oil deal. Or the time he grabbed the Uruguay zinc right off Kripper . . .'

If Guy had hoped that Nerine would now begin to get to know her parishioners, his hopes remained unfulfilled. She had heard of a case of measles in the village which made it quite impossible. 'Mama always kept me away from infection, you see,' she explained to Guy, 'so I have absolutely no immunity.'

But though Guy was so preoccupied, Nerine was far from bored. Owing to the tardiness of the League, Austria's case was not coming up until October. The wedding, therefore, was now scheduled for mid-November, but Nerine made no complaint at the delay. She had put her wedding dress out to tender among three of Vienna's leading couturiers and was busy examining the samples of brocade and fashion sketches which came by every post. Meanwhile, she had discovered a new and absorbing activity: she sunbathed.

It was a step not undertaken lightly, for her white skin had always been one of her greatest assets. But while she had kept entirely aloof from the opera company, and would have been hard put to recognize a single one of its members, she had observed the excitement with which the Archduke and Monteforelli discussed the sunbathing soprano. If her eyes had not been so blue, she would have hesitated, but a bronze tan against the azure of her eyes . . .

So, now, Pooley was sent to find a secluded embrasure on the battlements. Mattresses were conveyed thither, an alarm clock, towels and bottles of ointment. And carefully, increasing the dosage each day, scrupulously turning herself so that nothing got overdone or underdone, Nerine gave herself to the sun.

The results, she could not help feeling, were spectacular. Wandering through the great rooms of the south facade, she saw reflected in the glass-fronted display cabinets, the suits of armour and the silver trays, a golden glowing nymph.

This happy and innocent existence was blighted in a few agonizing moments when one bright morning in early September, she opened the letter from her brother, Arthur, which was propped on her breakfast tray.

Arthur had gone home, not only to escort his relatives back to Pfaffenstein, but also to collect the documents required for Nerine's remarriage. It was while in pursuit of these, in Whitehall, that he had met an old friend, now in the diplomatic corps, who had told him that Guy Farne had been offered a knighthood – and had turned it down! 'Apparently he just got that Tremayne fellow to say, no thank you, by return of post! It's hard to believe, but the chap swore it was true. Mama has taken the news hard, as you can imagine . . .'

Never had Nerine dressed so quickly. A scant quarter of an hour later, she entered the library. 'Guy, I must speak to you. I have just had an extraordinary letter from Arthur. He swore that you had been offered a knighthood and had turned it down!'

'Yes, that's correct,' said Guy, putting down the papers he had been studying. 'A knighthood often goes with this kind of diplomatic stuff. It's almost routine.'

'But . . . you mean, it's really true? You could have

been Sir Guy . . . I could have been Lady Farne – and you refused!

'That's right,' said Guy cheerfully.

Fury enveloped Nerine. 'But you had no right! You had no right to do it without consulting me. I'm going to be your wife. You've deprived me of status, of a decent position. Why didn't you ask me what I wanted?'

'Because I wouldn't have been influenced, in this case, by your wishes. I bought Pfaffenstein for you, I have entertained and befriended a large number of titled people to whom, candidly, I wouldn't give the time of day, because I felt – and I do feel – that it is your right to be accepted by society. But I myself will go out of the world as I came into it. The name the Matron chose for me all those years ago is the name I will bear until I die.'

'But why, *why*?'

Guy shrugged. 'Call it pride, if you like. We foundlings are a funny lot. Yes, I suppose it's a kind of pride. I've always made my own name, lived without handles. Even Martha couldn't have made me change my mind. Not that she would have tried.'

'Even Martha! You mean that . . . that washerwoman would have had more influence on you than I?'

Guy's face had tautened, but almost at once he relaxed again and said quietly, 'No, Nerine. Just that Martha is unsophisticated – to her these things mean a great deal. Whereas you yourself must know how little all this means in the end.'

'Well, I *don't* know. You realize I could have had Lord Frith with a title that goes back to Domesday. You might have made it up to me.' She felt the beginning of tears and, with a great effort, suppressed them. Tears had worked well at seventeen, but of late she found that they made her blotchy. 'I suppose you're a republican like that ridiculous princess of yours,' she sneered.

Guy looked at her. 'Nerine, if you are not satisfied we can break our engagement. If you're unhappy, you have only to say so and I will release you instantly and without reproach. But I will not accept a knighthood. Not now. Not ever. Do you still want to marry me?'

Nerine glanced down at the enormous diamond winking on her finger, then at the towers of Pfaffenstein rearing outside the window, and the undeniably attractive man now holding her gaze.

'Of course I want to marry you, Guy,' she said, coming to kneel beside him. 'Of *course*!'

Meanwhile, in the Klostern Theatre, rehearsals for *Fricassée* continued to be dogged by disaster. The constructivist railway platform collapsed, precipitating five engine-greasers on to the stage below and the shock, with its memories of her own catastrophe, brought on palpitations in the Rhinemaiden, who had to be conveyed to the Rudlphino Clinic in an ambulance. The outsize Tyrolean cows turned out to have died in vain because Klasky, dissatisfied with the percussive balance, scrapped the drum and replaced it with twelve smaller ones. Herr Berger, who sang the capitalist mill-owner,

278

developed nodules on his larynx; Frau Pollack broke a toe.

Tessa's cheque book, under the onslaught, gave of its best. She signed a cheque for the reinforced railway platform, for the Rhinemaiden's hospital fees, for the replacement drums. She signed a cheque for a new safety curtain (the fire people having finally caught up with Jacob), for repairs to the revolve damaged by Rayner-Meierhof's unsentimentalized signal box, for a practical moon . . .

And as she crept home in the small hours to count up her mutilated cheque stubs, Tessa now faced a new hazard. For she had left her attic in the Wipplinger-strasse and waiting up for her, concerned and interested, were the aunts.

The Duchess and the Margravine had rented (from a distant and indigenous relation) a flat on the fourth floor of an apartment block overlooking the Central Cemetery. It was small, dark and inconvenient and the old ladies spent their days in an agony of homesickness for Pfaffenstein which they endeavoured to conceal, not only from Tessa, but from each other. Neither of them had ever shopped unattended, or travelled on a tram, or dealt directly with tradesmen. Now, they stood in queues at the butcher, pulled Quin-Quin in and out of the terri-fying lift that led up to their floor – and economized.

The economies were ferocious and secret, for their great-niece must have no inkling of what was afoot. The aunts had been unable to prevent Tessa from put-ting half her money in trust for them, but they were determined that every groschen they could save should be added to the sum that would revert to her after their deaths. So while Tessa was at the theatre they ate virtually nothing, sent away the maid the hausmeisterin had found for them, and sat by the light of a single lamp. Then, when Tessa's step was heard outside, lamps were lit, soup and topfenkuchen were fetched from the larder and Tessa learned that they had spent another most interesting and happy day.

'And you, Putzerl? How did you get on?'

'Oh, fine. Very well. I painted this bed shaped like a mouth . . .'

'Like a mouth?' enquired Tante Tilda.

Tessa nodded. 'To represent decadence. It's for the mill-owner's apartment.' She had picked up a letter which might well have been in Guy's handwriting, had she known what his handwriting was like, but was actually from a choreographer who wanted her to finance his ballet. 'Aren't you eating anything?' she said, looking concernedly at her aunts. 'This soup is so good!'

'You know we never eat at night, dear,' said Tante Augustine repressively, and continued to ply her niece with food until Tessa went to her room – there to lie awake and reflect that Madame von Meck must have had very strong nerves or just a great many paper mills.

For it wasn't only *Fricassée*, but everything, that was going wrong. Schalk, Jacob's arch-enemy at the State Opera, cancelled a production that was doing badly and put on *Bohème* instead. With Jeritza singing Mimi,

Raisa did not stand a chance. Jacob rushed out *The Barber*, but the production was old and tired and failed to draw the crowds. There were alarming rumours, too, about the lease of the theatre . . .

'It's as though there's a jinx on us since we left Pfaffenstein,' said Boris.

But even he was shaken when Jacob appeared, after a matinée of *Fledermaus*, and asked to be fitted with a blond toupee and a moustache so as to elude the creditors who waited for him outside.

'Very Aryan,' he said, with satisfaction, when Boris had finished.

Then one day in the middle of September, when Tessa walked into her bank as usual for another cheque book, she was told by a respectful (not to say obsequious) young cashier that the manager would be most grateful if Her Highness could spare him a few moments.

The homily now delivered by the portly Herr Simmelmann was unctuous in tone and seemingly interminable. Her Highness's initial deposit was now fully withdrawn and while he was aware that Her Highness still had other resources and would not, in fact, default on her commitment to the bank, he had to point out that at the present rate she would find herself in serious difficulties in a relatively short period of time. There was the further matter of Her Highness not being technically of age according to Austrian law, which meant that if it was felt that she was in unsuitable company and being victimized, her business advisors – of whom he was happy to call himself one – might feel it necessary (entirely in her own interest of course) to take certain steps . . .

Tessa thanked him, transferred another block of securities and said nothing to Jacob. Thus her ancestress, Hildegarde of Breganzer, who had leapt naked into the flames rather than renounce her faith. Thus Tessa now . . .

16

At No. 12, King Street, Byker, Newcastle upon Tyne, Martha Hodge was having a farewell party. Living beside the shipyard as they did, Martha's friends and neighbours (and she was a woman whose neighbours were all her friends) were not parochial. The hooting of ships down the Tyne was as familiar to them as breathing and many of them had men at sea.

Still, Martha was going to Vienna, and then further still, and she was going to the wedding of her foster-son whom they all remembered rampaging round the streets like a fiend incarnate, and who had turned out so well; so the beer was flowing freely and they had got to 'Cushy Butterfield' and 'Keep Your Feet Still, Geordie Hinny' well before ten o'clock.

Martha, busy by the range warming sausage rolls and cutting more sandwiches, was in two minds about going. She did not like the look of old Mrs Hookey at No. 3; there had been a blue look round her mouth that morning and if she died while Martha was in Austria,

Martha would never forgive herself. And she felt bad about the Ridley twins: she had offered to mind them while Daisy went to her mam in Middlesborough and that would now have to wait. There was the cat, too: a stray which lived wild on the dump behind the shipyard. Martha had kept her in scraps while she nursed her kittens and though Minnie in the corner shop had promised to see to her, Martha could not help worrying a bit.

But Guy had said he would not be married without her, and he wanted her to come for a bit of a visit so as to get to know Nerine, so that was that. She would have gone to the North Pole to see Guy wed, and probably it would not be too bad even if it *was* a castle. People, Martha had found, were people, wherever you went.

'But why won't you leave here, Martha?' Guy had said when he first began to make all that money. 'Why won't you let me buy you a nice bungalow? Nothing pretentious, just a bit of garden and a bright kitchen. You wouldn't have to go far away.'

'I like it here,' was all Martha had found to say. 'I just like it.'

And that was how it was. Others might grumble about the smell of the glue factory, but not Martha. Others might fret at the view of a sooty wall surmounted by barbed wire, but Martha looked above it to the tracery of the tall cranes and the red hulls of the new ships. Martha liked the children playing hopscotch on the cobbles, she liked the lean dogs. She liked Betty at

No. 5 who never stopped talking and she liked Gladys next door who never talked at all.

'And I like to be by the river,' she had said to Guy, looking lovingly at the garbage, the rotting sheds and the mud of the Tyne.

But there was another reason. It was to this house that Jim had brought her when they were married. If his spirit wandered, it would come here to this place where he had found work and comradeship and laughter, and he should not find her gone.

So it was hard to leave, even for a few weeks, but as she moved about in her quiet, comfortable way, serving sandwiches and cake, topping up drinks, she was filled with happiness. For Guy was going to be married; he had found the girl he loved in Vienna. Everything had come right for this foster-son whom she loved more than life itself.

The following morning she dressed very carefully, for she must not disgrace Guy. A plain two-piece she had bought in Newcastle, a neat cloche hat and the fox fur Guy had given her fastened with a diamond brooch because she knew she was a bit of a disappointment to him over his presents.

'Not that they'd take me for a lady,' she said to the neighbours who assembled to watch her get into the taxi. 'I've only got to open me mouth.'

But when the train had steamed out over the Tyne bridge, and Martha had settled herself comfortably in the corner of her first-class compartment, she pulled out the locket she wore round her neck to gaze yet again at the photograph of Guy. How handsome he was, how happy he looked! Nerine must have been with him when he had his picture taken.

Martha would have been determined, in any case, to love the girl that Guy had chosen, but there would be no need for determination. That she had suggested this most wonderful of presents already made her Martha's friend.

'That's the first thing I'll do when I see her,' said Martha to herself, closing the locket. 'Thank her for making Guy give me this.'

She had staunchly refused to be escorted on her journey, only permitting Guy to send one of his employees to take her across London and put her on the boat-train. And thirty hours later, having learned the life history of the lady in the next sleeper and received a proposal of marriage from an inebriated Swiss banker she had helped out of the dining-car, she arrived in Vienna.

The time of her arrival happened to coincide with an all-important meeting between the Chancellor of the Exchequer, the Foreign Minister and an envoy from Geneva – all of whom were informed by a polite but clearly immovable Herr Farne that at that particular hour he would be at the Westbanhof fetching his foster-mother.

The meeting was changed and Martha now saw him come towards her, his keen eyes picking her out at once. He was looking tanned and fit and wonderfully elegant in a new dark suit.

'Martha!' He was hugging her, half-lifting her, substantial as she was, off her feet.

Guy was not a person who did things by halves. It was a full three minutes before she could put enough distance between herself and her foster-son to look properly at his face.

'Oh, Lord!' thought Martha, gripped by sudden panic. 'Now, what's all this?'

She had seen the colour of his eyes.

The first glimpse of Pfaffenstein, which had so amused Guy and so awed Nerine, quite simply appalled Martha Hodge. The conviction that Guy had taken leave of his senses was the main thought in her mind as she was driven round the zigzag road up the crag, across the drawbridge and into the main courtyard in which one could have comfortably housed a battalion of the Tyneside Fusiliers.

Her misgivings continued as she was marched through the state rooms and up the grand staircase. All those statues and some of them not even decent; all those carved chests collecting the dust! But when they went through an old oak door and into the West Tower, she looked about with more pleasure, liking the plain, whitewashed walls and scrubbed stone steps, and when Guy opened the door to a round room seemingly afloat in the sky, her face lit up and she said, 'Ee, love, now that's a real, nice room.'

'I thought you'd like it. It used to belong to the Princess of Pfaffenstein. She preferred it to the grander rooms in the main facade and I thought you'd feel the same.'

But Martha, as she moved admiringly among the room's simple furnishings, was suddenly alert. She knew every intonation of Guy's voice, knew through her very skin what he was feeling. He had never been a child who lied, preferring to fight his way out of disaster, but there was a flat 'keep out' note in his voice when he was suppressing something.

'One of the castle servants is still next door, an old nurse, so you won't be alone. She'll get you anything you want.'

'Funny, you'd think this was just a lass's room,' said Martha casually. 'But she'll be quite old, I suppose? The princess, I mean.'

'Twenty last birthday,' said Guy. 'Now, I'll send one of the maids up to you. Nerine's still in her bath or she would have come herself.'

Martha gave him a look. 'You'll do no such thing, Guy Farne. I'll wash me own face, thank you, and I'll find me own way down.'

Nerine was waiting in the blue salon to greet Guy's foster-mother. It was a room she had made particularly her own. She loved the rich peacock-blue of the walls hung with Gobelin tapestries, the sumptuous embroidered sofas, the deep pile of the Aubusson carpet with its pattern of birds of Paradise. And she loved the mirrors: eighteen of them, arranged in reassuring symmetry down both sides of the room.

Though she was welcoming a woman only of the working-class, Nerine had taken no less trouble than usual with her appearance. Already dressed for dinner, she wore a softly flowing dress of moss green lace, Guy's diamonds were at her throat and Martha, walking across the Aubusson towards her, had literally to stop and catch her breath.

No wonder, thought Martha; no wonder Guy had gone off his head when he lost her! No wonder he had waited ten years until he met up with her again!

'Welcome to Pfaffenstein, Mrs Hodge,' said Nerine. 'I trust your journey was not too exhausting?'

She spoke clearly, articulating her words with care to make sure that the homely woman with the sandy hair understood what she said, and extended her hand. Martha, who had meant to kiss her, shook it.

'Why, no, lass,' she said comfortably, 'the journey was nowt. And I'd a done it on me 'ands and knees to see Guy wed.'

Nerine replied suitably, but her eyes were anxious. The woman's appearance was less dreadful than Nerine had expected. She was quietly dressed and her manner was neither obsequious nor impertinent. But the accent! A Scottish accent – especially a Highland one – could be passed off; an Irish one, too. But this . . . Here in Austria it might not matter much, but after all Pfaffenstein was a temporary measure. In the end, Guy must buy her a suitable place in England and if he then insisted on having Mrs Hodge around . . . And in less than a fortnight, her relatives were arriving. What would Mama think if she had to sit next to a woman whose speech made their lowest servants sound educated? And more important even than Mama, Aunt Dorothy!

But there was nothing to be done at the moment, with Guy standing there smiling that slightly mocking smile of his and watching her. They went in to dinner and she made no demur when Martha was seated at Guy's left hand, nor was she surprised when young David Tremayne (though he had been at Eton) began at once to make a great fuss of the woman. Young Tremayne would do anything to get on the right side of Guy.

It was after dinner, when they were drinking coffee beside the great porcelain stove in the blue salon, that Martha found the opportunity she had been looking for.

'I've had it in my mind ever since Guy wrote,' she said, 'to thank you for making 'im send me this. It's the best present I ever 'ad in the whole of me life,' said Martha, pulling out the locket. She undid the chain and pressed the catch, to reveal Guy's photograph. 'It's good of him, isn't it? Real canny.'

Nerine glanced incuriously at the portrait. 'Yes,' she agreed. 'But I didn't make him give you this. I should have thought he could have got you something more valuable, actually,' she said, dismissing the delicate filigree setting.

Martha said no more. But as she closed the locket, she was frowning. If not Nerine, then who? Had it not been a girl who had 'advised' him? Was she, perhaps, making the whole thing up?

No, thought Martha. It was a girl, all right. But what girl? And where?

During the days that followed, Martha's disquiet increased. Guy spoke to his fiancée with perfect courtesy, but it seemed to her that he took considerable trouble not to be with her alone, and to welcome every opportunity that took him back to his papers in the library. Since Nerine, without actually drawing her skirt aside when Martha passed, continued to address her as if she were a deaf mute, Martha could find little to enjoy in the magnificent drawing-rooms of the castle.

But soon she found a world in which she was wholly at home. On the third day, she penetrated the kitchens and subsequently the bakery, the dairy and the farm. Here she could do nothing but marvel and approve. The people who worked there were skilled, frugal and friendly. They knew their job and the foster-mother of the English milord was a welcome guest.

'The things they do with red cabbage, Guy,' she marvelled. 'You wouldn't credit it! With apples and caraway seeds and heaven knows what! The cook's going to give me the recipe. But mind, Guy, you ought to be sending a hamper down to the second forester's house – 'im that's next to the inn. He's got his two eldest lads down with measles and his wife's broken her wrist, poor soul, slipping downstairs. And would Nerine mind if I went to see old Mrs Keller – her that lives right in the forest – and took her some grapes or summat? They say she's pining after the young princess – well, it stands to reason, don't it?'

'Nerine would be only too glad, I'm sure. She prefers not to go into the village herself,' said Guy tonelessly. Then, his face creasing into a smile, 'Martha, how do you *know* that the forester's two children have measles? How do you know Frau Keller misses the princess? You can't speak a word of German, can you? And it wouldn't help much, anyway, with the dialect they use.'

'No, you know I can't. But . . . well, I divn't know, love, but there's no call to know German to know things like that. There's all sorts o' ways,' said Martha, and she continued to spend busy days learning the ways of Pfaffenstein, culminating in an afternoon of triumph when she baked a gugelhupf. 'Though whether they'd eat it back in Byker's another matter,' she confided to Guy. 'You know, I thought you'd gone clean out of your mind when you bought this place, but I'm not so sure now. There's some fine people working here, people as know their jobs,' said Martha.

It was inevitable that Martha should hear a great deal about the Princess of Pfaffenstein, who was so universally missed, and she soon found in David Tremayne someone more than willing to answer her queries.

'She sounds a real canny wee thing. Would she be pretty?'

'No . . . I don't know. Her eyes are beautiful. But she's so little and thin and she moves so quietly that at first you don't think . . . she's so unadorned, you see . . .' David shook his head, caught in the bewilderment of those who try to describe a personal enchantment. 'All I know is, Martha, when she comes into a room, it's as though a lamp's been brought in . . . or flowers.'

Martha looked at him with kindness, but without pity, for he was exactly the right age for a romantic love.

'But she's a bit of a snob, maybe? Well, bound to be, with princes courtin' 'er and all? A bit toffee-nosed?'

'No! She's the least snobbish person I've ever met. She'd marry a blacksmith if she loved him,' said David hotly.

Martha, who was learning to knit in the continental manner as shown to her by grandmother Keller, bent absorbedly over her sock.

'Guy will have got to know her, like, in Vienna?' she enquired casually. 'When 'e hired that opera company? Before 'e got up here?'

David frowned. 'I believe so. But he never speaks of it. He never mentions her at all, if he can help it.'

'Aye,' said Martha quietly. 'I've noticed that.'

Greatly to his surprise, for speed had not hitherto been a characteristic of Austrian legal life, Maxi heard almost at once from Herr Rattinger in the Borseplatz. The solicitor said he had been in touch with the Strasbourg office of the Land Compensation Board and put the prince's claim, and though it was not possible as yet to be certain of the outcome, a cautious optimism would not be out of place. Herr Rattinger went on to recommend that the prince withdraw Spittau from the

293

market, for the time being at any rate, since greater force would be given at the hearing if it could be shown that his last remaining dwelling could be made habitable only in the event of a successful outcome to his petition.

The news put Maxi into high good humour and even brought a wavering smile to the face of the Swan Princess, who had been in a vile mood since Tessa's refusal and was given to stalking round Spittau's nursery block like a prophet of doom bemoaning the death of the line.

The Wasserburg was at its best in autumn; the mosquitoes gone, the sunsets magnificent, the sky trailing skeins of geese, duck, snipe and pochard which it was once more possible to shoot, and it was with real emotion that Maxi surveyed his reprieved domain.

The day after receiving Herr Rattinger's letter, he went to Vienna and withdrew Spittau from the market. Then he went round to the Klostern Theatre to give the good news to Tessa and ask her out to lunch.

The backstage world of the theatre had become familiar to Maxi, but nothing could reconcile him to *Fricassée* and it was with a grimace of distaste that he clambered over the railway platform, made his way round the bed shaped like a mouth – and found Tessa in the scene dock painting the signal from which Raisa, in Act Two, was supposed to hang herself.

She was pleased to see him and overjoyed about the reprieve of Spittau. 'Oh, Maxi, I'm so terribly glad.' To her surprise, she had continued to see quite a lot of

Maxi, who had clearly taken his rejection in good part and often came to the theatre. 'It makes me feel less guilty about things. At least it makes me feel less awful about us not being married,' said Tessa, who felt that morning just about as awful about everything else as it was possible to feel. 'But what a miracle it all is! How did you hear about this Strasbourg Commission?'

'Herr Farne put me on to it.'

'Guy!' Tessa had spun round, her brush dribbling red paint on to the floor.

'Yes. I met him outside the agent's and he told me what to do. And I'm sure it's only because of him that they pushed it through like that. He rang up Rattinger himself. Farne seems to be like God with all these people; you would think he'd saved Rattinger's kid from drowning. Well, maybe he did, I wouldn't put it past him. They answered in two weeks, believe it or not.' He looked intently at Tessa. 'Are you all right, Putzerl? You look a bit odd.'

'Yes. I'm all right. Fine.' Tessa pushed her fringe aside with the back of her hand and began to mop at the spilt paint with a rag dabbed in turpentine. One day, she thought bitterly, in two or three thousand years, perhaps, she would be able to hear Guy's name without feeling as though she had been put through a wringer.

'Well, anyway, what I wanted to say, Putzerl, was that if you ever feel like changing your mind, I'd still be terribly pleased. I mean, Spittau's there and it wouldn't matter about the money now. Of course, we wouldn't have much but we could manage. You wouldn't be able to have any fuss – but if you decided, after all, we could ask down Father Rinaldo (the one who used to make such a pet of you when he was chaplain at Schönbrunn) and just a handful of people. I won't keep asking you, but . . . well, if you thought it might work after all, just let me know.'

'Thank you, Maxi, you're very sweet.' Tessa was genuinely touched. Her childhood friend seemed to have become nicer and more perceptive in the last weeks, and amidst the perpetual grime and dust of the theatre, Spittau, with its wide skies and fresh winds, seemed far from unattractive. 'I don't know what's going to happen . . . you've probably heard that things aren't very good here. I mean, I've spent a terrifying amount of money and the bank manager was really unctuous and beastly. And I don't know . . . I mean, I'm not quite as musical as the others and sometimes I don't feel absolutely sure that *Fricassée* is—' She broke off. 'But that's silly. I have to go on. I promised.'

'That's all right. I just want you to know there's somewhere to go. What about some lunch?'

'Maxi, I can't. We've got a costume fitting at one and then the publicity people are coming.'

'Well, if you can't,' said Maxi, flushing slightly, 'do you think your little friend would come? Heidi Schlumberger?'

'Oh, yes! What a good idea. You'll find her in the chorus dressing-room. It will do her good to have a treat; she's been looking a bit peaky lately.'

An hour later, therefore, Maxi sat opposite the

296

Littlest Heidi at a white-painted table beneath a golden lime tree in the Prater. Not, however, the Hauptprater, with its fashionable chestnut allées and formally tended beds, but the Wurscht'lprater – that lusty, noisy, bustling fun-fair with its shooting booths and round-abouts and the famous giant wheel which Maxi particularly adored. How he had yearned to ride up there when he was a little boy, compelled to sit stiffly between his parents in their embossed, gold-wheeled carriage as it rolled relentlessly away from the high hedge behind which the 'hoi polloi' disported them-selves.

The late September day was gentle: a golden leaf floated down and landed on Heidi's adorable blonde head adorned by a pink satin bow which matched her blouse. Heidi, like Tessa, had been delighted by Maxi's news, and now said shyly that she was sure Tessa would soon change her mind and become mistress of Spittau. 'She must do . . . I mean, one couldn't not . . .' she said, looking worshipfully at Maxi out of her huge blue eyes.

Maxi patted her hand. 'Have some more sauerbra-ten,' he suggested.

But Heidi, who usually loved her food, made a little moué and said, 'No, thank you, you're very kind, but I couldn't. And no more wine either, thank you.'

But though she felt so queasy, Heidi did not feel in the least like cutting short the meal. While they sat here quietly in the open air, she could manage without dis-gracing herself. True, the smell of hot engine-oil coming from the roundabouts was bad, as were the occasional disgusting whiffs of frying faschingskrapfen which once, incredibly, had been her favourite food. But here, under the trees, there was also a fresher, reviving breeze which came from the adjoining park and carried only the scent of moist earth and autumn leaves.

For the reprieve would not be for long. That Maxi would want to take her on the giant wheel was inevitable. He was in a festive mood and had already won her a fluffy blue rabbit in a shooting booth. Gentlemen always wanted to go on the giant wheel and Heidi knew just how to make it enjoyable for them: when to say, 'Ooh!' and 'Aah!'; when to be so frightened (about three jerks before their carriage got to the very top) that they had to put their arms round her. And at the moment when the wheel seemed to be stuck, on the way down, she had learned to give a little, terrified scream – though everyone knew, of course, that the man who worked the wheel did it on purpose and that they were not really stuck at all. It had given great pleasure, that scream; Heidi would have been foolish not to be aware of that.

Looking down at the amber wine which she could not have drunk for a year's wages, Heidi Schlumberger thought of all the satisfied gentlemen in whose arms she had gazed at the blue and golden panorama of her native city. Aldermen and councillors, industrialists and officers – ever since she was fifteen years old, she had not been without protectors. And now, all that was in the past. Since she had met Maxi at Pfaffenstein, she had not felt able to oblige a single gentleman. It was madness, of course, for there was the future to think of and the rent to pay.

But the future was best not thought of at the moment. Even the most obscure of the cleaning ladies knew that the writing was on the wall for Witzler's company. Tessa's small finger might be resolutely plugging the dyke, but the waves were breaking over the top. 'And anyway,' thought Heidi, managing at the same time to smile enchantingly at one of Maxi's jokes, 'who would go on employing me now?'

The moment had come. Maxi had summoned the waiter and was paying the bill.

'I thought we'd go on the giant wheel, eh?' he said happily. 'It's just the day for it, nice and clear and not too many people.'

'Yes.' She gathered up her blue rabbit, her handbag.

'You want to, katzerl, don't you?' asked Maxi anxiously, caught by something listless and apathetic in Heidi's usually quick movements.

'Of course I want to. Of course!'

She took Maxi's arm and together they walked towards the carriages of the great wheel, now swaying ominously in the freshening breeze.

Oh, Saint Theresa of the Little Flowers, Protector of the Poor and the Sorrowful, please don't let me be sick, prayed the Littlest Heidi – discovering as the Princess of Pfaffenstein had done before her, how really awful love can be.

17

At the beginning of October, Guy left for Geneva. If all went as he hoped with the loan, Austria would find herself on the road to financial stability, and his task completed. After which he would return to Pfaffenstein to finalize the plans for his wedding.

It was during his absence that Nerine's relatives, escorted by her brother Arthur, arrived in force: Mrs Croft, Nerine's mother, her Uncle Edgar, her Uncle Victor, her portly cousin Clarence and – preceded always by murmurs of obeisance and respect – her Aunt Dorothy, the aunt who was an Honourable.

The honour that Aunt Dorothy, the daughter of a textile manufacturer promoted to the peerage, had conferred by marrying Mrs Croft's brother, had never dimmed. Now widowed and in her sixties, obese, opinionated and petty, she still held undisputed sway over the family.

More of Nerine's relatives were due shortly, but even those who had arrived seemed to fill the castle. Speaking loudly in English on the assumption that foreigners were deaf, they gave orders to the servants, demanded mineral water and British newspapers and could be heard everywhere braying cheerily at their own jokes.

It was only when she was with her own kith and kin again that Nerine realized how much she had missed them, and their admiration of Pfaffenstein's grandeur was balm to her soul. Yet her pleasure was tinged with regret, for they had brought distressing news.

Just two weeks before their departure, an English nobleman, Lord St Henry, his wife and both his young sons had been drowned in a tragic boating accident off the Isle of Wight. Mrs Croft had waited until there was no further doubt – in other words, until the bodies of all four victims had been recovered, undoubtedly dead – before writing an agitated letter of condolence to Lord Frith in his crenellated tower in the Grampians. Frith's answer, received just before she left for Austria, had been suitably grief-stricken, but it had also been unequivocal. Yes, it was true that his elder brother, St Henry, had died, along with his two sons; the loss was one which had shattered not only himself, but his old father who had aged by ten years and was not expected to live much longer. And yes, Frith had added, it was true that he himself would now inherit his father's title, but as she could imagine being the Duke of Aberfeldy would mean little when set against the tragic loss of his brother, his two nephews and his brother's wife. He had ended, as always, with concerned enquiries about

301

Nerine, whose stay abroad must surely soon be coming to an end?

'You haven't told him about your marriage?'

Nerine shook her head. 'There seemed no point until afterwards.'

Mrs Croft frowned. She was in the state bedroom, inspecting her daughter's trousseau. The full-length chinchilla, the Russian sable, the jacket of Canadian lynx were spread across the bed. The diamond necklace, the double row of pearls and a few other trinkets which Nerine had picked up in Vienna were displayed on the dressing-table.

'And I'm getting this silver lily,' said Nerine. 'It's a Pfaffenstein heirloom and absolutely priceless. Arthur found out that the Museum of Antiquities in New York offered fifty thousand dollars for it, and that was before the war!'

Mrs Croft nodded. She could not blame Nerine for her choice, but the blow dealt her by Frith's news was hard to bear. 'My daughter, the Duchess of Aberfeldy.' How inevitable it sounded, how right.

'You would have thought God could have managed it better,' said Nerine, throwing open the wardrobe to her mother's awed gaze. 'Just when one's really happy He sends along something like this to spoil it.' She pulled out an ermine-lined theatre cape and held it against her body, watching the play of light on the gold brocade. Yes, she had made the right choice, but really life could be amazingly cruel!

If Aunt Dorothy was pleased with her first sight of

Pfaffenstein, its liveried retainers and sumptuous rooms, she received a nasty shock at dinner on the first night.

'It was a shock, Alice,' she said to Nerine's mother when they had retired to the blue salon. 'I was not prepared for it, you see. Though how one could be prepared for such a thing . . .'

'I can see that,' Mrs Croft replied, and Uncle Victor, Cousin Clarence and Nerine's brother Arthur all agreed that it had been a shock.

'I know, but you see Guy is so fond of her,' explained Nerine. 'There's really nothing I can do. He's taken Mr Tremayne with him and the head steward makes all the seating arrangements now, but even when everybody was here it was the same.'

'But right opposite me! At the head of the table!' exclaimed Aunt Dorothy. 'That accent! I could hardly understand a word she said!'

'Nor I,' said Uncle Edgar, who had been on Martha's right at dinner. 'I must say, Nerine, I think it's most unwise of Guy to foist her on you socially. Of course, you wouldn't expect him to forget her – that would be quite wrong. Money should be sent, and a hamper at Christmas. But I cannot help seeing it as an affront—'

'No!' Nerine was definite about that. 'Guy thinks it's the biggest treat in the world to sit next to Martha Hodge at dinner. He put the Austrian Foreign Minister there, specially, when he came last week.'

'Really?' Aunt Dorothy was increasingly disturbed by this turn of events. 'You see, dear, it's all right for

303

foreigners – they probably wouldn't notice her accent, though how one could fail to . . . Or her lapse with the finger bowls. But, after all, Pfaffenstein is only a stage, isn't it? In the end, to take your place in real society, you'll have to return to England. And if this Hodge person has become accustomed to living as one of the family you will find acceptance very hard to come by, especially in view of—'

Here she paused, unable to put into words the matter of the Fish Quay, the piece of sacking, and what she referred to as 'All that'.

'Yes, I see what you mean. I've worried about it myself, Aunt Dorothy. But if one dares to criticize her, Guy just flies off the handle.'

'My dear, there's no need to criticize her, that would be quite wrong. We must just make her see, without any rancour, that it would be best for everyone if—'

She broke off as a plump, homely figure appeared in the doorway. Arthur, who had instinctively risen at the sight of a woman, was frowned down by Uncle Victor and sank shamefacedly back on to the couch.

Watched in silence by everyone in the room, Martha said good evening, moved over to a low chair by the window and took out the sock she was proudly knitting with the wool hooked over the left finger as demonstrated by Frau Keller.

'It's a grand evening an' all,' she said pleasantly. 'I never seen stars like the ones 'ere. Not that you can see much doon our way, what with all the muck blowin' off the chimneys.'

No one answered and Martha lifted her head. For a moment her kind face puckered and a look of grief, as unalloyed as it was unmistakable, appeared in her soft, grey eyes. Then she bent again to her task.

An hour later she rolled up her wool, said good night and went to her room. Not a single word had been addressed to her all evening. The education of Martha Hodge, which was to have such far-reaching consequences, had begun.

In the days that followed the Crofts, led by Aunt Dorothy, avoided no opportunity of snubbing Martha. They stopped talking the moment she entered the room, raised their eyebrows when she joined them at table and greeted with pitying smiles her cheerful reports of events in the village.

Nerine joined dutifully in this policy of humiliation, but she found herself in a quandary, for she had discovered in this plainly dressed, working-class woman, an unexpected talent. Three days earlier, crossing the courtyard fresh from her afternoon rest, she had come upon Martha who had spent a most satisfactory afternoon teaching the innkeeper's wife how to bake a 'Singin' Hinny', and greeted her future daughter-in-law with a quick, involuntary shake of the head.

'What is it?' said Nerine sharply.

'Well, love,' said Martha, facing it out, 'it's the way that scarf's knotted. The suit's grand – that soft grey sets you off a treat – but the neckline's too fussy with that knot right in the middle. Maybe if you was to wear it open, sort of casual like, with the scarf just folded in a bit . . .'

'Yes,' said Nerine quickly. 'I've been worried myself. Come upstairs.'

There followed many absorbing sessions in Nerine's bedroom, for Pooley, usually so jealous, took to Martha Hodge at once. Together they pored over fashion magazines, selected braids and trimmings, pondered the precise tilt of a hat. Martha's taste was unerring, her attention inexhaustible, but she was not afraid to speak her mind and Nerine, parading up and down in her trousseau, listened to her suggestions with eager interest. If only she had been a servant, thought Nerine, how easy it would be.

As for Martha, who endured with gentle dignity the snubs and pinpricks she had to face downstairs, she found these sessions hard to bear. In her own way she understood that Nerine's greed and self-absorption were akin to those of an artist or composer who will sacrifice everything and everyone in the service of his own gift, only Nerine's gift was her own beauty. She also realized that since there was nothing evil or vicious in this girl which would sicken Guy and thus release him, he was doomed.

'I go to Schalk!' pronounced Raisa, sitting on the bed shaped like a mouth in which she would never, now, be ravished by the capitalist mill-owner. But her voice was forlorn and a tear forced itself out of her greedy almond eye and rolled down her cheek.

Disaster had struck the International Opera Company. Two weeks earlier, the owners of the theatre had given Jacob an ultimatum. In view of Herr Witzler's unsatisfactory record in the past, they were only willing to renew the lease – at a considerably increased rent, of course – if Herr Witzler could pay them six months' rent in advance. Failing this, they intended to offer the tenancy to Herr Kitzbuhler who, for a long time, had been looking for a theatre in which to play farce.

It was the cheque for this sum – which Tessa had insisted on writing – that had been returned three days earlier, with the information that Her Highness's credit with the Bank of Austria was now officially exhausted.

The incident led to a spate of calamities. Two black-clad gentlemen arrived in Witzler's office, claiming to represent the Princess of Pfaffenstein, and informed him that if there were any more attempts to obtain money from Her Highness an action would be brought against him for exerting pressure on a minor. Jacob's creditors closed ranks and the owners of the theatre wrote and ordered him to vacate the premises on the twenty-first of October, the date scheduled for the première of *Fricassée*.

Now the company was assembled on the stage of the theatre in a tableau vivant of despair. Outside, the newspapermen waited like piranhas, but inside it was silent and dark. The phone, with its endless, doom-filled shrilling, had been cut off earlier in the day; the great arc lamps, lined up for a lighting rehearsal of *Fricassée*, were extinguished.

307

'Cheer up, 'ighness,' said one of the stage-hands, giving Tessa's shoulder a squeeze. 'It aint *your* fault. You've bin a bloomin' marvel!'

'Yes, truly,' said the Littlest Heidi, forgetting her own troubles in order to comfort her friend. 'You're a heroine.'

But Tessa, perched like a disconsolate fledgling on a luggage trolley, was beyond comfort. Outwardly silent, inwardly she seethed with rage and frustration. If only she had been of age . . . if she had been just one year older, she could have defeated the beastly lawyers. There were still a few securities she could have sold. She could have kept going somehow till *Fricassée* redeemed their fortunes. As it was, she had failed art, her friends, everything . . .

Jacob, white with dyspepsia and guilt, paced between the scaffolding, occasionally coming to stand before his under wardrobe mistress like a whipped spaniel. Even now, the bailiffs were probably stripping his villa in Hitzing; prison was a distinct possibility, but he was used to it whereas Tessa . . .

The blow was shattering for everyone. Raisa knew perfectly well that she could not go to Schalk, who had his own stable of dazzling sopranos; nor would Pino be welcome at La Scala as he had frequently boasted. The stage-hands and technicians, close enough to the bread-line at the best of times, faced almost certain unemployment. Yet everyone now set themselves to comfort Tessa.

'Never will we forget your sacrifice!' declared the

Rhinemaiden. She spoke with authority on the subject, for her own pearls lay unredeemed in the pawn shop in the Dorotheagasse.

'Here, have a piece of this,' said Boris, handing her half his gherkin sandwich. 'I've told you, you don't eat enough.'

Bubi, who had been sitting at Tessa's feet, now raised his head. He had commandeered Pino's peaked porter's cap and was engaged in an engrossing game of tram conductors with Tessa's cheque stubs for tickets, but it had become clear to him that he had a contribution to make.

'Bubi loves Tessa,' he announced. 'Bubi loves Tessa an awful lot.' He pondered. 'More than vanilla kipferl, Bubi loves Tessa.'

But as Tessa, managing to smile, replied in kind, there came a clarion call from Raisa.

'Ver is beink Zoltan?' she enquired, in a voice throbbing with portent.

'Yes, where is Klasky?'

The conductor had stridden purposefully from the theatre at midday, promising to return quickly, but that had been many hours ago.

'I zink per'aps 'e 'as shooted into 'imself,' said Raisa, not without a certain satisfaction.

'Oh, my God!' Jacob rushed towards the phone, then remembered that it had been cut off. That Klasky had done himself some kind of injury was not impossible. To see the masterpiece he had created with such anguish brought to naught was quite enough to unhinge this sensitive genius with his wild Magyar blood.

'Go on! Klasky couldn't shoot a barn door from ten centimetres away,' said the first flautist whose vendetta against the Hungarian, originating in a dispute about tempi in *Meistersinger*, was now in its fifth year.

'Shall I go round to his house?' said Tessa anxiously, slipping down from the trolley. 'It wouldn't take long.'

But at that moment, entering dramatically from stage left, Klasky himself appeared.

One glance at his wild hair, his burning countenance, made it clear that the composer of *Fricassée* had been through some ultimate and purging experience, some dark night of the soul, from which he had now emerged to pursue a high and noble task.

For Klasky had not staggered haphazardly into the theatre. He was looking for someone.

In silence, they watched as he clambered over the railway platform, skirted the signal-box, fell over a fire-bucket and then righted himself.

He was making for Tessa. He had now reached her and come to rest before her as she stood quietly looking at him, puzzlement in her auburn eyes.

'Here,' he said. The word seemed to have been forced out of him. 'I've been to fetch it. It's for you.'

He had put his hand into the pocket of his suit to take out a small, black box. At this point, however, emotion overtook him and he had to feel in his other pocket for a monogrammed handkerchief with which to blow his nose. Then, with a last purposeful thrust, he put the box into Tessa's hand.

'No!' Tessa's low, startled exclamation was nevertheless audible in every corner of the stage. 'No, please . . . I couldn't!'

But the Hungarian was in control again. 'Yes,' he said gruffly. 'I want you to have it. To show my gratitude for what you tried to do. It's yours.'

Now, everyone had crowded round. There were 'Oh's' and 'Ah's' from all sides, and the Rhinemaiden sighed like the sea.

For the gesture that Klasky had made, torn as it was from the very depths of his being, was the right gesture, the only one. Something had been said to the Princess of Pfaffenstein which could have been said in no other way.

Thus Tessa, on her last day as Witzler's under wardrobe mistress, looked down at the object held in her trembling hand. Mottled, a little diseased-looking, frail – and valued beyond any jewel in Christendom – the waistcoat button of Ludwig van Beethoven himself.

Guy, with his entourage, reached Vienna on a misty, mid-October afternoon. His part in the negotiations had been successfully accomplished. The League had granted the Austrian Republic an enormous loan with which to stabilize her currency and put her affairs to rights. Patiently enduring the eulogies in the continental press, the banquets and fulsome speeches which followed, Guy had only felt compelled to decline, with scrupulous politeness, the Great Cross of the Order of St Stephen which the grateful Austrian government endeavoured to confer on him.

Immensely relieved to be done with it all, he stepped down from the Geneva Express.

'Hurry the stuff out,' he ordered David. 'There's a train at three, I think, that gets a connection to Pfaffenstein. Check the times – I'm going to get a paper.'

David was back in a few minutes. 'I've reserved a first-class compartment, and the cases are in. We leave in ten minutes.'

No answer. Guy was reading with total concentration an article in the *Wiener Presse*, his face drawn into its most satanic lines. 'Get the luggage out again,' he said, when he had finished. 'Take it to Sachers. Wait for me there, and Thisbe, too.'

'Is anything—' began David, but the only reply was the paper thrust into his hand. He read:

KLOSTERN THEATRE CLOSES ITS DOORS
PATRON PRINCESS RUINED
THE LOSS OF MY OPERA IS WORLD'S LOSS
SAYS KLASKY

'Oh, Lord!' thought David. He looked up but Guy had already vanished, lost in the crowd making its way to the taxi rank.

Jacob was in his office, clearing his desk. The Rhinemaiden, supposedly helping him, was sniffing dolorously over old programmes and mementoes of former glory, removing them from the waste-paper basket as soon as Jacob put them in. Under the desk, in a nest of discarded newspaper cuttings, Bubi was being a mouse.

Already, even in so short a time, the theatre bore marks of desertion. The posters with their 'Cancelled' notices flapped dismally; the red plush seats were shrouded in tarpaulins; there was dust everywhere and it was bitterly cold.

Into this dismal scene Farne burst unannounced, exuding energy and power and sending Jacob leaping exultantly to his feet.

'Herr Farne! Welcome, welcome! Come in! A chair for Herr Farne, liebchen!' he cried, sweeping a pile of music on to the floor.

His squashed, despairing face was transformed. Herr Farne had heard of their plight; this famous music-lover could not bear to think of the demise of the Klostern Theatre; he had come to pay the six months' rent; he was going to finance *Fricassée*. They were saved!

The illusion lasted exactly as long as Farne's first words.

'If you imagine I would sit down in the same room as you,' said the Englishman, raking Jacob with his disquieting eyes, 'you must be an even greater fool than I took you for. You deserve to burn in hell for what you did to Tessa.'

'I . . . she offered . . . I tried to refuse, but—'

'You don't seem to have tried very hard. Bankrupting yourself is your own business, but bankrupting a

313

girl of twenty happens to be another matter. It would give me the greatest pleasure to see you in jail.'

But Jacob had surfaced again. 'Herr Farne, quite a small sum, now, could pull us round. Well, a fairly small sum. Klasky's opera is undoubtedly a masterpiece and—'

'Klasky's opera doesn't interest me in the slightest and if you think I'd lift a finger to save you after the way you've behaved, you must be out of your mind.'

'But then . . . why have you come?'

'I came to find Tessa. Where is she?'

Jacob's eyes flickered. If Farne was interested in Tessa, there was hope after all. More than hope! If Farne married Tessa, then Pfaffenstein, that lost Paradise, would be most gloriously regained. But no . . . the date of the Englishman's wedding to the widow had been announced. A famous couturier had given an interview about 'The Dress'.

'She's not in the theatre,' he said. 'She came here this morning to see if she could help, but then she went to visit one of our dancers who has not been well, Heidi Schlumberger.'

Guy indicated his lack of interest in Heidi Schlumberger with a contemptuous shrug. 'Is she coming back?'

Jacob spread out his hands. 'There is nothing to do here, Herr Farne,' he said wretchedly. 'We are finished.'

'Then give me her address.'

'Number 15, Friedhofgasse, Apartment 4. It's near the Central Cemetery.'

Then, prompted by some evil genius to try once more, he said, 'Herr Farne, we did a beautiful *Flute* for you. Couldn't you just lend—'

Guy had reached the door, but now he turned. 'If you dare to come crawling to me ever again after what you've done, I shall personally throw you downstairs. What's more—'

He was interrupted by a heart-rending wail, followed by a storm of sobbing.

Bubi's peaceful existence as a mouse named Heini had been progressively eroded by the angry voices coming from above the desk. The voices of people who did not *like* each other, who were cross with Papa and who were going to make Mama cry. He knew all about people like that. They were people in dark suits and bowler hats who came to the house and took things away. He staggered out from beneath the desk, his blond curls awry, his small face contorted by grief.

'Bailiffs!' cried Bubi pitifully. '*Bailiffs!*'

'Oh, Lord!' The terrorizing of small children was not in Guy's itinerary. He picked up Bubi, carried him to the desk and set him down. 'I'm not a bailiff,' he said. Impatient to be off, he took a short cut to solace. 'Feel in my pocket,' he ordered.

'Which one?'

'Either.'

Bubi's starfish hand vanished and reappeared with a match-case of wax vestas, a propelling pencil and then, a most marvellous thing: a glittering, golden fish with shining eyes.

'Fish?' said Bubi longingly.

'It's a dolphin. Press the tail.'

Bubi pressed, and out of the wondrous creature's mouth there shot a steely tongue.

'Is it mine?'

'Yes,' said Guy. Abandoning without regret the gold and onyx cigar-piercer presented to him by the Brazilian President, he left.

He found the Friedhofgasse easily, but his first view of the aunts appalled him. They looked shrunken and unwell, quite changed from the autocratic ladies of Pfaffenstein. And Tessa was not there.

'We think she may have gone to see Frau Richter,' said the Duchess.

'She was a little bit upset,' said the Margravine. 'Not Frau Richter,' she explained, 'for whom it is no longer possible to be upset, but Tessa. There has been a little bit of trouble at the theatre, you may have heard. And she came back unexpectedly and—'

The Margravine subsided, frowned down by a look from her sister-in-law. But it had been a wretched business, Tessa coming back without warning at midday and finding them like that – she with her skirt hitched up, washing down the bathroom, and Augustine cleaning the windows. Tessa had been rather unpleasant and wanted to know what had happened to the maid, then she had started snooping generally, asking why the stove was unlit and what they had had for lunch. And while it was true that kneeling was bad for her arthritis, there had been no need for Putzerl to make quite such a fuss.

'Who's Frau Richter?' enquired Guy.

'She is a lady of whom Putzerl is particularly fond. But dead. In the cemetery,' explained the Margravine. She nodded at the vast graveyard, stretching away outside the windows.

We think she may have gone there because she didn't take Quin-Quin,' said the Duchess, motioning at the pug who, almost as homesick as the aunts, had let himself go and was wrapped in nothing more impressive than a blanket.

Compelled by the barest civility to give the old ladies the news of Pfaffenstein for which they craved, Guy did not reach the gates of the cemetery until a quarter of an hour later.

The Central Cemetery was vast, mossy and overgrown. He walked quickly between the serried gravestones of black marble and grey stone, past urns and faded wreaths, past lichened angels collapsed in grief . . .

The afternoon was drawing to a close. Tousled bunches of asters and marigolds glowed on the green mounds; trees of russet and gold stood out against the sombre darkness of holly and yew.

Though he traversed the paths systematically, passing Schubert's grave and Beethoven's sarcophagus, there seemed to be no sign of her. Then, at last, at the far end of the cemetery, he saw the small, well-remembered figure, sitting on a bench. A copper beech spread its branches over her bent head; a red squirrel played beside her on the grass. It was a scene of total silence, limned in the colours of autumn and in autumn's essence for her sadness, like those of the sculptured angels who wept and mourned over the graves, was unmistakable.

Noting, with a dull lack of surprise, the rapid beating of his heart, Guy walked with his silent, panther gait towards her. Then his foot disturbed a pebble. She looked up, saw him and instantly, incredibly, was transformed. Everything about her: the eyes, the line of her mouth, the set of her shoulders proclaimed an uncontrollable happiness, and she rose to her feet and waited silently as he came towards her.

Guy's face as he approached showed no answering joy but only shock. I must not touch her, I must not touch her once, he thought; not for an instant.

'I saw what happened in the papers,' he said. 'It's true, is it? You're ruined? All the money from Pfaffenstein's gone?'

'Well, not quite. Not *all* of it . . . But they said I wasn't of age and threatened all sorts of things. You know what lawyers are – everything that's awful and always for your own good.'

'Tessa, let me help you. That's why I came.'

She shook her head and some of the happiness drained from her face. For a moment she had thought, wildly, that he was free and had come to claim her.

'You were mad,' he said harshly. 'Mad to do it.'

'You did it at Pfaffenstein.'

'I have a great deal more money than you. And if I

318

had retained Witzler I would have kept him on a very firm rein, I assure you. As a matter of fact I did think of using Pfaffenstein for what you once said – serving music. I couldn't imagine that Nerine and I would want to live in more than a very small part of the castle, and anyway my work keeps me travelling a great deal. But when I found that Nerine didn't care for music, it became absurd, of course.'

'Yes.' She was looking down at something she had been holding in her hand: a single, russet leaf from the beech tree above their heads. 'When I was little,' she said, 'I used to try to stick the leaves back on the trees. I couldn't bear autumn. I couldn't bear them to fall.'

'And now?'

She shrugged. 'Look,' she said. 'Look what people have to bear.'

She led him a little way down a mossy path to a plain green grave with a simple headstone.

'Ah, yes,' said Guy. 'Frau Richter? Your friend?'

Together, they looked at the inscription.

IN LOVING MEMORY OF
Bertha Richter, died 1896 aged 75 years
AND OF HER CHILDREN
Hannah Richter, died 1843 aged 1 year
Graziella Richter, died 1845 aged 6 months
Herrman Richter, died 1846 aged 1 year
Brigitta Richter (Bibi) died 1849 aged 3 months
Klaus Richter, died 1865 aged 24 years

ALSO OF HER HUSBAND
Johannes Richter, 1st Hungarian Jaeger Regiment,
killed in action at Königsberg, July 1886
GOD HAVE MERCY

'Yes,' said Guy. 'God had better have mercy, there.'

'When things get bad,' she said, 'I think of Frau Richter who just went on living and living after all those children had died. Look, she lived to be seventy-five! Think of all the Bertha Richters in here . . . you can feel their courage, somehow, coming up through the ground.' She turned and led him slowly back to the bench. 'These are the people I come for when I'm down, not Beethoven or Schubert. The great people are for the times when it's good to be alive.'

'For God's sake, Tessa, let me help. It would cost me nothing to reimburse you.'

'No.' The word was bleak, unadorned and final. 'I have to do it myself, Guy. It's not just the mess at the theatre – it's the aunts too. I found out that they've been practically starving themselves so as not to spend the money I left in trust for them. Somehow, I have to find a way out.'

She shivered a little in her cotton blouse and Guy picked up the shawl she had left on the bench and managed to wrap it round her without once letting his fingers come into contact with her shoulders, an achievement which gave him a certain satisfaction. She thanked him. Then, forcing her voice to be casual, she asked, 'When is the wedding?'

'On the fourteenth of November.'

'Oh, so soon?' She was staring down at the leaf which was still cupped in her hand. 'I haven't forgotten about the Lily,' she went on. 'I'll see that she gets it. I promised.'

'There's no reason why you should. Nerine has enough jewels to sink a battleship.'

'No . . . the Lily's not like that. It's special. I never cared for jewels but the Lily's different. It's so old, you see, so incredibly old. I can't explain, but when you look at it you know . . . what went into its making.'

She was like a lily herself, he thought: the pale head, the slender neck, the incorrigible elegance transcending whatever clothes she wore.

'Is your foster-mother already at Pfaffenstein? Martha Hodge?'

'Yes.' Guy smiled. 'She's having a great time making friends in the village. Rudi eats out of her hand and grandmother Keller is teaching her some weird way of knitting socks.'

'Oh, I'm glad! I'm so glad!' The elfin face was suddenly alight. 'And Nerine, of course, will have—'

'Nerine doesn't go into the village,' he said tonelessly. 'She's afraid of catching an infection.'

'An infection?' Tessa's hand had sprung to her throat. 'Is their illness? Not typhus?'

'No, no, nothing like that. A few cases of measles, that's all.' He paused. 'Nerine is to be pitied, Tessa,' he went on quietly.

'Nerine! But she has *everything*!'

321

He shook his head. 'She's in love with her own beauty and with every hour that passes it fades a little. I've seen her, sometimes, looking in the mirror with panic in her eyes.'

'"It is a fearful thing to love what time can touch",' quoted Tessa. 'Who said that?'

'I don't know, but they were right. I would have done better,' Guy went on bitterly, 'to have spent three days getting to know Nerine rather than buying her a castle. I was in love with the past, with my own splendid fidelity. But she is not to blame. She is what she always was: a lovely, wilful child. It is I who made her into something else. And because of this,' he said wearily, 'I cannot now reject her.'

Tessa bowed her head. While she believed Guy to be infatuated, she could hope that he might wake. But he had already woken and still meant to keep his word, and so all hope was gone.

As they stood there, close but never touching, the red squirrel came cautiously down the tree, made as if to scamper away again, then calmed by their stillness, jumped down and settled on the grass, holding a beech-nut between his paws.

'What was that word you taught me at Pfaffenstein?' said Guy, his voice very low. 'For a wild strawberry place? *Smultronställe*, was that it?'

'Yes.'

She did not ask why he enquired, for she saw in his face what he was saying. That this place, now, had become a *smultronställe*. That any place where they were together would be such a place, be it a railway station, a rainy street . . . 'Here is my space', Anthony had said to his Egyptian queen, meaning what Guy meant now.

'Guy, when I came into the picture gallery at Pfaffenstein, when the aunts were telling you about the Lily . . . Nerine asked you then when you were born and you wouldn't say. You said you didn't know. But it was . . . Was it in June? Before the twenty-first? Are you a Gemini?'

'Yes.'

She sighed, like a child reprieved from punishment. 'I knew,' she said. 'I don't believe in astrology, of course. It has to be nonsense. But all the same, I knew.'

They had been together longer than they realized. It was dusk now and a very young moon had climbed between the trees, cradling the evening star.

'I must go – the aunts will be worried. Guy, I don't know if we will meet again, but—' Her voice broke and she tried again. 'Sometimes, when you're alone and you look up at—' Once more, she had to stop. Then she managed, 'If I cannot be anything else . . . could I be your Star Sister? Could I at least be that?'

Guy dug his nails into his palms. Everything in him rose in protest at the fey, romantic conceit. He did not want her in the heavens, linked to him by some celestial whimsy, but here and now in the flesh and after the death of the flesh, her hand in his as they rose from graves like these when the last trump sounded.

'Yes,' he managed to say. 'You can be my Star Sister. You can at least be that.'

He felt something on his wrist – a breath more than a touch – and looking down saw that she was laying the beech leaf, like a most precious gift, into his hands.

Then she walked lightly away, pulling her shawl closer, and vanished like Giselle into the mist between the tombstones.

'Did you find her, sir?' asked David when Guy, with absolutely no recollection of the journey, reached Sachers.

'Yes. But she won't let me help her. God knows what will become of her. Unless—' But the word 'unless' was more than he could bear. He turned away, then swung round once more to look intently into David's eyes. 'I never thought of that,' he said slowly. 'Would you have . . . David?'

David flushed. But when he answered it was without prevarication, his head held high.

'No, sir. I wouldn't even have asked her. She never had eyes for anyone but you.'

18

Guy arrived at Pfaffenstein the following evening and setting aside the servants' efforts to announce him, found Nerine and her relatives at dinner in the Spanish dining-room.

Though a small party, they were dining in style. Light from two rows of candlesticks glowed on the walls of Morocco leather, the Goya portraits. An enormous silver epergne of writhing horsemen, which it took two footmen to lift, adorned the centre of the elaborately set table.

'Guy, dear! We weren't expecting you!' Nerine was in white, diamond combs in her hair, one curl dancing on her throat in the way that had always enchanted him.

'Let me introduce my family. This –' Nerine's voice took on an awed tone – 'is my Aunt Dorothy. Mother you know, of course, but this is my Uncle Victor, my Uncle Edgar, my Cousin Clarence . . .'

The men half-rose, the women inclined their heads. Guy bowed punctiliously and shook hands.

His future in-laws at meat were an awesome sight and a disquieting one, for here and there on the dull and staring faces he could make out a curve of the lips, a line of the eyebrows which proclaimed unmistakably their kinship to Nerine. In sudden need of solace, he looked round and said, 'Where's Martha?'

Silence. Nerine's eyes slid away from his and she began to fiddle with her napkin ring.

'Is she ill?' Guy's voice had sharpened. 'Has something happened? Has there been an accident?'

'No, no, nothing like that. Guy, you must be starving.' She motioned to a footman. 'Hans, another set of covers, please.'

The digression was unsuccessful. 'I asked you a question, Nerine. Be so kind as to answer it. Where is Martha?'

It was Aunt Dorothy, throwing a glance of reproach at her dithering niece, who now replied.

'Mrs Hodge is dining elsewhere. It was felt that she would prefer it.'

'Where?'

The question was put quietly. Guy had not moved and his hand did not even tighten on the chair-back where it lay. Yet both footmen drew back, seeking the shelter of the sideboard, and Uncle Victor looked over his shoulder at the door.

'In the place to which her station in society naturally

calls her,' said Aunt Dorothy. 'And where she herself is most at home.'

'And where is that?' Guy's voice was still gentle, reasonable, quiet.

'In the kitchen, Guy.' Nerine was holding his eyes, appealing to him. 'She has made such friends with the servants and – Guy! *Guy!* What are you doing? Don't, don't—'

Moving softly and seemingly quite relaxed, Guy had bent over and gripped the handles of the great silver epergne with its rearing horsemen. Then he slowly and steadily lifted it up and held it – to the incredulous gasps of the footmen – for a long moment above his head, before hurling it with demonic force against the window.

'I thought you would prefer me not to hit you,' he said pleasantly to Nerine.

And without a backwards glance at the screaming women and the shattered glass, he left the room.

A few minutes later he entered the castle kitchens.

The spectacle which greeted him was not a particularly pitiful one. A long, scrubbed table ran the length of the room. Hams and salamis hung from the rafters; bright copper pans gleamed in the light of the roaring fire; the smell of onions, fresh bread and schweinebraten floated deliciously in the air. Rows of cheerful-looking men in white caps and apple-cheeked girls in snowy aprons were busy eating and cracking jokes. And in what was clearly the place of honour between the chef, Rudi, and old Otto who kept the wine cellar, sat Martha Hodge.

'Aufstehen!'

Guy's barked order was superfluous. One glimpse of the Englishman as he stood in the doorway, and every person present had risen to their feet.

'Not you, Martha,' said Guy softly. 'It is not necessary for you to rise.'

But she was already standing and as she faced him he saw, unmistakably, the hurt and distress clouding her gentle eyes.

'Fetch the head steward.'

'Jawohl, gnädiger Herr!' Rudi almost ran out through the vaulted doors and reappeared seconds later with the castle's most senior domestic servant.

'I am at your disposal, Herr Farne,' said the old man, bowing his head.

'Who gave the order that Frau Hodge was to eat with the servants?' And as the man hesitated, 'I asked you a simple question. Answer it!'

'The order was given by Frau Hurlingham, gnädiger Herr. She came with the other lady, the one who is her aunt, but the order came from her.'

'Thank you. You may go.'

In goggle-eyed silence, the servants waited for further explosions. But Guy now smiled charmingly and addressing the chef said, 'You will have to move over, Rudi, and lay another place. I shall be dining here today.' He wandered over, lifted the lid of the soup tureen and sniffed. 'Erbsen suppe!' he said appreciatively – and settling himself comfortably beside Martha, took the bowl and spoon proffered by an awed kitchen-maid, ladled out an enormous helping and began to eat.

That night, Guy slept little. It had become necessary to take certain decisions. Hitherto, his chivalry had been directed towards Nerine, whom it was necessary to protect from the consequences of his own disillusionment. Now it turned to the protection of Martha Hodge.

That Martha's own humility was such as to make it impossible for Nerine to wound her, that she regarded her banishment to the kitchens as not of the slightest consequence was something Guy was temperamentally incapable of perceiving. He had seen her hurt. Unaware that her pain was entirely for him and his unhappiness, he decided to act.

But how? Outside an owl hooted, a clock struck two, and still he sat sprawled in a carved chair, frowning in thought. Every so often, he irritably flicked away, like the ash from his cigar, an image which nevertheless continued to recur: that of Witzler's little brat emerging from under his father's desk to lift a tear-stained face to Guy.

'What the devil?' thought Guy, who less than most men concerned himself with the tantrums of young children.

Then suddenly he sat up. Of course! He reached for a notebook and pencil, jotted down a few instructions and, ten minutes later, was asleep.

At six-thirty he woke David.

'Go to Vienna,' he ordered. 'Contact Witzler. Tell him I want to see him at the Klostern Theatre tomorrow at three o'clock, with all the stage-hands and technical staff. Not the singers. Say nothing to anyone. And wait for me there.'

Nerine had dreaded meeting Guy at breakfast, but he was friendly and courteous and made no reference to the events of the previous night. Curiously, his loss of temper had made her more determined than ever to go on with the marriage, for the caveman streak he had shown was not entirely displeasing. It had always struck her as odd that men, having admired her beauty, then wished to destroy it by 'The Act' which alas inevitably followed marriage and which left her, however calmly she tried to take it, dishevelled and not at her best. But if the thing had to happen – and she had lived long enough to have no doubt of this – then better by far that it should be with someone like Guy, with his saturnine looks and power, than poor Frith whose freckled knees and sandy, thinning hair, made the thought of 'All That' particularly uninviting.

So she apologized and promised to reinstate Martha in the dining-room, an action made easier by the fact that Guy's foster-mother had made clear her determination to return to Newcastle as soon as the wedding was over and to stay there.

'That's all right, Nerine.' Guy, though obviously ready to forgive, looked absent-minded, even anxious. 'Look, my dear, I've had some bad news this morning.

It seems as though there are problems with some of my investments.'

Nerine paled. 'Guy! Nothing serious, I hope?'

'No, no. Absolutely nothing to worry about. Only I'm afraid I have to be away for a few days to see to things. You just go on preparing for the wedding. And don't listen to rumours – have faith, won't you?'

With these disquieting words, he left her. What he told Martha before he left, Nerine did not discover. It was certainly not to have faith, for that Martha would have faith in him was something Guy had known since he was six years old.

By lunch-time he had left, with Morgan, leaving Thisbe in charge – and no word came for several days.

'What,' said Tante Tilda faintly, 'is that?'

Tessa looked hurt. 'It's my wedding dress,' she said.

The aunts exchanged glances of anguish.

'Theresa, you are getting married, not buried,' said Tante Augustine, standing with her back to the streaming window of Spittau's state bedroom with its view of the vast and heaving lake. 'Where did you *get* such a dress?'

'From wardrobe.' Tessa's small head, with its wisp of veiling, emerged from the folds of the gargantuan and slightly dusty garment like a snowdrop surmounting an igloo. 'Herr Witzler said I could take anything I liked. It's from *Lucia di Lammermoor*, but it's not bloodstained. It's the nightdress that's bloodstained. She goes off after the wedding feast, you see, and it is then that she murders Arturo.'

Though presumably grateful for the information, the faces of the aunts continued to reflect complete despair, and another drop of water seeped through the leak in the ceiling and plopped into the Meissen soup tureen beneath. Maxi's compensation had been agreed but not yet paid, and though Spittau would soon be warm and dry, the autumn rains were making things a little trying.

'It's not the bloodstains I was worrying about,' said Tante Augustine, returning to the attack. 'It's the size.'

'I'm going to take it up,' said Tessa soothingly.

'And *in*. Like, perhaps, three metres,' said Tante Tilda, unaccustomedly caustic.

'Yes.' Tessa was gazing at her reflection in the mildewed mirror with every appearance of satisfaction.

'Tessa, *please* let us buy you a proper dress. There is still time.'

But the economy game played by the aunts was being turned against them with a vengeance.

'No. It's bad enough coming to Maxi without a dowry but I don't want to waste any more money. You'll see, it will look very nice. She picked up a flounce of the massive garment and as she did so the Spittau ruby, plucked from the crown of Horsa the Red in 1343, rolled from her engagement finger on to the floor.

Without stooping, Tante Augustine fielded it with the tip of her cane. It was an accomplishment which she had perfected having had, in the eight days of Tessa's engagement, a great deal of practice.

'And anyway, Heidi will look lovely – her mother's made her the prettiest bridesmaid's dress ever! She's coming in a minute to pin me; I'll get her to show it to you.'

The information that Maxi was to become the happiest of men had reached him by letter, during the last week of October. Tessa's instructions had been clear and businesslike. If he still wished it, she was ready to be married. She would like the wedding to be quick – if possible before the middle of November – and quiet, with as few relatives as possible. If he had meant what he said about asking Father Rinaldo to officiate she would be very grateful, he was so understanding and unfussy. And she was bringing Heidi Schlumberger along to be bridesmaid.

'A common dancing girl as bridesmaid!' shrieked the Swan Princess when the contents of the letter had been read aloud to her.

'Yes, I must say it's a bit much,' said Maxi, for once in agreement with his mother.

But Tessa, when he telephoned her, was unrelenting. If he and his mother were too snobbish to welcome Heidi, the marriage was off.

The dismay of Maxi and his mother was nothing to that of Heidi herself when she heard of the honour that was to befall her.

'No, *please*, Tessa – please not me! I don't know how to behave with all those grand people. There must be someone of your own kind to ask.'

'But it's you I want, Heidi. I want someone familiar . . .

someone to remind me of the good times I had here and how happy I used to be.'

They were in the deserted, freezing theatre, rummaging among the contents of the skips for garments Tessa considered suitable for her trousseau.

'But you're going to be happy now,' said Heidi. 'I mean, you do love the prince, don't you?'

'Yes, of course. Only I think perhaps it's best not to be too much in love when you get married,' said Tessa carefully. 'I mean, think how awful it would be seeing everything sort of fade and get less.'

'Yes . . . I suppose so.' The Littlest Heidi looked unconvinced. 'Oh, I'm sure it'll be all right; I'm *sure* it will!'

'If you come, it will,' said Tessa. 'I want you to travel down with me and stay until the wedding. The country will do you good.'

That Heidi should be overborne by the steely will of the Princess of Pfaffenstein was inevitable, but there was one subject on which she stood firm. She was not, as Tessa helpfully suggested, going to adapt one of her *Sylphide* costumes as a bridesmaid's dress. Not only would her old dancing clothes no longer fit her, but if she *had* to go she would be decently attired. So she had run home to her mother, who was a dressmaker in Simmering, and returned twenty-four hours later with a charming, pristine, three-quarter-length dress.

Tessa's decision to marry Maxi had appeared fully formed in her head the morning after she had parted from Guy at the cemetery. By marrying Maxi, she would get the aunts away from the Vienna flat, for of course they would live with her at Spittau. Spittau was not their beloved Pfaffenstein but it was the country and a familiar world. There would be maids to help them, and plentiful food without standing in queues. Not only would she be able to help the aunts but also Heidi, who had been looking so peaky, and Bubi who could come to stay. Oh yes, the advantages of marrying Maxi were endless. She would breed not only water spaniels but komondors, those enchanting woolly-haired puszta dogs. And if anything was needed to convince her of the wisdom of her action, it was a quick perusal of the railway timetable which confirmed that a churn of fresh milk put on the 6.05 from Spittau would reach Boris and The Mother in time for lunch.

Having taken her decision, Tessa became immediately and radiantly happy. Everyone knew that she was happy because she told them so. True, certain outward and traditional attributes of happiness were not entirely within her grasp. Since she found it difficult to swallow anything much larger than a pea, she lacked the plump, pink look of the more obvious kind of ecstacy, and her nights, spent underneath a pillow *not* crying, gave her huge, hollowed eyes a look which a casual observer might be forgiven for not recognizing instantly as one of pre-nuptial bliss.

Nevertheless, having made up her mind, she moved with such efficiency and despatch that a week after her letter to Maxi, she arrived at Spittau with her aunts, her bridesmaid and the pug in a carpet-bag.

Though Heidi had had an uncomfortable journey, alternating frequent visits to the toilet with frenzied searches on the floor of the railway carriage for Tessa's engagement ring, she was deeply awed by her first sight of the Wasserburg.

'Oh,' she breathed. 'How beautiful! How melancholy!' It was clearly the greatest praise she could bestow.

In the vaulted hall at Spittau, the servants were lined up in serried ranks to meet their new mistress. But the stab of misery Tessa felt as she confronted the pomp and protocol she had hoped to leave behind for ever was instantly suppressed. She smiled brilliantly, made (as she knew only too well how) the short, expected speech and swept up the stairs to universal sighs of satisfaction.

During the next few days Tessa was very, very busy. She visited the tenants, many of whom had known and loved her from childhood, listened to their grievances and determined that at least some of Maxi's compensation should come their way. She rowed over to a neighbouring bay to bespeak from a retired captain of Dragoons an enchanting komondor puppy as soon as it was weaned, and spent hours in the kennels bursting paper bags in the ears of the new pointer puppies to prevent them from being gun-shy. Everything, thus, was going splendidly and the fact that Maxi now kissed her on the lips rather than on the cheek when he said good night was absolutely natural – something she would get used to very quickly and, indeed, enjoy.

Maxi was being altogether most kind and attentive in every way and the only fault she had to find with him was his treatment of Heidi.

'Why can't you be nice to her, Maxi?' Tessa wanted to know. 'You weren't such a snob in Vienna. You were glad enough to take her out to lunch and to the cinema when I was busy, but here you hardly talk to her at all. You know how I hate snobbishness, and she's so sweet.'

'Yes, I know she is. But anyway she avoids me just as much. Look, just leave me alone, Putzerl,' said Maxi, who really had rather a lot to bear.

Two days after Tessa had given her aunts the benefit of a preview of her bridal gown, the guests began to arrive for the ceremony. The meanness of the Swan Princess, coupled with Tessa's request for a small and speedy wedding, kept the numbers down to a minimum. Waaltraut came and was offended because she had not been asked to be a bridesmaid; the Archduchess Frederica came and was offended because Tante Augustine had her room; Monteforelli arrived grumbling about the damp . . . and Father Rinaldo who looked at the bride through narrowed eyes, flicked her nibbled fringe with his fingers – and held his tongue.

Then, less than a week before the ceremony, Tessa heard the sound of muffled sobbing as she was passing Heidi's bedroom door.

She knocked, entered and found the Littlest Heidi curled up on the four-poster, her blonde curls damp and her face streaked with tears.

'Heidi! What is it, love?' said Tessa, bending over her anxiously. 'What's the matter?'

No answer: just a disconsolate shake of the head.

'You're still not feeling well, are you? You didn't have any lunch again. Heidi, please let me fetch a doctor. This has gone on long enough.'

'*No!*' Heidi sat up, a look of terror on her face. 'Tessa, I absolutely don't want a doctor. You mustn't *think* of it. I'm perfectly all right. It's just the first months – I'll feel better soon. My sister was the same,' said Heidi wildly, now concerned only to prevent a visit from the Spittau practitioner.

'Oh, my God! How could I be so stupid!' Tessa had dropped her friend's hands, aghast at her own blindness. 'It is really quite unbelievable! Oh, love, why didn't you tell me straight away? You know I would have helped you.'

'There's nothing to help with. It's all absolutely all right. My mother's very good, she won't turn me out.'

'But Heidi, won't the father—? I mean, does he *know*? Surely he would want to help you – or marry you? Goodness, anyone would want to marry you. Or is he married already?'

'No.' Heidi had turned and buried her head in her pillow, but not before Tessa had seen the deep flush that spread over her face.

'Do you know, Heidi, I think I must almost be a cretin,' said Tessa reflectively. 'It comes of being brought up in that ridiculous way, I suppose. I kept

338

wondering why Maxi was avoiding you. And he really doesn't know about the baby?'

'No, he doesn't. And he mustn't – not *ever*! Promise me . . . please! Everything will be all right after the wedding, honestly. I'll go away and not see either of you again. Just let us get this wedding over.'

'Ah, yes, the wedding.' Tessa was still sitting on the bed stroking Heidi's tumbled curls, but there was something in her voice which made Heidi lift her head and look carefully at her friend. Tessa was smiling and her eyes held a look that had not been there for many days: amused, mischievous, yet curiously serene.

'Oh, you *do* love him! I thought you didn't, but now I can see you do. You're really looking forward to the wedding, aren't you?' said Heidi eagerly, clutching at Tessa's hand. If Tessa was happy, she could bear it all.

Tessa bent down and kissed her friend's hot cheek. 'Yes,' she said, her voice light and lilting. 'I'm looking forward to the wedding very much indeed!'

For two days after Guy's departure, life at Pfaffenstein continued exactly as before. Parcels continued to arrive with wedding gifts. Magnificent meals were served to Nerine and her family, and every provision made for their comfort. Then on the third day, most mysteriously, the footmen were withdrawn, as were the gate-keepers and the innumerable dirndl-clad maids who had scuttled respectfully along the corridors.

Thisbe Purse, looking harassed, tried to explain the new state of affairs to her employer's fiancée. 'These are

Mr Farne's orders, Mrs Hurlingham. I'm very sorry. There's just to be a skeleton staff. Meals will go on being served of course, but the staff are only to come up by the hour. I'm afraid there may have been some kind of trouble, but we must just keep calm.'

Then on the next day the men came.

They came in three pantechnicons, driving into the courtyard without a by-your-leave and thrusting their way into the castle. Men in bowler hats and brown overalls with pencils stuck behind their ears, swarms of them, flicking with their fingers at the porcelain bowls, lifting up ornaments . . . And bursting into the blue salon where Nerine sat with her family.

'Good morning, ladies and gentlemen. Sorry to inconvenience you but we have orders to remove the contents of this residence.'

The man who spoke was clearly the boss: a tall fellow with a yellow complexion and a theatrically curving South American moustache.

'Are you mad? What do you mean by this? How *dare* you barge in here? Nerine had risen and confronted him furiously, while all about her came cries of, 'What is it?' 'What has happened?' from the Crofts whose German was vestigial.

'We're only doing our duty, gnädige Frau. It's to pay Herr Farne's debts. He's rolled up, poor gentleman. Here's our authorization.' He thrust a sheaf of papers, alarmingly splashed with red sealing wax, in Nerine's face. 'You lot start next door,' he ordered three of his underlings. 'And you two start in the hall. The marble statues are fixtures, more's the pity, but we'll take the rest. Stefan, Georg, Isidor, you stay here with me.'

'No! No! No!' Nerine was as white as a sheet. 'I don't believe it, it's a lie!'

Impervious to her distress, the men got to work. Ropes were brought from the lorries with rolls of hessian padding and crates. Moving with incredible speed and the unmistakable air of men thoroughly accustomed to the job, they stripped the walls of pictures, carried out chairs, coffee tables, ormolu clocks and began to roll up the Aubusson carpet.

'I told you so, I told you so!' screamed Mrs Croft as the sofa she had been sitting on vanished from behind her. 'Not just a piece of sacking but a piece of sacking in *Newcastle upon Tyne*!'

Only Martha remained unruffled. 'Ee, hinny, you don't have to take on so,' she said in her quiet voice to Nerine. 'Even if Guy's in a bit of trouble, he'll come round again. You stand by him and you'll see.'

Nerine turned to her. 'Don't you see,' she said furiously, 'that I cannot? I simply *cannot* be poor, I have no *right*.' Her hands flew to her face. 'Oh God, what shall I do?'

One man only, out of all the bailiffs, seemed to have some degree of pity for the lovely widow: a small, portly man whose long, blond beard and blond locks issuing from the brim of his bowler hat contrasted strangely with his black and soul-filled eyes. 'You want to watch your personal possessions, gnädige Frau,' he whispered as he passed her with an armful of petit-

341

point cushions. 'Jewels and suchlike. They're forfeit, too, by Austrian law if an engagement exists.'

'Oh, my God!' Nerine was totally beside herself. Her jewels! The diamonds Guy had given her, the pearls . . . her furs!

'Excuse me.' One of the men had brushed past her and was lifting the first of the mirrors off the wall, then the second, the third . . .

'No! Not the mirrors! *Not the mirrors*!' screamed Nerine.

Then she turned and ran for the door.

19

Tessa had the compartment to herself and as the train steamed out of Spittau, she put her hand into the pocket of her loden cloak to draw out the ancient leather casket once more, and gaze at its contents.

Yes, she had been right in what she had said to Guy. It was not like other jewels, the Lily of Pfaffenstein. The beaten silver was dark, almost dull, so deeply was it marked by time, but the delicate marvellously wrought petals, the proud curve of the stem, exuded an unmistakable air of majesty. If ever there was an ornament carved out of the very soul of the unknown craftsman, it was this symbol of fidelity and love.

One last task, then: to take the Lily to Pfaffenstein and give it to Martha Hodge. Thank heavens she would not have to get out of the train, not have to see the castle en fête for the wedding; not have to meet Nerine, hanging with proud ownership on to Guy's arm. Martha had promised to be waiting on the platform, and all Tessa would have to do was lean out of the train, hand over the heirloom and continue her journey to Vienna.

'You'll know me all right,' Martha had written in reply to Tessa's letter, 'for I'm as broad as I'm long! But to make sure, I'll wear my navy coat and skirt and my fox fur.'

The train had left the plain and the great, grey lake and was climbing past vineyards pruned for winter, past chequered fields, into the hills. Her own country, now: fir woods mantling green slopes, glittering rivers tumbling through ravines and high on the horizon, a constant pearly cloud that revealed itself breathtakingly as the first of the snow peaks.

An hour later, the train puffed into the station that served Pfaffenstein. Tessa had lowered the window and was leaning out eagerly, the casket in her hand. An old man with a basket of eggs climbed into the third-class carriage at the back; a young man and a black-clad woman with two children got out but the platform itself was curiously empty. Certainly no one as broad as they were long – no one at all now that the passengers had dispersed, which was strange because Anton, the station master, nearly always came out to have a quick chat with the driver.

Uncertainly, she opened the door of her compartment and stepped down. Martha had promised. The dates and times in her letter were perfectly clear. Already, doors were slamming again and the wheezing engine was giving its pre-departure squeaks. Then, running along the platform, came Steffi, the postmaster's ferret-faced son, the only one of the five boys who had turned out badly.

'Your Highness!' He touched his cap. 'There's a message from the English gentleman's foster-mother. She's ill. She can't come.'

'Oh, dear!'

A minute in which to act. To anyone else in the village she could have entrusted the Lily, but not to Steffi who had already been in trouble with the police.

Nothing for it, then . . . Quickly, she took out her small portmanteau, shut the door of her compartment and stood ruefully watching the train draw out. A few minutes later, she had pushed open the white wicket gate which led from the station enclosure and set off on the path along the lake.

At once, she was in a world of aching familiarity. Here was the hollow alder in which she had found a nest of curled-up, sleeping water voles; here the rock shaped like a bird; here the bush that in summer was ablaze with sulphur-yellow roses . . .

She crossed the road, wondering again at the absence of people, and began to climb the steep, circuitous Narrenweg. The first shrine, with the wreath of artificial poppies which had lain there since Frau Sussman's son fell in the war . . . the second, on which the quiet-faced Virgin's nose was inexplicably missing . . . the third, beneath which old Marinka had put, as she put each year, a great bunch of her orange dahlias before they caught the frost –

'Oh, God!' Tessa had stopped, put down her bag and

345

grasped the branch of an ilex beside the path, suddenly overwhelmed by a searing sense of heimat – that word which, though embracing it, means so much more than simply 'home'.

Then she set her chin, picked up her bag and ten minutes later was walking through the gatehouse arch.

There was no one on duty. The courtyard was deserted. Feeling suddenly extremely anxious, Tessa walked up the short flight of steps into the great hall and looked about her, puzzled. Where were the ornaments, the vases, the tapestry hangings? Then a door opened above her and, breaking the silence, she heard a furious voice.

'Who the devil has raised the flag on the flagpole? Who is the imbecile who is climbing about up there? I'm going to blast him out of existence if it's the last thing—' Guy had appeared at the top of the staircase. '*You!*'

He came down swiftly, the brows drawn in a dark bar across his face, and stopped in front of the small figure in the grey cloak. 'And what brings you here?' he enquired.

'I brought the Lily. For Nerine. Martha promised to meet me at the station and bring it up, but she wasn't there. There was a message to say she wasn't well. Is it anything serious?'

Guy shrugged. 'She was all right this morning, perfectly all right. In high fettle, in fact.' He gave up the puzzle. 'You came from Spittau?'

'Yes.'

He nodded, scowling. 'And the prince is well?'

'Very well. Guy, please would you take this, I want to get back,' said Tessa, proffering the box. 'Just take it and give it to Nerine . . . with my best wishes for her happiness.'

Guy took the casket, opened it and looked at it for a long moment in silent tribute. 'Yes,' he said, 'you're right. It's an extraordinary piece of work. I regret, however, that I cannot give it to Nerine because she isn't here.'

'Isn't here?' Tessa stared at him, completely bewildered. 'But where—'

'She heard that I was ruined and left. In case you're feeling anxious on her behalf, let me assure you that she managed to take all her clothes and jewels and a few other unconsidered trifles that were lying about. We have reason to believe that Lord Frith will soon be the happiest of men.'

Tessa's eyes widened. There was no point in feeling happy because Guy was ruined, which was sad for him. Moreover, he certainly did not love her or he would not keep glaring at her in that way. All the same, happiness continued to streak in small, uncontrollable waves through her body. To conceal it, she looked round the hall.

'Is that why the furniture has gone?' she enquired. 'Because you're ruined? Did the bailiffs take it away?'

'Yes.'

Tessa nodded. 'It looks better like this, I think – not so cluttered.'

She tried to concentrate on the subject of Guy's ruin and was rewarded by a brilliant idea.

'Guy, if you're ruined *you* must take the Lily! It's terribly valuable! You wouldn't think so because it's just silver, but it's the legend and all that. The Museum of Antiquities in New York offered my father a *fortune* for it! Then, with the money you can start again and get something to sell like—' But for the moment inspiration failed her.

'Shoelaces?' suggested Guy, the old teasing note back in his voice. But at once, the anger returned to his face. 'Oh, God, why didn't you *wait*!' he burst out. 'Were you so eager for the prince?'

Tessa, looking around for something to sit on, found the pedestal of her great-grandfather's statue which had been too heavy to move. At the same time it occurred to her that she could at this moment have walked barefoot up Mount Everest, which would have been a record and pleased people.

'I knew you'd gone to Spittau, but I thought I had time. And then they said the wedding had been bought forward—' He broke off and turned away.

'Yes,' said Tessa. 'I thought it would be a good idea. Heidi was so very pregnant, you see.'

'Heidi? Who the devil? Oh, that dancing girl. What's she got to do with anything?'

'Actually, Guy, I was wondering if I shouldn't train as an actress,' said Tessa reflectively. 'I never wanted to act before, but honestly I think I may have talent. I did the Stanislavski method before I came downstairs – you know, getting yourself into the part – and then I swept into the banqueting hall when they were all at dinner and called Maxi a vile seducer and pointed my trembling finger at him and everything. I think my bosom heaved too; I'm almost sure it did. And if I was a successful actress I could help you—'

Guy had walked over to her and pulled her up by the wrists. She smiled at him and he said, 'Don't smile like that, damn you! Tell me what happened.'

'Well. I found out that Heidi and the prince had been—' she flushed. 'You know . . . It was incredibly stupid of me not to guess, but I didn't because nobody brought me up to know anything useful.'

'Go on.'

'And, of course, it was obvious that they were just meant for each other, but Maxi isn't . . . you know, very resolute. So I made this scene – I wanted to do it in a night-dress like in *La Sonnambula* but I thought I might trip – and denounced him and said he had to make an honest woman of my friend. And then the Swan Princess screamed and said she was going to have a heart attack and everybody ran about except Monteforelli who said God was almost certainly too busy watching sparrows fall to arrange anything so providential – only *sotto voce*, of course, and—'

Guy put a finger over her lips, which was a mistake because Tessa turned white and stopped.

'Just get to the point.'

'Yes, I will. But you mustn't touch me when I'm trying to concentrate. So then I said, very well, I would take Heidi to her mother in Simmering and her unborn child would be raised to a useful trade, and the Swan Princess went into a paroxysm (which was her snobbery fighting with her blood-lust for babies) and her blood-lust won and she said no Spittau born or unborn was going to be raised away from the ancestral home, and then *she* told Maxi he had to marry Heidi! So then we had the wedding and I came to give Martha the Lily, only she wasn't there.' She broke off. 'Guy, isn't that Martha out there? Only, what *is* she doing?'

'Good God!'

Tessa was looking out through the double doors of the hall across to the chapel – round the side of which there had just appeared, crawling slowly on hands and knees, the plump sandy-haired figure of Martha Hodge.

Guy was across the courtyard in a moment. 'Martha, have you gone completely mad?'

His foster-mother crawled another painful yard, then rose stiffly to her feet. 'Ee, I dunno,' she said, shaking her head. 'Rudi said as how I'd feel better when I'd done this penance, like, and I've ruined me stockings right enough and bruised me knees. But what the Reverend Ridley would say in Byker—' And as Guy continued to look at her in stunned amazement she went on. 'It's what King Louis-the-something did when he got on the wrong side of the pope, crawled three times round the church, only on 'is stomach. It was all those lies I told, see – saying I was poorly and getting young David to call away the station-master and all that faddle so as to get the lass up here. And me not even knowing if she 'adn't married the prince, like they all said . . .'

It was Tessa, coming up behind Guy and thoroughly familiar with the problems of guilt and retribution, who now took charge.

'That wasn't telling *lies*, Martha,' she said earnestly. 'That was strategy, like in a war.' Then she exclaimed, 'Oh, you're wearing the locket! Isn't the picture good of him! You wouldn't believe the fuss he made about getting photographed.'

A great sigh of release and fulfilment now issued from Martha Hodge.

'It *was* you, then,' she said. 'I knew . . . I just knew . . .' and opened her arms.

But when the hugs and explanations were over and Martha had gone to change her lacerated stockings Guy and Tessa, seeking the shelter of the library, found themselves interrupted once again. Preceded by a fusillade of agitated knocks Herr Witzler, distraught and unannounced, burst into the room.

'Herr Farne, I have bad news! Everything else is all right, I *completely* assure you. Every single article is labelled and waiting in the warehouse in Neustadt to be brought back when you give the order. But I, personally, have broken a Dresden figurine. Boris warned me . . . I knew you only wanted the stage-hands and it is true that I myself am not actually used to moving furniture, but I wanted to come too. After all, it was my company.' And as Guy frowned, he added hastily, 'I was extremely well disguised: my Aryan outfit. There was no question of Frau Hurlingham recognizing me. But in the excitement, I dropped the figurine. I understand that it is very valuable. Will you accept the first takings from *Fricassée* as compensation?'

'No,' said Guy. 'Our deal was that I would get the theatre back for you if you carried out your task successfully. *Fricassée* was nowhere mentioned and I am not remotely interested in financing it.'

'Herr Farne, I assure you that once you have heard—'

'I'll talk to you later, Witzler. Now, go away.'

'Yes, Herr Farne.'

But Witzler had now seen Tessa, standing beside the Englishman and reminding him suddenly of Our Lady of Sprotz, glowing with candles as she was carried through the streets at Easter – a sinful and unforgettable sight he had beheld from his bedroom window while studying for his bar mitzvah. He bowed, left and rushed down the steps to where Boris was waiting.

'It's all right, it's splendid – it's all as we hoped! You should see how he looks at Tessa: as if she had at that moment been lowered from Paradise!'

'So he should,' said Boris gruffly. He had been so impressed by his own appearance as chief bailiff that he was growing a South American moustache, an enterprise still in its infancy.

'Tristan is a herring compared to him,' continued Witzler. 'You'll see, he'll deny her nothing! Our accounts he may audit,' Jacob admitted, 'but that is all.'

A great radiance spread over his Old Testament countenance as he looked into the future. The plate-lay-

ers' chorus wafting from the battlements . . . Raisa
soaking up the ultra-violet . . . Pino's uvula awash with
eggs . . . And later, *Cosi Fan Tutte* and *Figaro* . . .

'I shall learn to milk a cow,' said Jacob, and hurried
off to find a telephone and give his Rhinemaiden the
joyful news.

'Guy, I don't think I completely understand,' said Tessa,
when they were alone at last.

'It's quite simple. I decided that the time had come to
terminate my engagement to Nerine. However, I had no
desire to humiliate her personally, nor did I wish to be
embroiled in a messy breach of promise case. So I hired
Witzler's troupe to act as bailiffs and strip the place.
Your friend, Bubi, gave me the idea – bailiffs seemed to
be much on his mind. It was an absurd charade and
wouldn't have deceived anyone with the slightest faith
in me. Even Martha smelled a rat, though fortunately,
she held her tongue. But as you see, it worked.'

'So you're not ruined at all?' said Tessa, abandoning
with reluctance the free and roaming life with shoelaces
she had envisaged.

'I'm afraid not. In fact, I used the time to pull off a
couple of rather profitable deals. You're disappointed, I
see. Don't you think a wealthy husband might be quite
useful, in view of your penchant for succouring the
arts?'

Tessa nodded, seeing the justice of this. 'Only, I do
have this wedding dress which I think it would be a pity

to waste. It's from *Lucia di Lammermoor*, but it's not bloodstained. It's the nightdress that's—'

But the helpful exposition on the plot of Donizetti's masterpiece which Tessa was preparing, was cut short by Guy who now told her to be quiet.

'I'm going to kiss you, you see,' he explained.

Then he kissed her.

It was a very long time before he let her go. When he did, she looked up at him, hurt and bewilderment on her face.

'Why did you stop?' asked Tessa.

'I thought you might want to breathe,' said Guy carefully.

'Breathe?' said Tessa, shocked. 'I don't need to *breathe* when I'm with you.'

What came into his eyes then – eyes which seemed, at that moment, to have invented the colour blue – made her put up a hand as though to shield herself from so much joy.

This hand he now removed.

'In that case . . .' said Guy.

EVA IBBOTSON

The Secret Countess

ST PETERSBURG, 1917

Anna's world is under threat. The eighteen-year-old countess has lived in luxury all her life, but revolution is tearing Russia apart – and her family must escape . . .

LONDON, 1919

Now penniless, Anna is working as a servant for the aristocratic Westerholmes. But as she falls in love with the young earl it becomes harder to keep her true identity a secret . . .

Previously published as *A Countess Below Stairs*

EVA IBBOTSON

The Morning Gift

They were not supposed to fall in love . . .

Ruth lives happily in the magnificent city of Vienna. Then the Nazis invade and her world is turned upside down. Her parents flee to London, but Ruth is accidentally left behind. A family friend offers her an escape route: a marriage of convenience to be dissolved as soon as they reach England. But Ruth's feelings for Quinn soon take her by surprise, and her efforts to set him free do not go quite as she had planned . . .

EVA IBBOTSON

A Company of Swans

For Harriet Morton, ballet is the only escape from her dreary home and strict family. Then a Russian ballet master comes searching for dancers . . .

Defying her father, Harriet runs away to join the ballet on a journey to the Amazon. In a grand opera house, deep in the heart of the wild jungle, she performs *Swan Lake* – and falls in love with a mysterious British exile. But Harriet's father has tracked her down . . . and her new life is under threat.

A selected list of titles available from Macmillan Children's Books

The prices shown below are correct at the time of going to press. However, Macmillan Publishers reserves the right to show new retail prices on covers, which may differ from those previously advertised.

Eva Ibbotson

A Company of Swans	978-0-230-01484-8	£6.99
A Song for Summer	978-0-330-44498-9	£6.99
The Morning Gift	978-0-330-44499-6	£6.99
The Secret Countess	978-0-230-01486-2	£6.99
Journey to the River Sea	978-0-330-39715-5	£5.99
The Dragonfly Pool	978-0-330-45635-7	£5.99
The Star of Kazan	978-0-330-41802-7	£5.99

All Pan Macmillan titles can be ordered from our website, www.panmacmillan.com, or from your local bookshop and are also available by post from:

Bookpost, PO Box 29, Douglas, Isle of Man IM99 1BQ

Credit cards accepted. For details:
Telephone: 01624 677237
Fax: 01624 670923
Email: bookshop@enterprise.net
www.bookpost.co.uk

Free postage and packing in the United Kingdom